Pr

th

"It is clear from the outset of *Darksome Thirst* ___ s her characters well... She possesses the talent and ability to paint vivid portraits with an economy of words, allowing us to feel as if we know these people too."

Morgan Ploutz
www.horrorchannel.com

"Remember the name Morven Westfield... She's an exciting new voice in the Horror/Vampire genre. *Darksome Thirst* is her debut novel and what an entrance it is! "

Raymond Buckland
author of *The Committee*, *Cardinal's Sin*, *The Witch Book*, and others

"Tired of good vampires or bad ones who run in clans and act more like gangsters than the undead?... The author does a very good job of establishing atmosphere, and the evil force is nicely handled... the characterization was convincing and the story engrossing. Overall, a very promising debut."

Don D'Amassa
Science Fiction Chronicle Issue 240

"*Darksome Thirst* is Morven Westfield's entry into the world of fiction and is, hopefully, the beginning to a long career. It is a vampire thriller that preys on our fears of the commonplace becoming the unknown... Westfield has created characters that get our attention, [keep] our interest... "

Barb Radmore, Front Street Reviews,
www.frontstreetreviews.com

"...portrays a good positive look at a contemporary Wiccan training coven in an easy-going fiction setting..."

Rosemary Edghill
author of *Speak Daggers To Her*,
The Book of Moons, I, and others

"[Morven Westfield's] quick and entertaining descriptiveness along with her ability to flow from one transition to the other make this book impossible to put down... The realism of the settings and situations give you the feeling that you have just finished watching a fantastic Reality Television program... There are those who are born to write and Ms. Westfield was born not to only write, but to entertain as well. I enthusiastically and somewhat impatiently await the next book in her series."

Tommy Watson, Staff Writer
Cauldronliving.com

"Clearly the author has done a lot of research (either objectively or subjectively) on Paganism and Wicca, and the attention to detail and accuracy of the rites and correspondences included is impressive."

Pagan News, www.pagannews.com

"An interesting story about a vampire, his intended victim, and a witch who senses that something dark is on the horizon... I personally enjoyed the detailed workings of the 'vintage' computer environment."

Terri Paajanen
Pagan/Wiccan Religion section on About.com

"The story is engaging and down to earth... I feel for the characters in the book. [The book] is very realistic, with a good amount of suspense to keep you going. My only disappointment was that it was too short!"

Mischa Parrill
BellaOnline's Wicca Host

"Ms Westfield's lyrical prose and attention to detail make this an enjoyable read. I will have to admit, though, that I preferred to read this page-turner in the afternoon while sitting in the sunlight rather than at night before going to bed!"

Wren
Henge of Keltria Magazine

"Alicia is someone most of us can identify with...The story is told with an unusual twist, combining vampirism and wicca in a most unusual read..."

Morganna Davies
author of *Keepers of the Flame*

"The plot is engaging, at times allowing the author's sense of humor to add great color to the writing style. Morven also tosses the readers several surprises and the book builds to a potent climax..."

The Unicorn newsletter, www.therowantreechurch.org

"Vampires, Witches, and technology - an intriguing combination, and Morven Westfield has put them together in an ingenious and entertaining story..."

Elizabeth K
Horns & Crescent Magazine

THE
OLD
POWER
RETURNS

by

MORVEN WESTFIELD

HARVEST
SHADOWS
PUBLICATIONS™

THE OLD POWER RETURNS

copyright © 2007 by Morven Westfield

Published by Harvest Shadows Publications
PO Box 378, Southborough MA 01772-0378 USA
www.harvestshadows.com
Printed in the United States of America
ISBN-13: 978-0-9741740-7-5

HARVEST
SHADOWS
PUBLICATIONS

Cover design © 2007 by The Graphics Goddess
www.thegraphicsgoddess.net
Photographs © 2007 Harvest Shadows Publications

10 9 8 7 6 5 4 3 2 1

Long ago, in days gone past,
When shadows ruled the land,
The people gathered far and wide,
From hill and dale and strand.

Gather we now as long ago,
The circle strong, unbroken.
Hand in hand, in twisting dance,
As magic chant is spoken.

Gather we now as moon rides high
And incense smokes and burns.
Energy courses through our veins,
And the Old Power returns...

After a poem fragment attributed to Lucius in
Prolegomena to the Study of Greek Religion
by Jane Ellen Harrison, Mythos Edition, 1991, Princeton University Press.

Chapter 1

Southern New England,
in the early 1980s

The last time that Meg saw her, Alicia Anderson had been injured in a mysterious explosion. And bitten by a vampire.

Trying to act nonchalant, Meg MacMillan clasped a notebook in her arm and walked briskly into a nearby conference room. Once inside, she arranged her notebook and pen on the table, as if ready to take notes at a meeting, and then confidently dialed a number from memory.

She had taken a seat facing the door so that she could look out its small window and know if anyone was coming. She adopted a bored, slightly tired expression as she waited for the person at the other end to pick up, so that if anyone *did* look in, they'd assume she was on a business call.

Privacy was important. Such was the life of a witch in the modern world. Meg, whose witch name was Matricaria, kept that part of her life private. None of her co-workers knew. She preferred it that way.

At the other end, Janith, the coven co-leader and Meg's friend and confidante, picked up the phone and listened as Meg softly and swiftly told her about the young woman she had just seen in the hallway.

"Are you sure it's her?" Janith asked.

"I used to work with her, remember? I saw her every day." Meg twisted and stretched the coiled telephone cord as she spoke, then craned her neck slightly to look through the glass panel of the door, checking for movement.

"But it's been three years."

"Yes, I know, but I'm sure it's her. It's not just her looks, but her mannerisms, and the haunted atmosphere around her— "

"You mean her aura?"

Meg stopped playing with the telephone cord as she tried to visualize what the differences were. "Yes, I guess her aura. She probably looked completely normal to everyone else. But I felt an immense sadness around her, a hollowness." She thought back to the explosion, the smoke, the acrid smell of something foul burning, the two tiny marks on Alicia's neck that she had seen as the unconscious woman was taken away on a stretcher.

"So, what are you going to do?"

"I looked up her name in the company phone directory. No Alicia Anderson listed, but it takes a while sometimes for new names to be added. I could always call the operator and ask, but I think I'll just wait until the new directory comes out next week and look again."

"What if her name's not Anderson anymore? What if she's married?"

"Many people keep their maiden names now. You did. Alicia would have. I remember her talking about names when someone at work got married, about how she'd definitely keep her maiden name. She was very adamant. If the woman I saw is Alicia, I'd say there's a good chance she's Alicia *Anderson*. If not, how many Alicias can there be around here? Especially Alicias with long, straight hair, and that haunted look?"

"Okay, but proceed carefully. She was in shock for a while after the incident. It may have rattled her permanently. Seeing you might flip her out."

"I agree. That's why I didn't just walk up to her and ask. I'll let you know how it goes."

Meg hung up the phone and rose from the conference room chair. *Good luck, indeed. It might take more than luck to pull this off tactfully.*

On the way back to her desk, Meg recalled the last time that she had seen Alicia. Three years. Had that much time really passed? Yes, indeed it had, and now that she thought about all that had happened since, she was surprised it hadn't been longer. Three years ago Meg was a journeyman programmer starting a new job at Theoretic, a small research company. She was also training to be a witch.

No, not a green, warty-faced Hallowe'en impossibility, but a goddess-loving, nature-worshipping wielder of magic. Although she felt in tune with the worship of the old pagan gods from her first steps on the path, she hadn't initially believed in magic.

Or vampires.

How things changed. Oh, how things changed...

First, there were the dreams of an unrevealed danger. Then there was the tarot card reading with a too-real vision of blood pooling on the cards. By the time she and her covenmates figured out what was going on, her co-worker, Alicia, lay unconscious, having used a laser in one of the research labs to do battle with a vampire who had just possibly killed one of the security guards.

That was the last that Meg saw of the guard who was with Alicia. After he recovered from injuries, the direct cause still uncertain, he was trans-ferred to another facility. It appeared he had been hurled across the room, but it wasn't clear how. The safety report indicated that he was probably thrown bodily by the explosion, but rumor had it that the safety investiga-tors weren't really sure.

Rumor also had it that his new job was one with less responsibility, much less responsibility. Despite the fact that there was never a public announcement, the grapevine said that management held him partially at fault for the unexplained explosion. And then there was the question of Alicia. What was she doing accompanying him on his rounds?

Alicia's story was that they were walking together because she was on her way back to the computer room and he happened to be going that way, too. His story was that he couldn't remember. The doctors seemed to back him on that. Amnesia, due to trauma.

Although Alicia returned to work almost immediately, Meg never was able to ask her what happened. After the "incident" Alicia appeared so haunted and fragile that Meg hadn't dared ask. Her coven leaders agreed it probably wasn't a good idea. "When she's ready to talk, she will," Janith had said. Rob, the other coven leader and now Janith's husband, agreed. "And if she's not ready, and you try to force her to relive the experience, you can do more harm than good."

Six months later, Meg was offered a spectacular job at a computer com-pany. On her last day at Theoretic, she said goodbye to Alicia and gave her her phone number, with a casual, "Let's keep in touch, okay?" But Alicia never did.

And now here she was at the computer company where Meg now worked. What was it that Rob and Janith always said about fate? "If you're meant to deal with something, you will. And it will chase you until you do."

Apparently Meg was meant to deal with the mystery...

And Alicia was meant to make sure of that.

Alicia's Diary

January 25, 1980

I saw a woman at work today who looked a lot like Meg. I wanted to go over and say hi to her, but what would I say? "Hi, remember me? I was involved in that mysterious explosion at Theoretic."

But I've got to know what really happened and why... not just that day, but in the months leading up to it. Was Wesley really a vampire, or did I imagine it all? Am I still imagining it?

Sometimes there are just floods of feeling, or shadowy dreams like grainy black-and-white silent movies. Sometimes there's just a phrase on my lips in the night, which fades before I can speak it.

But it's real. Very real. And I need to find out what it was and what it all means.

And if it will happen again.

Alicia capped her ballpoint pen and closed the diary, wondering if writing in it was even worth it. What she had written was sheer pabulum, a worthless diatribe. But at least she was writing *something*.

The therapist said it would be helpful, but Alicia wasn't sure she believed that. How could writing it out help, especially when it seemed that lately she was just writing drivel? Melodramatic drivel.

"Just write," the therapist said, and so Alicia wrote. She wrote words that were alien to her. Dreamy, poetic words with no real meaning, no real substance. It was so unlike her. Alicia was pragmatic, logical, strong. Alicia had worked her way up from nothing, and had survived— survived what?

What? *What* had she survived? Alicia lit a cigarette, a nasty habit she had picked up since the incident, and inhaled deeply. *What was it* that she had survived?

Chapter 2

"Hey, Alicia. Want to sit with us?"

Alicia turned to determine the source of the voice. A few feet away she saw a jovial woman waving energetically. Norma. *Of course.* In every department there seemed to be one person who was the social glue that held the group together. In this department, it was Norma.

Being about twenty-five pounds overweight, with strands of gray showing in her permed hair, Norma looked like a very young grandmother, or a very weathered mother. Her white turtleneck and cardigan did nothing for her pasty complexion, and it was only her mascara, blue eye shadow, and pink lipstick that kept her from looking deathly ill. Ignoring the large, gaudy, plastic jewelry that was becoming popular, Norma always wore only a small cross on a thin gold chain and 14-carat gold post earrings. In style and manner, she exemplified "mom" and comfort and sensibility.

Alicia was never one for sitting and chatting in the cafeteria— not in high school, not in her previous job— but she was new at Universal Info and knew that it would be to her advantage to get to know her co-workers even though she had been raised to believe that school and work were not places for socializing. She had lived by those rules, but noticed that those who were sociable seemed to do better. They seemed to get the information and resources they needed. And so, more out of practicality than desire, she would force herself to be social. Instead of eating at her desk as she wanted to do, she had abandoned the emotional safety of her desk for the company's large-but-crowded cafeteria. Standing hesitantly at the entrance, her brown paper lunch bag clenched in a nervous hand, she had been nonetheless relieved when Norma called out to her. At least now she wouldn't have to invite herself to join in.

"Okay," Alicia said, sliding into an empty seat next to her co-workers.

Norma gestured to the two other women who were sitting with her. "Alicia, you know Betty and Carol, right?" Betty, unlike Norma, looked very un-grandmotherly. Her hair was blond, blow dried, and sprayed, her skirts short and tight, and her shoulder pads big. But like Norma, Betty came across as warm and friendly, not snobbish or bitchy like Alicia expected her to be, and she gave Alicia a hearty hello. Carol was somewhere in between Norma and Betty. Her clothes weren't as modest as Norma's, but not as daring as Betty's. Her makeup consisted of only eye shadow and lipstick. But like the other two women, she was pleasant and cheery, and it was that, Alicia surmised, that had drawn the three women together as friends.

As Alicia opened her brown paper lunch bag on the stark laminated plastic lunch table, Norma continued what appeared to be a conversation in progress. "So, Betty, when's the party?"

"Next Wednesday, around seven. Alicia, wanna come? It's KopperWerkes."

"Copper works?" Alicia didn't recognize the name.

"They sell copper things: household goods like candleholders, bowls, plaques, gelatin molds. Things like that."

Sliding her sandwich and cookies from out of the bag, Alicia pondered how to decline without hurting the woman's feelings. Her budget was limited. Paying a mortgage, even with a roommate, left little disposable income. Alicia was more apt to put any extra money in the bank, as a cushion against hard times, than to fritter it away on unnecessary things. "Uh, thanks, but I really don't need any of those right now."

Betty waved her hands in dismissal. "Oh, you don't have to *buy*. Just come along. We'll have snacks and dessert. You'll have a good time."

"Okay, I'll think about it," Alicia fibbed, thinking that she most likely would *not* think about it.

Norma seemed to sense that Alicia was just being polite. She looked at Alicia directly, re-engaging her in the conversation before turning away to another co-worker. "You should. Really. Just come for the party. No one expects you to buy anything." She smiled and then turned to her right. "Carol, did you go to see that psychic?"

Carol swallowed the bit of sandwich she was chewing and hastily washed it down with a gulp of soft drink. "Yeah. This guy is really great. He is soooo accurate. He knew about my aunt's surgery and my cousin's new baby and my boyfriend."

Normally shy, Alicia couldn't keep herself from butting in, not where logic was concerned. "Couldn't he have guessed some of that, though?"

Shaking her head, Betty chimed in, "Carol didn't tell him anything, and he just came out with the fact that her aunt's name was Audrey and that she was having her gall bladder removed. How could he know that?"

Alicia pondered the information. While it was true that gall bladder surgery wasn't that rare and therefore it could have been a lucky guess, how did he know the name Audrey? It wasn't that common a name. And how did he know it was Carol's aunt? She turned to Carol. "Could someone have told him your aunt's name?"

"How? No one knew I was going. I just woke up Saturday morning and decided to call for an appointment. There was a cancellation, so I got one for that night."

"Okay, but how did you know about him? Does a friend go to see him? Could he have heard about your aunt from a friend?" Alicia believed that people really could be psychic, but she also knew they could be con artists. He could be either.

"Nope. I heard about him from a friend where I used to work, and that was a year ago. I was lying in bed, thinking about things, you know, like where I'm going in life, and I remembered hearing about this psychic, 'The Wizard of Westville.' I didn't even know my aunt was sick. She just started having gall bladder problems last week."

Alicia had to admit that it didn't sound as though there was much room for deception. "Hmmm. It *does* sound like he couldn't have learned it through regular means..."

Norma mopped up the spaghetti sauce from her plate with a slice of Italian bread and continued. "Ever been to one? I'm going to try to get an appointment. I could make one for you at the same time."

Five years ago Alicia would have laughed at the suggestion, at the thought of paying money to someone who might have powers of perception, but who more than likely had the powers of a well-studied confidence man, but her encounters with the unknown had taught her that there were indeed things that were unexplained. She was getting nowhere trying to find her own explanations for what had happened three years ago. Her therapist, who still didn't know the full story of the explosion, had encouraged her to reach out more, to not try to do everything on her own. To ask for and get help from others if needed.

"I don't know. Is he expensive?"

"Nope, readings are just fifteen dollars."

Fifteen dollars was a lot for Alicia to spend on non-essentials. Even though the economy was beginning to improve after the gas crisis and other shortages of the last few years, Alicia needed to watch her budget. Fifteen dollars was about three times the cost of a movie or a meal. Still, if he *was* psychic, maybe he could help her figure out the inexplicable events of the past. "Okay, sure, why not?"

"Good! I'll try to book us some appointments. His Saturdays are usually booked in advance, so we'll have to do a weeknight. Are you free on weeknights?"

"Right now I am. I'm planning to go back to night school, but that won't be for another couple of months, after I'm here long enough to be eligible for tuition reimbursement."

"In a couple of months it'll be summer."

"I know. I'm going to sign up for the summer sessions."

Betty laughed a gentle, sincere laugh. "Wow. That's dedication. I couldn't do that."

"Sure you could— " Alicia stopped herself, remembering how often she had had this conversation with her friend Susie. Susie, who had disappeared one night, just before the explosion, leaving her daughter with her ex-husband. A sharp pain tore through Alicia's soul as the memories resurfaced. *Susie! What* had *happened to Susie?* She had been so absorbed with her own problems that she never asked, never followed up.

Carol's voice brought her back to the present. Alicia missed the first sentence or two, but caught her saying, "Okay, I'll call and let you know when he's available."

As the conversation at the table shifted to what had happened in the last episode of *Knot's Landing*, Alicia busied herself folding and refolding her paper napkin. The deep painful memories of Susie faded and she found herself becoming more excited by the prospect of the reading.

What if he *was* psychic? Then she would be only days or weeks away from the truth.

"Alicia?"

Alicia turned at the sound of her name. "Meg! What are you doing here?" *So, it* was *Meg!*

Meg smiled. "I work here. And you?" She stepped over to the side of the long hallway to let someone pass.

"Me, too. I just started a couple of days ago, in Manufacturing Systems."

"I thought I saw you in the cafeteria, but I wasn't sure. How have you been? Have you been at Theoretic all this time?"

Alicia flinched on hearing the name. *Theoretic.* For some reason, hearing Meg say the name was actually worse than working there. "Yeah. Maxwell left and the new manager was really good to work for, so I decided to stay until I got my Associates Degree. They finally promoted me to Junior Programmer—"

"Congratulations!"

"Thanks! So I stayed, but after a while I started getting itchy feet. And you?"

"Just before you came back from medical..." There was an awkward moment where pain flashed over Alicia's face. As if to break the moment, Meg quickly continued, "I could see what Maxwell was really like, and I didn't want to keep working under him. I had no idea he was going to leave. A friend of mine had started working here at UI and gave me a call when an opening came up. I interviewed and they offered me the job. I've been in the Marketing Systems Group ever since. So, where is everyone? Are they all still at..." Meg paused as she searched for a word to replace the company name that seemed to bother Alicia. "Are they still at the old place?"

Alicia flattened against the wall as two men pushed an object the size and shape of a refrigerator past them. Mounted on a wheeled skid, the blue metal cabinet and clear cover of the minicomputer held Alicia transfixed as it passed. As a programmer, she didn't see the actual machines these days. These days someone else mounted the data tapes, as she had once done, carefully lacing the cool ribbon of magnetic-coated plastic through the maze of capstans, tension arms, and rollers. Someone else— maybe even a young woman near her age— closed the clear plastic door, pressed the power button, and then listened to the click and whir of the tape drive as it tried to find *Beginning of Tape*. Someone else listened to the hammers of the print heads as they slammed against the night-colored ribbons; listened to the flat, white noise of the air conditioning and the hum of the fans in the computer. Listened for footsteps, for door creaks, for... *listened, listened, listened...*

Meg was looking expectantly at Alicia, no doubt a little troubled by her momentary lapse into dark reverie. Alicia recovered quickly. "You remember Joey? He called me about a year and a half after he got laid off. He's not in computers anymore. After the layoff, he went to Florida and worked construction with his cousin. He didn't want to work *outdoor* construction anymore— 'That stuff's too hard,' he said. He came back that summer to see what he could find up here for interior work. I had just made an offer on a house— "

"You bought a house? That's great!"

"Yeah. It's just an old single-family on the south side of town, not the best area. It needed a lot of work, and since Joey didn't have anything else lined up, we arranged a work-for-rent deal. He did that for a month or two until he got work on a regular site."

Another minicomputer was being pushed past them, causing the two women to pause in their conversation long enough for it to pass.

Meg looked down the corridor in the direction from which the computers were coming. Apparently satisfied that she wouldn't be interrupted again, she continued, "So where is he now?"

"He's still at the house, but I don't see much of him. He's got a girlfriend and spends a lot of time at her place. I asked him why he just didn't move in with her and he said that his 'nana' would kill him if he moved in with someone before marriage!"

They both laughed at Joey and his endearing fear of his nana. Nothing, not even his parents scared him as much as his old-world, immigrant grandmother. She barely spoke English, but she spoke it well enough to let him know what was right and what was wrong. An amusing thought darted through Alicia's mind... *Maybe I should have set Nana on Wesley...*

Meg's voice brought her back from her short musing. "So, how's the house going?"

"Okay. The house is old, it wasn't kept up very well, and it's in a bad part of town, but that means it didn't cost a lot. I still might need to take on another roommate, though. But it's what I wanted, a place of my own, something my parents didn't have."

Meg glanced at her watch. "Do you mind if we walk and talk? I have a meeting at the other end of the building."

Alicia pushed off from the wall that she was still leaning heavily against. "Sure, no problem."

Meg turned and began walking down the hall with long, deliberate strides. "So how did you end up at UI?"

Alicia stopped while she thought of the answer to the question and then remembered she should keep walking. "I wanted to move on, get some more experience elsewhere, but you know how it is. If you don't have experience on the right machines, you can't get a job. COBOL is COBOL no matter which computer you're programming on. Yeah, there are differences, but all you need is a few months to pick them up. But try convincing a headhunter of that. They wouldn't even think of sending me on interviews for jobs that required mainframes because I had experience only on UI minis."

It was the same old story, but some of the sting was gone. Alicia used to dwell on how unfair the business world was, not promoting her only because she didn't have a degree, not hiring her even though her job skills were highly transferable, but her therapist had helped her understand that that's just the way things were. It wasn't *personal*. Alicia had two choices: she could overcome the odds or be crushed by them. She could wallow in self-pity or learn to use her emotional energy for better things. She had chosen the latter.

Meg listened intently as Alicia continued, "One day I was taking a course here at UI and one of their operators was in my class. He said there might be an opening here for a junior programmer soon, so I gave him my resume. At first UI was a little wary of hiring someone away from a customer of theirs, but by then Theoretic had announced that they were moving the business lab to Atlanta. UI relaxed because it wasn't likely that Theoretic would have a problem with them hiring away a northeastern employee."

"Oh, I didn't know about Atlanta. Sounds like you moved just in time." Meg stopped at the intersection of another long hallway. "Well, here's where I turn off. Are you going this way?"

Alicia shook her head and pointed in the opposite direction. "No, I'm going to go outside for a cigarette."

"Cigarette? I didn't know you smoked."

"Yeah, I started when— when I was at Theoretic. Stress. I keep thinking that I should try to quit once I get over the new job terrors."

Meg smiled. "Well, good luck. It was nice seeing you. Maybe we could have lunch someday?"

"There's not really enough time to go out, but maybe we could get together in the cafeteria some time?"

"That would be nice. Well, I have to go. See you later."

"Bye. Good seeing you."

Alicia watched as Meg disappeared down the long beige corridor. Seeing her walk away reminded Alicia of Theoretic when Meg had joined the company. It had been a much simpler time when Meg started. But not when she left.

It was bitter cold when Frederick awoke, and that irked him. Not the sensation of cold, for he felt it not, but the fact that the cold drove people into their homes, into their cars, away from his grasp.

A few miles west lay a hotel that resembled a castle, turrets and all. He could easily wait in the parking lot until a female guest drove in. If she had out-of-state plates, he could just happen to appear at the right time and help her with her luggage. If not, he could walk ahead of her, opening the door for her and making small talk as he followed her to the hotel bar.

But the hotel was across a busy highway, two lanes in either direction, and although he had discovered the ability to move quickly enough to make it across, that alone could attract attention.

No, Frederick would hunt close to home tonight.

Chapter 3

When Norma called the Wizard, she was told that his schedule was booked through the end of the month. But once again, there had been a cancellation. Norma was able to book an appointment for a reading for all three of them that night. Too excited to wait until lunch to deliver the news, she excitedly stopped by Alicia's desk on her way to morning break.

Alicia pondered the coincidences. It had been sheer chance that she had decided to sit with the women at lunch the day before and that she had joined them when they were talking about the Wizard. And now there was the coincidental cancellation of an appointment. Coincidence reminded her of *synchronicity*, which she remembered from her college psychology class.

Was her presence at the lunch table and the fact that the Wizard had a free appointment an example of synchronicity? Was the universe attracting this coincidence to her for a reason? Was it telling her that she needed to accept that not everything in the world was rational? *No*, her logical mind argued, *it's more likely that the Wizard really isn't as booked as he claims to be. He tells people he's overbooked to make himself seem more sought-after.* But wouldn't he be found out? Wouldn't people notice that there weren't other people at his house getting readings while they waited?

Alicia let the thought go. If she didn't, she would have been arguing with her logical self for hours. Her ability to see both sides of an argument meant that sometimes she argued both sides so much that she bored even herself. And if there was something to be decided, she often argued so much that she froze in indecision.

Their appointment with the Wizard was tonight. Alicia worked through her lunch break, pushing to make sure she completed everything so that she could leave with the others. They wanted to leave a little early so that they could get something to eat first. *Darn, I should have waited a few weeks before making that appointment.* Even though they'd all be leaving after putting in more than an eight-hour day, she felt uneasy about leaving on time so soon after starting her new job. *I hope they don't think I'm another nine-to-fiver.* Working long hours was almost considered a moral duty among the programmers she knew. Leaving early could mark her as less than serious about her career.

I'll make up for it later, she promised herself, turning the page of the mind-numbing project description she had been reading.

Around three o'clock, her co-workers left their offices for their mid-afternoon coffee break. Alicia hung behind, telling them she'd join them in a minute. When the sound of voices died down and she could no longer hear any clicking of keyboards nearby, she made the call.

"Hi, can I speak with Mrs. Curtis? This is Alicia Anderson." She waited on hold, watching, listening to make sure no one was around to overhear her conversation. She wasn't embarrassed about seeing a therapist, but she didn't want her new co-workers to start wondering what had made her decide to see one. That was one question she wasn't prepared to answer yet. How would she explain the explosion, the stranger, the bite...

"She isn't? Okay, can I leave a message for her? Can you tell her that I have to cancel my future appointments for now because my new company's insurance won't cover them for ninety days? Tell her I'll give her a call after the waiting period is over. Thanks."

She knew that she wouldn't be calling for an appointment, even after the waiting period was over. She had talked about everything she *could* talk about. The nightmares persisted, she had no idea what had really happened, and a curious mix of dread and longing still clung to her soul. And with school starting soon, she couldn't spare the time or money for appointments.

And maybe the kind of help that she needed wouldn't come from her empathetic, professional therapist.

Maybe the kind of help she needed would come instead from someone they called "the Wizard of Westville."

At five minutes of five, Alicia, Norma, and Carol piled into Norma's car and drove westward to a pizzeria. While Carol and Norma went to the counter to order meatball subs and soft drinks, Alicia held the table. Gazing at the travel posters of Greece that adorned the otherwise plain walls, Alicia tried to compose the questions she'd ask the Wizard.

She didn't want to just come out and ask, "So, was that a vampire in the computer room?" She'd ask about something harmless first. Maybe she'd ask about her job, her career. If this Wizard character wasn't really psychic, he'd deliver some empty patter about future opportunities and leave it at that. And if he really *was* psychic, he'd talk not only about her job in the future, but about what had happened at her job *in the past.*

Their orders given, Carol and Norma returned and slid into the booth, opposite Alicia. Norma broke the silence, "Too bad Betty couldn't make it. She could use the Wizard's advice about that boyfriend of hers."

Carol frowned and then nodded. "I know. I have a feeling they're not going to be together much longer. I wouldn't be surprised if he was out by the weekend. Poor kid. She really does know how to pick them."

Alicia looked up, not wanting to intrude, but curious about why Betty hadn't joined them. Carol caught her glance and redirected the conversation. "Have you thought about what you're going to ask?"

"I think I'll ask about my career. I haven't been at UI very long, so this would be a good time to get some ideas on how to get ahead."

"What about *your* love life?" Norma flashed a coy smile at Alicia.

"Yeah, I guess that wouldn't hurt. No news there, though."

"Oh, no one in the picture?"

"No, no one." Alicia fidgeted with a jar of crushed hot peppers she found on the table. She hadn't really thought of her love life for quite a while, not since she and Kurt broke up. After the breakup, she had wanted to concentrate on her career, her life. But then there was the vampire, and the explosion, and life had been just a wee bit too strange for love.

A half hour later they were back on the road. Alicia stared out the window of the back seat as the car journeyed westward on Route 9. Although Westville was only fifteen miles away from Danforth, Alicia had never been there before she started working at UI. All she knew of Westville before UI was that it contained the boys' reform school and Westville State Hospital.

The porch lights of the trailer park and the security lights of the garden center lit the sides of the highway, and then there was darkness. Had it been daylight, she could have seen the buildings of the Westville Boys' Reform School set back on the right, not much-changed since it was opened in 1846. The school was no longer operating, but its large brick buildings and traditional white colonial farmhouses still dotted the landscape, though they were hospital administration buildings now.

The school had been a place of discipline, punishment, isolation— and despair. Children regularly escaped from the school. And were never found. Alicia wondered *why* they were never found. Did they lose their way and perish from natural causes in the then-rural countryside of Westville? Or did they die from *un*natural causes?

Could Wesley have roamed this area? It wasn't really that far away. And if he did, how long ago was that? How old *was* he? She tried to remember if he had told her where or when he was born, or when he had died, but not surprisingly, she couldn't recall. If he had said anything, she had probably not paid attention, for—almost until the end—she was sure she was listening to the ranting of a very mortal lunatic.

Norma turned off the highway. Soon they approached a small traffic rotary in what Alicia assumed must be downtown Westville. Compact, brick buildings no more than two stories high huddled around the rotary, their exteriors stained with the soot of the industrial era in which they had been built.

In the front seats, Carol and Norma discussed directions over the blare of a disco station on the radio. "I think it would have been quicker to take Route 30," Norma noted.

"I'll have to try that next time," Carol said. Pointing to a road sign, she directed Norma, "You want 135 east." Satisfied that Norma had heard her, she continued, "I've always taken 135. I didn't notice that 30 and 135 connected downtown. I really don't know Westville."

No, neither do I. Maybe no one really knows Westville.

After passing a few more houses, Alicia could barely see the landscape, illuminated as it was by only starshine and a pale moon. It looked as though it was farmland. *I'd love to live out here. Close to work, yet quiet.* Despite the peacefulness of the pastoral scenes around her, there was an atmosphere, a stillness that unnerved her. She had felt it as they passed through the small downtown. The unsettling quality was less noticeable the farther from town they traveled, but it was still there.

Their car approached a stop at a wide Y-fork. At the *STOP* sign, Norma glanced around, not just for cars, but for bearing. Carol, noticing her uncertainty, instructed, "Bear right, and then it's going to be a right."

As their car moved off from the stop, Alicia tried to categorize her emotion. It wasn't fear; after all, having faced the possible undead, what could she fear from a mere psychic? Anticipation was probably more accurate; she had never gone for a reading before, and this man might hold the key to the mystery that had been plaguing her.

"It's going to be just after that development," Carol prompted Norma, pointing to her right.

Just ahead, Alicia could make out a low wooden fence in the light of the car's headlights. The clicking of the turn signal confirmed their destination as Norma pulled into the driveway.

As she stepped from the car, the acrid smell of wood smoke, thick on the dry, arctic January air, bit into Alicia's nostrils. Pulling her collar tight against her throat, she followed Norma and Carol over the uneven flagstones that led from the driveway to the front door of a single-story cottage, its cedar-shake siding stained ebony black.

Honeyed gold light shone through the café curtains that draped both the door and the three front windows of the wood-frame house. Norma banged the antique cast iron knocker loudly on the Wizard's front door, jarring Alicia from a momentary reverie. As they waited for him to answer, the three shifted and stamped in the cold, trying to keep warm, their shoulders hunched against the bitter wind.

An unexpected creak announced the door's opening. "Hi! Come in, come in. You must be freezing."

Norma squeezed by the tall, firmly built man who had opened the door. He placed a friendly hand on her shoulder, guiding her in. Carol and Alicia quickly followed behind, and he closed the door against the icy draft.

His blond hair streaked with white, his vivid blue eyes twinkling, he wasn't what Alicia expected in a practitioner of the occult arts. He looked too young to be her grandfather, or even her father, but there was an elder authority about him. Wearing simple blue jeans and an Icelandic-patterned sweater, he exuded ease and comfort.

He motioned them to sit, "Would you like some tea?"

"Tea's good," Norma affirmed. Alicia and Carol voiced their agreement as they settled onto a small couch. The Wizard retreated to make the tea and Alicia surveyed the small room that served as his waiting room.

To her left was a wall of fully stocked bookshelves. *That's what I should do, just have Joey put up shelves along the walls,* she noted to herself. *Bookcases are too expensive.* Unlike her own bookshelves that contained only books, the Wizard's were dotted with trinkets, including an authentic-looking voodoo doll. Its body was made of black cloth, black yarn serving as the hair. A wrap of dark red cloth was its only clothing. Propped askew against a stack of books, its white button eyes stared out into the room, its yellow embroidered mouth impassive.

On the floor across from her stood a grandfather clock. Alicia noted that it was running and that the time was accurate, yet she didn't know how accurate the moon phase inserts were. *'Depending on phase of moon.'* Alicia smiled. It was a programmer joke used to describe erratic behavior that didn't seem to have a pattern, as in "The process would fail, depending on phase of moon, and who knows what else. We've never been able to figure it out."

The room, like Alicia, seemed dressed for the cold. To the right of the clock hung an antique bed warmer and Alicia found herself wondering if it were still in use. Although a wood stove in the kitchen threw warmth that extended to the waiting room, she couldn't imagine that the outer rooms were very toasty. A thick braided rug lay between her feet and the cold floor and a large patchwork quilt hung over the back of a rocking chair. Looking at the wide white pine floor planks, Alicia realized that the house was probably built in colonial times. Even if he had insulated it, as everyone did during the oil crisis years ago, it would never be completely airtight.

Antiques abounded: a tall antique milk can, a flatiron, a spinning wheel, a shoe scraper, a crude handmade broom, and a large iron cauldron. A stuffed cat "slept" peacefully in a wicker basket near the wood stove, and it was only as she stared at it that Alicia realized that it was not a toy, but a fine specimen of taxidermy.

"Okay, here's the tea," the Wizard announced. As he sat the tray of cups down, Alicia noticed the coffee table. A tombstone.

"Yes, it's real," he said, nodding towards the stone. "It's about two hundred years old."

Taking her cup from among the others, Alicia noticed for the first time a most unusual candle holder set in a large dish. A human skull... or a remarkable replica... sat dripped in wax, a candle mounted on the top. *He really goes for the gimmicks,* she thought to herself. *I wonder how much of his reading is just show.*

She would be long in finding out. Norma was first to sit for her reading, and then Carol. Alicia was last.

The Wizard walked Carol back to the waiting area and motioned to Alicia. "Ready?"

Carol slipped by Alicia, giving her a comforting squeeze on the shoulder. "You'll love him!"

As she passed the wall of books, Alicia noticed the voodoo doll out of the corner of her eye. Whereas before it had been propped askew, head lolling to the right, it now sat straight, head turned to the *left*. Its eyes seemed to follow her as she moved past it, and there was something about those eyes that seemed to say, *Yes, go ahead, explain this. How did I move?*

A hollow tightness deep in her sternum betrayed her logical mind, which was scrambling for an explanation. *Maybe Norma or Carol bumped it going in. Maybe the Wizard moved it...* The doll seemed to smile at her attempted sleuthing.

The Wizard gently steered her toward an old stuffed armchair. "Have a seat. This is your first time here, right?"

Alicia nodded.

"I'm Alfred. People call me 'the Wizard of Westville'. There have been witches in my family for generations." He spoke quickly, in an offhand, almost bored manner as he settled into a large wingback chair, its upholstery shiny and thin with age, its wooden feet dark and gleaming. He looked at her straight on, almost *too* straight on, as if he were reading her already. Just as quickly he looked away, fiddling with a pile of papers on the small end table to his right. "My father wasn't a witch, though. Sometimes the power skips a generation." He leaned forward, once again looking straight at her, again as if reading her. "It's fifteen dollars for a basic psychic reading. You can give me the money when the reading is finished. I do cards, too, but that takes longer. Since it's getting late, I suggest we just stick with the psychic, okay?"

"Sure." She was still trying to figure out the doll. Maybe it was mechanical. Maybe there were wires and pulleys and he had thrown a switch as he followed Carol out.

In front of her the Wizard leaned his head back and closed his eyes. He lifted his chin slightly upward, and sighed deeply. Alicia wondered if he would go into trance, like in the movies, and she started to feel apprehensive. She heard that the Wizard did séances and had bragged of his power to contact spirits. She had filed it away as his way of entertaining the crowd and promoting his services, but what if it were true? What if he *could* contact the dead— or the undead? What if he contacted *Wesley?*

The room darkened. Alicia reassured herself that it was just the furnace putting a load on the electrical system. It was an old house, and even with a strong fire in the wood-burning stove, he'd have to have the furnace on as backup so that the pipes wouldn't freeze. If the heating system was forced hot air, the fan circulating the air would be switching on, and if it were electric— if he could afford electric— the heating elements would be clicking on. *Of course, the lights would dim!* She could hear the ticking of the grandfather clock in the other room and the hushed, excited voices of Norma and Carol as they undoubtedly compared notes on their readings.

The Wizard stirred, his closed eyes fluttering, his head twisting slightly as though he were trying to listen. "I see a man. Sandy hair. Not too tall, not short. Stocky. Well-built. Good with his hands. Name begins with a K. Kevin?"

"No..." *Okay, he's fishing for names, but K! What a letter to pick! Not very common around here.*

"Kenny?"

Alicia started to respond, but before she could, The Wizard latched onto another name, and before she could reply to *that* one, she saw by the smile on his face that he knew he had the right one.

"Kurt! His name is Kurt. Who's Kurt?"

"He was my boyfriend." *How did he know he had the right name? He couldn't see my reaction— his eyes are shut! And Norma and Carol don't know about Kurt.*

"Kurt. Yes! Nice guy, nice guy. Wants the wife, the kids, the white picket fence. Dinner on the table when he gets home from work. Weekends fixing the house. Summer weekends at the beach. Good man. Not for you, though. Am I right?"

"Yes, that's Kurt." She smiled as she shook her head. Yes, that certainly was Kurt. Wanted just an average life, with an average family, and an average wife.

"Yes, that's him, but that's not you." The Wizard drummed the fingers of his right hand against the arm of the chair and Alicia noticed a thick silver ring with a dark stone.

"I see walls, long corridors. Linoleum. The floors are linoleum. Bright corridors. A hospital? You work in a hospital?"

"No." *Should I tell him I was* in *the hospital? No, that would be leading.*

"No, of course not. You were *in* the hospital. Not long. For observation— "

At this point, he stopped and she noticed his hands grasp the edges of the chair arms like talons. He inhaled deeply. Outside a tiny gust of wind rattled the ancient window frames. She realized that she no longer heard Norma and Carol chattering in the other room.

The Wizard paused and in the spaces between his deep breathing she heard the wind increase, furiously rattling the panes against the mullions. "No, I see the corridors more clearly now. They're not hospital corridors. You worked there, but it wasn't a hospital." His eyes were open now and he was looking behind and beyond her, as though he were watching a scene projected on the wall. "No, not a hospital. The halls are long, and bright, but they're deserted. There's no sound. No paging, no voices. You are alone—no, wait. There's someone with you. You're walking together, talking."

Alicia stared, jaw slackened, not sure what to say. She was breathing through her mouth now, rapidly, shallowly, and she could feel her heart quicken, quicken as it did that night, that night, that terrible night—

"There was an explosion... but no one died." He opened his eyes and looked to her for affirmation.

She looked down at the floor, hoping he couldn't see the fear, the confusion, in her eyes. *No one died? What about Wesley? Does this mean he's still around, or that he didn't die because he was already dead?* How could she ask something like that?

Again the light seemed to dim, but this time she was not so quick to pass it off as overloaded wiring.

"Someone walked away." The Wizard leaned forward even more, his voice steady, low, strong, and deliberate. "He *still* walks."

"John?"

He leaned back, shaking his head, rubbing his eyes, which were closed now. "No. Not John. There is someone else there, a presence, *an evil.* I can't get a name, but I know it's not John; no, not him. I can't see this person; he's just a shadow. There's a veil, an inky veil, between him and me. I can't see him. But I do know that he walks. He still walks. And he doesn't walk alone."

Back in the shelter of her house, Alicia pulled her sweater and then her turtleneck up over her head and off. She felt the static as the ends of her hair brushed her shoulder blades, both hair and skin parched from the dry, cold air of the New England winter.

Other than the comment about Wesley, she remembered little of the rest of her reading with the Wizard. As she told Norma and Carol the next day at work, he had wrapped up the reading talking about school and her career and how she could do anything she put her mind to. She joked that she didn't need to pay him to find that out, but conceded that it was very astute of him to pick up that she had been going to school nights. It wasn't that common. "Are you sure you didn't mention it to him when you made the appointment?" she had asked Norma, but Norma insisted that she told the Wizard nothing about his new client.

Alicia was relieved when Norma and Carol started talking about their own readings, moving the focus away from hers. She couldn't tell them that what impressed her most was not that the Wizard got Kurt's name right or that he picked up that she was going to school nights, but that he knew about the explosion. Telling them that would mean telling them a lot more that she preferred never to mention.

No, she could not tell them that, nor tell them the single most important revelation of the reading— that Wesley still walked.

And that he did not walk alone.

Chapter 4

In spite of the fact that the temperature outside hovered near freezing, the sun streaming through the windows earlier in the day had warmed Rob and Janith's apartment markedly. That, combined with the heat that rose up to the fourth floor made the apartment hot, so hot that they had the living room windows partially open. Looking out over the city, noting more open windows, Matricaria could see that this wasn't the only building whose ancient boilers were cranked all the way up to ensure that heat would make it to the top floors. In the next building over, she could see open windows on the top floor and glimpses of inhabitants clothed more for spring than winter. No thick wool sweaters for them; instead they moved around in tee shirts or lightweight long-sleeved casual shirts.

Matricaria wondered if these apartments were ever anything *but* hot. She remembered the humid heat of the past summer, the warm autumn that had followed, and the cozy Yule celebration six weeks ago. Yes, maybe it was due to the way the heating worked, but now she was thinking that perhaps there was another factor. Anytime she was there, the room was always packed with people, and the body heat and magical energy certainly helped to raise the temperature.

Tonight every coven member was in attendance: the leaders Rob and Janith, and Gabe, Patty, Amethyst, Merlin, and Sybil. Elders from a sister coven would be joining them the following week to celebrate Imbolc, the ritual of the returning sun.

Rob broke the silence. "Before we discuss Imbolc...Candlemas...we have a couple of things to go over first. We need to go over some things we need to do before you get Third." The students turned to face him. Their coven practiced a degree system, a structured system of learning and advancement that had the student pass from an introductory phase through three grades, or *degrees*. With the exception of Rob and Janith, who had already made the Third Degree, those present were all Second Degrees. They had followed a set curriculum, shown evidence of strength of character and purpose, and passed tests of ability and knowledge. They now were preparing to take the Third and final degree.

In some covens, students would have had to demonstrate that they could lead and teach before they could graduate to Third. Rob and Janith's coven didn't have that as a requirement because the opportunity to teach didn't always present itself and they didn't want to hold people back just because there weren't any suitable new candidates looking for a coven.

Janith picked up the discussion. "We've had a few inquiries from people who want to join a coven, so we've decided to start a study group. This won't be a full coven...we won't have initiations and teach oath-bound material...but we *will* have overview classes on Wicca and some of the related arts like divination, astrology, and so on."

Sitting down beside Rob on the couch, Janith continued, "In our tradition, a Second Degree can lead a study group under the direction of a Third Degree High Priest or High Priestess. We're looking for volunteers to co-lead this study group as preparation for future coven leadership. I want you to think about this between now and the next time we meet and if you're interested, let us know. "

Janith turned to Rob, to indicate his turn to speak. Rob put down his cup of herbal tea. "As we said when you first joined us, no one is required to teach after they reach Third. If you just want to be a participant and not a leader, that's fine. If you don't want to participate in coven activities at all after Third, that's fine, too. This is not a cult. We have no hold on you. You can come and go as you please, and you're not required to pass on the training to others. The only thing you're required to do is keep your vows and protect the Mysteries."

Rob waited to give the message time to sink in. It was important that they know that they had a choice. "But many of you will want to continue, will want to share what you've learned. If you're considering this, we strongly suggest you consider volunteering to be one of the leaders of the study group. It'll be a good opportunity to learn the ropes of organization and group dynamics without being under the pressure one feels when teaching the full path. We'll take this up again the next time we meet. So think about it, okay?"

Later that week, Matricaria again found herself climbing the steps to the fourth-floor apartment where her coven regularly met. Tonight it would be just those who had expressed interest in organizing the new study group. As she ascended the last flight of stairs, she heard the unlocking of the security bar and door locks of Rob and Janith's apartment.

The door swung open, and into the stale, slightly sour smell of the hallway wafted the smell of sweet incense. Dressed in jeans, his silver pentagram bright against the dark fabric of his sweatshirt, Rob stood smiling in the entrance.

"Hi! C'mon in."

"Am I late?"

"No, Gabe just got here."

"Is anyone else coming?"

"No, I think this is it, unless someone decides to show at the last minute." He closed the door and locked it behind her. "I think it's just you two, but that's okay. We can still get a group together. Maybe some of the others will get involved once we get started."

Gabe rose to greet Matricaria as she entered the living room, "Hi, Mat! You know you really should call yourself 'Mat' for short. Sounds like Ma'at, the Egyptian goddess of Truth. Easier for the newbies to pronounce."

Matricaria laughed. "What's so hard about Matricaria? It's pronounced as it's written: Mat-rih-care-eee-uh. No offense to Ma'at, but I chose the name because I wanted to invoke the benefits of the herb *matricaria*."

Sighing in mock exasperation, Gabe replied, "I know. 'Wild camomille.' You want to be gifted with both healing and the spirit of the wild. Okay, we'll just have to drill them on your name."

She smiled as she placed her tote bag on the floor and removed her gloves, scarf, and down jacket. Stuffing the gloves and scarf into the sleeves, she returned to the hall and placed them on top of similar outerwear hanging over large wooden pegs.

"Oh, good. We're all here." Janith appeared from the hall that led to the bedroom and gave Matricaria a welcome hug. "Want anything to drink?"

"Tea would be nice."

"Rose Tingler?"

"What's that?"

"It's a new herbal tea that just came out. Hibiscus, rosehips, lemon grass. It's good. You'll like it."

"Sure, I'll give it a try." Matricaria took a seat on the couch next to the spot where Gabe had settled.

Janith withdrew into the small kitchenette and returned minutes later with a thick pottery mug of steaming tea and a jar of honey. She set them down in front of Matricaria and took a seat. "Okay, I think we're ready."

Rob sipped his own cup of steaming brew before speaking. "The first thing we need to do is find students. You know that out of respect for all religions, Wicca has a law of no proselytizing. We can't go out on a street corner and recruit. We can only let people know we're here and trust that the gods will send students our way."

"And they do. We just have to help them a little by making ourselves available to be found." Janith sipped her own tea.

"You know the old joke," Rob continued. "Every day a guy prays to God to let him win the lottery. This goes on day after day, week after week, month after month, year after year, until one day God bellows from the heavens, 'Do me a favor...buy a ticket already!'" He paused while the others laughed. "It's the same with our gods. We can ask them to send us students, but our petition is more likely to be answered in a reasonable amount of time if we give the students a way to find us."

"The first step," Janith continued, "is to get the word out that we're starting a study group. We've already told several elders in the Wiccan community, but we need other ways to get the word out."

Gabe leaned forward, excited. "We can put up notices on the college bulletin boards. I've got friends who are still in school who'd put 'em up for us."

"Another good idea." Rob wrote himself a note.

"How about putting an ad in the *Free Weekly*?" Matricaria volunteered. "We can write something very vague: 'Wiccan study group forming. Write and enclose SASE for more info.'"

"Good idea. We can use the *Weekly's* mailboxes or our own post office box. Any volunteers to write these things up?"

"I'll do the ones for the bulletin boards," Gabe offered.

"And since it was my idea, I'll do the ad for the *Free Weekly*. Was that wording okay?" Matricaria asked.

Janith nodded, "Sounds good to me. Use what you said, plus the actual contact information."

"It'll take a week or two before we have any responses. When we get one, we'll ask which books the person has read. If they answer with things like *The Satanic Bible*, we know they're not for us. If, on the other hand, the person's read books from our coven's reading list, then we write back and ask for a phone number and arrange a face-to-face meeting."

"Rob and I can meet them first, in a public place, probably somewhere here in town. You're both welcome to come, but don't feel you have to. The first meeting is to get a sense of the person, to make sure we're not dealing with a psychopath."

"Yeah, don't feel you have to come to the initial screening," Rob added. "You'll have your chance to meet the person after. We'll want you both to give us your opinion about suitability. It's a very subjective thing; sometimes the prospect can be a good person and well-read, but just doesn't click. Interpersonal dynamics are very important."

"For example," Janith continued, "if you have a group of serious students and the applicant is very social, very lackadaisical, that person can drive everyone crazy. However, he might fit in perfectly with another coven that believes in a lighter approach."

Gabe interrupted, "Hey! Stop talking about me!" From the exaggerated pout and puffed-out chest, everyone knew he was joking.

Janith smiled. "And sometimes a serious group *needs* a lighter touch and it will all work out. It's just something to consider."

Rob gave Gabe a few seconds to settle down and then continued. "Also, this might not be the right path for the person. There are many variants of Wiccan and magical practice. Maybe he or she is really looking for a pagan worship grove or a High Magic lodge."

"We want to accept two to three more applicants than what we consider the optimum number for a group. You always lose some during the course of training. People leave because of school, work, health, conflicts with time, conflicts with loved ones, the commute, or because they have to move out of the area. Five students is a good maximum number for a new-to-moderately experienced leader. So, we want to aim for seven or more."

Rob looked up. "Any questions?"

Gabe and Matricaria shook their heads.

"Okay. Once we accept a group of applicants, then we'll decide when and how often we'll meet. After we find out their backgrounds, we can decide on the content of the classes. Our main goal with a study group is to get to know the person and to see how he or she interacts with others."

"Do you think we'll be able to find enough applicants?" Matricaria asked.

"We should. There are a lot of people out there that we don't know about. There's an old occult maxim, probably stolen from Eastern religions, that says 'When a student is ready, the teacher will come.' Likewise, when the *teacher* is ready, the *students* will come. We just need to put the wheels in motion."

Janith smiled. "Okay, now that we have that over with, why don't we go out and get something to eat?"

Rob and Janith slid into one side of the small booth. Matricaria and Gabe slid into the other, their progress hampered by a large unrepaired tear in the dingy oxblood vinyl bench seat that caught on Matricaria's jeans as she wriggled across.

Having never visited this diner before, Matricaria cast an inquisitive eye at her surroundings. Posters of local events, their edges curling away from the nicotine- and grease-tainted walls, seemed to be the only recent additions to the décor. Scuffed and tracked with sand and salt from the streets outside, the black and white linoleum floor looked as if it could have originally been laid in the 50s. The chrome trims of the counter stools, once gleaming when the they were installed thirty years ago, were now pitted and discolored, the tarnish like bruises. Dying plants hung in pots suspended by fraying macramé cord.

The mingled smells of frying oil, stale cigarette smoke, and body odor were cloying in the overheated, low-ceilinged room. Matricaria crinkled her nose as Gabe lit a cigarette.

"Bother you?" he asked, pointing.

"Yes and no. It's better than the other smells, I guess."

Gabe laughed. "You'll get used to them."

"The food's fine," Janith assured her. "Really. We eat here often."

Rob smiled. "And so does half the student population of Bristelton. Seriously, it's not bad."

Matricaria smiled back. Though she was no stranger to cities or student hangouts, the diner had caught her off guard. "I guess I've gotten soft, living in the 'burbs."

"No diners like this?" Gabe asked, leaning back as the waitress, a gruff woman in late midlife, slid scratched glasses of water in front of each of them.

"Well, yes, but I don't eat there."

"Snob!" Gabe teased.

"Need a few minutes?" The voice was harsh and loud above the background noise of clinking silverware, clacking plates, simultaneous conversations, and the sizzle of the grill behind the counter. Tapping a spare menu against her order book, the waitress waited for a response. Everything about her seemed tired, Matricaria observed. Her hair, apparently permed and colored in the not-too-distant past, was frizzy and dry and a dull washed-out brown. Her face was sallow and her bloodshot eyes blinked as if she could fall asleep on her feet.

"Just a few," Gabe said, turning to smile at her.

Matricaria was surprised to see the woman smile back. "Okay, hon. Let me know when you're ready," she said as she turned away.

"You've got a way with the women," Janith kidded when the waitress was out of earshot.

"Yeah, too bad I'm gay!"

"Well, if it gets us better service, your gift's not wasted," Rob kidded.

"Anything you'd recommend?" Matricaria asked.

"It's all the same," Gabe said. "Edible."

Matricaria examined the sticky, laminated menu, laying it out on the table before her. Grilled cheese seemed safe. Across from her, Janith put her menu down and stared across the room, her lips straightening from a smile. Rob noticed. "What's up?"

"I don't know. I thought I saw a shadow."

"Maybe it's the lights. Maybe the freezer kicked in out back and they dimmed."

"No, it wasn't an overall dimness like that. It was more distinct, more 'contained.'"

Gabe casually turned to his left, then looked over his shoulder.

"I don't see anything."

"No, you wouldn't. It's gone now."

Rob placed his hand on Janith's forehead. "You okay?"

"Yeah, physically I'm fine. The shadow was very fleeting. I don't think it's anything on the physical plane. I'll have to do a reading on it when we get back."

"You're not dizzy or anything?"

"No, it's nothing physical. I'm fine."

Satisfied that Janith was okay, Matricaria looked down at her menu to make her final choice.

A fat black fly stared back at her with its large compound eyes. A fat black fly. In February. In New England. Where the outside temperature was well below freezing.

It sat motionless for a second, and then began sweeping its forelegs across its eyes, in typical fly fashion. In less than a second, there were two flies. Then three. Then four. Then five.

Now there were six large black flies covering Matricaria's menu, preening in unison with their forelegs. As a unit they stopped, looked at her, and then continued. As one, they turned to her right, looked at Janith, preened, and then turned to look at Rob. Again they preened, and then turned once more, continuing their counterclockwise circle, to look at Gabe. Pausing again to preen, they then continued, completing the circle facing Matricaria, where they preened once again, and then tilted their compound-eye fly faces straight up at her.

Matricaria looked up to see Janith staring, her alarm showing clearly on her wide-eyed face. Matricaria looked down again.

The flies were gone. *All six, gone!*

"You saw that?" she asked.

Janith nodded. Rob nodded.

Gabe nodded. "Shit. Here we go again."

Matricaria slipped the record onto the turntable and carefully positioned the needle at its beginning. Pausing to see if she needed to adjust the volume, she listened to the lyrics of the first song on the Alan Stivell album that Janith had just loaned her.

The song was in French, but Matricaria was no stranger to the language. She had lived in France for six months on a programming assignment a few years before. Still, her fluency had faded, and she had to listen twice, manually placing the needle back at the beginning and replaying, before she could make out "jamais nous ne comprimes." A trip to the French/English dictionary confirmed her translation: "Never did we understand."

"How appropriate!" she spoke aloud, shaking her head. "We never understood."

No, as far as the flies and the vampire, they certainly hadn't. The flies had visited her before, and though Matricaria wasn't normally afraid of flies, there had been something disturbing about them both times. For one thing, they seemed to act as a unit. She knew that group activities weren't uncommon in the insect world. Bees, for example, had highly cooperative social patterns, but this seemed different, *felt* different.

She tried to remember details from the first time she had encountered the unnatural flies, when she had wondered if they were minions of the suspected vampire. They were angry— visibly and audibly angry. Someone in the coven had mentioned their resemblance to the swarms of buzzing flies haunting the house in *The Amityville Horror*.

But this time they weren't angry; instead it seemed as if they were there to observe, to spy.

Matricaria slouched onto the couch to listen to the music and review the notes she had taken during her meeting with the coven. *Do you know how insane, how paranoid this sounds? Flies spying for someone? The vampire is gone. They're just an unusual variety of fly with strange habits.* But they had turned in unison, in a circle— in a *counterclockwise* circle.

Grabbing a fresh piece of paper, she wrote herself a note. "Go to library and look up flies." As Janith always counseled, Matricaria would start with the mundane first. Only if there were no rational scientific explanations would she consider occult ones.

Chapter 5

After the numbing lows of the days before, twenty degrees seemed almost balmy. If the weather hadn't warmed as it did, Alicia would have reduced her Saturday errands to the barest necessities, rather than risk the aggravation of her old car not starting. But the sun was shining brightly and she felt confident enough to extend her food-shopping trip.

On her way to the supermarket, she stopped at the used furniture store across from the Italian restaurant. Her collection of books had begun to outpace her collection of *bookcases*. She was going to ask Joey how much it would cost for built-in book shelves, but thought that it wouldn't hurt to make the rounds of used furniture stores in case an inexpensive freestanding bookcase or two was available.

Driving into the parking lot, she didn't notice anything different. It wasn't until she left her car and started walking toward the entrance that she realized that the sign for the used furniture store had been removed. Curious now, she continued toward the glass storefront to read a small, hand-painted sign that said:

> Want to find fresh, healthy food at reasonable prices?
> Join the Danforth Food Co-Op.
>
> Volunteer work from our members keeps prices down. To maintain active member status, you must volunteer 8 hours a month. Volunteer work includes repacking bulk items, stocking shelves, unloading trucks, bagging groceries, putting away food at night, and cleaning up. But it's not all hard work. Volunteering is a great way to meet people. C'mon in and see what we have to offer!

Alicia never expected to find a food co-operative in Danforth. Danforth was a fairly conservative, blue-collar town. She couldn't imagine it being very friendly towards what the townspeople would most likely consider a hippie establishment.

Yielding to her inquisitive nature, she entered the store. She found herself in a single spacious, rectangular room with walls that were bare except for a few posters and bulletin boards near the cash register. Large cardboard barrels of oats, barley, millet, rice, and bulgur, with small hand-lettered squares of white paper labeling each barrel, stood to the left.

At the rear of the store, floor-to-ceiling shelves in one corner were laden with paper bags and gallon jars of herbs and spices. Had her nose not been stuffed up from the dry winter air, she would have smelled the spices long before seeing them, their rich contrasting smells vying for attention. She recognized the names of the more common spices like ginger, nutmeg, sage, and thyme, and some of the herbs like camomille and spearmint, but there were other unfamiliar ones with exotic names like asafetida, damiana, hyssop, and mugwort. Some of the spices, like cardamom and nutmeg were whole. Other than cloves, Alicia had never seen a whole spice before.

"Hi, welcome to the Danforth Food Co-Op. Are you a member?"

Alicia turned. A relaxed older woman in jeans and flannel shirt had appeared from behind the counter.

"Uh, no. Is that okay?"

"Sure. Non-members can shop here, but we add a ten per cent surcharge to all your purchases. Feel free to look around."

"Thanks. I think I will." She wandered through the aisles, noting things she missed on initial examination.

Her sense of wonderment increased as she looked around the room. In the center of the front of the store were vegetable bins and racks of canned and packaged goods, many of them foreign to her: couscous, tahini, hummus, tabouleh. To the right was a large refrigerated unit with glass doors through which she could see containers of milk, cheese, and yogurt. On the bottom shelf, chunks of tofu lay submerged in an open bucket of water. She had never seen whole tofu before, having encountered it only as small, fried cubes in Chinese dishes, and wouldn't have recognized it were it not for the label on the bucket.

As she continued to wander, she noticed volunteers in the back weighing and bagging dried fruit. One looked up at her and smiled. She thought she recognized him. "You look familiar. Are you Dick Gilder?"

"Yes. Hi."

Alicia introduced herself. They had been in a creative writing class together in high school. He was a year behind her, an aspiring guitarist and folksinger whom she admired. He had always been friendly toward her, even though she wasn't one of the "in" crowd and wasn't pretty or rich or talented.

"Yes, I remember you. Hi! What have you been up to since high school? Still writing?"

"Well, yes, but these days it's programs, not songs."

They caught up on each other's lives. She listened, envious as he talked about his modest gigs at local folk houses. She felt almost embarrassed to admit that any creative leanings she had had in high school had been sub-jugated to her desire to get ahead in the computer field. As memories often do, one surfaced unexpectedly: she remembered a guidance counselor tell-ing her that she was gifted in humanities and language and that her chosen career should be in one of those fields— and that the one field that she should avoid was the cold, dry field of computers. But computers had cap-tivated her and the income from a career in computers offered her the possibility that she'd never be dependent on the kindness of others again, as she had when her parents died...

Dick's end of the conversation started to wind down and, not wanting to wear out her welcome, Alicia made her apologies, saying she had other errands to do.

"Good talking to you," Dick responded. "Hope you'll consider joining. This is a good place. Good people."

"Yeah, I think I will."

Walking back to the front of the store, she reflected on how welcoming they all were, not like the store personnel at the grocery downtown who either ignored her or looked at her as though she might steal something. And not like the snobs in high school who were always looking for reasons to *exclude* you, not include you.

As Alicia passed the cash register, the woman who had greeted her held out a small brochure and a mimeographed application form. "So, would you like to join the Co-op? To be a full member, you pay $15 a year and volunteer eight hours a month."

"I'm not sure I can commit to eight hours. I'll be going back to school nights this summer, I hope. I'll have classes at least two nights a week and then homework."

"No problem. You can just pay the extra surcharge when you're short on hours or you can bank hours now and apply them to the months when you're unable to volunteer."

"Really? Okay, I guess I can give it a try." Even with the assurance that she wouldn't be held inflexibly to those hours, Alicia didn't like to commit to anything without research and contemplation, but this woman was so encouraging that she couldn't find a reason to say no. Alicia took out her checkbook and wrote a check for the membership fee.

"And if you find you can't make the hours, even with banking, and you don't want to pay the surcharge, you can always cancel your membership."

She should have felt even more assured by that information, but she wasn't. To Alicia, resigning would be quitting— she was already more committed than she wanted to be right now. On the other hand, it would be nice to get involved with people who were back-to-the-land. And it would be good to get out again, away from her memories.

Cluster flies. They were called cluster flies. Or, in some parts of the country, attic flies.

Matricaria shut the encyclopedia volume and walked over to the large, low shelving unit to replace it. The library on Saturday was noisier than she remembered it as a child. Were librarians getting lax in shushing their customers, or was Matricaria experiencing the common misremembering of childhood?

Matricaria sat back down at the highly polished library table and made some notes. Cluster flies seek shelter in the walls and attics of buildings in late fall, and then go dormant. The artificial warmth that makes buildings habitable for humans in the winter wakes the flies from their dormancy. Through random crawling, they find entrances to the living spaces, where they seek light and warmth. That part made sense; the diner was indeed warm, and she was sure the old building had many cracks and crevices through which they could gain entry.

She paused, letting her pen rest against the paper as she contemplated what to write next. Cluster flies were sluggish. They tended to crawl more than fly. And the only communal, social activity mentioned was the activity that gave them their name: when the air was chilly, they gathered in clusters.

So the flies were real. But there was something in their behavior that was unusual, un-flylike.

Matricaria returned to the shelf housing the encyclopedias and pulled out the volume for V— for vampire.

Vampires are all about control, Meg wrote in her notebook. *No references to vampires controlling insects per se, but they were alleged to have control over nature: wolves, the weather. And if they can control something as powerful as the weather or as intelligent as a wolf, then why not a fly?*

Meg put away her notebook and filled two bowls with cat food before starting to get her ritual gear together. Tonight they would celebrate Imbolc during the week, on the actual day, instead of waiting for the weekend.

To her coven and to other witches who shared their belief system, *Imbolc* represented the center point of the dark half of the year, midway between the Winter Solstice and the Spring Equinox. In temperate climates, snowdrops and crocuses would be poking their heads above the hard earth at this time.

Meg peeked out the kitchen window. Either the squirrels had made a meal of the bulbs over the winter, or it was just too early for the first stirrings of spring in New England. No green shoots. Yet she had noticed that it was now light when she left work in the evening, and that alone was cause for celebration.

She and her covenmates were not just witches, practitioners of magical arts, but were also Wiccans, followers of a relatively modern reconstruction of agriculturally based religious practices that had their origins in prehistory.

In some Wiccan traditions, the holiday was called Candlemas even though there were Christian celebrations by the same name, celebrated by blessing candles. Meg pondered the similarity for a second. She thought that the explanation she heard from the nuns as a child was a bit of a stretch— that the candles symbolized Christ's light and were there to remind the faithful of his birth at Christmas— but did it matter? It was comforting that these two inconsonant religions had similar celebrations, as did many others throughout the world at this time of year, no matter what their explanation.

Still peering out the window, she recalled the old English weather prediction:

> If Candlemas day be fair and bright,
> Winter will have another flight.
> If Candlemas day be shower or rain,
> Winter is gone and will not come again.

Americans had transferred this folklore to a local inhabitant, the groundhog. If he saw his shadow—that is, if the day was bright— there would be six more weeks of winter. Oddly enough, six weeks brought one to the next Wiccan holiday, the Spring Equinox. Once again, she was comforted, this time by the fact that the old beliefs lived on, whether people knew it or not.

Her comfort was shallow, however, for today had been one of the brightest, sunniest days since weather records were kept in the area, and she could only wonder how dark would be the next six weeks.

Chapter 6

Frederick liked to keep moving.

Three years ago, on the night of the explosion, he moved away from the warehouse that he and Wesley had made their refuge. Wesley had detested the plainness and grime of the old cement structure, dingy despite years of painting and repainting, and he had commanded that they move to a more refined habitat— a disused but elegant train station.

Soon after dark Frederick arose from the large crate that served as his bed. Wesley had already left the premises, presumably not wanting to spend more time than was absolutely necessary in those dreary surroundings. Frederick stood by the wooden shipping crate, stretching and yawning, thinking about what he'd do with his night. His thoughts were interrupted when he felt the blast and heard the sound of breaking glass and falling debris, followed soon thereafter by wailing sirens.

Cautiously he had left his sanctuary and ducked behind the evergreen bushes that flanked the warehouse door. He watched across the parking lot as the fire engines discharged their space-suited passengers, who then disappeared into the turbulent clouds of smoke that had obscured the building's entrance. He continued to watch as a crowd gathered outside in the wintry cold. Uniformed men emerged, pulling two people from the building.

Assured that the explosion hadn't endangered his hiding place, he left the warehouse grounds swiftly and went in search of sustenance and amusement. He returned to the warehouse just before dawn.

He slept late the following evening and was surprised that Wesley hadn't awakened him and lectured him for sleeping in. He was even more surprised the next night when he awoke late again, to the sound of whistling wind and nothing more, and realized that Wesley might not have returned to the warehouse at all.

It took his sleep-fogged brain a few minutes to make the connection between Wesley's absence and the explosion, and even then he couldn't believe his luck. *Wesley gone?*

At a local downtown bar that night, he managed to overhear enough conversation to put together the details of the incident. An accident in one of Theoretic's labs. Security guard seriously injured, but stable now. Female employee treated and released.

If anyone else had been in the lab, they would have been toast.

Wesley never stayed away overnight. He was a stickler about returning to his refuge each morning before dawn. The only explanation for his disappearance was that Wesley was dead. *Really* dead. Not walking *un*dead, but *dead*.

While listening to the conversations around him at the bar, Frederick had been barely able to contain himself, could barely hold himself back from jumping on a table and dancing in sheer joy. *Free! No more Wesley!* No more being nagged to get up and get out the minute the sun set. No more degrading comments about Frederick's disheveled appearance nor disapproving looks when Frederick returned from a night's hunt smelling of cigarettes, beer, and traces of women's perfume.

No more Wesley!

But with that joy came worry. What if Wesley— or his demise— left clues at the scene? Whoever was investigating the explosion at the research lab might also look in the warehouse. Frederick was no longer confident that his hiding place was safe. The warehouse might be too "hot." Frederick would have to find another place to stay, but he didn't want to go downtown to the old train station that he and Wesley had been preparing. It was too creepy and smelled of moldering pigeon shit. Besides, if Wesley was still alive— rather, *undead*— that would be where *he'd* go.

Rising quickly from his crate the next night, Frederick had then cautiously made his way outdoors and surveyed the area. If he moved far away, he'd be safest from investigations, but he'd never know if Wesley came back and never know what the investigations were turning up. He needed to stay somewhere nearby, where he could keep an eye on things.

Looking across the street he could see the peaked front entrance of the local sports club. He knew the building. He had played basketball and volleyball there, when he was alive. ALL WELCOME, the sign said, and Frederick took that to mean him. He walked in the front door and registered as a member. He had some money he had lifted from a woman's purse and he still had his license and mailing address from before...

The license was all he had left to remind him that he was once human. In December, in the weeks when the sun set before the Registry of Motor Vehicles locked its doors, Frederick had spent the night in the hobo camp near the train tracks, just minutes away from the Registry building. As soon as the sun had set, he had risen and sprinted to the line of tired, grumbling patrons who glanced nervously at the clock, wondering if they would make it to the head of the line before the clerk closed for the day. It had taken him three tries, something he never would have endured when he was alive, but he made it, renewing his license, his passport to the human world.

He hadn't been sure that it was even possible. Could he be photographed? Those old horror movies said vampires didn't cast reflections. Were photographs reflections? Could his reflection be captured? Wesley had never explained things like that. Frederick was left to discover the facts on his own.

With doubts nibbling at his brain, he had tried anyway, using his long wait in line to think about what he'd do if he *couldn't* be photographed. "Hey, maybe your camera's broken. I'll come back later..." Yeah, he'd just act as confused as everyone else and leave.

But that hadn't been necessary. He had been photographed— a little paler than usual, but then again, it *was* December at the time— and with that photograph he got a license, which meant that he was able to register at the sports club and allowed to enter as freely as any other paying member.

Once inside the building, he made a mental map of all the utility closets and locked doors. The following night, he found a hiding place just before closing time and then waited for the building to clear. When he was sure he was alone, he investigated. His first good find was the folding stairs to the attic crawl space. As he suspected, it contained a few boxes and enough dust and cobwebs to convince him that the place was rarely visited. Dry and relatively warm, it sure beat the warehouse, and it didn't take him long to figure out how to fold up the stairs behind him.

Having hunted earlier, Frederick had nothing else to do the rest of the night. He thought he'd dribble a basketball a bit. He hadn't played any sport since that fateful night that Wesley turned him into one of the undead, and he didn't know how his muscles would respond now that they were dead.

Casually he tossed the ball from hand to hand, noticing how light it felt. He knew he'd have to be gentle, but he didn't realize *how* gentle until his first attempt at a dribble.

He turned his hand over, letting gravity take the ball. When it bounced back up, he meant to bounce it gently downward. Instead, when he tapped it, it flattened against the floor, disintegrating with the force.

As he hid the evidence of the exploded ball, he was thankful he hadn't tried a dunk. *Shit! Darryl Dawkins shattered the backboard! I probably would have pulled down a wall!*

He found some more balls and practiced through the night until he had just the right, light touch that would allow him to play without destroying the ball.

Frederick was giddy with the thought of what could be. "Whoa, if the guys from Danforth High could see me now!" he bellowed in delight. He could just imagine them sidling up to him in that chummy guy way, could hear them flattering him and trying to cajole him to join *their* team. He winced as he thought of how many times it was the other way around: him slapping a buddy on the back, buttering him up with exaggerated praise, hoping to be chosen...

It could be so different now. With this previously undiscovered strength, he could be the best basketball player in the NBA! He could be bigger than Larry Bird, or Magic Johnson, or even Dr. J!

His visions of clamoring photographers, luxury cars, and throngs of adoring women trembling with admiration and desire faded rapidly as he realized his limitation: how far could he go before he'd have to appear in sunlight? Not all games were night games. And there would be practices, press conferences, team meetings, most of them occurring during the day.

As the night waned and dawn approached, he accepted his fate. He had the physical power to be the best, to be the strongest athlete anyone could imagine, to outdo every sports hero he had worshipped since childhood, but to survive, he could only be what he had been in life: mediocre.

Nevertheless, he could play the game. He could join one of the recreational teams there. Playing would give him something to do in the long, empty hours after the hunt and the camaraderie would help slay the loneliness that crept up on him as his undead life wore on.

It would be just like old times... playing with the guys, going for a beer afterward. Flirting with the women at the bar. Telling dirty jokes and making rude comments. Laughing. He would welcome that. He had spent too many nights with long-faced, serious Wesley.

And so Frederick spent the dark, cold winter months playing basketball and hanging with the guys a couple of nights a week. At the end of the night, when his teammates headed for the comforts of sleep and home, he would head for the bleakness and desolation of the hunt, followed by the silence and shadows of the unused attic crawlspace.

As a member of the sports club, it was easy enough for him to come and go in the evening, when the building was open to the public. Eventually he discovered other ways to get in, so that he was never locked out if he didn't make it back by the time the place closed.

There was always a way to get in before sunrise. There was always the pool. Swim teams practiced as early as 5 a.m. As long as some luscious lady allowed him to stay— and luscious ladies were usually the reason Frederick returned late— he never had to wait out in the cold. By May, though, the sun would start to rise before the pool opened and he would have to move on.

Often, on his way back to the club, before the pallid winter sun crept up over the frozen horizon, he would stop at the edge of the parking lot where he had a clear view of the warehouse across the street. There he would stand in perfect stillness, listening, sniffing the air, hoping that somehow he'd know it if Wesley had returned. That revelation never came.

Frederick had had to move from the club earlier than he had hoped. He had gotten into the habit of leaving back doors unlocked some nights so that he could sneak back in early to the warmth of the building, and the maintenance staff began to notice. He had also been, as he was in life, lazy about picking up after himself, and people began to observe that equipment, carefully put away the night before, was no longer tidily stacked and stored.

Staff whispered among themselves about ghosts, and more than one person cited the recent movie, "Poltergeist" and an older movie, "The Amityville Horror," suggesting that maybe poltergeist or demonic activity was responsible for the unexplained movement of items after hours. Other staff members took a more practical approach and decided that maintenance and security should patrol the building more frequently.

No matter which belief prevailed— psychic phenomena or intruder— the outcome was the same: Frederick had to move.

It was very early spring, before people started getting out the rakes and lawn mowers, so he managed to stay in the garden sheds of some nearby houses. They were cramped and uncomfortable and some weren't sunlight-proof. Where the sun managed to leak in and hit him, his skin was painfully burned. And where the sun intruded, so did the cold spring rain. But it was shelter, and it sufficed.

Every few days, at dusk or just before dawn, just as he had when he hid at the sports club, he stopped at the edge of the warehouse parking lot, and watched carefully to see if Wesley returned. Still there was no sign. He had checked the train station downtown and found that the vagrants and pigeons had returned. Knowing Wesley's desire for privacy and cleanliness, he doubted Wesley would stay in those conditions. It was looking more as if his hopes were realized: that Wesley really had been destroyed in the explosion.

No longer tied to the warehouse to keep an eye on things, Frederick started moving further away. Unlike Wesley, he didn't care if his refuge was or wasn't the same each night. After the sheds, his next stop was a beautiful old cemetery built in 1848, created in the romantic style popular at the time. Frost heaves had set a door to one of the outbuildings ajar, allowing Frederick entrance, but it wasn't long before the groundskeepers noticed. On the lookout for teenage drinking, they had begun to patrol more often, and soon Frederick left the lichen-covered gravestones of the old Grove Cemetery.

His next refuge was at the Marist Fathers' property a few miles away. A former seminary, it had closed six or seven years earlier. It was boring, not really Frederick's style, but it gave him time to think, to plan. It had lots of outbuildings he could use and the Fathers went to bed early, so if he bided his time, he didn't have to worry about them seeing him leave in the evening.

But they did rise early, which meant he had to cut his late nights short or leave the bed of a lover early, so a few months later, he moved on, setting his course toward where the action was: Route 9. Frederick figured that if he could stay where the action was, there would always be someone to feed on.

And Route 9 was the *last* place Wesley would be, if he were still around. Wesley felt that he and Frederick were safer downtown, especially in the places where the drunks, hobos, and poorer people were. Wesley said no one cared about *those* people and there would be less fuss if one of them disappeared. Wesley said they must stay away from, as he put it, "those of better station."

Maybe Wesley was right, but there were a lot of lonely, single people frequenting the clubs and bars on Route 9 who had no one to go home to. And "better station" or not, many of them had no one to miss them if they didn't return home.

And besides, it was more fun there. He'd take his chances.

Frederick's move up Route 9 was in steps. He had avoided going east because he knew that's where Wesley would go, east along the "Golden Mile" as it entered exurb, then suburb, and then became just another large thoroughfare in the city of Fenmore.

Instead, Frederick moved west. As long as he hugged Route 9, he could be assured of a large enough food supply. Route 9 east of Danforth might have held most of the area's retail shops and inhabitants, but the population was beginning to spread westward as well.

On his own way westward, he tarried a few months at the Raceland Estate. Originally the home of a wealthy businessman, the estate was eventually sold off in parcels, and in 1971, the town of Danforth acquired part of it for conservation purposes. Frederick had fifty-seven acres of meadows, wetlands, and upland forest at his disposal.

But it wasn't the beauty of the green nature preserve that attracted Frederick. For him the attraction was proximity to the highway. Route 9 provided ample opportunities for finding rides, people, and parties. At gas stations, he would approach truckers and ask for a lift, making up some story about his car breaking down and it being his girlfriend's birthday and him needing a ride to meet her at a club. Or he'd approach a van full of people out for a party and talk his way into joining them. After he managed to steal a couple of ounces of pot from a very stoned group of guys returning from a concert in the city, it was even easier to invite himself along. All he had to do was offer to share a joint.

And Route 9 being Route 9, the travelers were often transients. Opened in 1810 as the Fenmore to Worcester Turnpike, it had a long history of people just passing through. Becoming a free road in the 1840s opened it up to the local population, but a large proportion of travelers were still just passing through, which made it easier for Frederick to feed and steal without arousing suspicion.

Sometimes he would travel further west with his quarry, watching the lights fade as the scenery turned to farmland and then back to gas stations, restaurants, warehouses, and retail shops as they approached the outskirts of Worcester. Sometimes he would travel even further west along the old coach road as it passed Worcester, to towns he never knew existed, small towns that might have been far in the backwater for their charming lack of sophistication, yet were mere minutes from the second largest city in Massachusetts.

There he would stay for a few days, never having trouble finding a deserted building or a willing bed partner, and then work his way back east along Route 9 again, finding rides back to Danforth at gas stations, bars, or truck stops.

At Raceland, he rotated his hiding places through the sheds and old dog kennels. In summer, he found shelter in the thick dark of the white pine and hemlock woodland. Some of the bushes out in the back of the old mansion were so dense that local teenagers had trimmed them out underneath, sneaking in there at night for drinking and partying. A few tried to muscle him out of their secret hiding place, but they were no match for Frederick and he soon had a section to himself. Not trusting the bushes to provide complete protection from sunlight, he had dug a deep burrow under an outcropping of rock deeper in the woods, using his bush sanctuary for nighttime relaxation only.

Life was good, though it was a little dirty. His sleeping burrow left him covered with damp earth and bits of leaves and roots. His bush retreat left him covered with leaves and sometimes cigarette butts.

There was a large stream nearby, and Frederick soon adopted it as his own private bath. He would wade in fully clothed, washing both body and raiment at the same time. The water was cold, but so was he.

In the fall, Frederick moved again.

Frederick liked to keep moving.

The vast loneliness of the Raceland Estate had made Frederick realize that he was more a people person than a recluse. He had made few friends among the teenage bush visitors, who seemed wrapped in their own tight society, intent on playing out their own high school dramas and romances. Although he was a mere ten years older than them, he was ancient in their eyes, a perception not the result of his undead condition. He was merely an adult, and therefore *old*.

Not far northwest of the edges of the Raceland Estate, on his habitual east-west highway, lay a group of three apartment complexes. Much taller than their surroundings, they overlooked a large reservoir, a backup in a system of tunnels and aqueducts that transported water from the western part of the state to the eastern metropolitan area.

The three apartment complexes had distinct communities, differing mainly by who could afford the different tiers of rental fees, yet they had one thing in common: a large and often-changing population of people— mostly young— drawn by the ease of apartment life and the quick access to highways. To Frederick, the three buildings represented action, life, possible female companions, and an unending supply of sustenance.

Frederick preferred the last one, Reservoir Hills. With over 1,000 units, it was the largest, and therefore the one with the most possibilities. Its inhabitants were mostly younger than those of the other complexes, drawn by the comparatively cheaper rent and the amenities: a small house behind the back parking lot had been converted to a residents-only nightclub. Drawn, too, they were, by the fact that Reservoir Hills was full of people like themselves. Unlike Reservoir Terrace at the far end of the three groups of apartments, which attracted older, more settled dwellers, Reservoir Hills was THE place for up-and-coming singles.

For Frederick, Reservoir Hills had another amenity. During the day, everyone was away, at work. With the exception of the maintenance staff, there was no one to stumble upon Frederick as he slept. There were storage sheds in the back, behind the clubhouse and larger storage buildings on the grounds of the golf course behind that, where Frederick could seek shelter without being disturbed. He soon discovered that the doors to the large furnace room of the first apartment building were rarely locked, and the far corner of the room was well out of view and never visited.

At night, people were always walking to and from the clubhouse, even during the week. Danforth, being in the suburbs, gave them a false sense of safety, and often they'd walk alone. It was easy for a friendly guy like Frederick to win a lady's trust, especially if she had been a little self-indulgent with the low-priced drinks there.

The clubhouse was for "residents only" and their guests. Frederick regularly charmed ladies into taking him in as a guest, and soon he became so well-known that the bouncers started letting him in on his own, without showing a membership card.

And if Frederick should bring a guest himself, some woman from the truck stop or the strip clubs further west, and if that woman never appeared again, no one noticed, no one asked, no one told.

And if Frederick, in the heat of blood lust should bite too hard or drink too deeply, if the warmth of her body and her urgent pressing, open-legged, against him should stir him beyond control, then the brooding, dark woods beyond the outbuildings and the cold immobile waters of the reservoir, from which the apartment complex drew its name, kept Frederick's secrets best of all.

Yeah, life was good at The Rez.

Chapter 7

Alicia was sitting alone in the cafeteria when Meg approached.

"Alicia! Mind if I join you?"

"No, not at all. Some of the people in my department are going to be sitting here. They're getting their lunch now, but I'm sure they won't mind. You might know some of them already."

"Okay, if you're sure they won't mind. I'll go get my lunch. Know what they're serving today?"

"No, I never pay attention." She pointed to the brown paper bag and the sandwich she was pulling from it. "I always bring mine. Saves money."

"Probably a good idea. I should do that more often. I'll be right back."

"Okay."

Alicia withdrew a packet of homemade cookies from her lunch bag. She was glad Meg had chanced upon her. She had been meaning to get in touch with her for lunch, but now that her initial training period was over, she was so busy that she had started eating at her desk. It was pure chance that Norma and Carol had talked her into joining them for a change.

For a moment she worried that they would mind that she had invited Meg to sit with them. *This isn't high school, Alicia. Why would they mind? We're adults.* But adults or not, she had seen enough petty group dynamics to feel a slight apprehension.

Norma was the first to return to the table. "Wasn't someone here a minute ago?"

"Meg McMillan. She and I used to work together at Theoretic. Mind if she joins us?"

"No problem. Theoretic?"

"It's short for 'theoretical.' They do research."

"Oh. What does your friend do here?"

Alicia filled in Norma, and Carol, too, as she arrived, on what Meg did and where she worked.

Norma transferred her food from her tray to the table. "Good, it'll be nice to meet her." She turned to Carol. "By the way, did you hear Fergus's wife had the baby?"

Carol frowned as her plastic knife bent with her efforts to cut her chicken cutlet. "No. What did they have?"

"A boy. I don't know what they're going to name him." Norma dropped her voice to a conspiratorial volume and looked around casually to see who was sitting close to them. "Let's see how long it takes Fergus to get promoted *this* time."

Alicia cocked her head and looked back at Norma, puzzled. "What do you mean?"

"He gets promoted every time his wife has a baby."

"Really? Why?"

"Because he has another mouth to feed."

"But that doesn't mean he deserves a promotion! No, that can't be true. It's got to be coincidence, right? Personnel would never let them get away with promoting someone just because his wife had a baby."

"No? Okay, when was the last time he got promoted?"

"I don't know. I just started working here, remember?"

"Oh, yeah. Okay, it was two years ago. When his daughter was born. And the time before that? About two years. When his first son was born."

Alicia looked at Carol, who nodded.

"Are you sure it isn't just because he's been in the position for two years and has done well?"

"Maybe. But the timing's pretty suspicious. We'll see, won't we? How much do you want to bet that we don't hear about his promotion within two weeks of his kid's birth?"

Alicia was silent. She had hoped that UI would be different, that they would promote on merit, not on any non-business factor. They seemed to be egalitarian enough about hiring women.

"Do they promote women when they have kids?"

"Yeah, right!" Norma replied, snorting. "Women are lucky they don't lose their jobs for missed time from work."

Alicia was about to protest, to comment on the unfairness of it all, when Meg approached the table.

"Hi. Room for one more?"

"Sure. Meg, this is Norma..." Alicia remembered her manners and introduced everyone, but her heart wasn't in it, not wholly, for a little of it died along with her idealism when she realized that UI was probably going to be like any other business, progressive or not.

Alicia distractedly crammed bites of a tuna fish sandwich in her mouth while carefully doling out Moonshadow's food. She watched for a moment as the doll-faced Persian gently nibbled at the smelly mound, then tucked in with a little more vigor. He purred as he ate and she could think of nothing more desirable at the moment than to stand and bask in his gratitude. Unlike others in her life, Moonshadow was always content with what she did, grateful for every aid or comfort. "You're so easy to please, Moonie." He looked up, blinked his clear, bright green eyes, and then continued to eat and purr, eat and purr.

Glancing at her watch, Alicia grabbed her overloaded pocketbook and reluctantly left the house.

She had agreed to go to Norma's KopperWerkes home party to be supportive, and now she scolded herself for giving in. She didn't have money to spend on home decorations or fancy copper pots, and she really should be painting a room or cleaning the house instead of spending an evening looking at things she couldn't afford to buy. Alicia felt both resentful and guilty, just as she did when Susie used to coax her out to nightclubs.

Susie! At the time that Susie disappeared, Alicia had been caught up in the emotional maelstrom of the vampire and the explosion, and hadn't been able to ponder it much, but lately it seemed that everything reminded her of Susie and she realized how few answers she had regarding her disappearance. Susie was devoted to her daughter and sacrificed everything for her. It didn't make sense that she would suddenly run away with a man, which is the only conclusion the police could come up with.

"Darn!" she spoke aloud as she braked for a red light, "I should have asked the Wizard about her!" She made a mental note. She'd have to go for another reading. Her first one, no matter how amazing it was in its accuracy, hadn't given her many answers, and now she was finding more questions.

The light changed to green and Alicia took a left, then her first right into the parking lot. Norma had instructed her to park along the back, where there was plenty of visitor parking. The lot in the back was chunky with ice and sand, where the shade from the trees and buildings prevented the sun from melting the deep ridges and tracks. As she stepped out of the car, her left foot slid out from under her. Thinking quickly, she grabbed the car door and caught herself before she splayed completely flat. Even though she was wearing sensible winter boots, she was no match for the ice. The warmth of the day had melted just enough of it to form a thin sheen of water on top, making it even more slippery.

Walking with knees bent like a skier, Alicia trudged across the parking lot. The hint of coming spring earlier in the day had quickly retreated when the sun set, leaving just the cold and wind, which buffeted her as she walked. Through the top of the bony framework of a stand of leafless trees to her left, she could see a moonless sky just beyond the pale lights of the parking lot. Ambient urban lighting blotted out what stars might have risen, but the light was not bright enough to blot out a caul of menace that hung over the deserted lot.

Alicia tried to attribute this perception to the normal instinctual fear one felt in a empty parking lot. *There are enough real things to fear without imagining more.* A forceful blast of wind struck her head on, taking her breath away, and forcing her attention back to physical reality.

She stared at the ground as she walked, concerned about her footing on the icy ground, leaving her less aware of her surroundings. Concerned now for a different type of safety, she looked up. Motion to her left had caught her eye, and for a moment she thought she saw something, or someone. Reproaching herself for allowing herself to be so vulnerable, she scanned the periphery, holding her breath to hear better.

Except for the traffic noise from Route 9, the lot was quiet. Beneath the trees she could see fallen branches, wintered-over bushes, and pieces of litter. *Litter.* It was probably just flying litter, caught by a gust of wind.

Regardless, Alicia quickened her pace.

Again it was bitter cold when Frederick awoke, which meant that finding people out and about was unlikely. He thought for a minute about his options. He could, of course, try the strip joints further west, but he didn't feel like trudging that far in the cold wind. Or he could hang around the clubhouse out back and see if anyone was desperate enough to brave the frigid night. There would be the regulars, of course, but he didn't think it was a good idea to feed on those who could identify him. He doubted anyone else would wander in.

What the fuck. Worth a shot. Zipping the jacket that he wore more for show than warmth, he left the shelter of the furnace room and swung around back.

True to his suspicions, there were few people about.

He saw only one, a woman, face wrapped in a thick scarf, stepping cautiously as if she were descending an alpine mountain. *There's an easy target.* He looked around to see if there were any witnesses. When he looked back, his prey had covered considerably more ground and was almost at the rear entrance.

Damn! Too close to the door.

Frederick turned away.

Meg looked at the clock. *Still early. Maybe I should pack my gear for tonight now, so I don't forget. Can't forget the incense.* It was her turn to lead the full moon ritual the following night and she mustn't forget the incense. It wasn't that Janith and Rob wouldn't have any on hand at the covenstead, it was that this incense was special— she had made it herself as part of the general preparation for ritual.

Until Janith and Rob gave the incense-making class, she had thought that the process was relatively easy; you found herbs or resins said to be appropriate for the working, and then mixed them together, and that was it.

On incense-making night, however, she discovered that some herbs smelled absolutely foul when burnt, or gave off a smoke that caused everyone to choke and cough. And if you weren't going to be using a block of charcoal to burn your incense on, you had to have a binding agent to keep the ingredients together and saltpeter to help it burn. Although many pharmacies carried saltpeter, you had to ask for it at the counter. Its other use as an ingredient in gunpowder and its alleged use to quell male sexual desire made Meg want to avoid having to do that.

Fortunately for her, the coven had an ample supply of round self-lighting charcoal blocks, which meant that she needed only to choose and mix the herbs and spices, which would then be sprinkled over the lit charcoal. The coven had found the charcoal blocks at a church supply shop in the city where they also found other hard-to-get items like beeswax candles and incense made from genuine frankincense and myrrh. But they wouldn't be using that rare incense for this ritual. They'd be using hers.

She retrieved the jar of incense from a shelf in her closet, and gave it a gentle shake to further blend the ingredients. Opening it for one last sniff before putting it in her bag, she could still smell the previous inhabitants of the jar. *That's okay. Olives have magical uses, too.*

When she had first rinsed the olive jar and noticed that the sweet musky aroma lingered, she had checked her herb notes, just to be sure that olives would be okay. Rob and Janith would be asking her about which ingredients she used and why, and would probably smell the olives themselves when they opened the jar for inspection. Even though there were no olives to contaminate the incense, the fact that the smell lingered meant that the *influence* lingered, and in magic, influences were important.

Recapping the jar, Meg decided to dump out her ritual bag to make sure that she had everything. It wouldn't do to start the ritual only to discover that she was missing an important prop or ritual tool. She took a towel from the bathroom and spread it out across the bed, and then gently upended the duffel bag, allowing her gear to softly tumble onto the towel. *Robe, cheat sheet, wand... what's this?*

Poking out from underneath her voluminous black cotton robe lay a stout piece of wood, *willow* wood to be exact. Meg froze for a moment as she remembered when and why she placed the wood in the bag.

Three years ago she thought she might need to sharpen the soft wood to a point as a weapon against the vampire that haunted Theoretic, haunted Alicia, haunted her. She had never whittled that point, though. The coven had instead used magic to drive the vampire away.

As she stood holding the light-but-strong piece of *Salix babylonica*, she wondered how long their spell would last. Was he driven away forever, or just for as long as their freshman attempts at magic would keep him at bay?

And were there others? The silence of her bedroom seemed stronger, enveloping, as Meg's thoughts swarmed with possibilities. *No, we weren't even sure that he* was *real...*

But he had appeared...

—and the flies...

Meg held the unsharpened stake with both hands now, vertically, against her chest. She could feel the wood warming and could feel the energy flow from her hands into the wood, swirl, and then circle back again.

And somehow she knew that he *was* real and that the willow stick would find a permanent place in her ritual bag; permanent, that is, after a short venture out while she whittled the end to a sharp, deadly point.

"Hi, glad you could make it! We're just getting started." Betty motioned Alicia inside, where guests had already gathered for the party.

"Sorry I'm late. I didn't leave work on time and then had to go home and feed the cat."

"Alicia, you're always staying too late! You should leave work earlier!" Norma called as Betty closed the door behind Alicia and motioned to the small dinette table to her left. "There are chips and dips there, and drinks to your right."

Alicia handed her a large paper shopping bag. "I brought some more chips."

"Good. Put them on the counter for now, and come join us." Alicia placed the bag on the kitchen counter, noting the harvest gold color of the stove, refrigerator, and dishwasher. Although the color was pretty dated, it was nothing compared to the pink stove she found when she bought her house. And a dishwasher! At least Betty had a dishwasher.

"Hi, Alicia!" It was Carol. "Is your friend from Marketing Systems coming?"

"You mean Meg? No, she had other plans tonight. She said she wanted to see the catalog, though. Could I borrow this one and bring it to work tomorrow?"

"Absolutely! We have plenty. C'mon into the living room."

Passing quickly through the small kitchen, Alicia found herself in a similarly small living room, one much smaller than her own, but much nicer. The left wall was exposed brick; the right, smooth, painted plaster. The sculpted gold rug matched the harvest gold of the kitchen.

She recognized a few of her co-workers sitting on the sofa. Like her, they were single. Unlike her, they were very much interested in decorating their living spaces. She was still at the point of repairing and restoring hers.

Alicia found a spot on the floor where she could lean against the wall as the representative began the demonstration. As she sat watching, Alicia found herself both absorbed and repulsed. The pieces were beautiful, well-made, and reminded her of bygone days, when things were simpler, but she resented the materialism. Did she really *need* a reproduction porridge pot or Paul Revere bowl? Did anyone? But it *was* well-made.

After the demo ended, Alicia followed the general flow from the living room to the kitchen area for dessert and coffee. Carol was telling a friend about the readings they had had with the Wizard. "Alicia, you had a reading. What did you think?"

"He was pretty good. He guessed my ex-boyfriend's name and described the place I used to work. He had no way of knowing either."

"That stuff scares me," Carol's friend replied.

"Why?" Alicia was curious.

"I just don't want to know about the future."

"Why not? To know is to be prepared."

"Yeah, but what if he told me I was really sick or something."

"Well, then, you'd know to go to the doctor, right?" Alicia couldn't understand someone not wanting information. "I mean, if your car had something wrong, wouldn't you want to know? What's the difference? A mechanic uses his tools to find out what's wrong with your car. A doctor uses lab tests. A psychic uses his mind. Different tools, same principle." To her, it was logical.

The woman shook her head and put her hand up in a gesture of defense. "It scares me too much to think how he knows."

"It's just another sense. Humans use only eleven percent of their brain and there are hypotheses that there could be untapped powers of extrasensory perception hidden in the remaining eighty-nine percent."

The woman didn't even seem to be listening. "All I know is that all that witchy stuff scares me." At that she turned and started a conversation with someone else.

Alicia looked at Carol, who just shook her head and rolled her eyes. "Touchy subject, I guess."

"Yeah, I guess."

Frederick waited in the cold, watching. He had been right about the lack of traffic that evening. A few women showed up at the clubhouse, probably directly from work, but they arrived at the same time and walked across the parking lot together. Some men straggled in singly, but they were Frederick's age, and regardless of what Wesley had said about the drink not being sexual, Frederick didn't like taking blood from a man.

First, there was the problem of getting close. How could you get close enough to a guy to bite his neck, or wrist, without getting queer? Frederick knew some of these guys from previous jobs, and vampire or not, he didn't want them telling people he was queer. Wesley had some way of making people do what he wanted, without their remembering, but Frederick hadn't figured that out yet. Of course, he could wait until a guy was really shitfaced and *then* bite him, but he'd have a real hard time facing the guy again. He'd just feel too weird.

No, he didn't want to bite guys, especially guys his age or guys he knew, and there were a lot of guys his age here. He hadn't really thought that out when he moved here. He knew that Reservoir Hills was THE place for up-and-coming singles, and to him that meant *women*. He forgot that single women would attract single *men*.

His exceptional hearing picked up the distant crunch of boots against crusty snow. *Guards*. The complex had part-time security guards who walked the grounds, making sure everything was secure. Their main purpose was to be visible, to discourage vandalism. They would patrol, recording the time that they checked particular stations. Frederick knew a couple of them and they had come to recognize him. He was always friendly and tried to act natural when he saw them. Relaxed. Like he belonged there. Like he was a resident, which he was, albeit a non-paying one.

It was by watching the security guards that he had discovered the unlocked furnace room in the first building. One night he watched a group of the guards try to lure a late-season skunk out with dry cat food. After that, they kept the door closed, but still not locked.

Frederick assessed the situation. *Nothing here tonight*, he thought as he edged further into the tree cover and turned west. *Maybe there's something at the Kettle*. In addition to the regulars who came for the home-style dinners, the twenty-four hour truck stop on his side of the highway attracted truckers, club-hoppers, and transients. The Kettle's parking lot was too well-lit and too small for him to accost someone, but if a tractor-trailer rig was parked off to the side, at least he could talk the driver into giving him a ride to new hunting grounds.

The trucker would most likely be heading east, which was Wesley's territory— if Wesley were still around— but maybe it'd be safe if he didn't go far, just a mile or two. Maybe the college. Wesley didn't like the college. Too loud. Too busy. Too many opportunities to be seen. But unlike Wesley, Frederick wouldn't stand out in a group of college-age kids.

At least not until he spoke. Then it became obvious that Frederick wasn't one of them. He had barely finished high school and it showed. And, as Wesley told him repeatedly, he had no "wonder of the world." He didn't know enough or have enough curiosity to fake even a shallow conversation with the students on the hill. *Whoa, and I don't have to*. Shoving his hands into his jacket pockets to keep them warm, Frederick felt a plastic sandwich bag. He pulled it out just far enough to see what was in it. *Three joints. Should be enough.*

Some of the college kids were getting into coke these days, but there were still those who appreciated good weed and would follow him to a quiet place where the snow cover would muffle any sounds of a struggle, if there was one. If he played the game right, there wouldn't be. *And those sweet young necks will heal nicely...*

Yeah, tonight he'd try the college.

His destination decided, he veered north, and then westward, toward Route 9 and new opportunities.

Chapter 8

"Tonight we'll have you working on cheese." The volunteer coordinator led Alicia to the back of the co-op. "There's a sink through that door. You'll be wearing gloves, but you should wash your hands first."

Alicia did as she was directed. The room was little more than a closet, but very clean, with white toilet and sink. Posters of food-related subjects hung at eye level on two of the walls. *SYSTEMIC PESTICIDES. THEY WON'T WASH...* and *VOLUNTEERS MUST WASH HANDS AFTER USING THE TOILET AND BEFORE EACH SHIFT...* A wood-framed mirror hung over the small pedestal sink.

She returned to the main room to find the coordinator hefting a wheel of cheese to the counter top. "Okay, here's the cheese. You want to cut it in approximately 1-pound sections. Here's the knife. If you switch cheeses, you've got to wash the knife and the gloves thoroughly. There's wax paper on the scale. Change that if you change cheeses. I'll show you how to take a tare weight. Have you done any of this before?"

"No, but so far it looks simple."

"Okay, good. Here's where you adjust the weight on the scale."

The sound of a small bell as the front door opened distracted them for a moment. Silhouetted against the entrance light outside, a slight man in a ski jacket stamped the road salt and sand off his feet as he entered. The volunteer coordinator adjusted her glasses. "Hi! I forgot you were coming in tonight. You can help our new volunteer."

The newcomer wriggled out of his jacket as he approached them. "*Alicia?*"

Alicia gasped slightly. "Todd!" He hadn't changed. He was still the slight, tentative, nervous person who had worked for Ernst Maxwell at Theoretic and had been assigned to cross-train with her. She had heard through the grapevine that Maxwell, having taken over her group after their manager died unexpectedly, wanted to replace her group with his own people, and that the cross-training exercises were merely a ruse to spy on Alicia's group. But Todd had given a fair and honest assessment of her, and Maxwell had to leave her at her job. Of course, that was before the explosion.

"You two know each other?"

"Alicia and I used to work together."

"Oh, excellent! I'll have you help her with the cheese. We just got a new wheel in."

"Okay." Todd unwrapped his long wool scarf and stuffed it into the sleeve of his ski jacket as he walked toward the back room. "I'll be there in a second."

The coordinator turned to Alicia. "Here's a calculator and the price per pound for each cheese. Let's see, labels, marking pen, yeah, I think that's it. Todd's done cheese many times before, so he can answer any questions. I'll leave you to it and get back to my paperwork, okay?"

"Sure, fine with me."

Alicia heard the water shut off as Todd finished washing his hands. Seconds later he reappeared and joined her at the counter. He divided up the work and they were well into cutting chunks of rich, fragrant cheese before he started any casual conversation.

"So where are you working these days?"

"Universal Info. I haven't been there that long, but so far it seems okay. Good benefits. Pay's decent. Hey, remember Meg MacMillan, one of the programmers? She's there, too."

"Oh, yeah. I remember her. Nice person. Really knew her stuff."

"So, what about you? Where are you these days?" Alicia smoothed the label on the cheese wrapper.

"I'm at Casualty Insurance. The pay is lower at insurance companies than at a lot of other places, but you get better benefits: more days off, more vacation time, cafeteria with food service, and they send you out to classes a lot."

"Yeah, I've heard that. Do you like it?"

Todd paused as he tried to get an accurate reading on a cheese wedge. "It's a job. Beats unemployment."

Alicia handed him a label as she waited her turn at the scale. "So how long have you been volunteering at the co-op?"

"Almost since they opened. I like to give back to the community and the co-op is involved in some food distribution programs for the needy, too."

Alicia pondered what he said. She had always thought of Todd as rather pro-establishment and material-minded, and here he was volunteering to "give back to the community." *I guess people aren't what they seem. Maybe I should ask him about that night the power went out... Maybe there's more to him than I thought. He sensed something the night Wesley first appeared.*

He was also the one who, while searching the premises a few days after the explosion, had found evidence that someone had been in the warehouse: two boxes partially filled with packing foam and compressed shredded paper that showed the impression of a body, and contained traces of rich, black dirt.

Maxwell had sent him in search of boxes of computer paper and Todd had stumbled upon this find, one that he had revealed only to her. It wasn't much longer after his confession that he left Theoretic. Because she didn't know him well and because he worked for Maxwell, Alicia had never confided in him that she knew who inhabited those boxes.

Maybe it was time.

Returning from his trip to the college, Frederick found a set of keys in the parking lot. He didn't know which apartment they belonged to, but the key to the outside door was invaluable.

For one thing, once inside he could get to the laundry room. It was warm in there, dry, and he could wash his clothes. The scruffy look of the 70s was disappearing and he noticed that women expected men to be more dressed up, neater. And the more people saw him in the laundry room, the more they would think he lived here, which meant that he could walk the grounds and the hallways without suspicion.

And maybe, just maybe, he might meet a lady there, doing her laundry, and strike up a conversation that he'd pick up later at the clubhouse and then later still at her place. *Always thinkin'. That's the key. What do I need Wesley for? I can figure it out. Just keep thinkin'. Wesley. Ha! Always telling me that if it wasn't for him, I wouldn't survive. Well, I seem to be doing pretty damned good on my own these days since he skipped off. All I have to do is keep thinkin'. And looking for opportunity.*

He felt that Wesley was always putting him down, making him feel small, making him feel as if he couldn't fend for himself— just to keep him in his place. And he was right. Wesley had kept him under control, and not with any unearthly powers, but with psychology. Sheer psychology.

But Frederick was learning a bit about psychology himself. Although the college trip had been successful, he knew he didn't fit in there. And when one didn't fit, people noticed. And vampires couldn't afford to be noticed.

Sometimes being invisible was just a matter of psychology. Sheer psychology.

Alicia copied the price from the calculator to the label in a careful, neat script and then looked over at Todd. "Uh, I need to ask you about something that happened at Theoretic."

"Sure. Shoot." His voice was calm and level, but a quick movement of his eyes revealed uncertainty and almost fear.

"Remember the night the lights went out in the computer room, just before the departments merged?"

Todd looked away as he responded. "Uh, yeah, I think so."

"You said you felt something."

"Umm, that was a long time ago."

"And after the explosion you found those two crates in the warehouse where you said it looked like someone had been."

Todd stared ahead as he dropped his pretense of forgetting. "Yes. I remember."

"You thought it was vagrants. But there's no way vagrants could have gotten in and out of that warehouse without the guards seeing them, right?"

Todd stared down at the cheese. "Well, it's possible that someone could have snuck in one night as the guard came in to do rounds and then snuck out again when the next guard came."

"Possible but not *probable*, right?"

"Right."

"Did you notice anything else in the warehouse?"

"No, I wasn't there long enough. I just did what Maxwell told me— looked for computer paper— and got the hell out of there. Something in that warehouse gave me the creeps." He gave Alicia a shallow grin.

"Like what?"

"I don't know. I mean, you'd think it was a very safe place, right? Locked, with guards checking it. But it just felt spooky."

"Maybe it was the lighting? Or the tall stacks of things?"

"No, that usually doesn't bother me... " Todd stopped in mid-sentence, his mouth open.

"What is it?"

"This sounds stupid, but you've heard about the ghost dogs, right?

"You mean the story about the second shift guard and his hunting dogs? The one where one of the dogs disappeared in the warehouse one night?"

"Yeah."

"So you heard the dog howling?"

"No, but I felt something. Like someone watching. But it didn't feel like a dog... ghost or not. It didn't feel like a dog."

"Do you think it was the story that spooked you? That because you heard that the warehouse was haunted by a dog that you felt something?"

"No. No, I don't."

"Then what?" She *knew* what spooked him, but she wanted to hear it from him, in his own words. Only if she heard it from him would she know she could trust him with the knowledge of what she herself had seen.

Todd inhaled slowly. Alicia wondered if he, too, practiced yoga, and then scolded herself for drifting off on a tangent. Todd spoke, looking directly at Alicia. "I can't tell you what it is. I know I tend to be nervous around people," he said, shyly looking away. He bit his lip before regaining his composure and continuing, "But when I'm by myself, I'm usually calm. Relaxed. So when I walk into a quiet place and instead of embracing the solitude, I fear the dark, then I know something's up. I don't know if I can explain it any better, but I just knew something wasn't right."

Alicia paused to read Todd's body language. He didn't look as if he were joking. His face wasn't tight, as if hiding a smirk, but instead his jaw hung slackly, slightly open as he stared straight ahead at the cheeses. He was leaning onto his arms, locked at the elbows against the work table, not standing cocky with his chest puffed out or his arms folded in symbolic challenge. No, he didn't look the court jester. Instead he looked like a man burdened with a weight, one heavy like her own.

"I believe you." She took another deep breath. "Todd, what if I told you that I saw something in there, too. Something that wasn't normal, wasn't natural. What would you say to that?"

"I'd say I have a friend that you need to talk to."

With a lazy, slug-like motion, Frederick drew his jacket sleeve across his mouth, then checked for blood. He had just hunted in one of the small towns west of Worcester, leaving a small-time party girl with a probable hangover and a definite mark on her neck. He doubted she'd remember much when she woke.

When he had walked her home, staggering away from a dingy second-rate bar, she had already forgotten a lot. Like who she was. And where she lived. And the fact that her mama must have told her never to let a stranger walk her home.

And after he managed to get enough clues out of her to find her place, he had walked her there and carried her up three flights of stairs to a squalid, stinking one-room apartment, where she passed out on a stained, unmade bed.

She was young, very young, probably no more than nineteen, if that. She would have shown a fake ID at the bar, if they had asked, and Frederick doubted that they did. Young girls such as she, blonde, thin, and dressed, as they say, "for easy access," weren't too uncommon at the bar where he found her.

When he had entered the bar, she was sidling up to someone who was probably one of the regulars, a balding older man in a plaid flannel shirt, with a pasty complexion and unkempt hair, who was gulping down a bottle of beer from the side of his mouth while he stared at the girl, mesmerized.

Frederick could hear the small talk, the man's voice almost trembling as he asked what a nice girl like her was doing in a place like that. She was giggling, and even without engaging his preternaturally sensitive hearing, Frederick could clearly hear her tell the man that she was new in town and just looking for a place to keep warm, that her apartment was really cold and the landlord wasn't doing anything about the heat.

The man smiled a greasy, creepy smile, saying *he'd* keep her warm. Instead of withdrawing, she leaned further into him. "Would you? I'm so cold."

Frederick tried not to be obvious as he watched the man run a stubby, calloused finger up her thin, bare legs. Was she even wearing anything under that coat?

He watched as she dipped her hip to grind into the man's knee. "Ya know what might help me warm up a bit? Would you mind buying me a drink? Sometimes whiskey helps."

Whiskey. She wasn't fooling around. No Sombreros or White Russians for her. She wanted to be drunk. Whatever she had planned, she couldn't face it sober.

The man raised a finger, and the bartender, obviously watching the scene, too, was immediately there, taking the order, and pouring a double shot of a generic whiskey from the lower shelf. Yes, she was serious about getting drunk, all right. Didn't even ask for a whiskey by name. Didn't care.

Enraptured, Frederick watched as she picked up the glass, downed all of it immediately, and then firmly ran her tongue along the rim. The man in the plaid shirt was watching, too, and Frederick could see him almost faint with lust. *So that's her game. She's in it for the money.* Frederick was surprised that he hadn't known it from the start.

"You havin' anything, bud?" The bartender's voice startled him.

"Yeah. Miller."

After the bartender walked away, Frederick found himself turning back to the scene in the corner. The man was standing now, and Frederick could see the girl whispering as she lightly tongued the edge of his ear. Frederick turned away. He didn't want to see any more, and certainly didn't want to hear it.

The bartender placed an open bottle of beer in front of him. "One-fifty." Frederick slapped two dollars on the counter and motioned the bartender to keep the change. He turned back to see the girl walking out into the biting cold. The man in the plaid shirt was sliding off his stool, waving to the bartender. "Gotta get going. See ya tomorrow."

"You take care," the bartender replied, and Frederick could see just a little bit of concern on the bartender's face.

Shit! What an opportunity. Everyone saw the guy leaving with the girl. If he could follow them, then maybe, after she concluded her business, he could convince her to go with him. He'd act as if he were looking for some action himself, and damn, he was. Watching her grind against the old guy's knee so wantonly had made him hot, really hot.

Frederick downed the beer in two gulps and then slipped off the bar stool and out into the night. At first he heard nothing, but concentrating on hearing, he soon caught the sounds of heavy breathing and a cooing, sultry voice. "You like that, huh? Bet your old lady never does this for you, does she? Oh, yeah, you like it, I can tell."

Frederick looked around to make sure there'd be no witnesses. He wasn't sure what he'd do. He could wait until they were finished and the old man was on his way, or he could walk over there now and throw the useless turd clear out of the parking lot. No, that would scare her. He'd wait.

Not wanting to be obvious, he started walking casually away from them. If he chose to, he could tune in on their conversation, but he chose not to. He didn't want to hear what she was saying, hear the man's moans and heavy breathing. *Shit! Why is she doing this?* She was pretty, really pretty. Maybe she needed the money for drugs. Addiction he could understand.

His need for blood was more than just a need for sustenance. It was a deep, driving need more like drug addiction than hunger, more like raw, lascivious desire.

He heard the sound of a shop door opening and looked to see a patron exiting a liquor store up ahead. *Maybe I'll get her drunk.* When they were drunk, they didn't struggle as much. And if they were drunk enough, they didn't remember. Reaching into his pockets, Frederick found some loose change and some bills. It wasn't much, but he didn't think he needed much. And obviously he didn't need to worry about quality.

It didn't take him long to make his purchase. He returned to the parking lot just in time to see the old guy drive away, and the blonde straightening her coat as she stood unsteadily in the dirty snow that edged the lot.

"Drink?" he asked, proffering the bottle.

"Thanks," she said, grabbing it. "Hey, it's not even open."

"Open it. That's what I bought it for."

She twisted the cap open with one snap, took a large swig, and then paused. "Mind if I take another?"

"Go ahead. All yours."

"You don't want any?"

"Nah. I'm already drunk. Drunk with the sight of you." *Damn, that's lame!*

"Fifty bucks."

"Whoa!" Frederick wasn't expecting that, at least not that quickly. And he didn't know why not. Why *wouldn't* she want to charge him?

"Too much?" She didn't look as if she were offering a discount. Instead she looked as if she were slightly amused.

Maybe he could play dumb. "Look, lady. I was just trying to be nice."

She looked him up and down. He wondered what she thought she saw. He was average, just average, in every way. Maybe she'd take pity on him. *Damn, why didn't Wesley teach me that mind thing?* He knew why; because then he would have been able to work it in reverse, work it against Wesley. He'd just have to try good old charm.

"Yeah, sure." She looked at the bottle and then at him. "Want this back?"

"Nah, as I said, it's all yours."

He watched as she took another large swig. He could see that her eyes were getting glassy, and she was wavering slightly, forward and backward. *Damn! What should I do?* He wanted her so badly now, for her blood, for the sex... But he knew he had to play it cool.

She smiled at him and shivered. "Cold out here."

"I was thinking the same thing myself. Maybe I'll go back in the bar and get warm."

She took another swig from the bottle, her eyes working him over again. "You got a car?"

"Nah, I'm hoofing it tonight. You?"

"Walking."

Damn, this is going nowhere! Maybe he should walk away, then circle back and grab her from behind. He knew he was strong enough and quick enough. He had done it before. But then he would be forced to kill her so that she wouldn't tell. No, he had to seduce her, make it her desire, too.

One more try. "Hey, I've got to get moving or I'll freeze. If you want someone to walk you home, speak now."

In the eternity of the silence, he watched her take another swig, watched her eyes roam over his body, saw her resolve stiffen as she tried to stand up straight. She had drunk the bottle past the halfway mark now, and the whiskey was hitting her hard.

"Yeah, I think I'd like that."

He waited for her to come to him, her feet wobbly on the pockmarked surface of the parking lot. She stumbled into him. Frederick didn't know whether she meant to do that or not, but he did know that he couldn't contain himself any longer. Not caring if there were witnesses, he kissed her and pulled her to the side of the building, where he pressed hard against her, mouth and body.

"No, not here," she said, her voice thick and slurred. "Let's go to my place."

He didn't remember much of the walk. He remembered that he was walking very, very fast and that she was so drunk now that he was lifting her more than holding her as they walked. She was getting drunker every minute, and couldn't remember exactly where she lived. After a couple of false starts, they were at her place, where he indulged both the fire in his loins and the one in his throat. It took all his restraint to hold back, to remember his strength, and to drink just enough to take away the knife's edge of his craving.

When it was over, he had checked to see if she was still alive. She was. With any luck, she'd have no idea how she got home. Or who had been there with her. And the bruise on her neck? If she was able to focus enough in the morning to see it, she might assume that it was just one of the many bruises that he had discovered sullying her pale young body, bruises that he didn't make and didn't want to learn the history of.

After letting himself out, Frederick walked to a late-night coffee shop hoping to find a truck or car heading east. The parking lot was nearly empty, but he went in anyway, ordering a coffee and donut, hoping to bide his time until opportunity arrived.

An hour later he knew that his possibilities of hitching a ride that night were slim.

He decided to walk east, determined to find another coffee shop or truck stop on his way. Miles later, walking along in the empty, silent darkness, boredom set in. The streets were deserted, and what few buildings dotted the empty vista of Route 9 were dark. He couldn't even look in people's windows for amusement. There were no voices, no sounds, no movement. Nothing. Nothing to entertain him.

The tediousness of the walk rankled him, producing an anger like a festering sore. *Stupid place!*

As he passed a used car lot, he had an idea: he could hotwire a car.

He had learned this simple skill while still alive, when the ignition switch went on his old clunker. One of the guys at work had showed him how to pull the wires and reconnect them manually.

Damn! Miss those guys. Frederick winced as he remembered his friends at work, the camaraderie, the practical jokes. He remembered a weekend when they all went to Eddie's to help him replace an engine. With all the beer and tomfoolery, it took much longer than it should have to lower in the replacement engine and connect the various systems, but they did it, and stood in the meager light of Eddie's garage and marveled at their accomplishment. *Damn.* Eddie knew his stuff, and he was always willing to share his knowledge. Unlike Wesley. *Eddie, this one's for you. Thanks!*

With a quick look east and west along Route 9 to make sure there weren't any police cars nearby, Frederick moved to the edge of the lot, past the bright security lights, looking for a likely target. He knew to avoid the newer models, with their steering locks and ignition kill-switches. The cars at the front of the lot looked too new to mess with, but he knew there had to be older cars, too, trade-ins. There were always people who couldn't afford new cars and drove everyone else's castoffs, and when fortune shined on them, they traded up, for a newer castoff.

Glancing quickly toward Route 9 again to check for cops, Frederick moved away from the highway. *They probably keep the rust buckets out back where they won't scare away the customers.*

At the back of the building, Frederick saw that we was right. *Bingo! There's my baby!* A rusted older Pontiac sat among three or four similar cars, so buried in snow he couldn't tell exactly how many were there. The fact that this one car was cleaned off was a good sign. It was probably working.

Dy-na-mite! It's got plates. He didn't know why the registration plates were still on the car. He hoped it wasn't because the car was just in for repair and wasn't running. But if it was drivable, at least he wouldn't have to take any additional time to steal plates.

Glancing toward Route 9 again, cocking his head and engaging his preternatural hearing, Frederick listened for traffic. Satisfied that there was none close enough to be a problem, he checked the door. Surprisingly, it wasn't locked. Not everyone bothered to lock their cars. *Sheesh, you'd think they'd lock it if it was sitting on a lot. I would. Damn. Not good, not good.* Maybe it wasn't running, after all. Or maybe it didn't have all its tires. Quickly he checked the driver's side and then the passenger side. All four were there, and they weren't flat.

Cocking his head again, listening with his vampiric senses, he checked once more for sounds of approaching cars. He could hear one now, and stood motionless as he listened to it coming closer and then continue to move down the road, never slowing.

"It's now or never," he half-sung as he readied himself. Careful not to jerk it too hard in his nervousness, he pulled open the dilapidated door, pausing only briefly to listen to see whether the loud squeak of its hinges had attracted any attention. Once settled on the hard, frozen seat, Frederick realized he didn't have any tools. *Shit! Okay, okay. No problem. I'll just connect the wires underneath.*

Looking around again, listening, Frederick moved only when he was satisfied that no one was near and then ducked under the dash, feeling behind the ignition. He was surprised that even in the dark, the deep unrelenting dark, he could *see.* Not well enough to distinguish the exact colors of the ignition wires, but well enough to tell which two were the same color.

Tensing his arm, he readied to pull them out. *Easy, now. Remember the freakin' basketball.* Gently he tugged with just his wrist, and the wires pulled free. Holding them in his hand, he righted himself and listened again for approaching cars. None. Using only his sense of touch and his fingernails, he stripped the plastic coating away from the end of each wire.

He touched the wires together and the starter kicked in. The chilled battery was weak and the engine cranked wearily, slowing with each successive try. *C'mon, c'mon. It's not that freakin' cold.* He held the gas pedal to the floor and sniffed the air, hoping he hadn't flooded the engine. He could smell gasoline, but hoped it was just his heightened sense of smell.

Okay, one more time. Angrily he pumped the pedal as the car cranked, slowing, slowing, and then, with a cough and a sputter, it finally caught with a small backfire. *Jesus!* Frederick looked around nervously, sure that one of the neighbors would be pulling aside a curtain to look for the source of the noise, but the dimly-lit windows of the nearby houses showed no movement.

Cautiously he revved the engine, gently easing off the gas every few seconds to see if it would stall. Assured that it wouldn't, he twisted the wires together, leaving them dangling under the dash, and drove away, toward home.

Of course, Frederick being Frederick, he had forgotten to check the gas gauge before he took off. The tank was nearly empty and he didn't get far before he had to stop for gas. The gas station looked closed, but he had expectantly walked up to the door of the small service station and convenience store, peering in for signs of life. He figured that if anyone was still there, he'd beg him to sell him just enough gas to get home. The station, though, was empty.

In his resulting anger, Frederick had discovered something he had only half-realized before: he was strong. Really strong. *Stronger* than really strong.

Discovering that no one was there, he had rattled the doorknob and then jerked the door. With a loud crack, it came flying off its hinges, landing him flat on his butt.

Frederick sat up, dumfounded at first, and then scrambled to stand. At first he couldn't figure it out: Why did the door come off? Were the hinges broken? Was someone doing work on the door? Was this a setup?

He lifted the heavy reinforced door, but it felt no heavier than a cardboard cutout. When he realized what had happened— that he, Frederick, had torn the door off the hinges— he couldn't believe it. *I just pulled this freakin' door off its hinges! Holy shit!*

He knew from his rediscovery of basketball that his strength was more than it ever had been, but even exploding basketballs didn't hint at what he was witnessing now. Could he be getting even stronger?

For a minute he stared at his right arm. It didn't look any different. The curve of the biceps under his jacket was the same since he was in high school; not bigger, not smaller. But the strength! Maybe the door was fake, a temporary covering? He examined the edge. No, this was a real door. He could see from the splintering that it was real wood, and could see that it was hardwood, maybe oak. He pressed gently with his thumb and forefingers and thought he felt it give. He tried again, with more pressure. The wood crumbled and compressed like a foam coffee cup.

Something was changing in him. He wasn't sure why, but he obviously wasn't a wimp anymore.

The staccato sound of a truck downshifting on the highway snapped him out of his reverie. "A bird in the hand's worth two in the bush," he spoke aloud to no one. His new-found strength was no reason to waste an opportunity. If he hurried, he could turn on the pumps, gas up, and get out before anyone saw him.

As he flicked the switches for the pumps, he noticed some money in the open drawer of the till. It wasn't much— just a few singles and a five— but along with the rolls of quarters, it added up. *Bingo! Cash problem solved!*

And so, quite by accident, Frederick escalated his posthumous life of crime. With his strength, breaking and entering was easy. Almost fun.

And it filled the lonely hours when he didn't need to feed and the ladies had other plans.

Chapter 9

"Evan won't be easy to reach," Todd had told Alicia. "He just moved here from North Carolina and he's staying with different friends until he finds a permanent place to live. It could take a while to track him down. I'll leave some messages around for him to contact you."

But now that the mystery of the vampire was being revisited, Alicia couldn't sit still. She *had* to know more. Having exhausted the Danforth Public Library and the local used book stores when she first encountered Wesley, she now turned to the House of Astrology.

Located on the lower floor of the local shopping mall, it was a strange yet comforting place full of mixed messages and fascinating items. The other shops on the ground floor of this outdoor mall had large plate glass windows and doors, with no more architectural decoration than the shop's sign. The House of Astrology was different. Its large plate glass window was dressed with a display of tarot cards and crystal balls, a small divider halfway up shielding most of the interior of the shop from view.

Instead of a typical large-paneled glass door, the door to the House of Astrology was more like a cottage door: white wood, with a lattice-work window at the top. The shop's logo, a golden Moorish or onion dome similar to Moscow's St. Basil's Cathedral or India's Taj Mahal, was securely attached to the lintel.

Alicia automatically took a deep breath and opened the door to the shop. A string of small bells sounded as she entered. Sitting to her left, in a cashier's area slightly raised above the main floor, one of the co-owners nodded to her in acknowledgement. Large, swarthy, with dark hair and substantial gold and diamond rings on pudgy fingers, Sonny had seemed ominous to Alicia the first time she entered the "House of A." After a few visits, though, the uneasiness had faded. She returned his nod with a faint wave and hello and continued inside where the shop's eclecticism continued.

To the left of the cashier's area was a peg wall of joke shop items: Halloween masks, magic tricks, fake vomit, and other novelties, none of which had anything to do with astrology or the occult. They always caught her eye when she entered, and this time she stared longer than usual and realized that she was looking for the strange voodoo doll she had seen at the Wizard's house. *Could it have been a magic trick?* She walked closer to the wall.

"Ten percent off on packaged tricks this week," Sonny called out to her without even looking up from a pile of paperwork.

"Okay, thanks." She wondered if she should ask about the doll... "I know this is going to sound odd, but do you have any voodoo dolls that move?"

Sonny looked up at her without speaking, his face frozen in what she could only imagine was disbelief. "Move? What, like jointed?"

"No, like move on their own. Like, oh, I don't know, a trick where you put them on a bookcase or something and move them without people seeing, like maybe a marionette—"

Sonny snorted softly and smiled as he shook his head. "You mean like at the Wizard's house?"

"You *know* him?"

Sonny shrugged, his smile now turned into a smirk. "Who doesn't? He's a big deal around here."

Alicia stared, trying to figure out if Sonny was being sarcastic, but he just shrugged and turned back to his paperwork. "No, he didn't get that doll from me. That's for sure."

She wanted to ask more, ask if it were a trick, but the way that Sonny turned back to work was so dismissive that it made her think that she wouldn't get much more out of him. She continued her walk through the shop. Just beyond the magic tricks were incense and incense holders. She picked up one of the blue and white boxes and sniffed, the smell taking her back to her high school years when everyone was burning incense. It was so exotic then. Everything was so exotic then.

Alicia put down the pack of incense and continued past a standing display unit in the center of the shop that held astrological greeting cards and what seemed to be overflow items from the other sections. A large, hollow, clear acrylic pyramid with copper framework hung from the ceiling.

Passing a display case containing pentagram necklaces and other occult insignia, Alicia continued to the far wall, to books on witchcraft by Sybil Leek, Louise Huebner, and Paul Huson. The names seemed familiar, and Alicia remembered seeing articles in the newspaper, probably around Halloween, that proclaimed these authors to be witches.

When Alicia had first started coming here, she focused more on the books on ESP and unexplained mysteries, ignoring this section. Now she was drawn to it.

On a shelf above the witchcraft books, she saw a shelf that she hadn't noticed before, one labeled WESTERN MYSTERY TRADITION. Wondering what that could be, she browsed the titles: *Applied Magic, Practical Occultism in Daily Life, The Training and Work of an Initiate, Psychic Self-Defense*. Eagerly she pulled the last book from the shelf and scanned the table of contents. Signs of Psychic Attack. Analysis of the Nature of Psychic Attack. Projection of the Etheric Body. Vampirism...

Alicia stared at the word. *Vampirism*. She turned to the section and read quickly, hoping for answers, but this author thought vampires were merely psychic manifestations. What had happened to Alicia was *physical*. Without thinking, she moved her hand to her neck. Although the external scars had faded, she knew they were there. She had seen them, felt them. Felt the pain and soreness. Had seen the bruising, felt the tightness...

Not sure if the book could help her, and not having the money to throw away on books that didn't, she slid it back onto the shelf.

"Good book. She's one of the grand dames of the occult."

Alicia jumped, startled by Sonny's voice being so close.

"Oh, I've never heard of her."

"She died in 1946, so she's not on TV much," Sonny joked dryly. "Her books are still the best on the subject."

He continued to the back of the shop, where he unlocked a glass case and removed an item for another customer. Alicia picked up the book again and skimmed a few pages. The writing seemed dense and theoretical. Uncertain what to do, she put the book back. Maybe she'd wait and ask Todd's friend Evan.

She turned to leave the store. Books on astrology crowded the shelves to her left as she walked back toward the front. In addition to the popular sun sign books, there were books and supplies for the professional astrologer: ephemerides, tables of houses, chart pads, and calendars indicating planetary aspects and moon signs. She wondered for a brief, swift moment if astrology could help solve the riddle, but whose chart would hold the key? Hers? His? Alicia bit her lips to suppress a sneer as she played out the scene in her mind. *Oh, yeah, and just how would I get his birth info? Excuse me, Mr. Vampire, sir. Before you bite, could I just have your date of birth and location? Thanks. I appreciate it.*

Another customer entered the shop, forcing Alicia to duck in next to a revolving glass showcase of exotic jewelry to allow him to pass. Fake glass eye pendants, silver winged Isis necklaces with matching rings, and chunky rings with large, dark stones glittered on the mirrored shelves of the showcase. AMULETS, the sign said, TO WARD OFF EVIL. *Hmmm, maybe next time.*

As she slid out the door, she thought she saw movement on the revolving display. A quick glance back told her she was right.

A glass eye pendant had turned on its chain so that it now appeared to be watching her as she walked out the door.

Alicia knew that he wasn't former Beatle Paul McCartney, but the man who had just walked into the food co-op could have been a stand-in. His sad, puppy-dog eyes, turned down at the edges, were what first made Alicia think of McCartney, but there were other similarities, too. Not just his eyes, but his face was shaped like the singer's: long, oval, with perfect arched brows hiding just beneath fringes of thick, dark hair; a strong chin offset by thin, sensitive bow lips.

With slow, elegant movements, the man strode over to one of the produce tables. As his intelligent eyes scanned the information card above the bin, his long fingers and delicate hands caressed an imported winter melon.

"May I help you?" the manager on duty asked.

The stranger smiled and spoke, his voice soft, gentle, and melodious. "Hello. I'm Evan, a friend of Todd's, and he said that Alicia might be working tonight."

"Yes, she is. She's right over there." The manager motioned her over.

The stranger smiled again as he removed his thick wool gloves to shake hands. "Hi, I'm Evan. I'm a friend of Todd's."

Alicia removed her own gloves, disposable sanitary hand coverings that the volunteers were required to wear when handling food, and shook his hand. He was tall, pleasantly slim, and his blue eyes shone, oddly reminding her of the high beam indicator on her dashboard instrument panel.

He paused and turned slightly, looking around him. Alicia wondered if he was looking for the manager, who was walking back toward the register. As if he were waiting for everyone else to be out of earshot, Evan paused and then continued, "Todd mentioned an experience you had and thought we should talk."

"Hi, yes. Thank you for coming." Alicia was going to mumble something about this not being the right place to talk, but she was delayed by the distraction of his eyes. They smiled even more than his lips, while at the same time being coolly serious. Before she could speak, Evan voiced what she was thinking.

"Obviously this isn't the time or place. I noticed an Italian restaurant across the street. Maybe we could meet there tomorrow? If we get a table in a corner, we should be able to talk freely. There should be enough ambient noise to cover our conversation."

"Okay. What time? I could get out of work at 5:30, so I could be there around 6 or 6:30."

"Why don't we make it 6:30?"

"Sure. See you then."

He smiled a gentle, friendly smile, nodded slightly, and, in one swift movement, pivoted on both feet before stepping away. *How strange*, Alicia thought to herself.

As she watched him walk to the exit, she noticed that he deliberately thanked the manager and said good-bye. She was amused to find that she was thinking something that only parents thought: how polite and well-mannered he was.

Turning back to bagging the dried apricots, she realized that he was different in another way, too. He was refined. He wore a sweater and jeans like anyone else, and his long wool coat could have come from the thrift store downtown, but there was something about Evan that hinted of private schools, crisp white shirts, and evenings at the symphony.

She wondered how someone like that could know anything about the dark, dank, and desolate places that hope has fled and fear has annexed. The places where Wesley dwelled.

Although Alicia arrived at the restaurant early, there was already a waiting line. Doubtful that they'd get a table, she walked up to the hostess anyway, and started to leave a name. "It's an hour wait, hon. Got a big party from a wedding rehearsal."

"Would you like to go somewhere else?" It was Evan, behind her.

"That might not be a bad idea." She thanked the hostess and then she and Evan wove their way through the growing, loudening crowd.

Outside, the cold mid-February air felt surprisingly good.

Evan rocked on the heels of his feet, his hands deep in his pockets, moving as if to keep warm. "Any suggestions? I'm not from around here."

Alicia thought for a moment. Although she had lived in the area most of her life, she didn't know that much about restaurants. Her parents had both worked, and were too tired at the end of a day to go out. It was much easier for her mother to whip up a simple meal than to change out of work clothes and find somewhere to go. On weekends, neither of her parents felt like driving somewhere and then waiting in line at one of the few restaurants in Danforth, and they rarely wandered far from Danforth. She and Kurt had eaten out quite a bit at Kurt's favorites, but Alicia didn't want to go there and risk running into him.

"How about Chinese food?" Kurt wasn't too fond of Chinese food. Alicia's parents had never braved foreign food, but she and a high school friend had visited China Sam's often in their last two years of high school, after her friend got her driver's license. She hadn't been there in ages.

" *Wo ai zhongguo ren.*"

"What?" Alicia couldn't be sure, but she thought...

Grinning, his voice warm and eyes sparkling, Evan translated. "'I like Chinese.'"

Alicia was incredulous. "You speak Chinese?"

"A little Mandarin. I have a fervent interest in Eastern thought and culture. I've been trying to teach myself Mandarin, but I actually learned that line from a Monty Python song."

"Monty Python! Of course!" Once again, she could thank her high school friend for the exposure. While her parents had rarely crept beyond the working class American cultural milieu, her friend had been more cosmopolitan, exposing Alicia to British comedy and music. *What an interesting guy*, she thought. "Okay, let's do Chinese."

Evan clapped his gloved hands together. "Great! How far a walk is it from here?"

"Walk? In this cold?"

"Sure. I walk everywhere."

"You don't have a car?"

"No."

"Did you walk here?"

"No, one of my friends dropped me off."

Alicia's mind was filled with questions, but they were more in the line of scoldings, so she kept them to herself. How could he stand depending on people for rides? That would drive her crazy! Didn't it drive his friends crazy? What if his friend dropped him off and she hadn't shown up? How would he get home? She suddenly felt like his mother. She couldn't hold it in. "You don't mind being dropped off? How will you get home?"

Evan shrugged his shoulders and smiled a broad, warm smile before a relaxed, dreamy mask fell over his face. "I never worry. The universe provides."

What a strange guy, Alicia thought.

"Okay, we're getting off the subject." Janith smiled apologetically at the coven members as she tried to reign in the conversation. They had been discussing who would plan and lead the ritual for the next sabbat, that of the Spring Equinox. Somehow, as often happened among this group of close-knit coven members, the subject had veered off course and they were now discussing a new movie about an American werewolf in London.

"Janith's right," Rob interrupted. "We need to assign the Spring ritual to someone, set the date, and decide if we'll invite other members of the larger family or if it'll be coven-only. We can chat after, when we take a break."

Gabe rolled his eyes, feigning offense. A coven member behind him poked him good-naturedly as the chatter stopped.

Janith continued. "Spring is one of the four lesser sabbats, one of the more joyous ones, but don't be misled and think we can just breeze through it. Although it's true that Spring is a joyous time, where we celebrate the greening and rebirth of the earth, there is a darker side. With Spring, the tides of the universe grow stronger, but this strength is a double-edged sword. The tides grow, the sap from the trees runs again, and life stirs again— but it's *all* life: physical, mental, psychic, good, *evil.* Yes, the old power returns, but this power can be for good or evil, and we are the guardians of the transformation. On your path in the Craft, you have been gifted with many things: the ability to read the cards, raise the power, and give healing and comfort to the sick. With that power comes a great responsibility. We must not only use our power for good, but we must also defend against evil. And at the Equinox, when the energy of equal day and equal night stand in delicate balance, we must be most alert."

The room was silent for a moment as everyone reflected on Janith's words. She looked around the group and spoke again. "I don't know why, but I have a feeling that this year's psychic spring tide is especially precarious and that if we're not careful, the balance could tip in the wrong direction."

Somewhere far away the elder vampire smiled easily. They were amateurs, students. Playing games, caught up in their own world of ritual and regimentation, hierarchy and pomp. And easily scared. They were no threat to him. Wesley knew that he was safe.

Alicia drove. Evan had gracefully folded his six-foot-plus frame into the passenger seat of her Chevette and belted himself in. She was pleased that he used seatbelts without being asked and didn't make fun of the low-end, no-frills subcompact car that she had bought when her previous car died. It was the first new car Alicia had ever owned, and it fit her fine. Like her, it was practical, plain, and dependable. And unlike some of the large clunkers she used to own, this one was just big enough: she called it "me-sized."

At the front of a run-down shopping center sat China Sam's, its presence announced by a large, lit yellow plastic sign with red lettering. Similar lettering in cling letters spelled out the name on the glass front of the building. In the dirty and rutted snow along the sidewalk in front of the restaurant, an abandoned shopping cart from an adjacent department store stood frozen and unattended.

As they neared the door, to Alicia's surprise, Evan reached ahead of her and opened it. More to her surprise, she didn't mind. She firmly believed that whoever got to the door first should open it unless encumbered by heavy packages or physical infirmity. It usually annoyed her when men opened the door for her because she saw it as an insinuation that women were too weak to open doors themselves, but with Evan it was different. With him, it seemed natural.

They scuffed off the road sand from their boots on a large rubber mat just inside the door. It didn't seem to be a question of manners, though Evan certainly had those. It was as if Evan cared enough, respected the owners enough, to not want to track in sand and road salt.

When the waiter appeared, Evan bowed slightly and mumbled something, presumably a greeting in Mandarin. He was quiet, unpretentious, and confident in his foreign greeting, and Alicia got the sense that he wasn't doing it to impress her, but rather was doing it because it pleased him to do so. The waiter replied in kind, also unpretentiously, while pulling out two menus from a short, dark busing station. Without another word, he showed them quickly to their table, as if it were not unusual to have a very tall, very

Caucasian, American greet him in his own tongue. For a moment, Alicia wondered if she had imagined it.

Like many of the Chinese restaurants in the area, China Sam's was Polynesian/Chinese. On the far side of the restaurant was a small bar with a thatched "roof" overhanging the counter. Large, almost comic reproductions of Polynesian masks decorated the dingy white walls. In the center of the restaurant, a family of five picked at a pu-pu platter, the children entranced by the burning blue gel in the center.

As she passed them, for just the slightest moment, like a ripple in time, Alicia once again had that feeling that she was imagining it all as she saw not the white, working-class family in jeans and sweatshirts leaning hard against a modern steel and laminate table, but a more primal, aboriginal scene around a low-flamed campfire.

Alicia ordered a dish that her high school friend always ordered: Egg Foo Yung. Whenever Alicia had been able to convince Kurt to eat Chinese food, Kurt would always order sweet and sour pork, so that even on those rare occasions that they ate Chinese food, Alicia rarely had Egg Foo Yung. To Alicia's surprise, Evan didn't order off the menu at all. Instead, he asked the waiter if the cook could make up something Szechuan-style.

Again, she was impressed. She never would have thought to ask for something off the menu, and she never heard of Szechuan. As she asked Evan to describe it, she noticed him carefully moving the knife and fork off to the side and tearing the paper off a package of wooden chopsticks.

As the dinner progressed, she became even more impressed than she was already. Evan told her that he had come to the area to attend one of the commercial computer schools. As they talked about computers and careers, she nearly forgot why they had agreed to meet, why Todd had sent him to her. Evan was interesting in so many other ways.

But Evan remembered. "Todd mentioned that you had an unusual experience back at your old job. He thought maybe I could help you make sense of it. What happened?"

Alicia told him the whole story, from the beginning, starting with Wesley. At first she wasn't sure that she should, but something told her that she could tell this worldly man anything and he would not be surprised, would not be shocked, would not be judgmental, for here was a man alive with a hunger for knowledge, and to him, all knowledge would be good, and all experiences would be exciting. This was a man to whom she could reveal herself.

Skillfully scraping his bowl and gathering rice with his chopsticks, Evan paused long enough to interrupt her. "You know that there are some people, very human, who are just *psychic* vampires..."

"Yes, I've read about them, and while some of it seems to fit, it doesn't explain how he could appear and disappear in a mirror."

"Hypnosis? He controlled what you thought you saw?"

"Maybe. But what about the wounds on my neck?"

"Fake fangs, or his real teeth whittled to a sharp point?"

"Hmmm. Could be. Getting through locked doors?"

"Picked the locks?"

Alicia was silent. Had she imagined it all? Had she set a laboratory on fire and possibly killed a man— his body was never found— because she *imagined* that he was a vampire? She thought back to the moment that she knew, knew that she was dealing with more than a man with a psychological aberration, knew that she was dealing with powers beyond her own, knew that she had encountered something that could not be explained away...

"Okay, what about this..." And so she told him about the warehouse, told him how she found his coffin, found Wesley awake. Told him that Wesley had her in his thrall, how she felt she could not move or breathe and then, just as his face was a fraction of an inch away from hers, the guard entered the warehouse. The coffin lid had slammed shut beside her. All thirteen nails flew up from the floor, back to their original places, and the boxes rearranged themselves with instant-replay accuracy.

Evan was silent, poker-faced.

From there Alicia moved on to tell of the last time she saw Wesley. The lab. She described how the guard had been hurled through the air by the force of the explosion.

"What about the person that you think was a vampire? Was he thrown?"

"I don't know. He could have been."

"Was he thrown out a window?"

"No..." *What an odd question.*

Again Evan was silent. He carefully set his chopsticks down and wiped his lips gently with his napkin. Leaning back, he tented his hands, staring straight down into some distance she could not see, could not fathom. Gently he closed his eyes, drew a deep breath, and opened them again, staring straight into Alicia's own.

Mocking the actor who delivered a similar line in *Cool Hand Luke*, Evan calmly replied, "Then what we have he-ah... is a failure to de-fen-es-trate."

The waiter refilled their glasses. Evan again spoke softly in Mandarin. The waiter gave a short bow in acknowledgement.

Evan was sitting in the same position, hands tented, as Alicia tried to make sense of what she had just heard.

Defenestrate? To throw someone or something out a window? Alicia tried not to react. *He didn't really say that, did he?* Here she was, telling him the most difficult thing she had ever told anyone, and he was making a pun of it? Didn't he know she was serious?

Before she could gasp in shock, or stammer in anger, Evan was smiling at her; no, more than smiling at her, he was *glowing* at her. His eyes sparkled and his face flushed slightly as he clasped his hands in obvious pleasure. He looked down for a minute, shaking his head, then looked at her directly, penitent, but still smiling. "I'm sorry. I know this is serious, but I couldn't help myself. I'm a compulsive punner."

She tried to be angry, she honestly did, but the more she looked into his deep sapphire eyes, the more she felt like laughing, like she was a child again, the child she never really was. Evan gently laid his hand on hers. "Forgiven?"

"Forgiven." A smile fought its way out of her stony expression, and she had to laugh. Hard. Evan did, too.

What a strange man!

When they stopped laughing, Evan returned to the subject of Wesley. He admitted to Alicia that her situation was something that he had never encountered before. "I'll do some research and let you know. I have friends who know about these things. I can call them. I think their coven is meeting tomorrow night."

"Coven? They're witches?"

"Yes, but not the types you read about in story books. They're good witches." Evan deftly scooped up one last morsel of rice before laying his chopsticks at the top of his plate, points to the left.

Alicia wasn't sure it was polite to ask, but she had to know. "Are you a witch?"

"Yes, I consider myself a witch." He paused and smiled conspiratorially. "I usually don't advertise the fact; I tell people on a need-to-know basis."

She wanted to know more, a whole lot more. How did he become a witch? Why? Could he do magic? Could witches tell her if Wesley was gone for good? But the night was wearing on and they had finished their meal, and she had to work in the morning.

"I'd like to know more about witches."

"I'm not sure how much there is to tell. I'm not part of a coven anymore, but I adhere to some of the same beliefs, hold a similar worldview.

But I also subscribe to many Taoist and Buddhist philosophies. When I get some answers about your vampire problem, we can get together again and talk more about it, if you want. It probably won't be until after I move, though."

The waiter returned, bill in hand, and placed it in front of Evan. Alicia, trying not to get angry at the sexism implied in assuming that she was being paid for, opened the bill in place and looked at the total.

"When are you moving?" Alicia asked as she reflexively leaned back to let the waiter remove her plate.

"I don't know. I need to find a place somewhere in Danforth. I'm starting a computer course in a couple of weeks at CC downtown and because I don't have a car, I have to find somewhere nearby."

"Really? The Computer Center has a branch downtown?"

"They will. It'll be about a block from the train station."

"Wow! That's only about a quarter of a mile from my house, and it just so happens that I need another roommate. If you're interested, we could go to my place now so you could see the room and then I could give you a ride back to your friends."

Evan clasped his hands tightly and shivered with apparent joy. "See? The universe provides! The universe *provides*."

Maybe it does. Alicia thought, but then she thought of all that the universe had provided for her in her life, and added, *But sometimes the universe has a sick sense of humor...*

Chapter 10

Joey had the mid-sized room next to Alicia's, which meant that Evan got the small one at the top of the stairs, opposite the bathroom. *At least he'll have a closet,* Alicia observed as she transferred an armful of clothing to her room. Her own room had none— it retained the original bare, square outline from the day it was built— and so Alicia had appropriated the small room's closet as her own.

The closet was all that Evan's new room had going for it, really. The carpeting of the ten-by-ten chamber was a thin, indoor/outdoor industrial variety, probably scrounged from scrap by the previous owner. Its grayish black color showed no dirt or wear, but showed no beauty or style, either. The small window on the left as one entered looked out on her neighbor's similarly gray-black asphalt-shingled roof. The small window across from the door looked out on the back yard and the dimly lit row of houses beyond it that belonged to the next street.

Alicia returned for another armful of clothing, stopping for a second in the middle of the room to stretch. It was late and silent. The traffic on the main road two streets away had thinned to almost nothing. Even the wind noise had died down. For a minute, it was easy to forget that Alicia's house bordered the busy downtown area of the largest town in New England. For a minute, it was easy to forget that there was anyone at all around her.

Returning to her task, Alicia noticed movement straight ahead. *Wait... the windows are closed. I weatherstripped that window. There's no way it could be drafty enough to move the curtain like that... But the curtain didn't move by itself...*

She stood motionless, breath held, ears alert, and tried to convince herself that it was something explicable, something that one would expect in a house built in 1892, but she couldn't shake the memory of Wesley and how he had appeared in a locked computer room... And what had she read about vampires? That they could change shape, that they could turn into dust motes or bats—

No! It's something normal!

But what? Taking the smallest, shallowest breath that she could, so as to not make noise, she eyed the edge of the left curtain panel, where she had seen the movement. Nothing moved. *Okay, I don't have roaches, and it would have taken a very large cockroach to move that curtain.* Anxiously she examined the edge of the window molding, from the left, then up, then down the right, then around the bottom sill. Nothing.

But the curtain didn't move by itself... Maybe it's a mouse.

Wondering if she should get Moonshadow and ask *him* to investigate, she cautiously stepped forward. Her mind stretched back to another time when she moved so quietly and cautiously, in a similarly gray and white world, in a warehouse, searching for a crate...

Her instinct now was to turn and run, run through the cold white February of Danforth until she found the nearby safety and the people of the twenty-four hour convenience store down by the lights... *No! This is something normal, and you can take care of it! You can't run for help anytime you can't figure something out right away! You've got to take care of yourself!* For Self was the one thing that she could depend on, the one constant, the one thing that never deserted her or died on her—

Again, her mind slipped back in time, back only three short years when she had *not* been able to rely on Self, when Self had deserted her like all she ever loved, like everyone she had ever loved, when Self had crumbled—

No! You're strong. That was an aberration!

Inhaling sharply this time, more to steel her resolve than to fill her lungs, she yanked back the curtain—

Nothing.

Alicia stared, breath held, waiting for the smallest movement.

Nothing.

As she looked for possible invaders, her eyes settled on a tiny steel ball sitting on the top of the lower sash. While her mind tried to determine what device would use such a small ball bearing and what it would be doing *there*, her eyes found the small, starburst-edged hole in the windowpane.

Someone had fired a BB through her window.

While she was in the room.

Her Inquisitive Mind working, Alicia wanted to know who, how, why— and she wanted the answers now! Somewhere in the deep recesses of Self, her Practical Mind was still buried, for she felt a strong urge to charge into the February cold, slipper-shod and coatless, into the dark, soulless night, where someone waited with a gun... a BB gun, yes, but a *gun* nonetheless.

Fortunately some part of her Practical Mind held sway, and she left the house by the front door, stealing quietly down the driveway on the right side of the house, peering over the fence gate cautiously before entering the back yard, her soft slippers making no sound on the cold, crusty ground.

All senses on the alert, she scanned the yard, looking from the top of the gap-toothed stockade fence to the bottom, behind the clothesline, and to the small garden shed to its right, directly ahead of her.

Nothing.

She paused to listen, straining for the sounds of breathing or boots on patches of crusty snow.

Nothing.

Turning toward the house, she looked at the bulkhead door leading to the basement. The light from the second story room above it caught her attention. She looked up to where she had stood minutes earlier.

She could clearly see the tiny BB hole, could clearly see the emptiness of the room, could clearly see that when standing at the window— and when standing here now, with not so much as a coat to protect her— she was a target, *a very clear target...*

And not just for someone with a BB gun.

Even though they hadn't even selected students yet, Rob and Janith had asked Matricaria to start preparing a lesson for the study group. It would be an introductory class, one that would give the students an overview of witchcraft. It had to be something that was not oathbound; that is, something that was generally open to the public, not something that was taught under the oath of secrecy that Matricaria and others had taken when they joined the coven.

At her kitchen table, a steaming cup of herb tea beside her, a contented cat curled in her lap, Meg, who was "Matricaria," looked over her notebooks. When she had first met Rob and Janith, there hadn't been a study group. She had found them, through friends of friends, just after they had chosen a group of possible students, all found in much the same way. At that time, the thought of a public study group was unthinkable. At that time, you were chosen to join a secret coven.

Now the trend was to gather interested students in a public place, teach them a little, get to know them, and watch them interact as a group before asking them to join and come to your home. Rob and Janith didn't have a public place to use yet, but they were working on that. While they did, they wanted Matricaria and Gabe to start preparing to teach.

Rob and Janith would do the first class, the one where they introduced the topic and tried to clear up the misconceptions of witchcraft that were a holdover from the days of the Salem Witch Trials. In 1692, petty jealousies, boredom, and disquiet over a frontier war seventy miles away were the real evils. Most of the people, if not all, who were accused, were not true witches, but just unfortunate people caught up in a frenzy of fear and the dynamics of mob rule.

Rob and Janith would patiently explain that modern Wicca was not devil worship and that they didn't even believe in the Christian devil, although they did believe in, and sought to avoid, evil.

Evil. Matricaria thought back to the ritual where the vampire had tried to break through their circle. Before then it had been a concept, an intellectual category, but now it was a reality, an undeniable threat. What she had felt come through the circle that night had been pure evil, and the vampire— or whatever he was— had been the center of it all.

"Focus!" she admonished herself, straightening up and unsettling her cat. "Sorry, sweetie." She stroked the feline's soft, plush, rabbit-like fur, evoking a strong, drooling purr, and settled in again to the task at hand.

As part of Matricaria's own training, she had had to pick an area of specialization. It could be in any subject that was part of their training, but it was to be a skill that the coven could use in time of need. It could be a method of divination, healing, or a specific practice of magic. For example, Gabe had chosen the spirit board. Matricaria had chosen herbs. *Maybe I can give them a short history of herbal use*, she thought to herself as she stared at the pad of lined paper before her, *or the tarot...*

Although herbs had been her specialty, she was also required to learn a divination method. Whether they chose divination as their specialty or not, the coveners were all expected to choose a method to use in daily life. They experimented with pendulums, spirit boards, crystal balls, and, of course, the tarot; for the tarot, in addition to being a divination method, was also a book, a story of life's journeys, and a meditation in itself.

That deep complexity had captivated Matricaria and she had chosen the tarot as her personal divination tool. *I could bring my cards and demonstrate one of the simpler readings...* Gently moving Luna off her lap, she walked to a small cabinet next to a comfortable old wingback chair in the living room.

To the casual eye, it was just a convenient side table, its dark polished wood and black knob blending in seamlessly with Matricaria's antiques and other furnishings. Behind its beveled door lay carefully stacked boxes, each containing some treasure of magic. A few short years ago, all her ritual gear fit in a single duffle bag. Now she needed the duffel bag, a closet shelf, and this cabinet.

As she pulled the deck from the cabinet, one lone card slid loose of the black silk in which they were all wrapped. One lone card, which fluttered face-down to the floor.

Matricaria picked up the card and gasped. One lone card representing change, conflict, and catastrophe.

The Tower.

The police arrived quickly, which is what Alicia would have expected for a report of a gunshot, even though, as she kept reminding herself, it was only a BB gun.

As one officer checked outside, a second interviewed her. He asked the standard questions— did anyone else witness this, where was she standing, what did she see and hear— all the while looking around the room, at the ceiling, the walls, the molding, the baseboards. *As if he'd find the perpetrator there*, she thought.

"Well, I think it's just kids. I wouldn't worry about it," he said, returning the tiny silver BB to her. He turned as the other policeman entered the door to the tiny room. "Find anything?"

"Nope. Nothing."

Turning to Alicia, he said, "Okay, I guess that's all. If they do it again, call us."

"You're not going to try to find them?"

"No. Look, it's just a bunch of kids, and boys will be boys... "

"Boys will be boys? *They shot at me!*"

"Look, miss. It's only a BB gun. It could have been a lot worse."

"But it's still dangerous. What if that had hit me?" She held out the round metal pellet. "What if I had been looking out the window when it happened? What if they shoot at someone else? Can't you stop them? Can't you talk to the parents?"

The officer edged closer to the door. "We'll keep our eyes open. If we find the kids, we'll see what we can do."

Alicia stood dumbfounded. They weren't going to do anything. Nothing. She tried to stammer a protest, but she couldn't think of what to say. How could they just leave her so, so *vulnerable*?

"Call us if they come back. In the meantime, you might want to keep the shades drawn and keep away from the windows."

Yes, I'll do that. I'll keep away from the windows. And figure out how to protect myself, because it looks like I'm the only one who will...

In Matricaria's brief experience with the tarot, the Tower had been the one card that she and her covenmates feared the most— not Death, the skeletal card used in horror movies to indicate danger, but the Tower. Whereas Death indicated an end, and by extension, a new beginning, the Tower represented catastrophic change. Complete disruption of life as one knew it.

Matricaria stared at the card. Maybe there was an alternate meaning. *Not likely.*

She remembered an exercise from the coven's tarot experimentation. Everyone picked a card and described the scene and what it meant to them personally. Maybe if she tried that, the answer would come to her. Matricaria laid the card out in front of her. In the deck she used— and there were many different designs— the Tower was set on a black background. *Black. Darkness. Night.* Her mind flashed to three years earlier, when she had chosen a card to represent their strange visitor. It, too, was dark, and of the night. Could this be a return?

Lightning. Flames. Fire. Were the flames in the card the flames of the fire at Theoretic the night of the explosion? *Two figures fleeing the flames by diving from the tower...* An image of Alicia and the guard at Theoretic flashed into her mind. Although they weren't diving, they were certainly fleeing the flames.

The card definitely seemed to point to the event at Theoretic, but this wasn't an example she could use in front of the study group, not without giving away a secret that the coven had decided not to reveal. As she shuffled the deck to find a different card, Meg realized that she had inadvertently skipped some steps in her reading. Because the card fell out on its own, she hadn't had the opportunity to formulate a question in her mind. And because she wasn't using a layout, which would indicate which cards represented which areas in a querent's life, she was missing a most important detail—

Did this card represent the past, the present— *or the future?*

Frederick needed more cash.

Although his vampire life was a freeloader's dream, Frederick had *some* expenses. Like buying ladies drinks or meals, or paying basketball team dues. When he first started his vampire life, he relied on petty theft. If his victims were drunk, drugged, or otherwise impaired, Frederick wasn't above lifting a couple of dollars from their wallets, especially if he could do it without arousing suspicion. It wasn't much, but he didn't need much.

During his coincidental robbery while in search of gasoline, he discovered more than a new talent: he found that he experienced great pleasure and satisfaction from the robbery itself. *He got off on it.* The sense of danger was a thrill, as was the pleasure of succeeding at a task— something he didn't always do when he was mortal— but the greatest pleasure came from the *power* he felt.

As a mortal, Frederick had been fairly powerless. He was subordinate to his bosses, the law, and even his parents. He had still lived with them until they moved to Florida, just before he met Wesley. Until he finally stood up to them the day they left, he did what *they* wanted, not what *he* wanted. "Frederick, take out the trash." "Frederick, you can't be coming in here at 2 a.m. on a weeknight. You live here, you come home at a decent hour." "Frederick, stop bringing those women around." "Frederick, I need more rent money."

They controlled his life. But now *he* was in control. He had the freedom, and the strength.

He became an expert in nighttime B & E— breaking and entering. At first he kept to gas stations in small towns, then moved on to convenience stores and other small businesses. Once in a while, he even hit clothing stores for new clothes and shoe stores for new sneakers or boots.

Frederick always moved around, never hitting the same town twice in a row. He had discovered that he could walk much faster and longer now, so it was no problem covering fifteen miles or more on foot. Farther than that, he just hotwired cars. If the door was locked, he would use a screwdriver or chisel to punch out the driver's side lock and pull the door open, securing it shut once inside by ripping off the door panel and tying a rope from the cross-braces of the panel to the seat posts. Neatness didn't count.

At first he watched his money carefully so that he wouldn't have to steal that often, reducing his chances of getting caught, but as time wore on, he became more confident that he *wouldn't* get caught. He became freer with his cash, taking his dates to better restaurants, tipping more handsomely, and buying expensive jewelry as presents now and then.

Even though he was careful to rotate his targets, the frequent thefts in small towns didn't go unnoticed. At least Wesley was right about that: in small towns, they noticed things. And took action. It wasn't long before the businesses in small towns were taking more care in securing their establishments and police were increasing their patrols at night. Some businesses were even installing surveillance equipment and alarms like they did in the city. And more drivers started using steering wheel locks.

And so, Frederick found himself standing with a pair of purloined pantyhose, dressed in dark clothing, and considering a different *modus operandi*. Armed robbery.

"When something works, stick with it." That's what Frederick's dad always said, and as Frederick stood pulling the stolen pair of pantyhose onto his rough hands, he had second thoughts about robbing an attended gas station instead of committing his usual B & E.

Simple breaking and entering had served him well, but business owners were starting to get wise, leaving little of value in the stations overnight. Frederick had been forced to consider doing his plundering before the last worker left in the evening.

It seemed like a good idea when he thought of it, but now as he stood in the cold shadows of a weather-beaten, grime-splattered building that housed the local real estate office, fear was settling in. What if the attendant recognized him? What if the attendant had a gun?

Frederick still wasn't sure he believed the immortality stuff. After all, Wesley had disappeared after a nasty explosion. Was Wesley mortal like everyone else? If so, then Frederick would be, too. Maybe Wesley didn't die. Maybe he just went somewhere else. But until Frederick had proof of that, he had to assume that Wesley, and therefore, he himself, could be destroyed.

He took a deep breath and blew it out through pursed lips as he prepared himself for the task. He didn't know if he was immortal, but he knew that if he had to, he was strong enough to overpower any gas station attendant anywhere, anytime— as long as the sun was down— and tonight he would use that strength to his advantage... if he could just overcome his jitters.

Two doors down he could see the gas station, see the attendant sitting at the desk, reading a magazine, could hear the sound of tires crunching on scattered spots of grimy ice crust as a car approached the pumps, hear the *ding ding* of the gas station bell. The attendant zipped his jacket and pulled on some heavy winter gloves as he left the shelter of the warm building. After a quick word with the driver, the attendant selected the grade of gas and inserted the pump nozzle into the filler neck.

Frederick watched all of this with rapt attention. The fact that he would soon attack this man made the whole commonplace scene of filling a gas tank so much more real, so much more vibrant. He felt as if he was watching a movie, or maybe was *in* a movie, waiting for his cue to enter the scene.

Calling upon a level of discipline Frederick never before possessed, he forced himself to look away, to survey the surroundings, to make sure that there wasn't another attendant, wasn't someone walking a dog, wasn't a police car patrolling nearby.

As the car left the pump, Frederick started moving closer. He stopped short when the gas station bell announced another customer. A pickup truck rolled in, and in seconds the attendant had the order and was filling the tank.

Slowly, deliberately panning a wide circle with his eyes as he waited, Frederick saw that the town was quiet, that no dog walkers or night strollers marred the frosty night. As the attendant counted out the change to the driver, Frederick edged closer.

His eyes were wide now, and his superior senses were ablaze. He suddenly realized that he could hear a car or person approach long before they could see him. And with his newfound strength and speed, he could be gone before they arrived...

Emboldened, he dashed across the lit pavement, taking a mere second to cross the lot, and before the attendant could reach the door, Frederick was behind him, his finger stuck hard and cold into the attendant's back.

"This is a gun. I want everything you've got in your pocket. No funny shit or I'll shoot."

"Jesus!" The attendant moved his hand to his pants pocket.

Frederick pushed the index finger of his right hand harder into the attendant's back as he grabbed the man's arm at the biceps. The arm was trembling and Frederick could smell something different than the man's aftershave and dirty hair... *Fear.* He could smell fear. And he liked it.

Frederick let go and took one step back. "No funny shit!"

"Okay, okay!" The attendant pulled out a wad of bills. "Look, man. There's not much here. Is it worth it?"

"Don't be a fucking hero. It's enough. Now go in there and lie down on the floor, hands behind your back. Count to 100 before you move. You move too early, I shoot. Got it?"

"Okay, okay. Whatever you want."

The attendant shakily did as he was told. He lay flat on the greasy floor, now wet from ice melting off customers' boots, and stiffly brought his hands behind his back.

Frederick, of course, saw none of this. He was nearly a mile away before the man reached the floor.

Frederick was halfway back to Danforth before he realized it. He had covered nearly ten miles at speed without effort, without noticing, without so much as a leg cramp or a labored breath. *Shit! What's happening to me? This is so cool! I'm strong and, man, can I run now!*

As he slowed down and moved off to the shadows of the trees on the side of the road to count his money unobserved, Frederick considered his new-found strengths. *Have I always been this way? Why the fuck didn't Wesley tell me? Shit!*

He thought back to when he first met Wesley, when he first... died. He couldn't remember how it felt, though if he had to guess, he would have thought it felt like a hangover, that he felt like he did any Sunday morning— nauseated and weak, with his pulse pounding in his aching head...

Maybe his new-found strengths were always there, but because he felt crappy that first day, he just expected that he always would feel that way. And maybe because Wesley kept him down, kept belittling him, kept him in line, he was never able to discover these strengths on his own.

That fucking bastard! With a renewed sense of rage, Frederick whirled and punched the nearest object, a hardwood tree nearly two feet in diameter...

... and sent it crashing to the ground.

Chapter 11

"I can't believe they just said 'boys will be boys' and let it go at that. You could have lost an eye!" Norma shook her head in disbelief.

"Yeah, I was a little shocked, too." Alicia took another bite of her tuna salad sandwich, wiping a tiny smear of mayonnaise from her lip with the knuckle of her right hand.

"Maybe you should call the station and report the cops," Carol offered.

Alicia grimaced. "And get them in trouble with their boss? That's the last thing I need, a couple of cops mad at me."

"Alicia, they're cops! They're supposed to protect us!"

"I know, I know. That's what I thought, too, but when you think about it, what could they do? Whoever shot the BB gun was long gone by the time they arrived. No one was hurt, and I'm sure they had more important things to do. I'll just have to stay away from the windows in the back of the house when the lights are on, that's all."

"Aren't you afraid?"

Alicia thought for a second, but only for a second. Her emotions were close to the surface and easy to access. "No, I'm more pissed off than afraid. Now I have a window to fix, and since I can't afford to pay someone to do it, I have to figure out how to do it myself. I taped over the hole with masking tape for now, but I'm going to have to fix it eventually, and I have enough house repairs to do." She sighed and took a sip of water. "Maybe I can get Joey to do it, if I can catch him at home."

Norma looked at her sternly. "Alicia, forget about the repair. You're alone in that house most of the time. What if something happens?"

"I won't be alone as much now that I'm getting another roommate. At least he'll be there, and maybe just having someone else in the house will make the kids think twice about doing it again."

"You know it was kids?"

"No, but that's what the cops thought. Why would an adult shoot a BB at someone?"

"Why would *anyone* shoot a BB at someone?" Norma was shaking her head again. "Kids these days. They're out of control. They have no respect. What's this world coming to?"

Alicia smiled.

"What's so funny?"

"Oh, nothing." She paused, and then continued. "I just remember my English teacher reading something similar in class. Let's see, how did that go? '...They have bad manners, contempt for authority; they show disrespect for their elders.. They contradict their parents, chatter before company, gobble up their food and tyrannize their teachers.'"

"Sounds like my kids!" Carol playfully poked Norma with her elbow.

Norma was not amused. "Okay, so kids have been rotten for a few years. That doesn't mean it's right."

"No, but maybe the cop was right. Maybe they were just being kids, like kids have always been kids. That quote was from Socrates, in the fifth century B.C."

"Just because it's been going on for centuries doesn't mean it's okay. It's gotta stop before someone gets hurt!"

Alicia stared down at her cookies. Norma was right. The cops were right. Socrates was right. And so was she.

The only thing she could do was to protect herself, and not rely on others to protect her. It never paid to rely on others.

Never.

Maybe she could rig a dark blanket over a drapery rod or something so she wouldn't cast a silhouette at night.

"Anything good?" Rob lifted Janith's crossed feet from the couch, and slid under them.

"Not really. Most of them are looking for thrills, not covens." She smiled back at her husband and magical partner, giving him an affectionate rub with her foot. "Listen to this: 'I'm tall, dark, handsome and like dinners for two and walks on the beach. Looking for a special woman... '" Janith shook her head. "How could he get THAT idea from our ad? We said nothing about romance."

Rob took the letter from Janith's outstretched hand, shaking his head, too, as he read. "Maybe he figured that if it was in the *Free Weekly*, it had to have something to do with dating or sex, even if he couldn't figure out exactly what?"

"Oh, maybe. Here's a good one. 'Yeah, I'm interested in Wicca. What is it?'" Janith flung the letter at Rob, snorting with laughter. "Do you believe this?"

"Well, at least he— or she— is open-minded!" Rob snuggled closer and rubbed her shoulder. Janith smiled and sat up, snuggling into him, permitting her long, strawberry blonde hair to caress the fingers that gently massaged her.

"Wild and crazy is more like it. Oh, gods, this is creepy! Listen to this: 'I am interested. Please give me directions to your coven so I can join you. I am signing my name in blood so that you will know that I am sincere.'"

"He didn't!" Rob leaned over to look at the letter. A look of disgust formed on his face even before he saw the faded brownish red scrawl at the bottom of the parchment-like paper. "Oh, gods!"

Janith started to throw the letter into the trash, but stopped. "I suppose we should hang on to these letters for a while in case the people contact us again, trying a different tack. I'll keep a separate folder of rejects."

"Good idea. It might also be helpful in case one of the other covens ask us if we've heard of these people."

Stuffing the letters back into their envelopes, Janith noted, "I know it's said that when the time is right, the student will find the teacher and vice versa, but this doesn't look very promising."

"Patience, hon. The ad's been out only a week. We agreed to run it for one complete moon cycle before giving up." Rob picked up a pen and textbook from the coffee table. He opened the text to a bookmark and began reading, jotting notes in the margins.

"Yeah, I just hope that now is the time and that we're not wasting our energy."

"Remember physics: energy is never lost. It's true in *meta*physics, too. Even if we don't get the results we want this time, the energy we put out there isn't wasted."

Janith pondered Rob's discourse for a minute, crinkling her brow in thought, before relinquishing her concern. "You're right. At this point, it's in the hands of the universe. All we can do is wait."

While her clothes spun in the large stainless steel commercial dryer, Alicia flipped through a trade journal for information systems professionals.

The day was fading and as it got darker outside and brighter inside, Alicia felt a little of the fear and vulnerability that she had felt a few nights ago when someone shot the BB into her window. Sitting in a dingy orange plastic shell of a chair facing a large plate glass window, she could feel her heart beat faster and her throat tighten until she had to move to the end of the room where a large table shielded her from the view of passersby.

There was no reason to think anyone would follow her here, gun in hand, but Alicia couldn't stand in front of a lit window anymore, not without the fear returning. If she forgot to close the shade at home, she'd turn off the light first before she'd walk near a window. She'd much rather risk a stumble in the dark than being a target against a lighted room.

She didn't understand it. She wasn't very afraid when it happened, but the fear seemed to deepen each day— no, each night, when the sun went down and she was exposed to the dark world outside. Night. Everything seemed to deepen with the night...

For the quickest, most fleeting moment, she could see Wesley's face, could feel the cold emanate from his skin, could see the blackening darkness as she had struggled against loss of consciousness... *No!* He was gone. This fear was a *new* fear, a fear based on a real experience, proven by real evidence.

She closed the trade journal and opened the copy of the *Free Weekly* that she had picked up at the co-op, hoping that maybe it would contain something to capture her interest, but there was so much that didn't really concern her. City politics. Complaints about incomplete snow removal on side streets during the last snow storms. Art reviews. Book reviews. Events. She passed quickly over the events section. All the events were in the city and she had no use for cities. Cities were dirty, dangerous, and noisy. And devoid of nature.

Her philosophy was that if she couldn't find what she needed in Danforth or the towns surrounding it, then she didn't really need it. Danforth was a big-enough town for her. Maybe too big. Her real dream was to live further out, toward the central part of the state, where large expanses of trees lined the edges of the major reservoirs. Of course, that dream was diametrically opposed to her other dream of a successful career in high technology, which tended to be closer to cities due to their colleges and larger labor pools.

Eventually her disdain of cities led to a fear of cities. She didn't know if it was her lack of appreciation that made it hard for her to get to know them and therefore understand them, but she did know that she feared them, and avoided them.

She had even coined her own word to describe herself— *metrophobe*— and then discovered that metrophobe meant the fear of poetry. Then she found *urbanophobe*. It fit. She was an *urbanophobe*, someone who was unduly fearful and contemptuous of cities. And though normally she vigorously excised even the tiniest shade of intolerance from her thoughts, this was one bigotry she allowed herself, even luxuriated in. Cities were evil and the root of crime, suffering, and violence. She was free to hate them.

Alicia stopped flipping pages at the Classified section. The *Free Weekly's* classified section was famous for its unusual and risqué ads. She remembered one summer evening at Susie's, all of them drinking piña coladas, the ice clinking against their glasses as they shook with laughter at either the ads or their own lewd commentary. Once again, she paused with the pain of remembering Susie, and the anguish of wondering what happened to her.

Shaking her head as if she could shake off the loss, she flipped the page. There, under Miscellaneous, sandwiched between an ad for tarot readings and one for astrology charts, was a short ad that read:

New Wiccan group forming. If interested, write, giving details of books that you've read and any previous experience. *FreeWeekly* Box 7501.

Wiccan... There was something about that word that seemed familiar. Alicia wished she had a dictionary with her. *Wiccan.. Wicca... Wik— Wit— Witch!* She wondered if they could be the people that Evan knew... How many witches could there be in the area?

While doing her research on vampires, she had leafed through, with fascination, some of the books on witchcraft that were also in the occult section. There, side by side with book after book of similar retellings of the rather fantastical Salem Witch Trials had been books that claimed that witches lived today and that they weren't green-faced, warty-nosed, stooped old hags, but rather normal people with serious beliefs, and an understanding of the esoteric laws of the universe. People with knowledge.

And power. Power to control events around them, protect themselves from danger. Protect themselves from evil.

Staring at the ad in front of her, she tried to remember where she saw those books. Were they in the library or the used book stores? She thought she had seen one, the diary of a witch, in the library. The other one, about mastering witchcraft, was at the House of Astrology.

She wasn't interested in joining the group listed in the ad— they were in the city and, besides, she'd be going back to night school soon and wouldn't have much free time— but maybe they'd be willing to talk to her and help her solve the mystery of Wesley.

Even without wearing her contacts, Matricaria could tell that the dark charcoal shape that seemed to tumble from the woods behind her house was a deer.

And that its left hind leg was bloodied.

Retrieving her spare eyeglasses from the bedroom and peeking out the window there, she could see now that the deer's hind leg, at the knee joint, was indeed dark and bloody.

Coyotes attack deer. She remembered a coyote that she had seen staring down her neighbor's now-gone cat just before winter came. *And so do cars...* On the other side of the small wooded area that bordered her land, there was a busy highway. It made sense.

Still, the appearance of a bleeding deer in the back yard was unusual— and unnerving.

Somewhat irrationally, she found herself thinking, *What if it hadn't been a coyote, or a car?*

"So where did you meet her?" Lynnie placed a cup of jasmine tea on the low rattan table. Evan sat cross-legged on the floor behind it, inhaling the steam from his own cup.

"She used to work with Todd. She just joined the co-op."

"And when did this all happen, and why is it coming up now?"

"Three years ago. She's been trying to figure it out all this time, but hasn't had anyone to talk to. You don't just walk up to someone and say, 'I think I might have a vampire problem.'"

"Of course not, silly boy!" Lynnie gave Evan a playful kick as she placed her own cup on the table. Stepping on the hem of her long, pastel blue clouds-and-sky silk bathrobe as she did so, she tripped, falling into him. Evan caught her immediately, his reflexes tuned from years of tai chi practice, and held her in a gentle hug, smiling. She smiled back contentedly at

Evan's dark blue eyes as he tenderly stroked her face, collarbone, and chest with his long, graceful fingers.

The world stilled as they drank in the sensuousness of the moment, the sweet delicate scent of jasmine tea caressing their nostrils. In the background, Pachelbel's "Canon in D Major" played softly, the two independent melody lines twining sensually over and around eight chords that repeated hypnotically. Lynnie kissed Evan gently on the lips and then righted herself. Evan watched intently as she turned to stir her tea.

They had met in college, dated a little, and then gone their separate ways. When Evan had decided to pursue a computer career, Lynnie had convinced him to come to Fenmore. He had stayed with her the first couple of days, abandoning himself to her charm and attention, but quickly found a reason to visit other friends, not wanting to deepen their relationship too quickly. Watching her now, he was tempted to rescind that self-promise of avoidance.

"I can ask my guides during my morning meditation tomorrow. You're welcome to stay and join me." Lynnie poked a playful finger into his side and raised her eyebrow suggestively. Evan responded by stroking her arm gently and shaking his head.

He spoke softly, sweetly, his voice deep and indulgent. "That's very tempting, but I have an interview at the school in Danforth, so I'll be staying with Todd tonight."

"I'm jealous," Lynnie teased, pulling away.

Evan pulled her back for a long, soulful kiss. "We could do a different kind of meditation right now..."

"Ummm... a meditation on the nature of ecstasy?"

"Hey, you're new here." It was a tired line, a tired routine, but with a little persistence, it always broke the ice. Frederick put on his best smile, threw back his shoulders, and moved in closer to the ash blonde who had just entered the clubhouse.

The woman smiled faintly, no doubt trying to think of how she could back away gracefully, having heard the line *from* strangers almost as many times as Frederick had uttered it *to* strangers, but Frederick had learned a thing or two in his endless nights of clubbing. She was wary. Play on it.

"Oh, hey. I'm sorry. You think I'm coming on to you or something." Still holding a beer in one hand, he put up his arms in a distancing gesture. "Don't mind me. Just trying to be friendly, that's all."

Of course he had her then. He didn't even have to look, but he couldn't resist a peek from under the lock of hair that had flopped over his eyes. Yes, her attitude had softened, visibly softened.

"No, that's okay. I don't come here often. My boyfriend didn't like clubs."

Boyfriend?

Not catching the past tense in her response, Frederick asked, "So you left him at home watching TV?"

"No. We split up."

Bingo! Can I pick 'em or what? Frederick was proud of what seemed to be his increasing powers of perception. He had thought that he felt a singular edge to her as he walked in— as if he could feel her *feelings*— had felt the loneliness of separation, the sharp edge of lives disconnected, the want and hurt of loss.

He continued his approach, making small talk, edging physically closer, so close that occasionally the hand that held the beer bottle— more a prop than anything these days— brushed lightly against her upper arm and shoulder. He could feel the warmth of her body and longed to press it against his cold skin, to bask in her warmth like a lizard on a desert rock.

As the evening wore on, he could see the effects of the sweet cocktails that she had been drinking. She gently melted from a rigid form to a fluid, swaying figure, and he knew that soon he could make his move. Should he let her think it was her idea, or would she be flattered if *he* suggested it? She was looking at her watch and Frederick knew he'd have to make his decision soon...

"Look at the time! I've got to work tomorrow."

"How late is it?"

She stretched out an unsteady wrist before him.

"Man, that's late! I've got to get going, too." So that would be how it played out. They'd just leave at the same time. He wasn't worried that they'd be seen leaving together, for tonight he'd take just a little, just enough to whet the edge of his appetite. She'd be fine in the morning— except for the hangover. And she would blame all her agony on that.

"Yes, that's true," Janith said to Matricaria. "The Tower most often represents unforeseen catastrophe, but it can also mean the fall of selfish ambition or an overthrow of power."

"I didn't remember that."

"It's in one of my books on the Tarot. Want to see it?"

"Yes, that'd be great. I'd like to believe that The Tower can be something other than complete and utter destruction."

Janith got up and retrieved a paperback from her bookshelf. "Here. Why don't you take this home, read up on it, and meditate on the meaning before we bring it up to the group. Tonight we're doing the healing for Amber's mother and I don't want to invoke negative energy or get sidetracked."

Matricaria slid the book into her tote bag. "Good idea. No, we don't want to be thinking about the Tower while we do a healing. And we certainly do get distracted easily!" It didn't take much to get the group off-track. They had been working together for over three years and conversation came easily.

"Yes, we don't want to bring in the energy of the Tower to our healing. You should take a few minutes now and deliberately clear it from your mind."

Matricaria nodded, straightened her shoulders, and closed her eyes in meditation. Focusing on her breathing, she cleared her mind of all else, becoming aware only of inhalation, exhalation. The traffic noises outside faded as her concentration deepened.

The buzzer sounded, jarring her to alertness. As Janith left the room to answer it, Matricaria took a sip of the herbal tea that she had made on arrival.

Later that evening, when she was free to allow the dark image of the Tower to enter her mind again, she would reflect on the other meanings that Janith had mentioned and they would give her hope that maybe things wouldn't be as bad as she feared. Then the only questions would be just who was in power? And was his or her tumble from its lofty heights of power a good or a bad thing?

Think, man, think. Frederick held the door for the blonde as she left the building. She had warmed to his flattery earlier. Maybe with a little more effort, he could wrangle a goodnight kiss from her. And while kissing her...

They were nearing the back door to the apartment building. "Well, hey, it was really nice to meet you," he said, smoothing his hand gently down the thick fabric of her coat over her right arm. He could feel only the slightest momentary flinch at his touch. *Good, she's not too uptight.*

Inside, she walked to the elevator and pressed the up button, turning unsteadily to face him. "Ooops. I guess I had more than I thought. I'm going to regret this tomorrow." She giggled, still swaying.

Frederick stepped close to steady her. *Play the protector— yeah, she'll be okay with that.* "Hey, are you okay? Let me walk you to your door. Don't want you passing out in the hall."

A slight unfocused look of wariness flitted across her face, creasing her forehead, knitting her brow. "No, that's okay, I'm fine...", but as she stepped into the opening of the elevator doors, she stumbled, and Frederick caught her.

"Okay, no more protests, little lady. I'm getting you home safely, okay?" He was careful to use all the right words: Home. Safely.

With glazed eyes, the woman looked up and nodded her acceptance as Frederick steered her into the back of the elevator.

"Betty. My name is Betty. Call me Betty."

"Okay, Betty, which floor?"

"Third."

Frederick pushed the button as the elevator door closed. Betty clung to him, her eyelids fluttering, her head lolling.

"Shit! I didn't think I drank that much."

"You know how it is. Those Sombreros go down easily."

"They weren't Sombreros. They were White Russians."

"Well, there you go! Vodka, coffee brandy. No wonder. How many did you have?"

Betty was lost in concentration when the elevator doors opened. Frederick shook her a little to get her attention. "Third floor, right? This is it."

She straightened her head and blinked, trying to focus. "Yeah. To the left," and then, as an afterthought, "Three. I had three."

"Three's not much. Empty stomach?"

Betty pointed to a door, and then fumbled for her keys. "Yeah, that's it. Empty stomach."

"Next time, eat something, okay?"

Betty looked up, trying to smile suggestively, "Well, maybe if someone would offer to take me to dinner, I'd remember to eat."

"Well, maybe I will." Frederick took the keys from Betty's hands and unlocked the door, something she hadn't been able to manage.

The apartment was like the others he had visited in this building: small kitchen, small living room with one exposed brick wall. If he had been the type of man to notice that sort of thing, he would have seen that the sculpted gold rug matched the harvest gold of the kitchen appliances, but Frederick didn't notice. He was too busy hyper-listening, trying to determine if Betty's neighbors were home and awake, trying to determine how much background noise was available to cover any screams or moans if she struggled.

Through the thin plaster wall opposite the exposed brick one, he could hear a television. *Good.* That provided *some* cover. The apartment on the other side was silent. He strained and found that he could hear a clock ticking there, but could hear no breathing. Most likely the occupant was out.

"Here, why don't you sit down," he instructed as he eased Betty onto the brown synthetic leather sofa. "You want some water?"

"No, I'm fine. Just need a minute."

Frederick maneuvered himself next to her. He could feel the blood lust rising, but held himself in check. He didn't want to scare her. If he could just bide his time, she would soon pass out.

Outside, the traffic noises stilled and then stirred again as the traffic light at the s-curve changed from red to green. Looking toward the noise, Frederick noticed that Betty's drapes were open. Frederick considered closing them, but then changed his mind. *Hey, we're on the third floor. And even if someone could see in, what're they gonna see? Someone kissing?*

Hesitantly he put his arm over Betty's shoulders. She stirred, and he could feel the smallest tensing of the muscles in her neck and shoulder. "Hey, it's okay. I'm just gonna make sure you're alright before I leave, okay? You sure you don't want some water or somethin'?"

Betty opened a glassy eye to Frederick, then spoke, her speech sluggish, her words slurred. "No, I'm okay." Frederick could see that she was fighting nausea. *Shit, the last thing I need is her puking on me.*

Gently he stroked her forehead. "You're okay," he said, wishing it as much as stating it, hoping her nausea would subside. As he caressed her troubled brow, he felt her relax to his touch.

She licked her lips and swallowed. "Yeah, I'm feeling better already." She swallowed again. "No, really, I am."

Frederick continued to stroke her forehead, not realizing that he also continued to wish, to *will*, that her nausea subside.

Betty turned to him. "You've got the magic touch. I'm feeling much better. Much, much better. In fact, I'm feeling really good."

Frederick met her open lips with his own, sliding his hand to the back of her head, weaving his fingers into her hair. From the dead weight of her head, he could tell that she was still quite drunk. *It's now or never, buddy.* Cautiously he eased his lips away, nuzzling his chin against hers, softly covering her cheek, her jaw, with light kisses as he inched his way down to her neck, down to the most vital and vulnerable part.

He could hear the lights change outside, could hear the drivers with manual transmissions shifting from neutral into first, hear them all easing up on the brake pedal, and as he heard them roaring away from the stop line, he bit lightly and firmly into her roaring vein, one hand clutching her head tightly for access, the other sliding urgently between her legs, for distraction.

With a quiet, carnal moan, Betty gave in to the bite, swooning into a light faint as Frederick drank the first precious drops.

Chapter 12

"'Morning, Carol." Alicia walked up to the large counter where the predominantly female clerical staff retrieved printouts from the computer room and stacked them onto shelves where they stayed until they were picked up.

Carol looked up from a batch of reports that she was separating. "Good morning! How are we today?"

Alicia grinned. "I don't know about 'we,' but I'm okay. How are you?"

"Not bad, not bad. What can I do you for?" She was cheery, but there was a level of distraction behind the smile. Instead of stopping to chat, she continued to separate the reports as she talked, tearing the green-striped paper at the perforation as she spoke.

"Can you tell me if a report got out yesterday?"

"I can check. What's the job name?" She stuffed a couple of reports into labeled pigeon holes on a shelf, her back to the counter.

Alicia wondered if she had offended her. *Stop being so paranoid. She's just busy!* "Um, I think it's MKT-0500. It was supposed to run at 4."

"Okay. Let me look." Carol turned to a long folding table behind her, opened a dark blue pressboard data binder, and began thumbing through sheaves of more green-striped paper.

As she waited for an answer, Alicia thought back to her days as an operator, when she had free access to the Holy of Holies, the computer room. At Universal Info, programmers weren't allowed in there at all. She wondered if any of UI's staff had encountered what she once had during those dark and silent nights.

Was *that* why Carol was distracted? Trying not to be obvious, she looked for signs. Her complexion *was* a little pale and she did look a little tired, but no more than the average person. Maybe she was out late the night before. Or coming down with something. There was nothing of the marked pallor that Alicia had seen when she looked in the mirror after the bite. Still, there was something wrong, some subtle tension in the air.

Running her finger down the rows of data, Carol stopped and looked to the right of the page. "Yup. It ran, and Betty initialed it as *Distributed.*"

"Speaking of Betty, what time are you guys going for lunch?"

"No Betty. It'll be just you and me, kiddo. Betty called in sick with a sore throat."

The sunlight easing through the north window had woken Betty around 5:30. Her first thought was, "Did I leave the drapes open?" and her second was, "What am I doing on the couch?"

She woke stiffly. Her neck hurt and her head ached. She was exhausted. As she turned her head to look toward the clock, she felt a pull on the skin of her neck. As she reached to feel for the cause, her earring post brushed her hand. *Shit! That's what I get for sleeping with my earrings in. Must've scratched my neck.*

Her mouth felt dry and cottony, and her throat sore. *Maybe I'm coming down with something.* She tried to remember what happened the night before and how she ended up on the couch. White Russians. She remembered drinking three White Russians, creamy drinks with coffee brandy and vodka. And that guy. What was his name? Rick? No, Frederick. That guy who helped her in.

Yet why was she so drunk? She remembered part of a conversation about an empty stomach, but it still didn't make sense. She had drunk those three drinks over a five-hour time period. And their milky base should have prevented the alcohol from hitting her bloodstream too fast.

But hit her they had, and as she lay sprawled out on her couch on this, the morning after, she had a dreamy remembrance of Frederick, and of a long, languid, kiss. And of urgency and desire. Of nothingness.

As she pushed herself to an upright position, a wave of dizziness hit, and she felt a tightness around her skull. *That's it. I'm calling in sick.*

She left a quick message with the third-shift operator and, still dressed, crawled into bed.

And dreamed. Of Frederick.

"Why are you looking to change positions, Mr. Maxwell?" asked the recruiter, a man in mid-life much like Maxwell himself, as he reached for a pen and moved a pad of lined paper into position.

Leaning forward a bit, his left hand anchored on the chair arm to give him leverage, Maxwell replied, "I don't think I'm being given a chance to prove myself. I've been there two years and I have no increase in budget, no additional headcount, no resources. How can I do anything without resources? What kind of a future do I have in a company that doesn't want to invest in management systems?" In the next four minutes he described his current position, careful not to sound as if he were complaining or shifting blame, which indeed he was, for in Maxwell's eyes, it was always someone else's fault, always someone else holding him back.

"Ah, yes. Tell me a little about your previous position. That's Theoretic, right?"

"Right. I was really whipping things into shape there. I had just taken over control of another group, and was in the process of cutting their costs, eliminating deadwood— you know, cleaning house— and then there was an explosion in one of the research labs. Upper management put everything on the back burner while they investigated the incident."

"Was this lab part of your organization?"

"The data processing lab was, but not the scientific lab." He continued, building a believable tale of his managerial success, winding up by describing his vision for Theoretic, and concluding that he had the big ideas and that Pete, the previous manager, was just happy to do what he was told and get home to his wife and kids after work. "I've got what it takes. I see the big picture and I know how to get results."

The recruiter, apparently impressed by Maxwell's spirited delivery, scribbled a few quick notes before asking more specific questions about responsibilities, how management was structured at Theoretic, how many people Maxwell had reporting to him, and at what levels. Maxwell sat up straight, his eyes alert, for this conversation, boring to so many, was what got his juices going. He rattled off numbers and organizational details like many men rattled off sports statistics. He was vibrant, alive.

"Okay, Mr. Maxwell. I think we have enough to go on. I'll call some contacts and try to set up some interviews. I think we might have something for you."

Taking the cue, Maxwell stood, smoothing his suit coat, extending his hand for the closing shake. He knew his manners, knew the rituals of business, knew his place in the world.

"Thanks for your time. It's been a pleasure."

"Same here."

Maxwell turned to the door, his heart pumping, his fingers tingling. *This time I'm going to make it. All I need is a chance.* As he waited for the elevator, he thought of Theoretic. And wondered: what really happened the night of that explosion?

Sore throat. As Alicia waited for Carol to join her at the lunch table, again she recalled that day in the computer room when she saw the two perfect marks on her own throat. *Silly! Betty doesn't have THAT kind of sore throat...*

Still, she couldn't shake the image. *It's just your mind, having a play on words.*

Alicia firmly pushed the vision from her mind as Carol and another woman approached the table, but a momentary echo of the vision persisted, an afterimage that would fade eventually, but in the meantime would block the center of all vision, the center of her life.

She needed more information. Now.

"So, Evan's moving in?" Todd asked, peering intently at the scale as he measured out a half pound of unsulfured dried apricots.

"Yeah, he said he's spending the weekend with a friend, but should be over sometime Monday night." Alicia waited for Todd to slide the apricots off the scale before placing her square of waxed paper in place. "He's starting at the Computer Center next week." She paused to read the weight of the unblanched almonds. "Thanks for hooking us up. I really needed another roommate, and he needed somewhere within walking distance of the CC."

"Oh, you're welcome. Did you talk to him about the warehouse?"

"Yes, I did— " Alicia paused as a customer neared the weighing area. Todd looked up, and then silently continued writing out the price label for the apricots.

A wiry man with full beard, and hair to mid-back, examined a package of miso soup powder, placed it in his shopping basket, and moved on.

Alicia waited for him to move out of earshot before continuing. "Evan said he had some friends that might know more about these things. He said he's talking to someone who does channeling, whatever that is— "

"I've heard that it's sort of a new term for mediumship. The channeler gets into an altered state of consciousness and becomes a channel for a spirit entity or alien being from alternate realms to come through."

"Ah. Well, he's talking to that friend this weekend. He said he'll also contact some witch friends of his and arrange a meeting. He's very interesting. How did you meet him?"

"Friends of friends. He went to college with some people I knew who were friends with someone I went to school with."

More witches? Alicia felt it would be impolite to ask. She scooped the last of the almonds into a bag. "Looks like I'm almost finished. Do you need any help?"

"No, I'm almost through here."

"Then I think I'll see if I can leave early. I have some more things to do around the house before Evan comes over, so I'm going to try to get up early tomorrow."

"Okay. I think you'll like Evan the more you get to know him."

Thinking back on their Chinese dinner, Alicia found herself smiling. "Yeah, I think I do already."

"Okay, we have some more replies to the ad in the *Free Weekly*. They just came today, so I haven't read them." Janith grabbed a small stack of envelopes from the coffee table.

Matricaria settled into her chair, notebook open, as Janith began to read aloud.

"I think we have a ceremonialist here, and not a modest one, either." She held up a business-sized envelope covered in angular esoteric symbols, "Let's see what our magician has to say...'I am the reincarnation of Aleister Crowley, The Great Beast. Do What Thou Wilt Shall Be The Whole Of The Law. Love is the law. Love under will. Magick is the Science and Art of causing Change to occur in Conformity with Will. Teach me your magicks and I will teach you mine.'"

Gabe smiled suggestively. "Does he like men? Crowley liked men. Maybe I could interview him?"

Rob laughed, "Sure, Gabe. We'll save him for you."

"I don't think he's what we're looking for— or vice versa." Janith picked up the next letter. Only a small white rectangle was left around the mailing address, the return address, and the stamp. The rest of the envelope was covered with tiny flowers, grass stalks, butterflies, and fairies hand-drawn in green ink. Janith turned the envelope around to look at the drawing as it continued onto the back.

Rob looked over her shoulder, eyebrows raised. "Wow. Very detailed work."

"Yes, either we have an artist here or someone who spends their days in altered states of consciousness— "

"—or both," Rob added.

"Let's find out...'my name is changeling childe. i've been able to see fairies since i was a little girl. no one could see them but me. in school everyone made fun of me but i ignored them and kept to myself with no one to talk to but the fairies who were always there for me in the morning and at night and when i walked to school and never left me and were my true companions and let me see them and their world that i've drawn for you on the envelope but you cannot show it to anyone. my mother said i must be a witch if i can see the fairies so can i join your coven?'"

"I wonder if this is a child writing?" Janith said, passing the letter to Matricaria. "The artwork is very accomplished, but the handwriting looks very childlike."

"Maybe it's someone who's emotionally still a child?" Matricaria looked briefly at the letter before passing it on to Gabe.

"Could be. Okay, one last one." Janith ripped open the envelope and unfolded the letter. "No fairies or Thelemic sigils on this one." On the plain white paper was a neatly typed letter. As Janith scanned to the bottom of the page, she gasped.

"What's wrong?" asked Rob, trying to peer over her shoulder.

Janith didn't reply. Instead she passed the letter to Matricaria.

"Oh, my gods. It's Alicia!"

"Read it to us," Janith directed Matricaria, who was still sitting silently, staring at the letter.

Matricaria took a deep breath and sat up straight. "Okay, here goes. 'Dear folks at Box 7501: I saw your ad in the Free Weekly and although I'm not interested in joining a coven, I was wondering if you could help me or refer me to someone who could. Three years ago I had a strange encounter with a being who may or may not have been supernatural—"

"That's an understatement!" Gabe cut in.

Matricaria smiled, took a sip of tea, and continued reading, "I would be happy to give you more details in another letter. (It's a long story.) The reason I'm writing is that I've been feeling that there's something going on

again and recently a psychic reader told me that the being that I encountered is still around. I need to talk to someone about this to try to understand what's going on. I know this all seems a little crazy, but I'm a normal,
sane person with a responsible job and I'm not one to imagine things. Any
help you could provide would be greatly appreciated. I've enclosed an SASE
for your reply. Thank you, Alicia Anderson." Matricaria took another breath
before looking up at Janith and Rob, who were staring thoughtfully off into
space. Even Gabe was silent. "Well, that definitely sounds like her. Even if
more than one Alicia Anderson reads the *Weekly*, that's her."

"Do you recognize the address?" Rob asked.

Matricaria looked at the address block of the letter. "No. Just a post
office box— 228. But it's in Danforth, and Alicia's in Danforth. It's got to be
her."

"What do you want to do? Normally we meet candidates in a neutral
place, in public, but since you know Alicia, we could invite her here."

"But she doesn't know *us*. I don't think she'd be foolish enough to meet
strangers in an apartment. And I'm not sure I want her to know about me
yet. She seems like a reasonable person, but I'd hate to let her know that
I'm a witch and then find out that she's a religious fanatic. We work in the
same building. It could be very uncomfortable, or even worse. She could
tell people at work, leave tracts on my desk, start sermonizing in the halls.
Do you think that you and Janith could meet her first and find out a little
bit about her attitude towards witches?"

"Sure, we can do that. We'll meet her for supper. If she seems okay, do
you want us to make arrangements to meet her here?"

Matricaria paused, mouth slightly open, as she tried to think through
the situation.

"We're getting together again next Wednesday. You could come in a
little earlier and we could have her come over then."

"That is, of course," Janith added, "if we feel she's okay with this after
we meet her."

Matricaria nodded. "That sounds good."

"Okay. Gabe, any objections?" Gabe was on his way to the bathroom
when Janith addressed him.

"Nope. Sounds like a plan to me."

"Excellent. Then it's settled. We'll scrqeen her, and then invite her here.
Okay, the next order of business— after Gabe returns —is starting to plan
our Beltane celebration."

Chapter 13

On Monday, Evan moved in.

April in New England is a tricky beast; in some years, snow still slaps the hand that would reach for spring. This year, however, the temperature was in the high 60s when Alicia came home from work early to let Evan in, warm enough to open the upstairs windows and let in the fragrant spring air.

Moonshadow perched in the bedroom window that faced the street, catching the strengthening rays of the sun. Nine years old now, the cat who had seen her through Wesley's visit seemed none the worse for wear. He moved less quickly and slept a little more these days, but otherwise he was the same, constant Moonshadow.

Alicia gave him an affectionate pat and hug. He responded with a deep, throaty purr. Thus distracted, neither of them saw Evan's friend drop him off at the curb... nor saw the deep, soulful goodbye kiss in the car. The first that Alicia knew of Evan's arrival was the sound of the doorbell.

Joey, who was at home waiting for a phone call from his girlfriend, answered the door. He offered to help Evan with his stuff, but there wasn't much: a knapsack, a duffle bag, a bedroll, and a box of books. "I travel light," Evan explained. "I like to be fluid."

"Yeah, man, I know what you mean," Joey said, picking up the box of books. "Follow me."

He led Evan up the front stairs. At the top, Alicia waited, empty-handed. She felt guilty for not helping. Joey led Evan into his room and set the box of books on the floor. "Here's your room. Hey, you guys interested in some pizza? I was going to go get one."

"Make mine cheese. I'm a vegetarian," Evan said as he unrolled the bedroll next to the far wall.

"What, you just eat cans of green beans and stuff?"

Evan smiled, his blue eyes bright and patient. "No, I eat fresh vegetables, bread, pasta, fruit, cheese, and eggs. Just no meat or fish."

"Wow, man. That's weird. Why? Don't you like meat?"

"I used to. But raising animals for food wastes land, water, energy, and other resources, which is unconscionable when hundreds of thousands of people die each year from malnutrition."

Alicia watched as Joey listened, a veil of confusion draping his face. Evan patiently explained vegetarianism as he saw it, why he embraced it, the plight of animals, and how a vegetarian diet was more spiritually evolved.

"A vegetarian diet is cheaper, too." Alicia interrupted. "When the price of meat went sky high a few years back, I bought a book that showed how you could get enough protein without meat."

"You know about this stuff, too? Wow. I don't believe you guys. This stuff is too weird. I'm going to get the pizza. Alicia, you okay with sausage, pepper, and onion?"

Evan held up a finger, gesturing for Joey to wait. "If you could just leave the sausage off half, I wouldn't mind pepper and onion. Is it meatless sauce?"

"Sure, I can get plain sauce."

Alicia nodded. "That sounds good to me."

"Okay, half with sausage, half without. Plain sauce, peppers, and onions on your half. You guys are strange!"

Evan and Alicia chuckled softly as they scrounged money for the pizza. As Joey left, Evan smiled at Alicia and said, "Tomorrow I'll cook. I make an excellent stir fry. We'll show Joey it's more than just canned vegetables or pizza."

"You 're on!!"

And he cooks, too! What a guy!

It's a good thing it's cold enough to wear scarves, Betty thought as she fastened one around her neck with a gold-tone stick pin.

She had run into Frederick again, at the clubhouse. At first she didn't know how to act. She didn't usually sleep with men on the first date, and she wasn't even sure that she had slept with Frederick anyway; there were no physical traces, but if he had used a condom, there wouldn't have been. All she knew was that she had been drunk, very drunk, and he had come into her apartment and was with her on the couch. And that she kept dreaming of him, kept desiring him. And that she had a small hickey on her neck.

So when she had seen him again at the clubhouse, she played it cool at first, ready to be the one to snub him if he showed the least bit of coolness.

She didn't have to, though. Frederick was warm and friendly. *Really* friendly.

"Hey, lady," he had called out to her as she entered the clubhouse. "I was worried about you." It could have been a line, probably *was* a line, but her need for companionship was so strong that she dared to hope, dared to look into his deep brown eyes.

He had draped his arm around her shoulder, gently kissing her with a barely parted mouth. She remembered thinking that he could use a mouthwash. But after a couple of drinks, it didn't bother her anymore, and she had nestled in close as they talked.

Frederick wasn't like the wimps at work. He was well-built and energetic, almost edgy. He didn't talk about obscure albums that she never heard of or strange movies. He was just a guy, a regular guy, who talked about basketball and hockey and seemed to know most of the guys in the clubhouse. She had felt instantly at ease with him, even when he was being vague, like when she asked him what he did for a living. "Construction," he had said, but that was all. And he wasn't specific about where he lived, either: "Around here," was all he said.

Picking up a can of hairspray, Betty paused as a horrible thought surfaced. *Damn, I hope he isn't married.* Usually when guys were that vague, they were. *Maybe he just doesn't want to get too close.* But when she had invited him home after they met again, he had been close, very close, as they merged naked on her bed, locked in wild, passionate lovemaking that both scared and excited her.

But having a wife would explain why he didn't sleep over, why he kissed her goodbye soon after their lovemaking and left in the still cold night. Yes, a wife who wouldn't, couldn't, tolerate a passion so strong and wild that it left bruises on her hipbones and neck. Sadly, it made sense. Too much sense.

It was Thursday before Alicia was able to stop at her post office box on her way to work.

UI, like many high tech firms, had implemented what they called "flex time." Theoretically that meant that an employee could start anytime from 7 until 10 AM, and work eight hours from there, but a programmer's day was never just eight hours. Many programmers arrived around 8:30 AM, for even if you ended up staying until midnight, if you got in much after 9, the managers, who all started early, thought you were lazy.

So, at least until she could prove herself to be a hard worker, Alicia, too, was trying to get in by 8:30. Though she was never *late* for work, she wasn't a creature of habit and rarely left the house every day at the same time. Sometimes she'd arrive at work twenty minutes before that, other days she'd make it in with just a minute to spare. All this week she seemed to be leaving just in the nick of time.

On Thursday, though, things fell into place. She had found the time to make her lunch the night before, when she had also chosen and laid out her clean clothes for the next day, and Moonshadow didn't leave her any fur balls to clean up in the morning. Joey was at his girlfriend's and Evan was sleeping late, so there was no line for the bathroom. And her car, thanks to it being a relatively new model, started on the first try.

As Alicia entered the post office lobby, she reflected on how many things had to go just right for her to arrive on time. She couldn't fathom how working mothers or people with long commutes did it. Mothers. She thought again of Susie, her friend, who had disappeared just before the explosion. Susie had been a single mom. How did she ever do it? And what had happened to Chrissie, her daughter? Chrissie would be nineteen now, and on her own.

As she fumbled with the combination lock on the postal box, Alicia felt a profound sadness. She had never given Susie due credit, or appreciated her own parents. How had they managed to get her to school, get her ready? To get her and themselves out the door every day, at the same time?

Can't do anthing about that now; no use wallowing in guilt. After the explosion, her therapist had suggested that she pinpoint the things that she regretted. If she could do something to make amends, do it, but if not, let it go. *Maybe I need to let it go.* Maybe she'd try another exercise the therapist had suggested: Write a letter to your parents and tell them what you were never able to tell them while they were alive. Yes, she'd do that. It would be Mother's Day soon. And Father's Day after that. Maybe she'd use those days as inspiration and write something in her diary, if she could find the time to write in it again.

As she opened the postal box, she tried to convince herself that she had no reason to feel guilty about Susie— no one knew for sure what happened to her— but Alicia couldn't help feeling that there was some connection between Susie's disappearance and the vampire, the vampire that had stalked Alicia. She remembered the vision she had right around the time Susie disappeared. Alicia had been asleep. Something woke her, though the room was silent and dark when she had surfaced from the depths of sleep. She had felt around on the bed for Moonshadow, thinking that maybe he was up and had knocked something over, but no, he was right beside her and she could tell from his tensed muscles that he, too, was awake, and listening, looking.

In the dim light provided by the lit face of her alarm clock and the light that had leaked through the sides of the cheap ill-fitting roller shades on the windows of her old apartment, she had seen Moonshadow's ears rotate into listening position, had felt his neck turn. When he had stopped turning, she looked in the same direction as he was looking, just as he let out a loud, snarling hiss—

There, at the foot of her bed, stood Susie in a long black dress, blood smeared across a jagged gash in her neck. As Alicia watched breathlessly, mouth agape in a silent scream, Susie smiled and waved her hand from side to side.

And then she disappeared.

Alicia had dismissed the vision as being related to her recent thoughts about Wesley and her research on vampires, but after Susie failed to pick up her daughter at her ex-husband's, Alicia wasn't sure. Her therapist, of course, believed that Alicia had been dreaming, and that her dream vision just seemed real to her. But she had never had a dream that real, and she was sure that she was awake when she saw Moonshadow react...

Alicia felt around in the cold metal of the postal box, finally touching paper. She withdrew a plain, white envelope with the return address of a post office box in Bristelton. *Bristelton? I don't know anyone in Bristelton.* She hooked her thumb under a corner of the flap and tore the envelope open as she tried to think who she might know in Bristelton, but no one came to mind. She unfolded the lined piece of notebook paper and read it:

> Alicia, You responded to our ad about a Wiccan group. We'd like to hear more about your experience. Would you be able to meet us at Smiley's Roast Beast this Friday night? If so, give us a call and we'll set up a time. Regards, Janith

Alicia looked at the bottom of the letter where a phone number had been scribbled, almost as an afterthought. Bristelton. That was a part of the city. Alicia hated cities, feared them. But this time she'd have to overcome her fears. The meeting was much more important than her fears.

Although she had put in eight concentrated hours by 5:30, Alicia felt guilty for leaving that early twice in one week.

"It's not like you'd be the only one who leaves on time on a Friday," Carol had counseled her. "Even Meg leaves on time on Fridays. And look at Fergus— since the new baby came, he's left on time *every* day."

Alicia knew she was right, especially about Fergus, but Fergus had a reason, and she had always felt in her previous job that if you didn't have a reason to leave on time— like a family— you were expected to work as late as you could. Maybe Carol was right, and maybe UI was different than Theoretic. Either way, she'd have to leave soon or call the number in Bristelton and tell them she'd be late.

Concentrate! You need to get going! She hated leaving early— actually on time— and hated driving into the city, but this was her chance to find out about Wesley. With a deep breath, she typed in BYE and waited for her computer terminal to show the logoff message before turning off the power.

When Alicia had called the number, the woman on the other end of the phone identified herself as Janith. She had sounded nice enough, and confident that Alicia would be able to find Smiley's Roast Beast. "It's right off the Pike. Just make sure you don't miss Exit 18— it's the left exit— and then bear left towards Bristelton..."

All day long she had dreaded the trip, worried that she'd get lost. She stopped to fill her gas tank on the way in, just in case. Even though it had been five years and two cars ago, Alicia remembered too clearly running out of gas in winter because her gas gauge didn't work. She had run out in Danforth, in her own town, where she knew where to walk, knew where the gas stations were, knew which sections of town to avoid.

When she was growing up, they had only one car, the car that her dad drove to work. Her mother walked or took the bus, as did Alicia. After her parents died, her foster parents were similarly restricted. Alicia's world had always been limited geographically, something that rising gas prices and then shortages in her early adulthood had only reinforced. *C'mon, if Meg can do it, so can you!* Meg often went into the city to see friends. She drove in alone, even when she was dating someone. Alicia wondered why her boyfriend never went with her... *Enough!* Alicia recognized her escapist technique of getting caught up in intellectual puzzles and guessing games. She forced herself to stop and pay attention to the task at hand.

The night before, she had emptied her handbag of anything valuable, leaving herself just enough money for gas in the morning and food at Smiley's. She slung the now-lightweight bag over her shoulder and stashed her briefcase under her desk. No use bringing work home this weekend. Joey and Evan were going to install the dryer and she'd finally be able to do loads of laundry without running to the laundromat to dry them. And maybe she'd show Evan around Danforth.

At 5:45, Alicia finally left the building.

Not knowing the traffic patterns during the rush hour, Alicia had polled her co-workers for advice. Would the Mass Pike be busy at that time? Should she try Route 9 instead? She wasn't used to driving to the city and she knew she'd find a traffic jam nerve-wracking.

"You worry too much," Fergus had said. "So you're in traffic. So what? It's only a few minutes, when you get on 495 and then when you get on the Pike."

Carol rolled her eyes and shook her head. "Men," she whispered under her breath. "When I go into the city, I go east on 9 and pick up the Pike at Exit 12. There's usually less of a line at that entrance."

Alicia wanted to ask Meg what *she* did, but she hadn't seen Meg since she had received the letter. There was no reason to assume that something had happened to Meg, but Alicia always feared the worst when people disappeared. Her therapist had said something about "abandonment issues" tied to her parents' deaths, but Alicia thought it was connected to more recent events, like layoffs or Susie's disappearance... *I wonder where she is... Stop being so paranoid! Meg's fine! She's just in meetings.*

In the end, she took Carol's advice and entered the Massachusetts Turnpike at Exit 12 off Route 9 East, just west of the apartments where Betty lived. Waiting in line for the toll ticket, Alicia looked in her rearview mirror and tried not to panic about the mounting traffic as car after car joined the evening rush hour lines. Her mind wandered to Betty, who had been out sick again. Carol had confided to Alicia that she was worried. Betty had a new boyfriend and they seemed to be out late a lot. She had taken a couple of sick days and wasn't getting into work as early as she should when she *did* make it in. But it seemed that Betty managed to make it to work often enough to avoid getting a warning, and her work logging, sorting, and distributing reports was easy enough that she could do it in her sleep, so her manager hadn't said anything. But Carol was worried. And so was Alicia. There was something about Betty's new relationship that didn't seem healthy.

Hoping to calm her increasingly rattled nerves, Alicia grabbed a cigarette. As she pushed in the cigarette lighter, she chastised herself for worrying. *Stop worrying about other people. You're going to meet a group of witches! Think about that— what will you say to them? What will you do if they're absolute weirdos?*

The car ahead of her pulled away just as she touched the glowing ring of the lighter to the end of her cigarette. The car behind her honked and Alicia panicked, stalling the car in first gear, the cigarette hanging ungainly out of the side of her mouth. Still holding the lighter, she quickly restarted, racing the engine, and squealing the tires a bit as she pulled forward.

Holding the lighter in her right hand, which also grasped the steering wheel, she rolled down the window with her left and snatched the toll ticket from the attendant, who just shook his head and smiled. "Thank you," she called out, wondering if her manners marked her as a hick who didn't take the Pike that often. *At least he's not pissed off at me for holding up the line.* With both hands nonetheless tightly gripping the wheel, Alicia found the correct lane and successfully merged onto the eastbound section of the Pike.

Her cigarette was still dangling from her mouth and the smoke was searing her nostrils. A large chunk of ash fell in her lap. *Darn!* Keeping her eye on traffic and her speedometer, she used the side of the fingers that held the lighter to feel for the hole where the lighter belonged. *How do commuters manage this?* Replacing the lighter, she found the ashtray and put down the cigarette. Her window was still rolled down and the cooling evening air was chilling her. With her right hand now free to hold the wheel, she rolled up the window.

Having won the challenge of the toll booth, Alicia began to think through the upcoming evening, approaching it as she would a computer program. *Okay, what's the worst that could happen? They could be weirdos, and armed and dangerous.* She thought back to a self-defense class that she had taken. *I'm meeting them in public, though. Just don't go anywhere with them. Make an excuse that you have to leave and don't go anywhere with them. And make sure they don't follow you to your car when you leave.*

A lumbering pickup truck obstructed the lane ahead of her. Alicia flicked on her turn signal and carefully passed the truck, taking a deep breath and hoping that the driver of the other car in the passing lane was paying attention to the traffic and not some radio program. Back in the slow lane, she continued her analysis. *Okay, so if they seem normal, what do I say?* As she settled back into driving, it struck her that maybe they'd think that *she* was the weirdo. What if they could feel her nervousness? Would they think that *she* was dangerous, like that guy who hung around the train station downtown who always kept looking around him? Would *they* squirm in their seats and make excuses to leave early? Would she lose the opportunity to get the help she needed to solve the mystery?

She'd have to proceed carefully.

Had Alicia been less of an urbanophobe and traveled eastward more often, she would have realized that the Bristelton area did not have the demeanor of a city proper. With Fenmore University bordering it on one end and Fenmore College on the other, it was more like a large student village than a part of the city of Fenmore.

Had she been less intent on finding her destination, she would have noticed the students frequenting their favorite watering holes and eateries, or entering and exiting the three- and four-story Georgian and Tudor Revival apartment buildings that marked the area.

But she *had been* intent on finding her destination, and she was distracted by her fear— not of the witches, but of the city. For her, this was still The City, and cities meant stolen cars, muggings, and worse.

She was grateful that her directions included hints on where she might find free parking, and even more grateful that a car had left almost immediately in front of her. It was parallel parking, and though many of Alicia's coworkers had been spoiled by large parking lots at work and at their apartment buildings, the space in front of her house where she parked often required her parallel-parking skills. *Well, at least that's one thing I know how to do in a city,* she comforted herself.

Lengthening the strap on her handbag, she pulled it on bandolier-style, over her shoulder and across her chest. She looked around to make sure she had remembered to lock the passenger door and the doors in the back and then looked in her rearview mirror to make sure no cars were coming before exiting from the driver's side.

Alicia stepped into the cold rain. She was relieved that the downpour had waited until she had parked the car. Although her car was fairly new and the wipers and blades worked perfectly, she had too many memories of torn blades and failing wiper motors not to worry when it rained. All her cars— and there had been many, for they didn't last long— had been clunkers, and though she now had a car just a year old, her old fears still took time to unlearn.

She took a quick glance at the directions to orient herself and set off at a brisk pace. Fear, not the rain, drove her to walk quickly. Her self-defense teacher had told them that to avoid trouble when in an urban setting, one should walk fast, with a purpose. It wasn't long before she arrived at the restaurant.

Smiley's was on the corner of Harvard Street and Bristelton Avenue, two main thoroughfares in the Bristelton area. The restaurant was in an old building. Alicia could see through the fogged windows to where students crowded the small interior. Janith had told her that there would be two of them, herself and the other coven leader, Rob, and that they would both be wearing navy blue outer coats. Alicia worried for a moment that they might have decided to change into raincoats, which might not be the same color, but then remembered that the rain had just started and that they would already be inside or surely already on their way.

Janith would be easy to pick out. She had described herself as having long, curly, strawberry blonde hair. Rob would be a little more difficult; having dark hair and glasses, he could have been any of a dozen people she could see through the window.

Gathering her courage, she entered the warm, noisy restaurant. *We're supposed to be able to talk here?* Slightly to her left, she saw someone who fit the description of Janith, sitting next to someone nondescript with glasses and dark hair.

Just as she saw them, they saw her. "Alicia?" the woman mouthed.

Alicia nodded and walked toward them. She had expected them to be older, much older. She expected the leaders of a coven to be in a wizened state: gray, wrinkled, with cataract-glazed eyes peering through thick spectacles, their frail arthritic hands clasping teacups for warmth.

Instead, they looked to be no more than a couple of years older than she, and were certainly not wizened or arthritic. Rob's hair was still full and dark, and his glasses no thicker than the average college student's. If Janith had strands of silver threaded in her strawberry golden locks, they were invisible in the pale light cast by the large lighting globes hanging from the tall, Victorian-era ceiling.

Janith nimbly scooted out of the tall booth, and Rob followed, until they stood in front of Alicia to greet her. Both were dressed simply in jeans, in dark winter colors, but not the jet black she had expected of witches. The smallest, delicate star hung from a silver chain around Janith's neck. Alicia could see a larger-gauge chain disappearing beneath the opening of Rob's college-logo sweatshirt, and she assumed that he, too, sported the same.

"Hi, I'm Janith, and this is Rob."

Alicia responded with a hello, but wasn't sure if she should shake hands. At work, she would have quickly proffered her right hand and given a quick, firm shake, to show that she meant business and that she was a woman of strong character. But these were witches, not managers, and she wasn't sure what to do, so she stood with her hands casually clasped in front of her and merely nodded as she responded.

"Is this okay?" Janith asked. "I know it's a little noisy, but that's actually a good thing. Sometimes noise can afford a lot of privacy."

"Uh, sure." Alicia replied, not being sure at all.

Janith turned to Rob, who scooted back into the bench. She scooted in after him, and Alicia did the same on the other side.

"And the food here is good and cheap," Rob offered, straining to look at the menu board across the room.

"You're not a vegetarian, are you?" Janith asked, suddenly anxious.

"No, but funny you should mention that. I just got a new roommate, and *he* is. I'd like to eat more vegetarian meals, but for now I'm still a carnivore."

"Good. Though there are quite a few places around here that can accommodate vegetarians, Smiley's Roast Beast isn't one of them!"

"What'll it be?" The waitress appeared from out of nowhere.

Rob started to order, but Janith stopped him with a gentle tap on his arm. "Alicia, do you need more time?"

"No, go ahead. I'll be ready."

Rob and Janith quickly gave their orders: roast beef sandwiches, fries, and colas. Alicia ordered the same, minus the cola.

As the waitress disappeared into the growing crowd of students and other patrons, Janith and Rob turned to face Alicia again.

"Now," Janith asked, leaning forward and placing her arms on the table, "What is it you wanted to ask us?"

Much to Alicia's relief, the traffic on the way home was negligible and once she had navigated her way back to the Mass Pike, it felt no different than driving Route 9 late at night— minus the traffic lights, of course. Relieved that she was on the right road home, she loosed her white-knuckled grip on the steering wheel and relaxed her hunched shoulders.

The evening had gone better than expected. Not only were Janith and Rob *not* weirdos, they were kind, patient, and caring. They listened carefully to every word— not interrupting, as she would have (*I need to stop that*, she noted), but letting her get every word out. And after the briefest pause, they'd filled the silence that she dreaded so much with thoughtful questions or words of encouragement. They never treated her as if she were odd, and even more important, though they were college graduates with fine, rich fields of study and she was just a lowly technology night student, they treated her as an equal.

And best of all, they knew what she meant when she talked about Wesley, for one dark night three years ago, at the height of a desperate ritual to bind an unknown evil, they had seen him, too.

Chapter 14

Ernst Maxwell stood, not wanting to wrinkle his suit by sitting down, and rocked on his heels as he surveyed his surroundings. The executive area was bright and modern, and characterized by a singular simplicity, frugality, and avoidance of comfort and luxury.

The secretary who had taken his name sat behind a simple beige steel desk. The smoky charcoal in-baskets, pen holder, and supplies organizer were plastic, not wood. The carpet was a typical low-pile commercial-grade gray; no thick oriental rugs on polished hardwood floors like the ones at the insurance companies he had interviewed at the previous week.

Maxwell had expected something a little more lush, based on the salary the company was offering. *Probably spending their money on salaries instead of furnishings and supplies. Well, that just means more for me, doesn't it?*

He gazed out the large window to the left of the secretary's desk. Past the landscaping and parking lot, he could see Route 9 and then nothing but trees on either side. *Overhead's probably low, too,* he mused. *Land costs are much cheaper here than in the city or even in Danforth.*

As he waited, he mentally rehearsed his explanation for why he wanted to leave his current position. More opportunity. Chance to advance. The usual. The words and phrases he needed came quickly to mind. He had used them before and would use them again.

Explaining why he left his previous job, at Theoretic, would be more of a problem. Things had been going well until the explosion, but then the ensuing investigation soured his relations with the higher-ups, enough so that he was continually passed over for promotions. His budgets were regularly cut while other departments got what they asked for. The explosion wasn't his fault; upper management was too cheap to pay for more than one around-the-clock guard for the whole building. *Tone it down, old boy. Don't want to sound like you're a complainer. Say that there had been budget cuts and upper management had thought that one guard could cover everything because it was a locked facility.*

"Mr. Maxwell? Mr. Westar can see you now."

Maxwell straightened his tie and followed the secretary to a cluttered, unremarkable office.

"So, what happened? Did you meet her?" Gabe was his usually exuberant self, eyes wide and alert.

"Yes, we met her at Smiley's, " Janith replied, as Rob got up to answer the buzzer. As always, Matricaria and Gabe were there early, waiting for the others to arrive.

"Did she have any trouble finding the place?" Matricaria asked. "I heard at work that she was really nervous about driving into the city, asking a couple of different people for directions and worrying about traffic."

"No, she said she didn't have a problem. She *did* seem nervous, though. Is she always that way?"

"She doesn't like traffic and she has this thing about cities."

"Yeah," Rob said, rejoining them. "She told us, almost proudly, that she was an urbanophobe."

"Urbanophobe! Love the word!" Gabe leapt up for hugs as three of the coven members arrived, shaking rain off their coats in the hallway before entering the apartment. "Hi!"

Janith, Rob, and Matricaria stood, receiving the coven members with a hug. After everyone settled in, Janith continued her account of the meeting with Alicia. "At first, she seemed a little nervous, but, as Mat said, she's nervous about driving into the city, so that could be it."

"City? This is Bristelton!" Gabe threw himself back into the couch's ample cushions and rolled his eyes in mock exasperation.

"To her, it's still the city," Matricaria offered. "I get the feeling that she's never traveled much, and I wonder if she also has a subconscious fear of driving because her parents were killed in a car accident. She's usually pretty fearless, but driving to strange places seems to unnerve her. That, and wasps. She's got an almost unreasonable fear of wasps. We were talking about it at lunch one day and she said that she's never been stung herself. I asked if she had ever seen anyone get stung and she said that when she was very young, she watched a wasp fly up her cousin's shirt and sting him repeatedly."

"Interesting how the things that scare her are things that happened to *other* people." Rob said, picking up his tea and blowing to cool it.

"Hmmm. That makes sense. Sometimes we feel so helpless when things happen to *other* people. Is she the type who doesn't like being out of control?" Janith asked.

Matricaria laughed. "Oh, yeah. That describes Alicia. She doesn't ever try to control *other people*, but herself— that's another story."

Another coven member spoke. "Yeah, sounds like she has control issues, even if only with herself and life in general."

As another covener opened her mouth to make a point, Rob interrupted, saying, "Well, none of us are psychiatrists, so it's all just conjecture. Let's move on, okay?"

"Yes, just because we've all taken a course in Abnormal Psych doesn't qualify us as psychoanalysts." They agreed, and Janith steered the conversation back to the meeting. "Let's get back to the story. She told us everything, how this vampire— his name's Wesley, by the way— appeared, how he bit her— "

"He bit her?" Gabe sat forward, listening eagerly.

"Yes," Matricaria replied. "Remember I said that when I found her, I saw bite marks on her neck?"

"Oh, yeah. Wow." Gabe slouched back again.

"Did she tell you about the explosion?" Matricaria asked.

"Yes, she did."

"She doesn't think that it destroyed him?"

"She's not sure. She's been feeling uneasy lately, as if something very bad is going to happen, like she's waiting for the other shoe to drop."

"But that could be a sign of clinical depression, too, right?" One of the coven members asked.

Gabe again rolled his eyes. "Okay, I thought we agreed that we're not shrinks!"

Rob chuckled softly. "Yes, that's true, but it's a good point. It could be the paranoia and sense of doom associated with regular, garden-variety depression. But there was something about the way she spoke of it that made me think that there was something else behind these feelings."

"And let's not forget the reading," Janith said.

"Reading?" Matricaria asked.

"She said that she went along with some co-workers to a local psychic— the Wizard of Westville?"

"Yes, I've heard of him. Alfred something. Some French name. He's supposed to be good."

"He said that Wesley still walked."

"He called the vampire by name?"

"No, but it sounds like he meant Wesley."

"But what if it's not?"

"If it's not?"

"Yes, what if it's not Wesley. What if there's another vampire?"

"Ah, wait!" Janith bit her lip and shook her finger as if trying to point to something that was eluding her. "She said that the psychic said, 'He still walks. And he does not walk alone.' So maybe it *isn't* Wesley. Maybe there *is* more than one."

In the space of only a heartbeat or two, the room seemed to collapse in heavy silence as they all came to the same, horrific conclusion.

"So," Matricaria said, "Either he had a companion or— "

Gabe pounded his head with his fists. "Or the fuckers are multiplying!"

"You mean '*suckers* are multiplying'," one of the coveners said, trying to break through the pall with a little humor.

But no one laughed at the play on words.

The note was taped to one of the kitchen cabinets with transparent tape.

"You'd think that someone who works in construction and paints for a living would realize that masking tape is better on finished surfaces," Alicia complained, peeling away the tape without even reading the note, anxious to remove the tape before it could mar the cabinet. Moonshadow waited patiently at her feet, purring, lifting one paw and then switching to the other, as he often did, marking time in his own odd way as he waited to be fed.

Alicia opened the refrigerator while reading the note.

> Alicia. We still on for Saturday? I'll get my friend's pickup and be back at noon so we can go get the dryer. Evan said he'll be here to help. See ya. Joey.
>
> P.S. Almost forgot. My cousin got that job doing the vacation cottage in Maine. It's gonna go the whole summer. I'll be moving out at the end of March so I can go up early with him.

"Shit!" She placed the cat food on the counter and ignored Moonshadow's incessant weaving between and around her legs as the news set in. "Just like Poppa used to say— every time I get my head above water, some damned fool comes along with a swamp boat and mows me under!"

She had been looking forward to having two boarders in the house. The money from Joey and Evan would have helped replenish her savings and pay for some repairs and materials for small improvements to the house. But now Joey was leaving. "Well, as long as Evan can pay, we'll survive. Right, Moonshadow?"

Moonshadow, as always, just purred.

Alicia lit a cigarette.

The coven could have spent the entire evening discussing Alicia, Wesley, and how to proceed, but they had more to do that evening, so they shelved the discussion after an hour. Though Janith and Rob were the leaders and could, in theory, make a decision without *any* deliberation, they always tried to engage the group in the process.

In the early days of the coven, Janith used to worry that they might get frustrated when, after an evening's discourse, she and Rob would make a final decision that ran counter to the group's wishes, but eventually she had come to accept that this was the curse of leadership: to hear all sides, but in the end, to make the decision that was the best for the group, whether the group liked it or not.

The evening's discussion went mercifully better than that. They all agreed that Alicia was in danger and needed their help. And they all agreed that they wanted to help her.

Rob suggested that, considering her previous interest in ESP and her studies of the vampire, Alicia might want to join the study group to learn more about the unseen world and to learn how to protect herself. The only dissonant voice that evening was that of Matricaria, who gently reminded them that she worked with Alicia. "We don't know how she feels about witches. It's one thing to *consult* witches, but quite another to join them. What if she thinks that witches are devil worshippers and talks about this at work?"

"We'll do a reading," Janith suggested as she pulled her tarot cards off the bookshelf. "We'll ask if we should approach Alicia about joining the study group."

She withdrew the Queen of Swords from the deck, explaining, "I don't know why, but this feels right as the Significator, the card representing

Alicia." She placed the card in the center of the piece of black silk in which the cards had been wrapped. "And let's try something different. Instead of using the traditional ten-card spread, let's try some directed questions using the three-card past/present/future spread."

The group nodded and Janith continued. "For the past, what question shall we ask about the past?"

Gabe spoke up. "How about asking what her past experiences with the occult and witchcraft are? If the Devil shows up, she's outta here!"

Janith smiled. "Good idea. Okay, the question is, 'What is Alicia's past experience with witchcraft and the occult?'" She closed her eyes and shuffled the deck slowly, concentrating on the question. The group joined her in concentration, waiting for her to pull the card.

"Six of cups." She laid down a card showing six cups, each containing a single white, five-pointed star. In the center of the card, a boy was handing a small girl one of the cups, which was filled with flowers.

"Well, that says *past* and *childhood* to me!" Gabe said.

"True, but it also means 'the traditional.' If she has the traditional misconceptions about witches, that's not good," Rob replied.

"But it's also a card of pleasant memories, right?" Matricaria asked.

"True," Janith said. "Happy childhood, pleasant memories."

"So she could have happy memories of witchcraft, either in this life, or a previous life. There was an occult revival in the mid-70s. Maybe she dabbled with tarot or astrology."

"Good point. Let's look at the next card, the one for the present, and see how that previous experience has evolved." Once again, Janith closed her eyes and shuffled the deck intently. "The question is, 'What is Alicia's present opinion of witchcraft and the occult?'"

She laid down a card of a crowned man in robes seated between twin pillars, a sword in his right hand and scales in his left. "Justice."

Someone in the group inhaled sharply. "Legal problems? Like libel? Like she would speak out against us in public?"

"Could be. But this card also represents equilibrium and balance. It could mean that Alicia is viewing the facts and weighing her opinion. That is, it could mean that she is like a judge and looking at the facts objectively."

"That fits her personality," Matricaria said. "She's very much the type to gather all information before forming an opinion."

"Okay, final card. Let's see... The question is, 'What will be the outcome if we tell Alicia about the study group and invite her to come to a meeting?'" After a slow and deliberate shuffling, Janith laid the card on the cloth. "The Eight of Pentacles?"

Her comment was a question because, in her understanding of the tarot, the suit of Pentacles was most often associated with money, material gain, development, trade, or industry. It didn't seem like a suit connected to a question of the occult. "Rob, would you hand me *The Tarot Revealed?*"

Rob retrieved the well-worn copy of Eden Gray's classic book on the tarot. Janith turned to the page on the Eight of Pentacles. "Hmmm. This is interesting. If we stop thinking of money for a minute, this really fits. Gray says that the card can mean apprenticeship, skill. Maybe it means that she would be open to becoming an apprentice."

"And," Rob added, "remember that divinatory tools sometimes speak in puns. This is a card of 'craftmanship'— think of craft with a capital C, as a shortened form of 'Witchcraft.' If you think of it that way, it really fits."

Janith looked at Matricaria. "Since this affects you the most, I leave it up to you. What do you think we should do?"

Matricaria thought for a moment, biting her lip, taking a deep breath, closing her eyes for a second in deep supplication. "I think that the cards are fairly clear, and I think Alicia is in danger and really needs our help. It would be unethical for me not to come to her aid. I think we should do it. Go ahead. Ask her."

Rob reached over and gave her a brotherly hug.

Janith gathered up the cards and wrapped them in the silk.

"So be it. May the gods protect our Craft."

He was mid-bite when he felt it.

Though Wesley should have been swept up in the luxuriousness of his engorgement, instead his mind half-wandered to Alicia, and to the group of witches who had, unbeknownst to her, come to her aid when he had tried to lay claim to her.

Uncharacteristically, he allowed the blood to flow out the side of his slack-jawed mouth, quickly forming a dark, menacing patch of red across the blouse of the woman he held in thrall. When she felt the blood, saw the blood, she screamed, and Wesley withdrew.

Seeing his error, knowing that now he wouldn't be able to again hide his terrible secret from his victim, he did the only thing he could do:

He snapped her neck, killing her instantly.

Chapter 15

"Murphy's Law. I get a working dryer just when it's almost warm enough to hang clothes outside! Better late than never, though, I guess. Thanks, guys, for going to get it. You want pizza? It's on me and there's cold beer in the fridge."

"All right! Now you're talkin'. Evan, you want one, or don't you drink?" Joey was standing with the refrigerator door open, waiting for Evan to answer.

"Yes, I'll have one. Thanks."

"That's my man! Alicia, you want one?"

"No, thanks."

"No? You buy all this beer and you don't want any?"

"No, I don't drink beer."

"No beer?"

"No. Never liked the taste of it. I've got some Paul Masson chablis in there. I'll have some wine later."

"Paul Masson? Oooh, aren't we fancy?"

"What, it's just white wine. I don't like beer!"

"Hey, you drink what you want. I'm just yankin' your chain," Joey said, giving her a friendly pat on the shoulder. "You wanna call in the pizza? I'll pick it up." He took a swig and then started toward the door, beer bottle in hand.

"Okay, but you really don't want to drive with that, right?"

"Oh, right!" Joey laughed, and brought the bottle back to the kitchen, placing it back in the refrigerator. "Okay. Call in the order, and I'll be there when it's ready."

"Will do."

"That's okay," Evan said to Alicia after Joey left, "I like a little wine myself now and then."

"I'm really not trying to be a snob. I just can't get used to the taste of beer."

Alicia called in the pizza order as Evan disappeared upstairs. Had he lingered for a moment longer, she might have added that she had wondered aloud, during therapy, if the reason she disliked the taste of beer so much was that it reminded her of her father, who always drank beer. Someday that memory would pale, but for now she didn't enjoy beer, for whatever reason.

Evan bounded down the steps and into the living room. From the doorway, Alicia could see him remove a record album from its jacket, which featured the image of a long-haired, moustached face on a dark blue background. The graining of the photo and the style of the man's hair reminded her of the Shroud of Turin. "What's that?"

"Ommadawn, Mike Oldfield." Evan was kneeling next to the turntable. He blew on the stylus and looked at it carefully. "Is this in good condition?"

"I don't know. Even though I can run computers and wire a phone line, I'm not really good with stereo equipment. Kurt, my ex-boyfriend, handled that."

"Well, we'll give it a try." Evan carefully lowered the stylus arm onto the rotating album. Alicia noticed how long his fingers were and wondered if he played piano or guitar. She stretched out her own short fingers, remembering her past efforts on the guitar, and listened as the music filled the rooms. Ethereal and light, yet active, it was nothing like the folk or rock that she usually listened to.

Evan retrieved his beer from the kitchen and returned to the living room. "Like it?"

Alicia followed him. "It's very different, but yes, I do. I've never heard of him."

"He did 'Tubular Bells,' the soundtrack for 'The Exorcist'."

"Oh, right!" She could see the similarities now that he mentioned it.

As the bass thrummed and the strings became more insistent, she found herself almost transported. Evan had turned off the overhead light and sat in the half-dark of the front room, stretched out in a worn stuffed chair, the light from the streetlight outside zebra-striping his face as it leaked between the slats of the Venetian blinds.

Evan's eyes were closed. He was lost in the music, totally at ease with himself, as the driving rhythm of the piece continued. Alicia sat across from him, involuntarily relaxing as well, losing herself in the dark, moody music. "This music is really nice."

"It's New Age."

It sounded as if he said *new age*, but she thought that she misheard him. "New Wave?"

"No, New *Age*, as in 'music for a new age.' It's very spacey, meditative."

"Ah. I never heard that term. I usually listen to rock. Or folk."

"Are you going to the Elliott Folk Festival?"

"There's a folk festival in Elliott?"

"Yes. I heard that it used to change locations frequently, but it's been in Elliott for the last six years."

"Wow." Alicia was incredulous. She had lived in Danforth, the town next to Elliott, almost all her life and didn't know about the folk festival. How could she have missed it? Elliott was a town she knew. Her mother had lived there as a child and she herself had worked there once. And every year she made a pilgrimage to her parents' graves there. "I can't believe I didn't know about it!"

As Evan told her about the festival, she realized that this was the first time since high school that she had met someone who actually liked folk. Her friends had much different tastes in music. Susie preferred R & B and disco. Kurt was solid rock: Aerosmith, Deep Purple, Eagles, Led Zeppelin. Anthem bands. Top 40. The same type of music that Joey liked. The only music that she and Kurt had in common was Jethro Tull.

"And they have Morris dancers and contra dances for all levels—"

"Morris dancers? Contra dance?"

"Contra dance is sort of like square dancing, but not really. It's participatory and a lot of fun. Morris dancing is a traditional English folk dance performed by teams. They combine dance steps with hand movements— "

Evan jumped up to illustrate a Morris dance. He lifted one leg, bent at the knee, and held the opposite arm up, slightly bent at the elbow. "The dancers wear rows of bells below their knees, and hold handkerchiefs or sticks in one hand. They're usually men, but lately there have been more teams of women, and even mixed sides."

"Sides?"

"Teams."

Alicia was captivated as he hopped about, straight-backed. He was dipping and turning, shaking his foot to ring imaginary bells, and waving a similarly non-existent handkerchief. He skipped in a circle, explaining the tradition and how it was tied into agriculture, and spring. And life. She realized that she knew only American folk traditions, not European. It was all so new to her and Evan knew so much.

Evan stopped, taking a deep breath, and flopped back into his seat. "You should go. It's next weekend. I can give you directions. I'm staying with an old friend in town Friday night and then we'll come out on Saturday. Maybe we'll see you there."

"Sure. That'd be great. "

In the background, Ommadawn built to a climax, guitars screaming, drums pounding insistently, erotically. Synthesizer and electric guitar were joined by the unlikely company of uilleann pipes.

She could feel the vibrations in her breastbone, her throat, her life. She felt breathless, as if she were poised high on a mountain, with one foot out, ready for a step across the wide unknown. She could almost feel the cool mist of the high clouds across her face and the heat of the sun on her scalp. She was soaring, yet standing still, frozen in that moment of boundlessness, life stretching before her.

Months later she would recognize this image as she laid down the tarot card representing the past:

The Fool.

Alicia picked up the phone on the second ring, a habit from her days as a secretary. "Hello, is this Alicia?"

"Hello."

"Yes..."

"This is Janith, from Bristelton? We met a couple of weeks ago?"

Alicia sat down on the kitchen floor beneath the wall phone. "Hi, yes. How are you?"

"Fine, thanks. I don't know if we mentioned this when we met, but Rob and I are forming a study group. It's not a formal coven, but just a group for people who want to learn more. We thought that this might be a good place for you to get some more information to help you deal with your, uh, situation. We're meeting Wednesday. Would you like to join us?"

Alicia sat up straight, excited. This could be *very* helpful— a group of people whose brains she could pick— but what did she know about these people? She had met them only once. "Oh, wow, that sounds great, but I'm not sure... " She thought quickly, "Things aren't too busy right now, but I'm going to be taking some summer courses at night school, and I don't know how much time I'd have."

"This is going to be a really informal group, and because people go away over the summer, we won't be meeting that often. I don't want to pressure you, though. One of our tenets is to *not* pressure people, to *not* proselytize. This is not a cult. We wouldn't have even called you except that *you* came to *us*. Before you decide, maybe you'd like to meet the rest of the group? Rob and I won't actually be leading it. It'll be two of our students. We met you initially because we're the ones who usually do the screening."

Alicia relaxed a little. If they were worried about *her*, it indicated that they had at least a partial grip on reality. "Okay. It probably wouldn't hurt to check it out."

"Super! I'll mail you directions and details. As I said, you can meet us and then decide. No commitments, no strings. The only thing we ask is that you honor our privacy and not reveal the identities of any of the people you meet. The general public often thinks that all witches are evil-doers and some people have had windows broken or received death threats—"

"Death threats?"

"Usually it's from fundamentalists who take 'Thou shalt not suffer a witch to live' a little too literally and aren't aware that the word *witch* might have been a misunderstanding to begin with. Some scholars think that it should say *poisoner*. At that time, witches and magicians were the main sources of all herbal preparations, good and bad, so the word was translated as witch."

"And they actually threaten to kill people over this?"

"Mostly in the South, though. Death threats are rarer here. But not job losses. Many of us have conservative jobs and wouldn't have them for long if our employers knew of our interest in witchcraft and the occult. So, we'd appreciate discretion."

"Sounds fine to me. I know how you feel. I don't think I'd want it spread around work that I thought I was bitten by a vampire!"

"Yes, I thought you'd understand. Okay, I'll get the details about the study group and the meeting location into the mail tomorrow. I just need to photocopy the directions first. We look forward to seeing you. Have a good week."

"You, too, and thanks for calling."

Hanging up the phone, Alicia felt as though her life was at a pivot point now, about to wheel, whip, and whirl to a new direction. She felt scared, but also special, different.

And alone. For there was no one she could tell about this, no one with whom she could share the exhilaration of progress.

No one would understand. Except Evan, and he was out with his friend.

It was an effortless drive to Elliot High School, where the folk festival was being held. Alicia relaxed as she drove straight down Route 135, parallel to the train tracks. The day had seemed dreary and overcast as she passed the abandoned train station downtown, but the further she drove, the lighter things seemed.

Downtown Danforth, by the train station, seemed dark, crowded, and derelict. As she followed the straight spine of what was originally built as the Old Central Turnpike, the area opened up. To her left, on the other side of the tracks, was a long dirty brick building built by the Para Rubber Company at the start of Danforth's industrial era. The sight of the old building, usually so familiar that she barely noticed it, took on a foreboding aspect as she wondered about its past, about the vampire Wesley's past. *Was he alive then? How long* has *he been alive? Is he still alive?*

Not far from Para Crossing and the competing auto graveyards on either side of the road, the scenery changed again. Modest two-family wooden houses and an Italian-American grocery store clung together on her right and only trees, weeds, and the iron spine of the rails flanked her left.

Shortly after that, the houses thinned and a few miles later she came to the small pond on her right that signaled her right turn. She turned next onto Pond Street. When she was still a good half mile or more from the school, she could see the cars backed up almost to the cemetery where her parents were buried.

Alicia pulled onto the grassy shoulder at the edge of the cemetery and parked. To her right lay the skeletal teeth of the tombstones, and beyond them the placid glassy waters of yet another pond. Drawn in by the peace of it all, she thought of visiting her parents' graves, but then decided to wait until afterwards. *It's not like they're going anywhere.*

Checking her side mirror before opening the car door, she saw families emerging from the cars that had parked behind her. For a moment she reflected on the fact that *her* family never went on outings like this. Her mother and father were always too tired after working a full week at hard, physical jobs... *Not their fault, not their fault. They did the best they could.* Alicia opened the car door before she could become trapped in self-pity, and joined the now-steady stream of people heading toward the school.

Just looking at their clothing, she realized how insular she had become. Limiting herself to her job, school, grocery shopping, and an occasional visit to a co-worker's apartment, Alicia was used to a world of homogeneity. People wore similar clothes and hairstyles. Here they ranged from the nondescript folksy type—wearing jeans, sweaters, and hiking boots— to aging hippies in similar, but more colorful clothes, the women in long dresses and wearing lots of beads— to families of different levels of affluence, wearing more updated sweaters, thin leather jackets, and designer jeans. All ages were represented: babies hung placidly from denim slings, children skipped alongside their parents, and elders leaned on walkers and canes. It was so different from the narrow range of ages that she dealt with in a high-tech company.

And because they were all so different, because there was no norm, Alicia suddenly felt like less of an oddity. It wasn't that she *fit in* any more than she usually did, but more that she didn't feel as *out of place* as she usually did.

Sheep-like she followed the crowd, knowing that they'd know the way in. When the crowd stopped, she knew she must be at the correct entrance and fumbled for her money.

"Are you a member of EFFA?"

"EFFA?"

"Elliott Folk Festival Association."

"No, why? Do I need to be?" For a fleeting moment, she was embarrassed, afraid that she had trespassed. *No, I'm sure that Evan would have mentioned it!*

"Oh, no. It's just that if you're a member, you get a discount." The woman at the ticket table smiled and handed her a festival program and a mimeographed brochure. "If you want to join, here's the membership information. First time?"

"Uh, yeah..."

"Oh, you'll love it. Just relax and make sure you check out the food vendors. There's some Scottish shortbread that's just divine."

"Thanks." Alicia took the program book and brochure and moved off to the side where she could study it without getting in someone's way. The food stalls were marked as nearby, but she didn't need a map of the site to tell her that: strong scents and spices permeated the air— garlic, cinnamon, and the smell of freshly baked breads.

Events were listed as running simultaneously in three dance halls and a full-time music room, all close to where she stood. "Ah!" She whispered to herself. "Morris!" Morris dances were listed for an outer courtyard, but not until later in the day. She glanced at her watch for the time, then stuffed the program booklet into her handbag. *Okay, first, food!*

As she lined up to try *colcannon*, a hot, creamy Irish and Scottish dish of kale, cabbage, and potatoes, she looked around for Evan. Tall as he was, he should be easy to find, especially with his graceful, lanky stride, but nowhere in the sea of jovial festival-goers could she see him.

"Hi, can I help you?"

"One colcannon, please."

Maybe he wasn't there yet. It was early, only a half hour after opening. She'd wait for him.

"What time do you want to go to the festival?" Lynnie asked, crawling back into the bed that she and Evan had shared. In the background, soft ethereal music played, and the daylight passing through the incense smoke suffused a warm golden glow about the room.

"Hmm?" Evan snuggled close, stroking her thick blonde curls away from her smiling face.

"The EFFA festival. What time do you want to go?"

"Oh, anytime. The Morris dancers aren't until the afternoon, and if we don't catch them today, we can catch some tomorrow." He wrapped his lanky frame around her, cradling her head in his arm.

"Didn't you say that you told your housemate you'd be there today?"

"Well, I said we'd be going, but I didn't say the time. She's a big girl. She can find it herself. That reminds me. What do your guides tell you?"

"About you? They say a lot about you," she teased, snuggling into him, pulling the Chinese silk-covered comforter over her bare shoulders. Evan traced a lanky finger over her fine collarbone.

"They do, do they? I'd like to hear about that in a minute," Evan kissed her forehead and squeezed her close, "But did your guides say anything about the vampire?"

"He is an infant soul, stuck in the needs of survival, and he is not making progress in his cycles of reincarnation."

"But is he really a vampire?"

"My guides don't communicate that. They do not judge or label. They say merely that he is an infant soul. He is not evolving; he is gathering experiences, learning lessons, and fulfilling agreements, but he is not evolving."

"What about Alicia?" Evan felt Lynnie tense under his embrace, but ignored it, thinking that she was just reacting to the cold rush of air as the silk comforter slipped suggestively from her soft white shoulders.

"What *about* Alicia?" Lynnie asked, staring deep into Evan's eyes.

"What do your guides say about Alicia?"

"She is here at this time, in this incarnation, because she is meant to be. She has agreements to fulfill."

"We all do. That's all they said?"

"Yes. Her journey is for her to discover. Speaking of journeys, I'm going away next weekend to a channeling retreat. Are you interested?"

Evan propped himself up on one elbow. "I'd love to, but I have to work at the co-op on Saturday. I need to get my hours in before I start my classes. Sunday I'm going to dinner at some old friends of my mother's."

Lynnie thrust out her bottom lip in a mock pout. "O-tay. Maybe next time, then."

Evan leaned in to kiss her. "Yes, maybe next time."

And in doing so, Evan completely missed the fact that the mock pout was *not* mock, and that Lynnie, for all her protestations of modernity and openmindedness, was thoroughly and old-fashionedly jealous.

Chapter 16

Betty stopped and stared at her bologna sandwich, wiping a blob of mayonnaise from the crust and smearing it onto the thin single-ply paper napkin that she had appropriated from the condiment area. "Yeah, I think he's married. We never go to his place, he won't give me his number, and he always leaves before morning." She was almost tearful as she confessed her fears to Norma at the lunch table.

"It doesn't sound good. And he's never around for holidays, right?"

"The only one so far was Easter, and yeah, he couldn't come over for Sunday dinner." Betty wiped a stray tear from her cheek as Norma looked on, concern darkening her eyes. "Why does this always happen to me? Why do I always pick the losers, huh?"

"Did you ask him? Did you *ask* him if he's married?" Norma asked.

Betty shook her head.

"Well, ask him! Maybe there's another reason he's never around."

"Yeah, right."

"There could be, y'know! Maybe he's on the run. Maybe he's the guy doing those gas station robberies. Or maybe he's in the Mob. Yeah, he could be hiding from someone."

Betty laughed a weak, unenthusiastic laugh. "Norma, you crack me up."

"No, seriously. There could be some other reason besides him being married. I think you should ask him. Don't just let him get away with it. He's treating you like you're a slab of meat and it isn't right." She gave Betty a good-natured squeeze on the shoulder. "Talk to him. Just ask him why he won't take you to *his* place or introduce you to his buddies. Just ask him." Norma looked up and turned back to Betty quickly. "Here come the others. Are you okay?"

"I'm fine."

"You sure? Hey, you're looking a little pale. Maybe you should take some vitamins. Your iron might be low."

"Yeah, you're right. I'll get some later."

"Promise?"

"Yeah, I promise."

Norma gave her one last pat on the shoulder before greeting Carol and Alicia.

A thin, blonde woman in a well-tailored suit addressed the group of new employees gathered in the conference room as she handed out small white cards. "That ends the official orientation at Universal Info. We're handing out free lunch passes for the cafeteria. You can pick anything on the menu. Just give the pass to the cashier."

Returning to the front of the room, she continued, "You need to turn in your W-2 forms before you leave or we won't be able to cut you a paycheck this week. The insurance forms need to be in by Friday. If you have any questions, just call me. My number is listed in the front of your New Employee Handbook. Okay? Have a good lunch."

A stocky manager in front of her politely refused the lunch pass. "No, thanks," he said as he straightened his already-straight tie. "Are there any good restaurants nearby?"

She laughed. "Good? In Westville? There's hardly anyplace to eat to begin with, never mind *good* places! But if you head west on Route 9, there's a little place called Henry's. They have great fried clams and fish and chips. They're on your right, at the first intersection."

"Thanks."

As Alicia and Carol settled down at the table, Betty furtively blotted her eyes with a napkin.

Norma quickly engaged the new arrivals in conversation, distracting them from Betty's reddened eyes. "So, did we do anything fun this weekend? How about you, Alicia? Don't tell me you just did housework, laundry, and errands?"

Alicia chuckled slightly. "No, actually I didn't, not this weekend."

"Good!" Norma coached. "I told you, ya gotta get out more."

"Well, I did. I went to the EFFA festival."

"EFFA? As in F'in'?"

"No, no. As in Elliott Folk Festival Association." Alicia told them about the exotic foods, the bright costumes of the dance performers, the fun she had with the participatory dance.

"Oh, sounds interesting. Not my cup of tea, though. Me, I'm more Hall & Oates, Kenny Loggins." Norma popped the tab on her soft drink and stuffed a straw into the hole.

"Yeah, me, too," Carol added. "I love Hall & Oates. Oh, did I tell you my cousin picked out the song for her wedding?"

As the conversation turned to weddings, christenings, and home parties, Alicia felt singularly alone again. She had just had one of the more fun weekends she'd had in years, and they weren't interested. It wasn't that they didn't care about her that bothered her, but more that they had such a narrow set of interests. Would she always be an outsider?

"Alicia, you should come to the next one."

"Next what?"

"Tupperware party."

"Why? I don't need any more plastic bowls. There's just me."

"Just you? What about your roommates?"

"We don't eat together. Joey goes to his girlfriend's on weekends, and Evan was away with a friend— "

"A girlfriend?"

"No, just a friend. I don't think it's a girlfriend." She hadn't actually thought of it at all. Maybe it *was* a girlfriend. That would explain why he never showed up at the festival.

"You can put some away in your hope chest."

"My what?"

"Hope chest. You know, a cedar chest you use to collect linens and household stuff for when you get married. You don't have one?"

"No. If I did, it would be more like a hope*less* chest."

"Believe me, you're not the first one to say that. I had a cousin who was 35 and got so tired of waiting that she opened the chest and started using the things herself. Hey, why not? The towels were beginning to rot and the copper was turning green."

All of a sudden the bread in Alicia's sandwich felt very dry. Marriage. It was never really a goal for her. Career and education came first. But still, in the back of her mind, she had always thought she'd be with someone long-term when she was older. Just how old was *older?*

"Oh, guess what I heard!" Carol said, tapping the table in front of Norma to get her attention.

"What?"

"Rumor has it that we're getting a new Director of Management Information Systems."

"Yeah, I heard that, but it's probably not true."

"No, it is. He started today. I can't remember his name, but I hear he's a real jerk."

"Couldn't be worse than the one where I used to work," Alicia said, shaking her head.

"Well, I guess we'll soon find out."

The conversation stopped temporarily as Meg approached the end of the table. "Hi, ladies."

"Hi, Meg. Join us?" Alicia moved her sandwich wrappers to clear a space for Meg.

"No, sorry. I have to get back to my desk and prepare for a one o'clock meeting. Hey, Alicia, guess who I saw leaving the orientation room?"

"Gee, what's this, quiz day?" Norma said, laughing, in a loud aside to Carol. "Everyone's asking us to guess something!" Her comment brought a warm smile from around the table.

"Who?" Alicia asked.

"Our old boss, Ernst Maxwell."

"That's the name!" Carol said. "Ernst Maxwell! He's our new Director."

"Oh, my God." Alicia closed her eyes in a deep wince.

"Oooh. I didn't realize he was going to be in *your* department." Meg gritted her teeth in an obvious grimace. "Sorry to hear that. Well, I've got to get going. Let me know how it goes with him."

"Oh, yeah. I'll let you know!"

The table was silent as Meg walked out of the cafeteria.

Alicia stuffed her half-eaten sandwich back into her brown paper lunch bag, turning away from the table as she did. "I need a walk."

As she hastily left them, Carol followed her with her eyes. Turning to Norma, she said, "Shit."

Betty, Norma, and Carol were walking back from the cafeteria when Alicia returned via the side door.

"Hey, lady. You okay?" Norma asked.

"Yeah, I'm fine. Just needed some air. And a cigarette," Alicia replied.

"So what's the scoop with this Maxwell guy? Is he really bad news?"

Alicia took a deep breath. *Do I tell them that he blames me for his failure to get ahead at Theoretic? That he blames me— rightly, unfortunately— for the explosion? No, that would mean telling them about Wesley, and I'm not ready to open up about that just yet. Lucky for me, he's got enough faults to talk about without even touching on the* real *problem.* "Well, I'm a bit of a feminist and he's a bit of a chauvinist."

Betty laughed. "Oh, like we don't have those here already? Remember, our manager promotes men when they have a new mouth to feed, whether they deserve it or not. Around here you'd think it was still the 60s, not the 80s."

"True, true. But it's more his attitude when he does it. At least our manager treats us as *people*, even if he doesn't treat us as *equals*."

"So he's got an attitude?"

"He's an arrogant bastard."

"Alicia! I'm not used to hearing you swear!"

"Well, the situation called for it. There's no other way to describe him."

As they neared their work area, Alicia added one last comment. "And he's not the kind who would be happy to see people standing around talking instead of working." Alicia looked around nervously. "I'll talk to you later."

Alicia felt someone's presence and looked up to see her boss at the cubicle doorway. "Hi, Alicia. Sorry for the short notice, but there'll be a meeting at 2 in the Sumac Conference Room to meet the new Director of MIS."

"Which room is that?" All the conference rooms were named after trees, and Alicia could never remember which was which.

"That's the large one on the second floor, just above us. It's a department-wide meeting, so we needed a big one. You know how to get there?"

"That's the one next to the pizzeria, right?"

"Right."

"Yes, I know where that is."

"Good. See you there."

"Okay."

Alicia glanced at her watch. One-thirty. *Short notice indeed! Typical Maxwell style: I'm important. Drop what you're doing and obey me.* She wondered how many people had to cancel or leave existing meetings to accommodate him. And how many night shift workers were phoned this morning and had to drag themselves out of bed hours early just to be here.

There was no way she could avoid it. Maxwell would recognize her. In the time since she had left Theoretic, she hadn't changed her hairstyle, nor much of her wardrobe. She still had the same sweaters, turtlenecks, and jeans that she had worn the winter before and the winter before that. Yes, she had added a piece or two, but today she was wearing something that he was sure to have seen her in. Maxwell certainly would recognize her.

Alicia always made it a point to arrive a few minutes early for meetings, so it was with great distress that she hung behind in the ladies' room, hoping to slide into the back of the large conference room just before the meeting started. He'd still recognize her, she was sure of that, but at least he wouldn't have time to say anything to her.

Staring at her watch, which she had set according to the telephone time announcement just ten minutes earlier, she waited until it showed exactly 2 p.m. before leaving the restroom. The conference room was just a few doors down, and the low hubbub of conversation leaking through the open door told her that although it was now time, the meeting hadn't started.

Darn! She considered returning to the ladies' room, but Carol and Norma saw her from inside and were waving her in.

Concentrating on joining them and getting seated before anyone saw her, she didn't notice the man standing inside, to the right of the door.

"Ooops. Excuse me." *Maxwell!* The one person she was trying to avoid!

In the thin, frail second that she looked at his face, she could see the recognition change to fear, to anger, and then to cold, hard detachment. "Alicia! I didn't know you were working here." His condescension was so very evident.

"Just started. Uh, Welcome to UI."

"Thank you." The voice was greasy with smugness born of power and distaste. "Nice seeing you."

He patted her slightly on the upper arm, more to move her along and out of the doorway than as a gesture of goodwill. Alicia was more than happy to move on and quickly joined Carol and Norma.

"Ah, brown-nosing the new director, I see," another co-worker chided with a slight smile, getting a quick elbow from Carol.

Alicia didn't answer, but instead just shook her head and opened her notebook, preparing, as she always did, to take notes that she would probably never read. But it kept her focused, kept her mind from wandering during boring meetings, and this was one meeting where she certainly needed to stay attentive.

Maxwell's superior walked to the front of the room, asking for everyone's attention. Maxwell stood off to the side, straightening his tie and shifting his shoulders under his suit jacket.

Alicia tried not to make eye contact, as if he were a snake or wild animal, as if making eye contact would make him strike. In her notebook she wrote the date and subject of the meeting and then, in small script, as if writing it small could diminish its importance, she wrote, *Max is back.* And then, remembering a phrase from a movie,

We're doomed. Doomed, I tell you!

He was there, at the bar, as he said he'd be. Betty straightened her tight leather skirt as she entered the Club.

"Hey, babe," he called, extending a welcoming arm.

Betty gave him a peck on the cheek. Frederick immediately sensed that something was wrong, an impression that could have been born of his newly acquired sensitivities or remembered from years of playing the field. "Uh-oh. So what did I do now? Did I forget to call you?"

"No, you didn't call. You *never* call. And you've never given me your phone number."

"So, is that a problem? Maybe I don't like phones."

"Or maybe your *wife* doesn't!"

"My *what?*" Of all the things that could be bothering Betty, this was the *last* thing he expected.

"Your wife. You're married, aren't you?"

"No!" He held out his left hand. "Do you see a ring?"

"No, but that doesn't mean anything. You could have taken it off. Or maybe you never wear one. A lot of guys don't. My father never did. He got it caught on a wooden crate while working one day and it almost ripped his finger off. He took it off and never wore it again."

"Well, I don't wear a ring because I don't *have* a ring. I'm not married."

"Then why do we never go to your place?"

"It's a dump."

"So? Maybe I could help you fix it up. I'm good at that."

Shit! This is getting messy. "Look, right now I have a real dump of a place." Frederick thought quickly. "And a real asshole for a roommate. He's a cokehead. I wouldn't trust him around my lady."

He had his hand around her waist now, and he could feel her relax. *This is workin'. Good.* "Look, I've been thinking of moving out, and I was going to find a new place and then— "

Frederick paused to gauge her reaction. She was relaxing, and was looking trustingly into his face. *Shit! I wish I knew how Wesley did that hypnotism thing. Maybe if I just think the thought real strong, she'll believe it.* "I was going to find a new place and then I met you and, well, I didn't want to say anything yet, but I was hoping, you know, well, if things kept going as good as they are, that maybe we could talk about getting a place together or something."

Her eyes misted over. "Oh, Frederick!" She threw her arms around him in a big hug.

"Hey, now, let's not go too fast. We just met, right? We don't want to rush things." *Damn, I've got to stall her.* "My last relationship ended badly." *Yeah, she died in my arms. That was pretty damned bad.* "I need time."

Betty reached over the bar and grabbed a cocktail napkin. "Okay," she said, wiping her eyes. "Okay. I can wait. I've got time."

So do I, babe. So do I. "All right. So that's settled. Now, would a steak dinner cheer you up? I could go for a steak just now." His blood lust was rising. It was way too early in the evening to feed from her. Though she was now relaxed and trusting, she was too awake and sober. She'd realize what was going on. A rare steak might stave off his cravings just long enough.

"Okay. Sure." Betty removed a small mirror from her purse and blotted her eyes carefully. A half-moon of mascara clung to each lid, just below the lashes, giving her eyes a macabre look.

Frederick took a last swig of his beer as he swiveled off the bar stool.

"Let's go."

Betty kissed his cheek and then his neck. He stumbled with desire.

"You okay?" She asked, disturbed by his wobbling.

Frederick willed himself steady. "Yeah, just a little light-headed. I haven't eaten all day. Let's go get that steak."

Chapter 17

Alicia ripped the envelope open carelessly, yet the two sheets of paper inside survived her ravaging. She unfolded them gently. They were from Janith, about the study group.

The first sheet was handwritten, in Janith's stylistic hand, and Alicia wondered if Janith had taken calligraphy lessons. The sepia-colored ink reminded her of ancient tomes... or dried blood. She shook her head violently. *Where did* that *come from?* But she knew where it came from. For in the fractional part of a second that it had entered her mind, another image had entered— Wesley's face.

She shook her head again, as if in the shaking she could cast him out. She took a deep breath and focused on the letter.

Dear Alicia,

Enclosed are directions to the apartment and some information on the study group. As I said when I spoke to you on the phone, we think that some of the techniques you'll learn in the group will be helpful, even if you decide not to continue. Once again, though, let me stress that this is NOT a cult. You are not required to join and no one will curse you or anything like that if you decide not to join.

Please let us know if you plan to come so that we'll know how many handouts to make. Keep calling if you don't reach us at first. (We don't have an answering machine.) It's probably long distance for you, so feel free to respond by mail instead.

Janith

The second sheet was a blurred electrostatic copy on slimy paper with instructions for prospective students. Directions to the apartment where the meetings would be held were at the bottom and Janith and Rob's phone number was at the top. Beneath that was the date and time of the first meeting, a request to bring something for the potluck meal, and a brief list of the subjects they'd cover: Relaxation, Meditation, Introduction to Astrology, Introduction to the Tarot, and Spells of Protection. *So I'm not the only one who needs protection. I wonder if the rest of them have vampire problems, too.*

Alicia let the papers drop onto her lap, forgetting that Moonshadow was there. His left ear twitched and he looked up with that glare of aggravation that only a Persian cat can muster. "Sorry, Moonie," Alicia said as she smoothed his ruffled fur. He responded with a purr and pushed his head into her hand for more.

She remembered the night that Susie's ghost had visited, how Moonshadow had seen her first. "You'll warn me if any vampires are around, won't you honey?"

Moonshadow stopped purring. He withdrew his head, looked at her straight on with his pale emerald eyes, and abruptly jumped off her lap.

"Oooh. I guess that's a no, huh?"

The City.

Once again, Alicia's fears weren't of meeting a group of strangers who were also *witches*, but were of getting lost, mugged, raped, murdered, or killed in a car crash on her way to their apartment.

She was relieved to find that the apartment wasn't far from a road she knew well: Route 9. Though the locals referred to that stretch of road as "Huntington Ave," to her— and the map makers— it was still Route 9, and that little piece of familiarity strengthened her.

The directions were clear and, this late in the season, so were the road surfaces. As Alicia parallel-parked a couple of blocks away from the apartment, she wondered what she would have done if she had come in the dead of winter and the streets were clogged with snow banks. As it was, parking wasn't easy to find.

Deal with that bridge when you come to it, idiot, she scolded herself. *You don't even know if you'll be coming here again.* But that was her way: Worry first, and get it over with. Think ahead. For every Plan A, have a Plan B. Be prepared. Carry aspirins and adhesive bandages, just in case a migraine comes on or you get a nasty paper cut. Make sure you have pencil, pen, and paper (for those 'To Do' lists) and your address book in case you break down and need to call someone for help.

And after the Blizzard of '78, she always carried matches. You never knew when you might be stuck in deep snow and need to light a fire, even if you were on a major east-west highway in a heavily populated metropolis.

On the positive side, it meant she was never caught short. On the negative side, it meant that her pocketbook weighed a ton, and the last time she saw a doctor for a back problem she got quite a lecture about carrying such a heavy bag. But she couldn't give it up. It was her security blanket.

To her, every little trip, every little event, was like launching a battle campaign. *Be prepared. Hah! I never should have been a Girl Scout. Ruined me for life!* Alicia smiled, took a deep breath, and relaxed. *It's okay to be prepared. Just stop stressing about it, okay? Just prepare and then let go.* She worked on her anxiety in therapy and was finding it easier and easier to talk herself out of anxious situations, but there were still a few situations like cities and vampire encounters that were a bit challenging.

With her initial anxiety under control, she slung her pocketbook bandolier-style over her head and shoulder. Looking in the side mirror first, she exited the car, locking it as she did. *Okay, be confident. Walk like you belong here.*

As she walked, passing some of the many students who lived in the area, she started to relax. If they could feel safe here, maybe it was okay. She really didn't know the neighborhoods. Maybe this one was one of the good ones.

From the street, it certainly *looked* like a decent neighborhood. Though the impersonal quality of tall buildings made her anxious, her logical mind had to admit that the streets were clean and the architecture was pleasing. The tall whitish gray buildings in the block where the apartment was were tall enough to be grand, but not tall enough to be a threat.

Bounding up the steps to the doorbell, she steeled herself once more against the unknown. *You'll be fine. They're nice people.*

She pressed the buzzer and waited.

Although she arrived 15 minutes early, four people had preceded her.

"Am I late?"

"Oh, no, not at all," Janith replied, leading Alicia into the now-cramped living room. "They just arrived. You're fine."

Janith quickly introduced Alicia to the four, but even before she had finished, Alicia had forgotten the names. They were common names like John or Bob or Jane or Debbie and their owners were just as nondescript. They could have been one of any of the tens of thousands of students in the city with their jeans and pullover sweaters in muted colors.

Alicia always forgot names in the nervousness of introduction. Each time she promised herself to pay better attention and maybe try some of those name-remembering exercises she had heard of, not that they seemed very promising.

Rob's voice from behind her interrupted her despair at memorization. "Okay, we're just waiting for two more people and then we can start, but why don't you all get whatever you need and we'll— " The rasping low-pitched sound of the buzzer cut him short. "Looks like they're here." Rob walked over and pressed the button, holding it for a few seconds before continuing. "Of course, we'd *know* for sure if the intercom worked, but it never has."

He smiled and let go of the buzzer and walked to the door. "As we said when we first met all of you, we're not the ones who will actually lead the group. We're acting more in the role of advisors. The two people coming in now will be the leaders of the group. They're students of ours and are ready to start training others."

Alicia could hear footsteps and muffled voices echoing in the hallway as Rob opened the door. She didn't know what to expect. Would they be young like Rob and Janith, or wizened, as she had initially expected the coven leaders to be? Trying to act nonchalant, she opened her notebook and carefully wrote the date and subject of the meeting on the first blank page.

Not wanting to be rude, she looked up as Rob introduced the first person through the door, a vibrant, wiry young man who called himself Gabe, followed closely by someone that she immediately recognized—

Meg!

This time she couldn't *help* staring. Meg! What was she doing here? Was she coming to learn, too?

Alicia stared open-mouthed as Meg walked over to her, hand extended, saying, "Hi, Alicia. I'm *Matricaria*," emphasizing the name, not just for pronunciation, but, Alicia felt, as a signal to call her by that name and that name only.

"Whh-what?"

"I'm known as Matricaria. It's the Latin name for chamomile. I chose it because my specialty is herbs and I liked its properties: soothing, healing. That's the type of influence I want to have on the world."

"Yes," Rob jumped in, "People often choose magical names to use when they become witches. Hers is Matricaria. She's the other half of the leadership team."

Alicia was too dazed to notice that Rob, Matricaria, and Janith were staring back at her, trying to judge her reaction to this unexpected revelation. She didn't see the tense, quick glances from one to the other as they assessed the situation, nor the quiet communal release of breath when she finally spoke.

"Oh, hi! Well, it's good to see a familiar face— "

Before she could say more, Janith stepped up and took control. "Okay, we can get started. Gabe and Matricaria, if you want anything to drink, there's soda in the fridge and hot water for tea."

So Meg was the leader— and a *witch*! Alicia sat shocked, incapable of speech, dumbfounded. Meg! How many weeks, months, even years had they worked together, and yet she never knew! To her, Meg was the embodiment of a successful career woman: confident, analytical, logical, and— there was no other way to express it— *normal*. As Alicia looked around the room, she realized that they *all* were. Except for the tiny silver star that Janith, Rob, Gabe, and Meg— Matricaria— wore, there was nothing to set any of them apart from anyone on the street.

Gathering her senses, she continued to calm herself. *Okay, so they look normal. So do you! Who says that witches can't look normal? And maybe they are normal, just different...*

Out of the corner of her eye, she felt someone staring and looked up just in time to see a worried Rob look away. Janith, however, continued to look at her, but with a soft welcome smile that seemed to speak to her as Alicia would speak to her cat: "It's all right."

Rob moved to the center of the room. "Okay, let's begin."

It was a phrase that Janith, Matricaria, and Gabe had heard over and over during their training as Rob had called their affable group to order, and one probably used by covens and study groups just like this all over the country, all over the world, all over time. And though Alicia had probably heard the same thing or something similar at school or in meetings at work, for her this phrase now had a new meaning. Let's begin the meeting, begin the journey, begin the battle.

For the first time since that fateful night that Wesley had first appeared to her in the computer room, Alicia felt that there was order in the world and that once again she could control her own fate, her own destiny, that she was no longer at the mercy of forces unknown. For here were people who knew the unknown, who had, it seemed, learned from others who had trod the dark halls of the strange, and who had come out alive and unscathed.

Yes, Rob. Please, let's begin.

"I'm Rob and this is my wife, Janith. We're the leaders of a training coven that has operated in this area for about five or six years. We don't proselytize; that is, we don't push our beliefs on others. That being said, we do feel that what we've learned is valuable and we feel that it's our duty to pass it on to others. Many people get interested in the supernatural, the occult, without proper guidance, and some paths can be very dangerous."

Rob paused for a sip of tea, and Janith, true to habit, stepped in to fill the silence. "Yes, and some paths are quite safe. We have tried to guide people along the various paths of magic and spirituality." She nodded to Rob, who took over again.

"The training coven we run is a traditional coven with a set group of practices, beliefs, and rituals. Students follow a specific curriculum as they learn the craft of the witch and the ancient nature-worshipping religion behind it. This group, however, is not part of that coven. Instead, it's an exploratory group where you learn a little about the Craft, learn some magical practices, and decide for yourself if you want to further your studies. I want to make it perfectly clear that you are not committing yourself to anything at this point—"

Janith tenderly touched his hand. "Except secrecy. We ask that you not reveal the names or identities of anyone you meet here." At this point, she looked directly and almost pleadingly at Alicia. "We all have lives outside the coven, outside the group. We all work, at least part time. Some of our employers would not be amused to find that we are students and practitioners of the occult."

"Yes, as Janith said, we ask that you respect each other's privacy. If you decide to study further and ask for membership in the coven, we would then ask for an additional vow of secrecy because what you would learn in the coven situation are techniques that, in the hands of the unscrupulous or the evil-intended, could be dangerous. We would ask you to take a vow not to reveal them except to people who have been properly prepared and judged as morally fit and who have taken a similar oath. But that's the coven. Let's talk about this study group. Matricaria and Gabe, who are students of ours, will be the actual leaders of the group. Janith and I will be here at future meetings— because we live here— but we will probably go off in the other room and let Gabe and Mat run things on their own. This is part of their training— to learn to teach, to learn to lead, to learn to think on their feet. So, why don't we turn the meeting over to them. Mat?"

Rob gestured toward Matricaria in a fluid exaggerated grand motion and smiled.

"Okay. Hi, I'm Matricaria ..."

As Alicia listened to Matricaria detail her personal history and how she became interested in the craft of the wise, she marveled at the woman who was speaking. She was the same woman that she knew as Meg, with the same open, confident manner that she had exhibited in countless meetings and presentations at work, but there was something else this time; a presence, an attitude, yes, even a gentle warm power that emanated from her and filled the room. Alicia could feel it, almost see it, as an individual atmosphere or a radiant cloud stretching out from Matricaria and enveloping the room.

"... I've been studying with Rob and Janith for almost four years now..."

Four years. So she had begun her training just before everything began with Wesley...

"... and when they asked for volunteers to lead the study group, I volunteered." She paused. "I don't want to take up too much time with my background or history, but feel free to ask me if you have any specific questions. Gabe?"

As Matricaria tossed the virtual ball over to Gabe, Alicia felt a slight shift in the room. Matricaria's inner light, which had been so bright that it was almost beacon-like, was fading gently back into her body as she gestured toward Gabe.

But it wasn't just that she was stepping out of the spotlight. It was almost as if it were a deliberate gathering in, as if Matricaria felt what Alicia now felt, that someone outside was watching...

Again he felt it. It wasn't just the pull of the memory of Alicia, her intelligent brown eyes alive with defiance, but a sense of power behind her— literally behind her— a group of soft, indeterminate shadows, glowing slightly.

Wesley stopped in his wanderings. He had been walking the rain-sodden streets of the Southern city, hidden in the ensuing fog. He was a mere block away from the late-night revelers of Bourbon Street, among whom he could count many promising victims. But the indistinct vision from cold New England 1500 miles away kept assaulting his consciousness, breaking the concentration of the hunt, overpowering his vampiric senses.

The dusky, discordant smells of jambalaya, beer, and vomit in the alleyway into which he had ducked were soon overpowered by the clean, crisp olfactory hallucination of an early spring night in Fenmore, the only smells in common being the diesel fumes from cabs and buses.

Wesley closed his eyes and focused. He could see a room, a bright room, with nine indistinct shapes, moving, talking, laughing. He tried to focus, to see who was in the room, to understand the connection that held him, but it was as though he were looking through frosted glass or sheets of pale organza.

Of course! As Wesley strained harder to see through the haze, he began to realize what the haze was. On the astral plane, the plane of his vision, it looked for all the world like a cotton cocoon, a blanket of protection. And that's what it was.

It's the witches, and they're in a protected space. And this time Alicia is with them!

Gabe was next to introduce himself. Dressed smartly in designer jeans and new-looking sweater, he was nonetheless almost childlike in his exuberance, squirming in his seat, gesturing with his hands. His eyes, wide and expressive, were warm and friendly when he spoke of his finding witchcraft (which he called "the Craft"). They were outright passionate when he spoke of pagan rituals and the Goddess.

Alicia hadn't even known that there was a goddess involved. To her, witchcraft was just that, a *craft*. A craft or practice with methods that could help her find out the truth about Wesley and act accordingly. If this was a religion, she wasn't sure it was what she wanted. Her experience with the Catholic church had left her on the border of atheism. To her, religion wasn't logical, and she couldn't help thinking of the Karl Marx quote: "Religion is the opiate of the masses."

Meg— Matricaria— interrupted her drifting thoughts. "This study group will cover mostly the arts and sciences of the Craft, though it will, of course, touch on the religious aspects. But only slightly. So don't worry; in this study group, you won't be asked to embrace a new religion or anything like that."

Alicia noticed that the others also seemed relieved. Were they, like her, relieved that they wouldn't be studying *any* religion, or were they relieved that they wouldn't have to denounce their own?

Gabe resumed his introduction with an exaggerated air of defeat, "Yes, and you don't know what you're missing!" and then turned the introduction over to the person on his left. "Let's introduce ourselves— first names only— and say where we're from and what we hope to get out of the group. Why don't we go around the room— clockwise!"

"Yes," Matricaria said, "Clockwise, or, as we call it, *deosil*, the way of the sun. Get in the habit of thinking of moving clockwise because when we work ritual together we will always move in a clockwise direction." She gestured to the person at Gabe's left. "I'm sorry. Go on."

Alicia took notes mainly because it gave her an excuse to look down and not have to make eye contact with Matricaria. She tried to focus, tried to remember their names this time, tried to remember where they lived and what they were here for. Her mind kept wandering back to the explosion, back to Theoretic. Did Matricaria know what was going on then? Why didn't she step in to help? Did she just stand by and watch it all happen? *And what do I say when it's my turn to talk?*

"Alicia? You want to tell the group a little about yourself?" Matricaria smiled as she tried to pull Alicia into the discussion. As if she sensed Alicia's concerns, she quickly added, "You don't need to say much. Just tell us what you hope to learn here."

The others were smiling politely, warmly, and though Alicia knew she should feel comfortable and protected, she really felt like running from the room. Manners and the slightest bit of ego kept her firmly in her seat. She couldn't run out now and let them think she was rude.

"I'm Alicia, I live in Danforth, and I came to learn more about, uh, psychic things, psychic ability."

"Danforth? Where's that? Is that near 128?"

"West of 128. Between 128 and 495."

"Wow. I've never been out there."

Alicia smiled. At least she wasn't the only one who felt safer sticking close to home. "Yeah, if you look on the map, it's just after where it says, 'HERE THERE BE DRAGONS.'"

"Oh, like one of those maps from the Middle Ages!"

Relieved that they caught her allusion to medieval cartography, Alicia relaxed. She hadn't even been aware of it, but somewhere in the back of her mind was the fear that she wouldn't be able to hold her own against the people who had just introduced themselves as college students.

"'Here there be dragons.' That's a good one. I'll have to remember that," Gabe said as he looked over to Matricaria for a sign that she was ready to start. "You said you had something prepared, so I'm going to turn it over to YOU!" He patted her knee affectionately and then rose from the couch and headed toward the kitchen.

"Okay, I thought that for our first session... "

As Matricaria launched into their first lesson, Alicia thought back to what she had said and the warm reaction from the group. *Here there be dragons. Good one! You actually thought of something witty to say under pressure. Here there be dragons... Oh, my God...*

Dragons. From the Latin draco.

As in Dracula...

Chapter 18

"Did anyone else feel something?" Matricaria was picking up empty tea cups as she spoke, the clack of ceramic surfaces audible over the hiss of an antiquated steam radiator. The prospective students had left, leaving just the four initiates.

Rob cast a worried glance at Janith before answering. "Yes, I did."

Janith nodded, and Gabe, his exuberance dropping to solemn silence, also nodded.

"But you cast a circle before they got here, right? That's supposed to protect us?"

"And isn't the covenstead supposed to be fairly protected anyway, just from the amount of ritual we do here?"

"Well, if you want to get technical," Rob said, moving a pile of books on ancient Sumerian lore and Greek mythology aside before dropping onto the couch, "It *did* protect us. Nothing happened. We're all safe. He didn't get in."

"So, you felt it, too, that it was the vampire?"

"Absolutely."

"Great. What do we do now?"

"I'll call a coven meeting for Friday— "

"Uh, date!" Gabe said, pleading his case, rolling his eyes in an exaggerated expression of impatience.

"Gabe, if we don't do something soon, your next date could be with a vampire!"

Gabe appeared to be ready to toss out a witty reply, but stopped. He leaned back into the couch and started chewing on the side of his thumb, distressed at the tough decision he'd have to make.

Rob's worried face softened a little. "Okay, one day won't make a difference. Saturday. Can you make Saturday, say, seven o'clock?"

"Yes!"

"Good. I'll call a coven meeting for Saturday. We'll discuss the situation and we'll do a general protection ritual. Gabe and Matricaria, you should pay special attention to what we discuss and what we do. For your next study group meeting, you need to go over magical protection with the students. Make sure that they at least have the basics." Gabe nodded. Matricaria made a note in her notebook.

Janith sat against the edge of the couch back, her arm affectionately draped over her husband's shoulder. "Hon, maybe it would be a good idea if Matricaria gave Alicia some private lessons right away."

"Good idea. Mat, can you do that?"

"I'll see her at work tomorrow. I can ask her to come over. At the very least, I can give her some general instructions on visualization."

"Good. That should help. And tonight, before you cast your circle of protection around your bed, cast one remotely around Alicia first."

"Right."

"And we should all do some research on amulets of protection."

"Easy. Crosses and garlic! Not very attractive, but easy," Gabe pitched in.

"True, but I can't see her wearing either, nor us, for that matter. Besides, we're still not one hundred percent sure this guy's a vampire, that there's even such a thing as a vampire—" Rob paused as the lighting dimmed a lumen or two. He noted from the looks around the room that he wasn't the only one who saw it. "We just know that whoever he is, whatever he is, he's trying to get in, and we need to stop him. *Can* stop him. And that's important. Remember that one of the basic foundations of magic is *belief.* Starting now, we *have* to believe that we can stop him."

"Even if our minds tell us otherwise?"

"*Especially* if our minds tell us otherwise. We *can* stop him. Got it?"

As one who prided herself on being a careful driver, Alicia was embarrassed to realize that the twenty-plus miles from the covenstead to her house was a blur.

She remembered finding her way back to the Massachusetts Turnpike, but from then on she was on autopilot as she digested the evening's events.

Meg! They had spoken of a religious aspect tonight. Was Meg just in it for the religion, or did she do magic, too? Is that why she was so successful?

"Me-yow!" Alicia said aloud, to no one. "That's as bad as suggesting that she *slept* her way to the top! Okay, so Meg's a witch. She's still intelligent, capable, and a hard worker. I shouldn't assume that she used magic instead of her own skills to get ahead at work."

As she rolled down her window at the tollbooth, Alicia was brought back to the task at hand by the chilly night air. *Drive, dummy. You can figure out the rest when you get home.*

Home. Joey, for all intents and purposes, had left. He was sleeping at his girlfriend's apartment now. Only a few belongings marked his place at Alicia's house, and he had moved those into the smallest bedroom, giving Evan the larger room next to Alicia's.

She couldn't wait to tell Evan about the study group. "*The only thing we ask is that you honor our privacy and not reveal the identities of any of the people you meet*," Janith had told Alicia over the phone, and she had repeated it more than once tonight. *Okay, so I just won't tell Evan her full name. I'll call her by her first name.*

The house looked dark as Alicia pulled into the tiny gravel driveway. She craned her neck to see if Evan's light was still on at the back of the house. There was light, but only a faint glow. *Nightlight?*

She grabbed her handbag and butted her shoulder against the car door to open it. "Ouch!" She had forgotten that she had locked it when she got in the car, something she always did in cities, but never did at home. "That's going to bruise."

The gravel crunched and slid as she walked down the driveway to the sidewalk and then across to the front door. Alicia never took the shortcut across the small patch of grass between the house and the broken-teeth barrier of the brown picket fence. She wasn't fussy about the lawn, feeling that lawns were useless abominations that should be replaced with edible or fragrance-producing plants, but she wasn't about to wear away a path and let erosion carry away the topsoil, either.

Moonshadow greeted her at the door. "Hi, Moonie. You want din?" She whispered her usual greeting, wondering what Evan thought of people who spoke to their cats with more affection than they spoke to humans. She had tried to tone it down around Joey, whose affection towards animals was more often expressed in the raucous high-five way that he expressed affection towards humans.

With Moonshadow now fed, she grabbed her notebook and handbag and retreated upstairs. As she reached the landing, she saw a thin sliver of weak yellow light under Evan's door. Dropping her baggage at her own door, she paused to listen. Silence. Was he still awake? She didn't want to be rude and wake him, especially on a work night.

"Evan?" she called, tentatively. She thought she heard movement, and then seconds later, his door opened.

Behind him she could see the warm glow of candlelight. "You weren't sleeping, were you?" she asked, now more worried about a fire hazard than her possible breach of etiquette.

"No, I was just reading."

"By candlelight?"

"Yes, I need to buy a lamp."

"Oh, you should have said something! I have a spare one that you could use—"

"No, that's okay. I like it this way. Reminds me of olden times."

You remind me of olden times, she thought as she looked at the tall, slim figure before her. He was dressed simply, in loose, natural cotton pants and a matching long-sleeve thermal top. Although he was obviously dressed for indoors, he wore a black knitted cap, which matched his black cloth slip-on shoes.

As the candlelight flickered, she reflected that he could have been a man from the mid-1800s, or, as he squinted against the glare of the harsh hall light, a Chinese immigrant at rest after a day of working on the railroad. *Except that he's so tall.* Enraptured for the moment by history, she nearly forgot her purpose, and in the quickness of trying to recover, blurted it out inelegantly.

"I just met the witches—"

Evan grinned impishly, opening his eyes in mock surprise, "You *did?*"

"Yeah. Do you have a minute?"

"Yes. Let me just grab a shirt." Without moving much, he twisted around, reached in, and withdrew a thick, flannel work shirt that he pulled on like a robe. "Shall we? Or, why don't you just come in here? I've had the door closed and it's nice and warm. Well, it was..."

Alicia felt embarrassed by the inadequacy of the heating system. "I'm sorry it's so drafty."

"No, that's okay. This is New England. It's still barely spring. That's what you expect. Our ancestors survived much worse."

Alicia tentatively stepped into his room, feeling odd about entering, and then remembered that it *was* her house.

How different it looked in the candlelight. The modern, nearly garish orange-flowered wallpaper leftover from the previous homeowner receded into a background pattern that was almost pleasant. Completely lacking furniture, Evan had placed a bedroll and sleeping bag perpendicular to the wall containing the door. In one corner lay his ubiquitous backpack. In another lay a carefully stacked pile of clothes. Between them a line of books, with bricks as bookends, lined the baseboard.

"I didn't realize you were sleeping on the floor! If you want to sleep on the couch until you get a bed, please do. It folds out into a double bed."

"No, that's fine. This is the way I like it. Simple. Austere. I like to live simply. Here, have a seat." Evan pulled a large black throw pillow from his bed, where it had laid against the wall, pressed into duty as a backrest.

How different it was from her own surroundings. Suffering from want as a child, Alicia now cherished every possession that she had gradually accumulated. When Susie had redecorated— which was often— Alicia was the first one to raise her hand when Susie asked if anyone was interested in her giveaways. Susie! Again her name surfaced like a bad dream, and the deep, dark ache in the pit of her being reminded Alicia that she— indeed, no one— ever solved the mystery of what happened to Susie.

"You were saying?" Evan gently touched her arm with his long, elegant fingers.

"I'm sorry. Lost in thought there. Yes, I went into town and met that group of witches that I was telling you about."

"And they weren't warty and old, right?"

Alicia found herself laughing. "No, they weren't warty and old. They were normal people, and young, and very easy to talk to."

"You expected different?"

"I know you said that the witches you know— and you, yourself— are normal, but, yeah, I guess I did expect either old, wise wizards or weird, Satan-worshipping maniacs or some sort of psychopath that you'd read about at Halloween. Y'know, the type who would relish decapitating puppies, nailing toads to doors, things like that."

"I think maybe even the Satanists would have problems with that stereotype."

"But you know what I mean. I expected them to be eccentric, crazy, or downright spooky. And they weren't any of those. They were good people, kind people. Just people with an interest in the occult."

"Like you."

"Yeah, you're right. Like me."

Alicia caught herself staring at Evan again. Although she had initially thought he was a bit odd-looking despite the resemblance to Paul McCartney, the candlelight softened his features so that now his smiling eyes and sensuous mouth took precedence. He reached for a cup that sat next to his bedroll and again she was mesmerized by the liquidity of his movements. They weren't harsh or jerky like Joey's, or clumsy like her own. They were slow, languid, and sensual, even in the everyday act of picking up a cup.

"So, did they have any advice?"

"We didn't get into details. We'll do that in the study group. It's going to be informal and we'll learn some of the basics of protection and maybe tarot card reading and things like that."

"Sounds good." He smiled, winking both eyes in the process, and then took a sip from his cup.

Alicia found herself staring again, and an awkwardness crept over her along with a residual chill from the outdoor dampness of the evening. "Well, I have to work tomorrow, so I'd better get ready for bed."

"Okay. It looks like you're on the right path."

"I hope so."

"Sleep well." He smiled, his eyes shining.

"You, too. You sure you're okay on the floor?"

"I'm fine. It's good for the back."

"But it's cold."

"I have a thermal camping pad underneath," he explained, pulling back the rough wool blanket to expose a thick and probably expensive pad.

"Okay, but if you get cold or stiff, move to the couch, okay?"

"Yes, mother!"

Again, Alicia found herself laughing. "Okay. I get it. Good night."

"Sleep well."

"So what did you think?" Meg lowered herself into the hard cafeteria chair at the far corner of the room, away from the other co-workers.

Alicia casually looked around before answering. "I'm not sure about the religion part."

"Well, as we said, we're not going to cover much of that anyway in the study group, although Gabe would have preferred to. He's much more into the religious aspect than the thaumaturgy."

"Thaumaturgy?"

"The word actually means 'performance of miracles,' but in witchcraft, it refers to magic. I'm more of a balance person myself: magic when needed, religion as a normal part of my life."

"It's still going to take me a long while to not think of the Catholic church."

Meg smiled and sipped her coffee. "Don't worry about it. If you're not interested in the religious aspects, no one will force you, especially in the study group. And in your case right now, there's more a need for magic, though Gabe would disagree. He would argue that an appeal to the gods for protection would be in order. He may be right, but that's not your path, so we'll attack it from the other direction."

Alicia was silent for a moment as a group of people approached the table next to them and then, changing their minds, moved to another, further away. When she looked back, she noticed that Meg's eyes were slightly closed, her hands slightly raised, and her face frozen in concentration, but within seconds it was all gone and she was the same Meg that Alicia always knew.

Something connected in her mind and Alicia asked tentatively, "The people who almost sat next to us changed their minds at the last second. Did you, uh..."

"Did I think very strongly that maybe they might find another table more agreeable?" Meg smiled impishly behind her raised coffee cup. "Guilty. One of the basic tenets of our version of the Craft is that your magic should not harm people. It didn't really harm them to move over fifteen feet. It might have harmed us if they sat within earshot."

"Ah." Alicia took a sip of her own coffee, pondering. These witches certainly weren't evil as people would imagine them, nor fist-pounding religious fundamentalists. They were analytical, thorough, ethical. Like herself.

On the other side of their table, a new group of people sat down. "Ooops. Missed them!"

Alicia suppressed an outright laugh at Meg's joke. So these witches had a sense of humor about themselves, too.

"Look at the time. I should get back to my desk. We have a lot of things to talk about, but obviously the company cafeteria isn't the place. I'd like to invite you over to my place sometime. We could get Chinese or pizza or I could throw together something simple. Do you have any free time this week?"

"I'm not doing anything Thursday, and I'm really not picky about food."

"In that case, how about some leftover lasagna? I made a large pan for the last coven meeting and froze half of it. Around 7? I'll write up some directions and drop them by your desk."

"Lasagne is fine, and Thursday's fine, too."

Meg rose and Alicia followed, feeling more at ease than she could have imagined, and trying desperately not to bubble over with giddiness at the fact that Meg— Matricaria— just performed magic, out of the blue, right in the company cafeteria.

"So, did you ask him?" Norma looked up expectantly as Betty pulled the chair away from the table, both of them oblivious to Alicia and Meg walking by, just two tables away.

"Yup." Betty shook her head, staring at her lunch, hiding her face.

"And?"

"He denied it."

"Bastard!"

"Yep. What did I expect? God, Norma. I should know better."

"So, what was his excuse?"

"The usual. His place is a dump. His roommate is an asshole. They haven't cleaned in months. You know the story."

"Jesus!" Norma shook her head and exhaled forcibly. "What a jerk."

"Well, maybe..."

"Maybe?" Norma looked at Betty in disbelief. "Whaddya mean, 'maybe'? You just told me his lame excuses. He never lets you into his life, he won't give you a phone number, he never stays the whole night—"

Betty looked up and leaned across the table. Norma could see that she was smiling. "He wants to move in with me!"

Norma paused, breathless. "What?"

"He said that he wanted to move out of his apartment anyway, and that he didn't want to say anything to me yet, but he was waiting to see how it went between us and— "

"And you believe him?"

"I know. I shouldn't. But when he said it, it sounded so right, and it just felt so, so, I don't know, so strong. It's hard to describe, but at that moment I felt like whatever he said was the truth, and nothing but."

Norma unwrapped her sandwich, lost in thought, and then remembered her manners. "I'm happy for you, I guess. Did he say when?"

"Well, no, but I didn't ask. Maybe I should ask him, huh? Or maybe I shouldn't. I don't want to seem too pushy. Whaddya think?"

Norma dropped her shoulders and sighed. "Well, I think you might be wrong to believe him, but what do I know? I don't know him. I wasn't there. It sounds like a line, but, hey, he *could* mean it."

"Yeah, he could, he really could. You've got to meet him, Norma. I think you'd change your mind if you met him. Maybe you and your husband could come over some night and we could have dinner, or maybe we could go bowling or something."

"Does he bowl?"

"I don't know. He said he plays basketball and he used to play baseball, so I'm thinking he's athletic. I can ask."

"Okay, I'll see what night the old man is free. He's got his league, and he promised his brother he'd help finish their family room, but we'll figure something out."

"Great. I'll ask him tonight. Norma, I'm so excited!"

"Good for you, Betty. I'm happy for you."

She said it without sarcasm or rancor, but inside Norma felt quite the opposite. She didn't know why, but she just knew— *knew, knew, knew*— that Frederick was lying. And that somehow, sometime, and in a big way, Betty was going to be hurt. And hurt bad.

"So, she was in your *bedroom*?" Lynnie poked a playful finger into Evan's exposed, nearly hairless chest.

"Darlin', it's *her* house. She can go anywhere she wants."

Lynnie rolled over and up so that she now faced him. "I know. I'm just teasing."

"And what if she *was* in my bedroom, hmm?" Evan poked Lynnie in the ribs, causing her to wriggle off his chest. "Hmm? After all, you and I are just friends."

Lynnie made an exaggerated pout. "Just friends?"

Evan pulled her closer, her naked body tangling in the sheets as he did so. "Okay. *Close* friends."

"Yes, very close friends."

They kissed slowly, luxuriantly, for a few seconds before Lynnie pulled away. "So, tell me what she said about the witches."

"They sound legitimate. If they're who I think they are, they're from one of the more well-respected covens in the area."

"Which tradition?"

"Some branch of European tradition."

"Do you think they can help her?"

"I'm not sure." Evan wove his fingers through Lynnie's thick and wavy blonde hair as he thought aloud. "Maybe, maybe not. The leaders are relatively new at this. It's their first coven and it's been going only about four years. They're hooked into a network of other Traditionals, I'm sure, so they must have a lot of resources."

Lynnie rolled away slightly.

"Something wrong?"

"No. You know how I feel about some of these Traditional groups. They get caught up in their hierarchies, their procedures, their little games. You rarely see much real psychic talent in any of those groups. Or spirituality, for that matter."

Evan untangled his hand from her hair and pulled up to a sitting position. "Well, yes, their coven is part of a hierarchical tradition, but the coven itself doesn't seem very hidebound. I met a few of them at a friend's house in Harvard Square when I first moved up here."

"Well, maybe they're different. All I can say is that the few I met when I was at school were more concerned about where I came from, who I knew, and what 'degrees' I had. They weren't interested in hearing about my Guides and evaluating my experiences at face value."

Evan smiled and playfully pulled her chin up so that she was looking directly at him. "We're not talking sour grapes, are we?"

With one swift movement, Lynnie, too, sat up. "Okay, so maybe I was a little oversensitive at that psychic symposium last year, but I'm not the only one who's had to listen to these egotistical no-talents brag about their lineage and their Degrees. A lot of my friends have had the same problem. Remember I mentioned that Heidi had those people walk out on her crystals seminar? And what do these witches *do*, anyway? They chant and wave their wands and everything, but I've never heard one of them say anything about their Guides or their channeling. Are they even connected to the psychic realm?"

Evan put a gentle hand on her shoulder. "You forget that I'm one of them, too."

"Yes, from a completely different line, from a different part of the country. And you weren't stuck in a coven long enough to get a big head about it."

"Okay." Evan pulled her gently back toward him. She didn't resist. "But I was in the coven long enough to see people actually penetrate the mysteries and work real magic."

"If they were that good, why didn't you stay and complete your training?"

Evan rocked back until he was half-reclining again. "You know me. I don't like rules and strictures. Even though the witches I trained with were relatively loose, they still had a system, and I found it confining. I don't like to be confined."

"No, you don't," she said, nuzzling in to him. "I never understood how you lasted as long with them as you did. There must have been a love interest, huh?"

Evan playfully poked her in the ribs again, "Oh, so you think I'm *that* shallow?"

"Sometimes, dearie, sometimes." And, as if to prove a point, she kissed him.

He did not resist.

Chapter 19

"Yeah, okay." Frederick was looking down when he said it, but at least he said it.

Betty tensed, but her voice was calm. "You don't sound too excited."

"Uh, no, uh, it's just that I haven't been bowling in a long time. Don't want to make a fool of myself."

Betty put a playful hand over Frederick's hand. She could feel that he, too, was tense. "I'm sure you won't. You're a big, strong, guy."

"Yeah, that's what I'm afraid of."

Like Betty, he kept his voice calm, trying to hide the truth. He really *was* afraid of his strength, at least in the bowling alley. What if he rolled the ball with such force that it drove the pins out the other side of the wall?

Luckily for Frederick, Betty didn't ask what he meant, but instead continued lobbying for the cause. "You'll be fine, I'm sure. You'll like Norma and her husband. They're good people. C'mon, we never *go* anywhere. I'll try to set something up for this weekend, okay?"

"Sure. I'll practice my bowling." *Yeah, maybe I should. Shit, this could get hairy.*

"It'll be fun. We can go out to eat first, at that steak place you like."

Steak. Frederick felt a pang of hunger so deep he almost heaved. He swayed slightly, and grabbed the back of the couch to steady himself. Betty, true to form, noticed immediately.

"Hon, you okay?"

"Yeah, I'm fine." Thinking quickly, he tried to cover his unsteadiness with a joke. "Man, you mention that steak place, and I almost die thinking of it! Hey, have you eaten? I could use a burger or something."

"How about the diner? They're open all night, right?"

You're telling me. How many nights had he stood in the shadows of their parking lot, waiting for opportunity? Waiting for deliverance in the form of a lonely waitress, off work from her own job, stopping by on her way home. He never understood how they could eat in a place like that after working all night in some other hot, smoky hole-in-the-wall, grease as thick in the air as cigarette smoke, but they did. And he took advantage of that.

"Nah, I'm sick of that place. I used to go there all the time. Let's go somewhere different. There might be a place open on Route 9, or maybe that place at the service area on the Pike is open. I know how to cut through to the workers' parking lot so we don't have to pay the toll."

"What about that Irish place at the Center? I think they serve food until ten."

"Okay, and if not, we're not far from the back road to the service area."

Frederick gave Betty a friendly pat on the butt. She responded with a deep, ferocious kiss, so strong that its lust combined with his own blood lust nearly knocked him off his feet. He kissed back hard, so hard he drew blood from her lips, and the sweet coppery taste of it spread like fire through his body, his loins, and he wanted to ravish her right there; ravish her like an animal, tearing great shards of flesh and sinew from her neck, her shoulders, her breast—

"Hold on, tiger. You're getting a little rough there."

With the greatest amount of effort and a self-discipline that he had never known in mortal life, he pulled back, seconds away from her slaughter.

"Whew! You just get me so hot, babe. All hot and bothered." The blood lust rose in him again and he leaned forward, pushing his eager loins against her hips.

"Should we stay here, or do you want to eat out?" She smiled at her double entendre. Frederick felt the wave of blood lust wash over him again, harder, as he tried to shake that picture from his mind.

"Let's get going. I really need something to eat or I'm going to pass out."

Betty kissed him on the lips, but lighter now. "Okay. We can always pick this up later."

"Damn straight!" As he stared at her, he felt the lust grow again, and he thought of another woman who had stirred it in him, not too long ago, and of the last night she had been with him— had been with *anyone*—

"Earth calling Frederick! Hello! I think we'd better get you fed. You're starting to scare me. You sure you're okay?"

"Yeah, I'll be fine. Just need to eat. C'mon, let's go."

"Well, *I* can still go," Norma said, trying to cheer Betty up.

"But that would be only three of us. Are you sure your husband can't get out of helping his brother?"

"No, they've got to finish this up. He says it'll take only a few more weeks, and he's got to do it when he's got the time off. He's been lucky he hasn't had to pull a lot of extra shifts on weekends, but that's going to change when the weather gets nicer and he has to start covering for people on vacation."

"Yeah, I know. I suppose I could wait, but I want you to meet him."

Norma looked at Alicia, who had just sat down at the table. "Alicia, do you bowl?"

"Bowl? Well, I did a couple of times in high school, but that's it."

"What are you doing Saturday night? Do you want to go bowling?"

Betty looked at Norma and then at Alicia. "Yeah, do you want to go bowling? My boyfriend and I were supposed to go with Norma and her hubby, but he can't make it. We need one more person. Wanna come?"

"Well, I don't—"

"C'mon, Alicia. It'll be fun," Norma pleaded. "You don't get out enough."

Alicia winced. *That's what Susie used to say. Maybe she was right.*

Norma wouldn't let up. "It's just one night. After that, you can do whatever it is you normally do on weekends."

"I have errands in the morning. What time?"

"Well, we're going to meet at the Club," Betty said. "You know, the one at my apartment complex. How about six? We can have a drink and then go to that bowling place in Worcester."

Alicia tried to think of an excuse, but there wasn't any. She really didn't have anything urgent to do on Saturday. She was caught up on working co-op hours and her visit with Meg was on Thursday. "Sure, why not."

"Jeez, you don't sound too excited!" Betty said. "Frederick didn't, either. Maybe I should can the bowling idea."

"No, bowling's good. We just have a couple of lazy bones among us," Norma teased, looking at Alicia as if looking over horned-rimmed glasses. "They'll like it, you'll see." Norma punctuated her pronouncement with a light tap on the table. "And we'll *have fun*! Right, Alicia? A good time will be had by all! You'll see!"

Alicia wasn't surprised that Meg owned a house—after all, she did, too—but she was surprised that it was on the north, the more rural side of town. The more expensive side of town. Although she was sure that Meg was earning a good salary as a senior programmer, Alicia was still surprised that Meg could afford a house on the north side on her own.

Crossing Route 9, Alicia felt a curious pang of anxiety at the cluster of buildings near O'Toole's Irish Tavern. She attributed her uneasiness to the traffic that snarled slightly as it approached the environs of the college, and then clogged as it passed over Route 9, where cars were making nearly impossible left turns.

She attributed her uneasiness to the congestion, never wondering if any ghosts from the days before European settlement still haunted the grounds of this older part of town. She never wondered if the ghosts of native Americans, long dead from the tribal warfare of the early 1600s or the "malignant distemper" that ravaged this section of the land of the Nipmuck in 1616, still bothered, three hundred years later, to roam their former hunting grounds.

Did Old Jacob, who made his home on a hill near the Center that was still called Indian Head Hill, regret abandoning his indigenous gods for the Christian God of early missionary John Eliot, or did he sleep in peace, satisfied with the churches that now guarded his land?

It was unusual that Alicia, who filled her inner stillness with intellectual puzzles, never wondered about any of this, nor wondered if, in one of the cars that waited patiently to stream across Route 9, there were people she might know. People whose paths would someday cross hers more literally, more intimately than a chance passing on the road, who hungered for more than just a steak at the tavern.

The congestion lessened as she passed the old Common and its attendant cluster of historic steepled white churches, halls, and private residences, many dating from the 1700s. From there the houses were set further apart until she reached the section of road where housing developments from the '60s branched off. She could see the shadows of the single-story slab houses off to the sides, still not as close together as the houses downtown, but closer than the farmhouses she'd pass as she continued north.

Soon the road showed signs of habitation again, and even modernity, as Alicia braked for a red light at the first lit intersection since crossing Route 9.

"Left at the lights, then drive 3.7 miles..." Alicia strained to read her directions by holding them up to the dashboard lights.

She drove slowly, cautiously, looking in her rearview mirror frequently to make sure she wasn't irritating any of the drivers behind her. There was only one. She signaled, pulled over, and let him pass so that she could look for Meg's house in peace.

Alicia had lived in Danforth almost all of her life, but had been to the north side only once or twice as an adult. She didn't know anyone who lived there, and the area's lack of commerce meant she had no reason to visit. Had she known about its wealth of unspoiled land, open spaces, and even a state park, she might have visited more often, but the odd fact was that she *didn't* know of those amenities.

Like many, she knew less about her own town than she did of the rest of the world. Her ignorance was an ignorance sprouted not from apathy, but more from agoraphobia and a fear of not belonging. She had grown up knowing that the north side of town was the better side of town and that she, and the stock she came from, was not Better. And to her, that meant that the north side, so close in distance, was really quite out of reach.

So, tonight, in contrast to her white-knuckled drive into the city, was, to her, an adventure, one nearly as broadening as her adventure into the lair of the vampire itself.

There was no denying it this time. He could almost smell the crisp, clean air of New England's early spring, could feel the cool dampness on his cheek as, more than a thousand miles away, Alicia emerged from her car, now parked in Meg's driveway.

Wesley could feel all that, and feel the sea change of her life that she felt as she stepped into the semicircle of light that illuminated the side porch.

In one sense, it heartened him, for he knew that Alicia, in her journey, was journeying closer to him, and he looked forward with genteel fascination and just the smallest bit of physical attraction, to his next meeting with her.

Yet it also frightened him, for he knew, even more than she herself could know, the reach of a mind fueled by mystery. Not quite obsessive in her inquiry, she nevertheless was a formidable opponent and the dance of wills they had experienced in the past could soon become all-out war.

He was reminded of the words of an ancient military strategist, that war "is a matter of life and death, a road either to safety or to ruin." And with the strength of a coven behind her, the war could lean less in his favor.

But either way, it was a road that he would soon have to take.

Wesley quickly plotted his travel back to New England. It was still cool enough so that for most of the journey he could withstand an unrefrigerated railcar. Should he risk the passage of a hobo, taking shelter in railroad cars? He had traveled that way in the past, enslaving a footman to arrange the journey, to accompany him and smooth out any wrinkles in the journey. But the trains did not run as often as they had in those days and now the journey would be too long. Each hour on the rails increased the chance of discovery, exposure, and annihilation.

An airplane was quicker, but riskier. A footman could not stay with the casket on its journey. It would be on its own while it awaited loading, and also throughout the trip, during which time Wesley knew he would be vulnerable.

No, he would try again that which he had done on his initial passage south. Somewhere along a lone, deserted highway he would find a truck stop. He would observe and determine which trucks were refrigerated. And then he would select one and enslave its driver.

He shivered somewhat in disgust as he remembered his disappointment with Frederick, how common and crude the man was, how Frederick was not sufficiently disposed to be taught, disciplined, or tamed. Next time he would choose more carefully.

And after he had safely made his way to New England and the driver and his truck were suitably dispatched, he would seek another companion, someone with more intelligence and grace.

"I see you found the place okay." Meg welcomed Alicia into her home.

"Yes, your directions were fine." Alicia stepped in quickly so that Meg wouldn't have to hold the door open to the damp spring air. The wind had risen as she approached the house and she could feel the warmth being sucked out the open door.

"C'mon in. Maybe that's why my college advisor thought I'd be a good programmer— the first part of the aptitude test required you to give directions from one point to another. I've always been good at giving directions."

"Me, too— or at least I think I am!"

Meg turned down the hall and Alicia followed.

The house was an antique colonial, much like the neighboring ones that Alicia had passed en route, wood clapboard covered in white paint, with white trim and black shutters. Inside, it was white again: recent white plaster covered by white paint. Unlike Alicia's mahogany-stained door jambs and doors, Meg's were all painted, and painted white.

The end of the entrance hallway opened to a kitchen that appeared to be recently remodeled. Unlike those in the other colonial houses of the area, the kitchen was spacious, airy, and bright, even at night. Above the spot lighting, Alicia could see skylights and the dim silvery light of a moon just past full.

"What a large kitchen!"

"Big, isn't it? It's really great for entertaining— you know where guests always end up— "

"In the kitchen!"

"Right!" Meg took Alicia's coat from her and draped it over a contemporary-styled Windsor chair. "Speaking of the kitchen, that's where we'll start tonight. The lasagna is heating in the oven. Would you like some tea or soda or something?"

"Tea would be nice."

"Great. Have a seat. I'll put the water on."

As Meg strode to the other side of the kitchen, Alicia took in the details of her surroundings. Bright walls and skylights illuminated a décor that was very traditional, but in a European rather than a colonial American way. It had been over five years since the bicentennial, and for five years before that, it seemed, people had been decorating their houses in an old colonial style: turned spindles on chairs and stair rails, calico chair pads in beiges and browns, and cutesy handcrafted bric-a-brac everywhere. But Meg's house was different, more modern, and held an air of refinement, elegance.

Unlike many modern décors, Meg's hadn't forsaken greenery. Feathery branches of green asparagus ferns tumbled down from plain wooden sconces that had been painted white to match the plaster walls. A large, bushy green ficus sat in a corner, clearly having benefited from its proximity to one of the skylights. Huge matching rubber plants accented opposite sides of the long kitchen, while one specimen Swiss cheese plant stood sentinel to the side of the bathroom door. A large ceramic statue of a sitting orange tiger cat stood next to it. Alicia was about to comment on how beautiful it was when she realized it wasn't a statue.

She automatically stooped to a squat and gently held out her hand, making a kissing sound. "Hi, kitty. What's your name?"

"Oh, I didn't realize that he was down here. He usually spends most of his time upstairs on my bed. That's Sol, after the sun. I've got another cat, Luna, but she's not a people cat. She's likely to hide until you're gone."

Sol approached and sniffed Alicia's hand tentatively. Apparently deciding that anyone who already smelled of cat was probably a cat person, he now forcefully rubbed the sides of his chin and the backs of his ears against Alicia's outstretched hand. His golden fur was plush and soft, with striking reddish tints. A white bib and chin set off the deep rich colors of the red and orange. White fur surrounded the golden discs of his eyes, unlike the dark kohl eyeliner of Moonshadow's eyes. Sol's purring was loud and forceful. Alicia could see why Matricaria named him after the sun, for he was the sun incarnate, in both coloring and disposition.

"What color is Luna?"

"Black and white. She's got one white ear and one black, and half a moustache. I named her Luna after the moon— she's both black, like the new moon, and white like the full. And she's just as mysterious!"

"So, did you name them after their personalities, or was it the reverse?"

"Ah! You're smiling, but you know, that's often the subject of conversation among Witches! I know one household of people who will never name a puppy 'Loki' again!"

Even though Alicia wasn't that versed in Norse mythology, she remembered enough from high school English class to know that Loki was the god of mischief. "I'll remember not to choose that name for a cat!"

Alicia continued to pet Sol, much to his enjoyment. She noticed a name tag and a small silver disk with strange inscriptions. For some reason, it reminded her of the silver encircled stars that she had seen Janith and Rob wearing when she first met them.

Matricaria noticed her fondling the medallion. "That's an amulet of protection. We need to get you one. You're not a silversmith, are you?"

Alicia couldn't suppress a small laugh, "Uh, no... Is that a problem?"

Always assuming she's the problem. We have to work on her self-doubt. "No, not at all. Any object you make with your own hands has more power because it has your energy in it. So, if you knew how to work in silver, I'd suggest you make your own, even if it's not quite the right phase of the moon. Most of us aren't silversmiths, though, so we buy them. Do you know the House of Astrology?"

"Yes, I was there not long ago."

"They have amulets. You should try to get one as soon as possible."

"How much will I need to spend?"

"It depends. There's a magical 'law' that says that one shouldn't haggle over magical goods, but some argue that what it really means is that you shouldn't cheapen the goods. Get what you can afford. You'll probably want something small and on a long chain so that you can hide it easily under clothing. Once you get it, I'll show you how to cleanse and charge it."

"Charge?" Alicia asked, thinking of credit cards.

"Imbue it with magical energy. Energize it."

"Okay."

"Ideally we'd want to purchase and charge it while the moon is waxing— growing from new to full— but you need one now. I don't think that we should wait."

"Is it okay for me to wear one, even if I'm not a witch?"

"Typically, people who wear them *are* witches, but not always. In your case, your life is in danger. You need protection, and that need transcends custom."

The whistle on the teakettle blew and Meg turned to attend to the tea. Sol had had his fill of attention and now moved back to the potted plant to wash himself. Alicia took a seat at the table.

"I don't know what to call you. Are you Matricaria or Meg?"

"At work, I'm always Meg. I'm not out at work."

Alicia thought for a moment. "Out? You're gay?" She had just learned that term from Evan when he described some of his friends as being "out of the closet." She wasn't all that sure that Meg was using it correctly.

"No," Meg laughed gently. "Wrong closet. Some witches have started to use the same terminology as the gay community, except our closet is a *broom* closet. People who choose not to go public about being a witch are said to be 'in the broom closet.'" She smiled and continued, "So, at work, please call me Meg, and *only* Meg. When I'm with the study group or other witches, please call me Matricaria and *only* Matricaria."

"What if I slip?"

"Don't worry. You'll catch on. We've been doing this for ages, and people usually get in the habit quickly, and if they don't, we survive."

"Okay. Should I call you Meg now?"

"Yes, that would make it easier for you. Call me Meg anytime I'm not with other witches."

"Beautiful house, Meg. Have you lived here long?"

"Yes and no. This was my grandparents' house. We lived in it for a few years when I was growing up. After college I rented it from my grand-mother when she moved to Florida. Gramps had died the year before and when she died a few years later, I inherited the house, for which I'll be eternally grateful. Since I don't have a mortgage, I put the money I saved into major improvements like knocking down a wall to make one large kitchen and adding passive solar, skylights, and blown-in foam insulation. I'm still working on it, though. I'll have to show you the 'Before' and 'After' pictures sometime."

"Yes, I'd like to see those."

Meg carefully placed a mug of tea on a coaster in front of Alicia and sat down across from her. "I'm glad you could stop by. I thought it might be a good idea to meet alone, where we could talk freely without worrying about scaring the others."

Alicia smiled. "Yeah, I can imagine they'd be a little freaked."

Meg got up again and selected a box of cookies from a reproduction antique jam cabinet and started to lay them out on a white china plate. "Also, because of your, uh, experiences, you're probably more vulnerable than the others, which is why I suggested the pentacle. There's an old occult belief that when you start studying the unseen worlds, a call rings out on the astral plane announcing your arrival, ringing a sort of 'astral dinner bell.' Astral entities with nothing better to do sit up and take notice."

"Astral entities?"

"Beings on the astral realms. Spirits, elementals, elves— "

"Vampires?"

"Vampires. Because you and I have been exposed—"

"You?" Alicia stopped sipping her tea and looked up. "How were *you* exposed?"

Meg stopped her cookie arranging and looked at Alicia. "Oh, that's right! How could I forget! You don't know."

"Don't know what?" Alicia was confused, but not confused enough to ignore the cookies in front of her.

Meg slid the plate closer to her guest and then continued. "You remember that I arrived on the scene just after the explosion?"

"I heard that you were coming in to check on a job that was running."

Meg nodded. "The explosion happened just as I opened the door. I had seen your car in the lot, so I ran into the building to try to find you. Fortunately, the fire department was close behind me. The smoke was so thick that I don't think I could have rescued you." Meg paused. "Do you want milk in your tea?"

"Oh, no, thanks. I just take sugar."

Meg passed an artistically hand-thrown sugar bowl across the table. Unlike the powder or slate blue of the typical colonial décor, this was a rich, deep cobalt blue, the color of oceans and dreams. "The rescue team ordered me out. As I waited, suddenly things began to make sense. I had been having dreams of a presence, an evil presence. I had done a tarot card reading during a ritual and the cards appeared to be covered in blood. And then when they carried you out of the building, I saw the marks on your throat."

Alicia stiffened and edged away from the table.

"It's okay, Alicia, it's okay. I haven't told anyone outside the coven."

"I thought you probably knew, because I told Janith and Rob about it when I first wrote to them. No, it's just the memory of it, that's all. The marks have faded, but the memory... that's clear as ever."

Meg leaned in closer across the table. "It's okay. We're here to help. The night of the explosion we did a ritual to try to banish him, and we thought we succeeded. But recently we've begun to wonder. We've had sensations—nothing tangible—but sensations that make us think that we're not alone."

Alicia stared down at her hands, breathing slowly and deliberately, trying to calm the rising fear.

"So you've felt it, too. All this time I kept thinking that I was imagining it, that there was a rational explanation for it all, but the more I researched, the more I was convinced it wasn't hallucination, that it was real. And the more I thought about what a grand leap of logic it required for me to believe that, the more I doubted my sanity. I suppose I should be pleased that I'm not crazy." She looked up at Meg with a wan smile and sharply exhaled before continuing. "But I'm not. If this isn't my imagination, then it means that this could be real. That he really *is* a vampire."

"Yes, I'm afraid that might be true. The coven had examined other possibilities. Could he be a psychopath, could you be imagining it, could the wounds be the result of sex play?"

Alicia looked up, surprised.

"No accounting for tastes, you know. Some people like a little pain with their pleasure. It wouldn't be the first time someone had drawn blood, nor the first time that it was done without the other person's permission." She stopped to sip her tea and nibble her cookie before continuing. In the silence, a large grandfather clock ticked away the moments as the two women absorbed what Meg had just said. "But, anyway, we thought it all through. Although any individual instance that we sensed could have been explained away logically, taken as a whole, the clues weren't so easy to brush off. And then, just a few weeks ago, there were the flies."

"The flies?"

Meg opened her mouth to speak, but stopped, rigid and breathless, staring behind Alicia at the broad bay window. There, on the gleaming white-painted sill sat one, then two, then three, and as Alicia turned to see what had caught Meg's attention, a full complement of six flies assembled, preening, staring at the women, and then, as if they were all of one mind, they stopped. And stared back.

"Yes," Meg said as she turned her eyes back to the table to face Alicia. "The flies."

And when they turned back to try to determine what minature demons of hell they could be— the flies were gone.

The rhythmic tic-tic-tic of the clock was a dissonant counterpoint to the fast, crazed beating of Alicia's heart as she stared at Meg. "They're just flies— "

Meg didn't respond immediately. She looked around before speaking.

"Yes. They're called cluster flies, and they're not unusual indoors, even at this time of year. I looked it up in the library. But Alicia, did you notice that there were six— *exactly* six— and that they all appeared at once and then disappeared at once? Did you notice how they all moved in unison, as if they were one mind, or were being *controlled* by one mind."

"You think Wesley's controlling them?"

"Wesley?"

"The vampire."

"How did you learn his name?"

"He told me when I first met him."

Meg looked alarmed. "Alicia, this is important. Where did you meet him?"

"In the computer room."

"Did you invite him in?"

"No. He just appeared, but I know why you're asking. I've read that, too, that a vampire can't come in without being invited. But maybe because a place of business is a public building, he, by being part of the public, was invited in."

"But there's always a guard at the front."

"Maybe the guard invited him in! Maybe the guard was his, his Renfield."

"Yes. In *Dracula*, Renfield was his assistant and what better assistant than one with keys and complete access."

"But your house— and mine— aren't public, so we're safe inside our houses, right?"

"Yes, except for the flies. His minions don't need an invitation because they're still part of the natural world."

"You think they can harm us?"

"Not directly, no. They're still flies, even though they're under his influence. They're not vampires. But I think they're spies and that they report back on what we do." Meg must have seen the confused expression on Alicia's face, for she quickly added, "That doesn't sound right. I don't mean that they march in and give a verbal report. What I mean is that they can transfer impressions, maybe even thoughts, to him."

"Oh, okay. I *was* beginning to wonder!"

"Maybe now is a good time to teach you some of the shielding exercises that you'll be learning eventually in the study group. But you need them now. Have you ever done any meditation or guided imagery exercises?"

"Meditation, in yoga."

"Excellent. You'll need to relax and visualize, just like you do in yoga."

"That's it? No spells, potions, charms?"

"For now it is. You need to learn something that you can use at any time, any place. You can use these techniques at your desk, in your car, or, if you're in a public place, you can either go off in a corner or find the ladies' room. Okay, sit up comfortably in your chair. Try to keep your spine straight, but keep relaxed. You're not trying to be a Marine. You're trying to straighten the spine, the pathway of the life force. Let your hands rest naturally in your lap and close your eyes."

Alicia did as Meg directed, noticing how stiff her back and muscles had become in just the few tense minutes with the flies.

"Breathe slowly and naturally. I want you to imagine all the worries, fears, and anxieties draining down from your head to your toes and flowing down through the floor, past the basement, and into the deep molten core of the earth."

The steady tic-tic of the grandfather clock seemed to fade as Alicia visualized a sludge of anxiety flowing away, through her.

"Let it go, let it all go, and when you feel it's released, I want you to imagine a soft cocoon of white light, a fluffy cloud, surrounding your body. It's soft and comforting, it moves as you move, stretches as you stretch, goes where you go. Now I want you to visualize a similar cloud of light around this room, encompassing us both and all within it."

Meg paused and in the stillness Alicia could feel the white light radiating around the room, could really *feel* it. And whether it was her imagination or not, it felt good, and she felt safe, an ease which she hadn't felt in months.

"Each night before you go to bed, do the same. Start with the cloud around you and then create a larger one around your room. Any time you feel threatened, wherever you are, reinforce the white cloud around you."

Chapter 20

"Candlepin or ten-pin?" Frederick put his arm around Betty's waist as they walked back to the car after dinner. The steak had been perfect; the cook had taken his request for extra-rare steak seriously. Though Frederick still craved the sensuality of the bite, the meal had taken away the urgency. He could wait now. Wait until Betty was lost in the throes of passion. Wait for a short nightcap.

"Ten-pin."

"Dy-na-mite. I can do ten-pin." Frederick was relieved. Though he had played the regional variation of bowling invented in Worcester a century ago, he thought that the bigger, heavier balls of ten-pin might be easier for him to feel, to control.

Betty reached up to kiss him. "You wanna drive?"

"Sure, babe."

She had had a few beers with the meal, at Frederick's insistence. He had nursed his one beer throughout the whole meal. He took the keys from her and unlocked the passenger door.

Sliding onto the seat, she looked up at Frederick with glazed eyes. "Oooh. Those beers really hit me. Guess it's early-to-bed tonight."

Frederick leaned down and gave her an intense kiss on the lips. "That's what I was hopin', babe."

"Mmmm... I'll try to stay awake for that."

"Don't worry. I'll wake you."

"You can leave your boots by the radiator," Janith said, pointing to the wall on the right.

"How are we supposed to plan the Spring ritual when it's *snowing?*" Amber shook off her coat by the radiator and then hung it on the pegs with the others.

"Yes, it's always a challenge when the weather doesn't cooperate. Try this: We're the ancients, it's snowing, we don't know if it'll continue to snow until the end of time, and it's our job to stop it and to bring in the warm weather." Rob smiled and disappeared into the kitchen.

"That must have taken a leap of faith!"

The intercom buzzer sounded and Amber reached over and pushed it. "That's Mat. I saw her drive by, looking for a parking space." Amber opened the door to the hall.

"Hi. Find parking okay?"

"I'm a few blocks down, but it's not bad."

Noticing that she was the last one to arrive, Matricaria removed her boots, hung her coat, and made a quick stop at the bathroom before settling in with a mug of hot tea.

"Before we start talking about the ritual, I thought we'd hear from Matricaria and Gabe about how the new study group is going and talk about what we need to finish up before you all take Third. Mat? Gabe?" Rob took a sip from his own tea and waited.

"Things are going well. I gave a little talk on the religious aspects of the Craft and the Western Mystery Tradition."

"Were they still awake when you finished, Gabe?" Merlin patted Gabe on the shoulder, to let him know he was teasing.

"Awake? They were yelling for an encore!"

Rob smiled. "Mat?"

"I had them introduce themselves and then gave a broad overview of what we're going to cover and reminded them that they could leave at any time."

"How's Alicia doing?"

"I had her over to the house for a private instruction in shielding, as you suggested. While she was there, we had a visitor— no, make that *six* visitors. Six visitors with compound eyes, rubbing their little forelegs together."

"The flies? Where?" Janith had returned to the room.

"At my house."

"Maybe you need an exterminator?" Amber suggested.

"Could be. But there were exactly six, just like at the restaurant. And just like at the restaurant, they all moved in unison, all sat perfectly still, *staring* at us. I'm not an entomologist, but you don't have to be an expert to know that this isn't normal behavior for flies. Also, they all disappeared at the same time. *Completely* disappeared. All at once."

Rob was sitting quietly, his hands clasped at his knees. "This is the first time since we did the binding that we've had contact. Somehow, the binding's come undone. Matricaria, after we did the ritual, you took the poppet home, right?"

"Yes. Janith gave me a square of black silk. I wrapped the poppet in it and took it home, and then buried it."

"Did you put it in anything before you buried it?"

"No. Just put it in the ground."

"One school of thought says that the binding and the poppet must remain intact because they represent on the physical what happens on the astral. If the binding loosens on the physical, it also loosens on the astral. We might have made a mistake burying a doll bound with a cotton cord directly in the ground."

Janith bit her lip for a moment before speaking. "I'm wondering if we didn't think this through well enough. We should have thought about the duration of the spell. This one should have been forever."

"Or longer," Gabe mused.

"But the doll was made of wax. You'd think it would be okay, right? I mean, I can understand if the doll was made of cloth or unfired clay, then it might have disintegrated over time, but wax should have been okay, I would have thought."

"But the problem was the bindings. I'm so used to bindings being temporary things; you know, like binding an ex-lover from doing harm during a breakup just until he cools down, that sort of thing. I never thought about one that would have to last forever. Do you think you could locate the spot where you buried it?"

"Yes, it's near a large stone at the end of the yard. I should be able to."

"But, honey, why does it matter? The binding is obviously loosening, whether the poppet is intact or not."

"True, but if we find the poppet intact— and be careful, Mat, that you don't break it while digging it up— then maybe it's not the same problem. Maybe it's not the vampire at all—"

"Wesley. Alicia told me that his name is Wesley."

"Maybe it's not Wesley who's at the root of this. It could be something else."

"Like another vampire."

"Yes, like another vampire."

Frederick waited close to an hour after they locked up before he approached the building. He was surprised at his own patience and discipline. Five years ago, even three, he wouldn't have been able to stand stock-still in the dark, listening, waiting. But he had found, as time went on, that when you have all eternity, you no longer mind wasting time. At least *he* didn't.

Staying close to the shadows of the building, he trained his ears to the roadway and the sidewalks. No cars were approaching, no one drew near on foot.

The bowling alley was in one of the more run-down towns northwest of Danforth. Frederick had picked it specifically for that reason. With its high crime rate and low tax base, the town had but a small police force, and they kept busy breaking up bar fights and responding to domestic disturbance calls. No one was paying attention to a run-down bowling alley in a deserted part of town.

Frederick had thought long and hard about how he'd get in. He didn't think that the place was wired with an alarm, but what if it was? *Well, you run, dummy.* He knew that he could outrun any cop, any cruiser. And with his supernatural hearing, he'd hear them coming in plenty of time.

He could easily break a window, bars or no bars, but breaking glass was the type of sound that people heard, no matter what other sounds were assaulting their eardrums. Like a baby crying or a trapped kitten in a tree, breaking glass would be *heard*.

But doors being ripped neatly off their hinges wouldn't. For one thing, it wasn't a sound that people heard very often, so they wouldn't recognize it as a bad sound. So, that was his plan: to very casually slide over to the back door, jerk it up off its hinges, slip inside, and prop it back in place. Anyone passing by later wouldn't notice a difference, as long as he kept the lights off.

Cinch! Who needs lights? Frederick smiled. It seemed that the vampire was almost designed for crime. They were fast, strong, and could see in the dark. He moved forward a few feet and then stopped to listen. Nothing. Taking a deep breath, more out of habit than need, he swiftly approached the door, ripped it off, and slipped inside.

The sound had been minimal— a sharp crack and groan, but that was it. By the time it registered on anyone's brain, even the dust and splinters would have settled.

Still, he waited calmly in the doorway, just to be sure.

When you have eternity, you don't mind wasting time as much as you used to. At least he didn't.

"So what do you think we did wrong?" Janith asked, sitting down beside Rob on the couch after the last covener had left.

"I don't think we did anything *wrong*. I think it's more that we didn't think it through. Anything could have happened to that poppet. I don't know how deep Matricaria buried it, but if it wasn't below the frost line— or even if it was— the ground around it had to be subject to freezing and thawing, especially in the spring. Look at the weather we've been having lately— warm, then snow, then warm again ... I wouldn't be surprised if it surfaced. We would have to have put it a few feet under or in a strong metal box, and I don't think she did either. We just weren't thinking it through, that's all."

"Maybe part of the problem was that we didn't think he was real. My feeling of being choked in the circle, that could have just been my reaction to stress, and not a real physical manifestation."

"We still don't know if he's real. Until we actually see someone killed— gods forbid!— or see this person perform feats of strength or survive a killing blow, it's still a matter of opinion whether he's real or not."

Janith sat quietly beside him, not saying anything.

"I know what you're thinking, hon. The first time this all started happening, you said that maybe we should have called in Sumner and Tania, that we should have asked our teachers for help. Maybe you were right. I wanted to think we could do it ourselves, and I thought we had. I really thought we had."

Rob paused and turned to face his partner, his High Priestess, his friend. "Tell you what. We'll let Matricaria dig up the poppet. If it's compromised, then we know that's the problem, and we just do another binding."

"And if it's not?"

"Then we do some more divination to find out what it is that's haunting us. *And* we call Sumner and Tania. I'll call them myself."

"Sounds like a plan." She leaned over and kissed him gently on the cheek. "Love you."

"Love you, too, hon."

As he waited to make sure a silent alarm hadn't sounded, Frederick took in his surroundings. It was a small place, less than twenty lanes, but it still had a bowling-alley smell, that curious mixture of paste wax, stale cigarette smoke, human sweat, stale perfume, and beer.

The seats that were clustered around the scoring area were cracked and taped, the drapes at the windows on the far walls were sagging, but even in the dark, Frederick could tell that the highly-polished wooden lanes gleamed.

He could hear the drip-drip-drip of a poorly maintained faucet in one of the restrooms and the low hum of a refrigeration unit at the bar somewhere behind him. He recognized the steady click of a wall clock and the hum of a fluorescent light at the front entrance, but otherwise the building was deathly still.

To be able to practice unobserved, he needed to be at the *other* end of the lanes. That would mean that his only nearby exit would be the front door. "Shit! Didn't think that one through very well, did I?" He looked up, and when he saw the high windows to the right of the door, he remembered how Wesley had scaled the train station like a spider and wondered if he could do the same. The walls were painted-over cinder block. He was sure that his strong, lean fingers could gain purchase between them, just as Wesley's had with the rough-hewn granite blocks of the train stations. With any luck, he wouldn't need that option, but it was good to know that it existed. Frederick didn't like feeling trapped.

After a few more minutes of complete silence, he decided to make his move. He knew that he could run fast, but still he was amazed at the swiftness with which he traversed the room. Had he not been paying attention, he would have accidentally propelled himself through the far wall!

Pausing again, he listened. Silence. Not even a car. He wondered for a moment if the building was too soundproof for him to hear outside noises, and then, as if on cue, a car drove by. *442. Hemi. That guy's not taking his time, either.* And then a second car, just as fast, and nearly as powerful. *Cruiser!* Feeling more relaxed now that he knew that one of the city's police cars was engaged in chasing a speeder, Frederick approached the long rack of bowling balls.

Again he felt a pang of remorse. In life, he had been fairly active. Bowling was something he did every winter, when baseball died down and basketball wasn't scheduled. But here he stood, staring at the balls, not even remembering what weight he had used last time. How long had it been?

He picked a ball that looked suitably large and hefty, but with his vampire strength it felt light. He'd have to concentrate if he didn't want to be tossing it down the alley like a softball.

Frederick stepped up to the line and drew the ball up to his chin. His eyes misted over as he remembered his buddies in the back, cheering him on, in the years that he played in the league. He remembered the drinks afterward, the pranks, the jokes, the laughter. And now all was silent. Deathly silent.

"C'mon, man, snap out of it," he said aloud, as if saying it aloud could do more to coach him out of the blues than just thinking the words.

Breathing in, he sited the pins at the end of the alley, and drew back, then released, holding his posture like a statue as he waited for the ball to connect.

CRACK! Almost before he could see it, all of the pins were shattered in a puff of sawdust. "DAMN! And I wasn't even trying." He listened for a minute to make sure that no one else heard the crack of the pins, and then selected another ball.

He remembered the time someone dared him to bowl lefty and he could barely get the ball down the lane. He drew the ball to his face with his left hand, sighted his line, and released, but this time he was gentle— at least he thought so. The ball hit the pins with another resounding crack, but they didn't explode into dust and he could hear the ball gently drop down.

"That's better!" He grabbed another one, concentrating less on aim and more on controlling the release enough to make it seem more normal, more human. He hadn't bothered to turn on the ball return. There were enough balls, using each lane only once, for him to get the hang of it.

Even before he had run through the heavy balls, he thought he had it down, but he continued until the last heavy ball was gone. And then, grabbing one of the fresh towels that had been laid out for the next day's business, he calmly left the way he came, being careful to lodge the ripped-off door into the doorway, so engrossed in thought that he forgot to clean out the cash register, a matter that the police would find quite strange when they investigated in the morning.

Chapter 21

Meg sat at the kitchen table studying the weather forecast in the newspaper. She needed to dig up that poppet, and soon, but it was still too dark when she got home from work, and it would be too cold in the morning before she left.

Maybe she could find a reason to make a quick trip home in the middle of the day. Maybe if she said that she had a doctor's appointment, she could rush home, change into gardening clothes, dig it up, clean up, and get back to work in an hour or two. She could make up the time at the end of the day. No, too complicated. What if there was traffic? She'd be better off trying to do it before work.

She stared out of the large bay window into the dark, relaxing into her thoughts, when she began to drift into a near-dreamlike state. The background tick of the grandfather clock faded and the room began to dim as she moved gradually, by imperceptible degrees, into a full but lucid state of trance.

Recognizing her altered state, she seized the opportunity to astrally walk into the darkness of the back yard, out by the large protrusion of rock. In her mind, she could feel the damp cold moss, slippery new blades of grass, and small leaves of gill-over-the-ground as she walked across a patch of lawn where the snow had melted away. The ground had a greenish brown aura, except in one spot, to the left of where she thought she had planted the poppet.

There, instead of a soft, emanating light, she saw a dark swirling miasma of dissolution, decay, and death, and she knew: that's where she would dig for the poppet.

At six o'clock, Alicia was waiting outside The Club for Betty. Seconds later she saw her walking across the parking lot, tugging her coat closed against the wind. Arctic air and strong winds had followed a cold front that enveloped areas from the Dakotas to the Midwest and even New England.

"Hi, Alicia. My boyfriend said he'd meet us inside. Why don't we go on in?"

Alicia followed Betty into the warmth of the dark, smoky club.

"Hey, how's it hangin'?" Rico, the bouncer, gave Betty a hug. "So where ya been? I haven't seen you in weeks."

"Around. My boyfriend and I just haven't been in, that's all."

"Oh, so you and Freddie are a twosome, huh?" Rico pulled back, feigning surprise, but it was clear that he knew it already and was just trying to get more information without prying.

"Yeah, I guess we are." Betty was smiling shyly, but Alicia could tell she was proud. "Is he here yet?"

"Nah, not yet. I'll tell him you're here when he shows. He's a lucky man, and you can tell him I said so, okay?"

"Okay, I will." Betty smiled, flattered.

Betty started to walk in, with Alicia behind her. Rico put out a hand to stop her. "Betty, she's your guest, right?"

"Oh, yeah. Silly me. This is Alicia, my friend from work."

Rico extended a strong, very muscular hand. "Rico. Welcome to the Club."

"Hi."

With his other hand, he guided her in. "Hey, have a beer for me."

"She doesn't drink beer," Betty said.

"No beer? What do you drink?"

"Sombrero or some other drink with milk or cream."

"What a wimp!" Rico made a pretense of putting her down, but Alicia didn't feel insulted. Though he was built like Superman on steroids, and could act as tough as the next guy, he had a warmth about him that made Alicia feel *safe*, not threatened.

"Yeah, I know, but I don't like beer."

"Hey, have something for me anyway. I can't drink on duty."

"When you're off, we'll buy you one, okay?" Betty called back.

"Deal!"

As they entered, Alicia noticed how Betty seemed to know everyone and how friendly they seemed toward her. *Well, she lives in the complex. Of course she knows everyone here.*

A second later, though, she was back to being self-critical. *Yeah, and would you know everyone if you lived here? No, you wouldn't even know Rico. You'd be too shy to talk to even him.* As Betty introduced her to everyone that they encountered, Alicia's inner argument continued. *Yes, but that's okay. You're just not that social. Remember what the therapist said— it's okay to be different! So it's okay if you're not a social butterfly.*

As Betty continued to banter among her neighbors, Alicia flashed back to her friend Susie. This was just how it was when she went out with Susie. Susie would flit among the admiring crowd, trading pleasantries, asking how people were, lavishing compliments, and Alicia would trail behind, a mellow smile frozen on her face, wondering what she was doing there. *You're going bowling with Betty, Norma, and Betty's new boyfriend. That's what you're doing here.*

Norma! She tapped Betty gently on the shoulder. "Betty, what about Norma? Will she be able to get in?"

"Uh-oh, that's right! I'll go tell Rico."

"If you want, I'll tell him. I'm not doing anything. You stay here with your friends."

"Would you? Thanks! You're a doll."

Alicia threaded back through the crowd, relieved that she had something to do besides smile and forget names. In the few minutes since she and Betty arrived, the crowd had started to thicken, no doubt with people arriving after work. She wondered if they had enough exits if something went wrong. *Okay, stop that. You're fine. You've got a better chance of being bored to death than being trampled during a fire.*

When at last she made it to the entrance, Rico was welcoming people in, commenting on the weather, asking about boyfriends and spouses. *It's almost like a family,* she thought, and for a dizzying second she was pulled deep into the old whirlpool of depression, remembering that her parents were gone, remembering that she was an only child, and feeling abandoned, unloved, disconnected, until, with a snap of will and a shake of her head, she pulled herself out of it.

Just in time to spot Frederick.

"Hey, Freddie, my man!" Rico reached out and gave him a playful punch. But Frederick wasn't very jocular tonight. He had recognized the young woman coming toward the entrance.

Fuck! It's Alicia!! I thought Betty said her friend's name was LISA! Shit! That'll teach me to pay attention.

"Hey, man, you okay?" Rico turned Frederick gently by the arm so that he could see his face.

"Oh, yeah, sure. Whew. Just a little tired." *It's okay. She doesn't seem to recognize you. Just act cool!*

Frederick thought back to the first time that he had seen her. He had managed to get into the main building at Theoretic when a power failure distracted the guards and temporarily disabled the security systems. He had been cutting through the parking lot on his way somewhere else when it had happened. He had taken advantage of it quickly, not thinking what he would do once he got in.

He had walked quickly by the front desk, trying to get safely into the interior before the guards returned. He saw a door with a combination lock on it, and hoping that the power cut meant that the lock was disabled, he gave it a try. It opened, and he slipped in quietly, hoping to hide out for a few minutes until the guards returned to their stations.

In the dark he could see someone slumped in a chair. The sound of the door latch must have woken her, for she immediately stirred. She shivered, wrapped her arms around herself, slid off the chair, and walked to the thermostat.

Frederick being Frederick, he couldn't resist a smart-assed remark. "Cold, isn't it," he had said.

She had spun around, and she would have seen him if it hadn't been for the distraction of the power coming back on at that exact moment. The flash of the overhead lights blinking on and the loud thud of the power kicking back in gave him the cover to slip out the door before her eyes could adjust.

Yeah, that's right. She didn't see you. She couldn't have. The lights would have blinded her and you split the instant they came on.

Rico was speaking again, drawing Frederick back to the present. "Well, c'mon in, then. People are backing up behind you, and the door's wide open. We're not payin' to heat the whole state of Massachusetts here!"

Alicia stood back to let him pass. Frederick could see a perplexed look eclipsing her face, a look indicating clearly that she felt that there was something disturbing about the man; something that flittered just beyond her understanding.

And Frederick— being Frederick— couldn't stop himself from calling back to Rico, at the very moment he passed in front of Alicia,

"Yeah, cold, isn't it?"

Cold, isn't it?

It felt like a band tightening around her head. *Cold, isn't it?* Where had she heard those words? *Cold... isn't it... isn't it... isn't it?*

That night, that first night that she thought she saw something in the computer room... But that was Wesley, wasn't it? And this man in the black and yellow stadium jacket was *not* Wesley. This was just one of the guys. And it was mere coincidence that he said those words.

"Hey, what's your name again?" It was Rico, gently brushing her arm.

"A-Alicia."

"Alicia, that was Betty's boyfriend." He gestured toward Frederick. "Weren't you ladies waiting for him?"

"Yes..." *Yes, but... But what? Yes, but I don't want to meet him until I figure out why he gives me the creeps?* "Yes, but we're waiting for someone else, another—"

Just then Norma pushed through the door, exhaling loudly and stamping her feet. "Whew, cold, isn't it?"

Okay, see, she just said it! Everyone says it. It's just one of those phrases! Then why don't I feel strange, like I did when HE said it?

It was because *he* was cold! He had radiated cold like the walls of her house when she had returned home from work, having left the thermostat too low. A cold that followed you, enveloped you... *But he just came in from the cold. Of course, he's cold! Anyone would be, right?*

Trying to test her theory that someone coming in from the cold would radiate cold, she stepped closer to Norma. No, this was not the soul-sucking cold she felt when Betty's boyfriend walked in.

"So, are they inside?"

"Oh, yeah, sorry! Betty sent me here to get you, and I'm just standing here like a lump. Rico, she's another one of Betty's guests."

"Hey, I dunno, two guests..."

He was turned half-facing them and was leaning in toward them in what could have been a menacing posture, but he was smiling.

"G'wan. Tell Betty she owes me."

"Will do. C'mon, Norma."

As she walked Norma into the main room, she thought again of the weird sensation when Betty's boyfriend had passed. He didn't look threatening. He was very average of build, very casually dressed, but there was a sense about him that any moment the tides could turn, that *he* could turn. It made no sense. If she were to fear anyone tonight, it should have been Rico. Solid muscle from head to foot with forearms that could break concrete, he was a 3D model of power.

But Betty's boyfriend emanated a different power, a stealthy, darker power that lurked just below his civil exterior.

"Hey!" Betty called out, waving to them. Alicia and Norma headed toward her. When they reached the table, Betty began the introductions. "Alicia, Norma, this is my boyfriend, Frederick."

It was then that Alicia remembered. The last time that she spoke to Susie, she was getting ready for a date with her new boyfriend— Frederick.

"Hey, Alicia." Betty was reaching across the low cocktail table, grabbing the hem of Alicia's jacket. "Earth to planet Alicia. You okay?"

Alicia blinked as if awakening from sleep, then responded, "Oh, yeah, yeah, I'm fine. Just thought of something I need to do at work tomorrow."

"Work, work, work. You should chill out a bit, right, Frederick?"

Frederick had moved his beer to his lips, as if he would drink, but instead he was staring straight at Alicia, having caught her gaze, his eyes opening wider, his head and neck tensed, inclined toward her, and for the briefest of moments he was completely still, silent.

He hadn't fully figured it out, but he knew that if he thought hard enough, and stared long enough, sometimes people bent to his will. It was happening more and more these days, and seemed to take less time than it did when he first started trying to imitate Wesley's control over others. *You don't know me. You've never seen me before tonight. Everything's okay.*

"Frederick? Oh, geez, not you, too? What's the matter with everyone?"

You don't know me. You've never seen me before tonight. Everything's okay.

Betty gave Frederick a quick slap on the upper arm. "Frederick?"

He quickly snapped back to attention. "What? What? I was trying to see the TV over the bar. Any law against that?"

"Well, don't get too interested. We're going to leave for bowling soon. Alicia, you want a drink before we go?"

"No, that's okay. I probably shouldn't drink on an empty stomach."

"Gee, you really *are* a wimp!"

Frederick smiled behind his raised bottle of beer. *That's what I'm countin' on.*

"You know where it is, right?" Betty called out to Alicia as she slid into the passenger seat of her car, having once again turned over the driving to Frederick.

"Yup. Route 9 west. The road is on the right and then it's a mile down on the left."

"Okay, we'll meet you inside the door."

As she buckled her seatbelt and started the car, Alicia tried to process what had just happened. She had heard Betty's boyfriend's name, Frederick, which had reminded her of Susie's boyfriend. That was understandable. What had happened next was not.

It was almost as if Frederick knew what she was thinking—knew, saw, and feared it. She had looked at him, and from there the recollection was hazy. She could remember looking at him and she could also remember Betty asking her if she wanted a drink before they left. But somehow the space between those two events had taken on an extraordinary long shape and she felt as if there was something in there that she was missing, something important that she needed to remember.

Too soon she saw the set of lights that Betty had given as a landmark. She quickly pulled off the highway into the parking lot of the bowling alley.

Maybe she had just been upset over the remembrance of Susie. Maybe, in that short, quick, slip into sadness, it had just seemed as though the time took on special import. Maybe there was nothing wrong.

Why should she assume that there was any connection between her state of mind and Betty's boyfriend?

What am I getting so worked up about? I don't know him. I've never seen him before tonight. And everything's okay...

The predictable smells of stale smoke, fermenting sweat, and beer welcomed them to the overheated bowling alley. Frederick mused that of all the heightened senses that he had acquired since becoming a vampire, the sense of smell had to be the worst. He could smell the funky odor of old bowling shoes heavily laced with spray disinfectant even before he entered the building, and the smell of melted cheese from the pizza concession that mingled with the disagreeable odors of old hamburger grease and rotting garbage.

At the far end, in front of the snack bar, a group of young children were finishing up their game, their screeches and whines mixing poorly with the sounds of pins clacking together in the background.

One of the pre-school kids had rolled the ball so ineffectually that it looked as if it would stop before it even made it halfway down the lane. Frederick stood watching as the corners of the child's mouth turned downward in an ever-increasing frown, his lip quivering as the all-too-expected wails began. He dropped to the floor and rolled in a tantrum, more tired than disappointed in his athletic skill, his crankiness leaking out in a loud, wracking sob, tears mingling with snot on the highly polished floor.

"Brats!" Frederick's voice was low and saturated with disgust.

"Loverboy doesn't like kids?" Norma teased Betty, just out of Frederick's earshot.

"That's a relief!" Betty said, "I'm definitely not ready for that!" Her eyes conveyed a wistfulness that her voice belied.

Frederick, of course, could hear it all. Since his back was to Betty and he couldn't see the look in her eyes, he believed her lie. *That's good, babe. Not sure I could even make any if I wanted to.* Wesley had never mentioned what effect the vampire life had on a man's ability to father, and Frederick had never asked. It had never occurred to him. In his mind, he was still too young to settle down. Telling Betty that they might move in together was closer to settling down than he had ever been, and over the last few days he was beginning to wonder if that was a mistake. She had been getting more bossy lately, asking him where he was going, making plans for him—like bowling.

At the nearest lane, a tall brunette with long legs and ample frontage was bowling in a mini-skirt. Frederick smiled as he noticed the group of locals at the snack bar leering openly, their mouths agape as they casually moved closer to the lanes.

"Hey, hon, look at that. They have midnight bowling, with music and stuff. Maybe we should try it?" Betty was pointing to a large sign behind the cash register.

"Why don't we wait and see how this works out. You may not ever want to go bowling with me again."

"Hey, at least there wouldn't be any ankle-biters there." Betty's voice again belied her true feelings.

A teenage clerk approached the register. "How many?"

"Four," Betty said confidently, taking the lead.

"Pay here for the shoes, then wait at the rental counter and I'll be right over," the clerk instructed.

Frederick handed the kid a twenty before Betty could read out the total. "My treat."

"Hey, big spender, thanks!"

As the others thanked him, the kid moved over to the rental section. Frederick looked back at the brunette, thinking of how all it would take was a few minutes, a direct stare, and a little bit of thought, and she'd be leaving with him. Betty would kill him, of course— *if she could.*

A wave of giddiness started deep in his solar plexus and flushed over him. Betty couldn't hem him in— no one could. If he wanted, no one could stop him from doing *anything*!

Easy, boy. Easy. Thoughts like that could get you in a lot of trouble. He still didn't know if he could die, and what could kill him if he could. If Betty broke the top off a bottle and stabbed him in the neck, would he bleed to death? And what if he grabbed her and drank her blood? Could he drink fast enough not to bleed out?

"You want shoes?" The kid was in front of Frederick.

"Huh? Oh, yeah. Ten."

The kid handed Frederick a scuffed pair of gray and maroon rentals. Frederick held them as far away from his supersensitive nose as he could without being obvious and stepped aside from the counter.

Norma got her shoes next. As she walked away, past Alicia, she mumbled, "Still wet with disinfectant. I guess that's better than being still warm!"

Alicia laughed and approached the counter.

"Size?"

"Seven and a half."

"We just have them in whole sizes."

"Okay, eight, I guess."

"Eight."

"Alicia haven't you bowled before?" Betty asked as she stepped up for her shoes. "Nine."

"Yeah, but not very often and it's been a long time."

"Well, don't worry, we're just here to have a good time."

The kid handed Betty her shoes and pointed to the opposite end of the alley. "Lane six, as soon as it's open. They're almost finished."

"Six it is. C'mon, gang. Let's get some food first, and then wait over by lane six."

As they walked toward their destination, Frederick turned and took one last look at the long-legged brunette with ample frontage. *Meet me out back in two minutes*, he thought, staring hard with an intensity that sent waves of energy off his body.

The brunette let loose her ball, stood motionless until it connected, and then turned to Frederick—

And winked.

"Hey, hon, you want to get me a cheeseburger with fries? I've got to go to the little boy's room."

"Let me guess— extra rare, right?"

"You got it." Frederick gave her a quick kiss on the lips. "I'll be back soon."

Betty turned to Norma and Alicia, "You guys want to share a pizza? Pepperoni with extra cheese?"

"Fine with me."

"Sure."

Betty turned to give her order to the clerk. Norma dug in her purse for money. Alicia, who already had her money out, just happened to be looking in the direction of the rest rooms when she noticed Frederick stop, look around, and then take a slight detour out a side door. *I wonder where he's going...*

Betty turned to Norma, "So, what do you think?"

"What a hunk! And he's nice, too!"

"Alicia?"

"What?"

"What do you think?"

"Uh," she tried to think of something good to say. Even if she hadn't just seen him sneak out the exit, there was something about him that made her uncomfortable. Something hollow, yet edgy. "Yeah, he seems nice."

"Nice? Just nice?"

"Well, I just met him. We haven't had a chance to talk."

"Talk?" Betty laughed. "There's more to men than brains!"

"Some would say there's not even that," Norma kidded.

"Really?" Alicia smiled good-naturedly. Maybe in their world, brains weren't that important, but to her, they were *very* important. She couldn't imagine getting close to a man like Frederick, no matter how handsome or brawny he was. On the other hand, Evan, who was so slight that he was almost effeminate, was immensely attractive to her.

She found herself wondering how Evan was doing. He had said that he would be staying late at the computer center tonight, working on an assignment that was due Monday. She wished that she could be there with him instead of here. Maybe she could help him with his work. And she'd certainly be better at *that* than at bowling.

"Alicia, want to snag us a table over by six while we wait for the food?"

"Sure. If you need help carrying anything, just wave, okay? Oh, and here's some money."

Alicia dodged her way past the full tables to an empty one near lane six. Across the room she could see the signs for the rest rooms. The mystery of Frederick gnawed at her. Maybe he just went out for air. *It is pretty stuffy in here.* She had noticed how he wrinkled his nose when they first walked in. Maybe he just had a good sense of smell.

It's none of my business. He's Betty's boyfriend. But Betty's your friend.. You'd want your friend to tell you... Stop being so paranoid! He's probably just gone out for air. Then why didn't he just say so? He's a big boy. He doesn't have to ask for permission. But why did he lie about going to the men's room?

Alicia realized that her inner dialog was getting out of control and began to do some breathing exercises to calm down. Not wanting to close her eyes and appear odd in a public place, she looked in the general direction of the bowlers at the far end of the alley, pretending to watch. She began to slow her breathing and to imagine the anxiety and tension sloughing off her like dead skin. Feeling cleansed and relaxed, she tried the protection exercises that Matricaria taught her.

She imagined a soft, white protective cloud forming around her, shielding her and swaddling her, keeping her safe from the world and its evil. When she felt sufficiently cocooned, she blinked a few times and brought her focus back to the table, just as Betty and Norma arrived with the food.

She was waiting around back, as Frederick had instructed her, her arms folded tightly against her slim body in defense of the cold, her legs pressing against each other for warmth.

"Hi," she said, a little unsure. "I want you to know that I don't usually do this. I don't know what I'm doing out here."

Yeah, that's what they all say. "You're making a date, that's what!"

She laughed and tossed her hair seductively. "You seem to already have one."

"Oh, her? Yeah, but we're not, like, married or anything. We date. What about you?"

"No, I'm not married."

"So, whaddya say? It's not like I'm asking you to sleep with me or anything. Want to meet for a drink later?"

"How later?"

"Midnight?"

"Okay... Midnight. Where?"

"How about here? They have that midnight bowling thing, right?"

"Yeah, they do."

"Okay, so I'll meet you back here at midnight."

"Okay, midnight."

Frederick leaned forward and kissed her on the cheek. "Midnight it is, beautiful."

"Lane six is open," the voice on the loudspeaker was barely discernable over the music and clacking pins.

"Okay, guys, that's ours. We need to get balls. Anyone seen Frederick?" Betty was looking out over the alley.

"There he is," Norma pointed.

"What was he doing outside? I thought he said he had to go to the little boy's room?"

"Maybe he *went* outside!"

"Norma!"

"Frederick! Over here. The lane's open."

"Anyone see any blue ones? I always bowl with a blue ball. I know it sounds crazy, but I always do better with blue balls."

"Blue balls? Norma! Get your mind out of the gutter!"

Norma laughed. "Betty, this time it's *your* mind that's in the gutter! I was talking about bowling balls!"

Norma grabbed a marbelized blue ball and sat down at the scoring table like an old pro, slipping the score sheet under the metal clip, writing the names in the columns. "Betty, it was your idea, so you go first, then Frederick, then Alicia, then me."

"Can I go last? I haven't played in ages. I want to watch your technique."

"Technique? Ha! You won't learn much from me, but I'll put you last. There. Okay?"

"Thank you."

Betty nuzzled behind Frederick. "Oooh, you're cold. Were you outside?"

"You know me. I always feel cold, but yeah, I stepped outside for some air. It's really smoky in here."

"Yeah, I think it's that team at the far end. They've been smoking like chimneys."

Betty was leaning into Frederick seductively.

"Okay, Betty, save it for the bedroom. You're up."

Betty pretended to scold her friend and co-worker as she walked to position at the top of the lane. "Norma! How rude!"

Frederick watched as Betty released the ball. She was as physically attractive as the brunette he would be meeting at midnight, but with the brunette there was a sense of adventure, of danger, of the unknown. What would she smell like? What would she look like, close up and in the light? Would all the guys who were watching her now be watching him, wishing they were him? Would she take him home...

"Frederick, wake up!" Norma seemed to have taken on the role of team leader. "Your turn."

Frederick causally walked over to the ball return. As he picked up the ball, its lightness reminded him to bowl gently. He remembered his experience with the basketball. And the door he ripped off the gas station. And the bowling pins that disintegrated into sawdust just a few nights ago when he practiced.

Easy, boy. E-a-s-y. He stepped up and released the ball, lightly, slowly. Yet still it sped down the lane and hit the pins dead center, with a resounding crack. "Stee-rike!" Frederick called, more in the voice of a baseball announcer than a bowling commentator.

"Way to go, Frederick! Way to go!" Betty was beside him, hugging him. Feeling proud and expansive, he returned the hug and kissed her gently on the forehead. "Yeah, not bad, not bad."

"Okay, out of the way, Carmen Salvino," Norma said as she pushed through to position, smiling at Frederick and Betty, who stepped back to the scoring table.

Her first ball downed seven pins. Her second downed the last three.

Betty recorded Norma's spare. "Alicia, you're up."

As Alicia moved into position, Frederick noticed something strange. There was a fuzzy, indistinctness to her, as if he was looking at a photograph taken through gauze. He looked away, to the other bowlers, thinking that maybe it was a trick of the lights that he hadn't noticed before, but they all looked normal. Frederick looked back at Alicia just in time to yell, "DUCK!"

She had adopted a reasonable stance, but when she drew back her arm, she accidentally let go of the ball, which flew at full speed into the chairs surrounding the scoring table.

Alicia's first concern was the bystanders. "Oh, my God. Is everyone okay? Did I break anything?"

"Alicia, you're dangerous!"

"Yeah, I know. I warned you. I'm not very coordinated." She looked around at the chairs and the tables behind the barrier that separated the lanes from the general bowling alley.

"Do you do this all the time?"

"No. Usually I just bowl gutter balls. I got fifteen in one game, once."

"Fifteen? Alicia, there are only twenty balls in a game."

"Yeah, I know. I told you I wasn't very coordinated."

Alicia approached the chairs, looking for the errant ball. Frederick handed it to her and as she took it from him, she noticed something odd: he was staring. And he almost looked frightened. They stood opposite, each looking into the other's eyes, for what seemed like an eternity before Norma took charge.

"Alicia, come with me. The grip's too loose on that ball and the drilling is probably too wide for your hand. Let's find one that fits better." Norma led Alicia away from Frederick, but not from the puzzle.

Why did he look at me that way? I know I just let the ball loose, and people could have been hurt, but he must know that wasn't deliberate... Maybe he doesn't?

"Let me see the hand you bowl with," Norma demanded.

Alicia extended her right hand.

"Just as I thought. Small hand, short fingers. The ball you had was more a guy's size. Okay, let's look at... this one."

Norma handed Alicia a ball to try. Frederick stood behind Norma now, and once again he was looking at Alicia, almost squinting, as if he couldn't see properly.

"How does it feel, huh?" Norma was tapping Alicia's shoulder.

"It feels a little tight."

Alicia handed the ball back, and looked again at Frederick. He was still staring, but this time it was an intent stare, a stare directed squarely at her.

"Okay, let's try another one."

When Norma stepped away to get another ball, Alicia could see that Frederick's hands, by his sides, were slightly clenched. Intellectually, she found his posture disturbing, but emotionally it was as if she were watching someone on television, or someone miles away.

"Okay, try this one. This looks more your size."

Alicia slipped her fingers into the ball, but her attention was on figuring out the strange situation with Frederick. There was a fierceness to Frederick's stare that just didn't seem able to penetrate her, as if—

As if she were surrounded by a protective layer!

"Yeah, yeah, this one fits."

"Are you sure? You don't sound sure."

"Yes. Look." She rotated her wrist to demonstrate.

As Norma leaned over to check the fit of the ball, Alicia looked up at Frederick. He was still staring, but now a look of surprise and puzzlement washed over his face. He turned quickly away.

"Yeah, much better. Okay, let's try again. Since you weren't anywhere *near* the lane that time, we won't count that first ball, okay? You guys all right with that?"

"Just as long as she doesn't do it again!" Betty was now standing behind Frederick, pretending to use him as a block.

"Sure. Fine with me."

But Frederick didn't look fine, Alicia thought. He looked worried. Alicia stepped into position and let the ball roll.

"Six pins! See, Alicia, that's all you needed was a good fit! No one ever told you to check the fit when you kept letting go on the backswing?"

"No. My ex-boyfriend just told me I was doing it wrong."

"If he had been just a little more helpful, you would have learned how to bowl well. Maybe you guys would have joined a league or something. Maybe you'd still be together."

"Maybe." *Yeah, just what I needed. A life of boredom at the lanes.*

Alicia bowled the next ball of the frame, hitting the remaining four pins.

"Spare! See, Alicia, you're not bad!"

"Well, I didn't say I was bad— I said I was dangerous!"

"Well, now that we've figured out that it's a grip problem, you aren't *dangerous* anymore, either. Hey, maybe you should go bowling more often. Might meet someone."

Yes, someone who likes to hang out at bowling alleys.

"Betty, you're up."

As Betty approached the ball return and Norma recorded the latest score, Alicia stole a furtive glance at Frederick. He wasn't staring at her this time, but he was definitely troubled. His mouth was straight, his jaw set, and he stared straight ahead into the lanes, not really focusing, not really there.

Betty stepped up to the lane and looked back at Frederick, too, and Alicia could see that she, too, was puzzled by his demeanor. Betty opened her mouth as if to talk, but then turned back to the lane.

She bowled a four, and then a six. Earlier, Frederick might have congratulated her on the spare, but now he just stared ahead, not even noticing.

"Spare!" At least Norma was paying attention. "You keep this up and you might come in second. Okay, lover boy. You're up. And in first place, too! Frederick?"

Frederick responded to his name and the jovial trickster was back. "First place, huh? Well, I'm just going to have to make sure I stay there. Let's see... A couple of strikes should do it."

And a couple of strikes it was. Two in a row. And then another. Betty was overjoyed, jumping and clapping her hands when she wasn't wrapping herself around Frederick in a showy hug. Norma kidded him about joining her husband's team.

Alicia just stood back and wondered: What had disturbed Frederick and why wouldn't he look in her direction anymore?

Frederick, of course, won. Betty and Norma had given him a good fight for the title. Alicia had been solidly in last place the entire game. But she had managed not to let the ball go on the backswing again and had only two gutter balls, and that, for her, was a big improvement.

Frederick seemed more relaxed after his win, buying a round of drinks. As Alicia sipped cheap white wine from a plastic cup, she noticed something odd. Frederick seemed distant from her, *physically distant.*

"Alicia, you need to practice! Want to come bowling again sometime?" Norma had placed a friendly hand on her shoulder.

"Thanks, but school's going to be starting soon— "

"School? It's going to be summer soon."

"I know. I'm going to try to get in a course or two during the summer session."

"Gee, what a wet blanket!"

"I know. I've heard that before. My friend Susie used to say it all the time."

Alicia hadn't known she was going to say it before she blurted it out, but as she did, a confused thought had crossed her mind regarding Susie's mysterious boyfriend.

She looked over at Frederick, and if it could be possible, he looked paler than usual—and afraid.

Alicia finished her post-bowling drink as quickly as she could without drinking *too* fast, and then made her move to leave.

After her comment about Susie, Norma and Betty had reproached her, saying that she needed to get out more, that she was working too hard, and that she was going to be an old maid if she didn't do something.

Frederick had stood by silently, staring. His look of fear changed to grim acceptance and then resolution.

She didn't know what his resolve entailed, but she knew that she had to get out of there and home, where she felt that somehow she would be safe.

Remembering her manners, she thanked them all for the evening, and thanked Frederick for the drink. He looked at her— sadly, it seemed— and mumbled "No problem" or something similar in a flat, colorless voice, before turning away to order another round for the rest of them.

In the parking lot, a strange sense hit her, one that she knew she had felt before. In a few minutes she had traced it to a summer evening, just before Wesley had arrived.

Now, as then, the dark seemed to move and the sense of *déjà vu* was so strong that it was annoying, making her head buzz.

The night air smelled of exhaust fumes and wet earth. It was so different from the stuffy, stale air of the bowling alley. Above, a moon just past full slowly dragged itself toward zenith.

And then the night stood breathless, immobile. Somewhere off to her left she thought that she saw something; a shadow, too fleeting to present any tangible danger, but there, in the darkness, a shadow.

Paranoia?

Or a glimpse of what was to come?

After they had drunk the second round on Frederick, they left the bowling alley, Norma driving away on her own, and Frederick squiring Betty back to the apartment complex. She had just kicked off her heels and hung up her coat when he said, "Hey, look at the time. 11:30. I'm bushed. I'm just going to go home tonight and get some sleep, okay?" He gave Betty a hug and a long, tender kiss.

"Sure I couldn't convince you to stay for just, say, half an hour?"

"Nah, babe, you know what would happen, and then I wouldn't be able to get up in the morning."

"I've never known you to sleep past dawn."

"Well, tomorrow I would. I don't know if it's the bowling or the beers, but I'm really wiped out."

"You could just sleep, y'know. We don't have to do anything. Why don't you stay?"

Frederick shifted on his feet, irritated at her well-meant relentlessness. *Won't she ever give up? She's like a freakin' bulldog.* "Nah, I didn't bring any clean clothes, so I'd have to get up early and shower. I'll just go home and crash."

"Okay." Her voice betrayed her disappointment. "You coming over tomorrow?"

"You bet, babe. I'll be over around 7:30. How's that?"

"Okay."

She didn't look too happy about his plans, but Frederick wasn't about to make any concessions.

"Hey, I'd better go before I fall asleep standing here. I'll see ya tomorrow night, okay?"

"Okay."

Betty walked him to the door and gave him another goodnight kiss, but Frederick smoothly cut it short.

As he stood waiting for the elevator, he thought again of Alicia...and her friend... *Nah, it can't be the same one! Sue's a common name. Well, maybe not 'Susie,' but, hey, close enough.*

But what if it *was* the same person? How much did Alicia know? What had Susie told her? *These chicks tell each other everything.*

The door opened and Frederick was glad to see that the elevator was empty. He was in no mood to ride with strangers. *I don't need to deal with this shit. I'll just do that mind control thing.* Except that Alicia seemed immune to his power. It was almost as though she were standing behind glass or something. First there was that weird effect of her looking soft and fuzzy, and then it was as though he couldn't connect, as if she were shielded.

But, Frederick being Frederick, by the time the elevator had traveled the few floors to the lobby, he was thinking of something else...

Frederick would be thinking of a tall brunette with long legs and ample frontage who would be waiting at the alley for him.

Frederick could hear the pounding disco music as he traversed the parking lot. He stopped at a truck's side view mirror to check his appearance. "So, what's the deal about vampires and mirrors, huh?" he asked no one. "I can see myself perfectly." He pushed a few stray hairs back with his right hand. "Yeah, look. Solid as a rock. It's not like I'm a ghost or anything."

As he stared into the mirror, Frederick thought about how a ghost might look. At that very second, at that very moment, his image began to fade, to become more translucent, until it looked like a double exposure on a photograph.

"Hol-y shit!"

He looked around to make sure that no one was watching him, just as worried about someone finding him talking to himself as about someone seeing his disappearing image.

He looked again. His image was back to being normal. Solid. Did he imagine that he saw himself fading? Again he thought of what a ghost might look like, and as he stared, his image began to pale.

"Okay, okay. So what would it look like if I was invisible?"

He continued to look in the mirror, thinking of what his reflection would look like if he were invisible.

His image continued to fade, until there was *no* image, and he was staring in the truck's mirror, seeing only the cars parked behind him.

Okay, so am I invisible to everyone or just to the mirror?

A car door slammed, and then another, just a few feet away.

Time to check this out!

A young couple, bowling bags in hand, approached the entrance. Frederick stood as still as he could, making no noise until the couple were less than five feet away. At that point, he jerked his head up, in a signal of recognition.

"How ya' doin'," the man said to Frederick.

"Not bad, not bad."

Shit! They can *see me.*

Frederick was a little disappointed with his discovery. *Invisible Man, now* that *would have been cool!*

Still, he had other talents. He shrugged his shoulders and turned to face the double glass doors of the entrance. Inside, the lights were lowered, and a disco ball and black lights lit brightly colored posters on the walls.

The brunette was sitting alone at a table, watching the bowling, trying to look cool. Frederick thought of going in there to meet her, as they originally planned, but, for once in his life, he decided to think things through.

If he went in there, people would see him, and for what he wanted to do to her, he didn't want witnesses of any kind.

In the mood for experimentation, he thought of a different approach. She would come to him. *I wonder if that brain thing works long distance?* If it didn't, he could turn around and go back to Betty, and no one would ever be the wiser. However, if it worked...

He looked around the parking lot to make sure that he was unobserved. He could see a couple in a BMW in the middle row, but they were too busy snorting coke to notice anything else.

Frederick turned back to the glass doors, and in his best movie vampire style stared through the doors at the brunette with ample frontage. As he stared, he thought, *Come to me. Come to me. Out back where we met before. Come to me.*

She had been watching people bowling, but now she dropped her head slightly to the side as if she heard something. Before she could turn all the way around, Frederick stepped away from the glass doors and walked quickly to the back of the building, where they had met earlier.

Waiting for her there, he thought of what he'd do next. The couple entering earlier had seen him there. If there was an accident or if she was injured, they might remember him. Maybe it was better if he stood her up and picked someone else.

As he heard her low heels crunch on the pea gravel of the path, he had an idea. He stepped off to the side, behind some thick evergreen border plantings. As he waited for her, something wild, something salacious rose in him, and he decided to have a little fun.

Stop right there, he thought, and she did. She was less than ten feet away from him now, but she couldn't see him hiding in the dark, dense foliage. He could hear her breathing, hear her heart pounding, as she tried to understand what was happening to her.

Take off your coat. Even though he wasn't speaking aloud, she looked around as if trying to find a source for the sound.

Frederick persisted. *Take off your coat— now!* Still looking around, she dropped her fine leather jacket to the ground.

Okay, now the sweater.

She stood, arms clasped, not moving.

Frederick thought harder. *Off with the sweater— now!*

The brunette stood defiant, not moving.

Okay, what the fuck's the problem? This mind thing's been working on you all night, and now what? Rage rose, and Frederick was ready to pounce on her and throw her against the hard stucco wall when he gave it one more try. *YOU... WILL... take the fucking SWEATER off... NOW!*

This time she obeyed, pulling her expensive cashmere sweater up over her head and dropping it to the ground, where it fell on the rough edge of the path.

Yeah, yeah, that's better.

Even in the dark, Frederick could see her shiver, see the goosebumps rising on her arms, see a slight glint of light reflecting off the satin straps of her white bra. She had become subdued, still, as if the force of his mind was weakening her resolve.

Now the bra. TAKE OFF THE BRA!

As she reached around to undo the hook, voices from the parking lot startled her, and she stopped, mid-frame. She looked in the direction of the parking lot and then down at her partially clothed body. A look of horror and confusion contorted her lovely face. "Jesus! Oh, my God!"

Bending down, she grabbed the jacket and the sweater, pulling the jacket over her exposed chest, stuffing the sweater over her handbag, and ran, feet twisting on the unstable gravel, until she reached her own car. She jumped in and drove roughly away, peeling rubber.

Behind the bushes, Frederick was rolling on the ground laughing, nearly pissing himself— a human function he still retained— rolling, laughing, drunk with the power, drunk with the control that he had.

"Shit, man. Woo, shit. A little more practice, and I could rule the freakin' world!"

Chapter 22

In spring the sun moves into the sign of Aries, the Ram, a fiery active sign of force, energy, and determination. But even though it was now in the sign of the Ram, the sun had risen ashen and pallid, as if it were shining through a dense fog.

Dressed for warmth, Meg silently let herself out of the house. Pausing at her back doorstep, she checked for onlookers before walking across the grass to the garden shed. Her neighbors weren't particularly nosy, but she was sure that they would wonder why she was out so early on a damp morning before work, digging a hole in the middle of her lawn.

The thermometer outside the bay window had registered just above freezing. With the weak sun, the day was crisp. A slight breeze and occasional chilling gust stirred the red buds on the maple trees.

She reflected that somewhere, even in this chill, avid gardeners would be tilling the soil in sunny patches or in raised vegetable beds. Taking advantage of the spring rains, they would plant peas, which love the cold ground of early spring. With muddy fingers, gloved or ungloved, the gardeners would be repeating the phase of the agricultural cycle as people had done in this area for at least a couple of hundred years. Unlike their modern counterparts, the early settlers and the natives before them weren't looking at thermometers or weather forecasts, but instead would have been looking to the earth for Her signs, looking to the trees and the skies for wisdom.

Later Meg would plant a small vegetable garden, her way of connecting to the earth and its spirituality, and getting fresh food in the process, but not now. Not when it was a good five to six weeks before the last frost. No, not even peas. The soil was much too heavy to work at this time of year and the sun rose too late for her to get in much before-work gardening.

But this morning, instead of bringing new life into being, instead of *expanding* life and the promise of life, she would be digging up a symbol and vehicle of constriction.

Meg clumsily fitted the key to the rusting lock of the garden shed, and unlocked it on the first try. She opened the door quickly and slipped inside, pulling it closed behind her, forgetting how dark it would be. It was deep cold dark, and Meg suddenly found herself worried what could be there in the dark with her, what could have slipped in despite the lock or found another entrance during the cold winter months when the shed had stood undisturbed. Her anxiety would be short-lived, though, for the previous owner had thought to fit the shed with one bare electric bulb. Meg frantically batted the air, her unreasonable fear mounting by the moment, until she found the pull cord and switched on the light.

She stopped to calm herself. *That was silly. What could get in? The door was locked. Field mice? Chipmunks? Squirrels? Garter snakes? You're not afraid of them! And anything else would have been too big, right?* But in the few seconds before the light illuminated, she had had a vision, a disconcerting vision, of a man, a very pale man, using bags of grass seed for his bed, and lengths of row covers and plastic mulch sheets as his blankets...

Erasing the image from her mind, Meg picked up a four-tined spading fork, her usual choice for deep digging, the same fork that she had used to dig the hole to bury the poppet initially. She considered it the most useful of her garden implements; the sharp, strong spines could bite easily into the thick clay of the New England soil, and, using leverage, she would be able to quickly dig out a large plug of earth.

Her mind flashed to a co-worker who had told her how he had repeatedly speared potatoes right through while trying to dig them up using a spading fork, and she reconsidered. The fork might be strong, fast, and efficient, but with it she could spear or break the poppet, thereby loosening the spell, and inviting potential disaster.

Turning to a small bucket on the floor, she grabbed a trowel and a small garden fork instead, and then a foam kneeling pad. The work would be hard and slow, but she couldn't run the chance of breaking the poppet and letting loose the restraints that held back the vampire.

The shed door flew open and for a moment she was breathless, half expecting the vampire to be waiting, half expecting *anyone*, anything to be standing there, a physical manifestation of her fear, but it was just the wind, a brief gust that had pulled the light shed door open as it passed through the yard.

Steeling herself, Meg stepped out, long pull-cord in hand, and turned the light off only when she was standing in the daylight, wan and pale as it was. Pushing the hasp closed and hanging the open lock through it as precaution against the wind, she turned to the task at hand.

Again she scanned her surroundings, looking for curious neighbors more than anything else. Now fueled with the adrenaline from the wind gust, she looked more closely for anything out of the ordinary.

Satisfied, she stepped away from the shed and then remembered something that she had learned in her training. They had been talking about spells of invisibility. Janith and Rob had mentioned the theory that the spell-casters were never really physically invisible, but that they had just seemed to be so. Rob had asked how many times they, in real life, had felt so ignored that they felt invisible. He asked them to think of a time in their lives when, for example, a store clerk or waiter might have ignored them, and then, upon seeing them, exclaim, "Oh, I'm sorry. I didn't see you there!"

He had explained that the theory was that the invisibility spells of old were really more illusion, mass hypnosis, and stealth, and that the spells and formulae of the old grimoires, those ancient mystical books of spells, acted on the mental plane, not the physical.

And so she relaxed and stilled her mind into that meditative state that she used for spellwork. She imagined that her muscles, now tensed with the cold, were instead fluid and flexible, and that she could move with such grace and ease that she would not attract even the slightest attention. She exhaled forcefully and imagined her body becoming less dense to onlookers; imagined that, in a trick of light, she would seem more translucent, and less noticeable against the greening landscape. And then, just for good measure, she imagined a cloud of energy around her that would obscure her from view as well as protect her should she accidentally loosen the bindings on the poppet.

Thus prepared, she set off across the lawn to the large rock at the back. Gently placing her kneeling pad and tools on the ground, she held her hands out, palms down, a few inches above the soil as she tried to 'feel' where the poppet was. Starting just to the left of where she had 'seen' it earlier, at first she felt nothing. Then, as she slowly moved her hands above the ground, she felt a scant tingle in her palms that gradually grew to a low throbbing, and she knew that she had found the spot. With her right hand she used the tip of the trowel to mark out the area, continuing to feel with her left.

When she was finished, she had marked out an oblong shape slightly larger than she remembered the poppet being. Taking a deep breath and beseeching the gods for aid, she thrust the trowel into the cold, waiting soil.

Hundreds of miles south, Wesley had no such problem with the cold. During the day the temperature had risen to the mid-70s. Now, in the last few hours before dawn, it had cooled, but still not much.

Wesley stood just off the edges of light at the truck stop, watching as the trucks arrived, looking carefully at the drivers. He wanted a strong man, one who could, with a little ingenuity, place Wesley's casket on a hand cart and push it up a ramp into the refrigerated section.

He didn't really need a coffin, unlike the vampires of film and stage, but he found it most practical. When properly shut, it would keep out the sun. It was durable, and its very nature made people less prone to approach it. And, if it were the proper model, with satin pillows and deeply padded lining, it was quite comfortable.

Wesley's choice of a thrall would need to obtain that coffin for him, and before daylight. He would then need to spirit Wesley and the coffin away before the funeral home owner could recover and realize what had happened.

Wesley would need to act soon. As he watched a possible specimen, he felt a tug, far away, again from the land of quaint white-steepled churches, colonial architecture, and deep woods. This time it was more of a tap, and somewhere in the back of his mind he could hear the distinct sound of metal against earth, as Meg's trowel dug closer to destiny.

A thin crust of soil resisted, but once past the tiny layer of frost, the trowel went in easily until, further down, it encountered hard, frozen soil again.

Meg stopped and appraised the situation. She had been digging painstakingly for at least ten minutes. Though she had made some progress, she still had not recovered the poppet. Worried that she would impale it on the trowel, she had been careful to test the ground, not just with the tip of the trowel, but also with her psychic sense, again spreading her hand over the soil for a reading.

If she continued much longer, she would be late for work. Maybe it would be better to stop now, and leave the ground exposed, where the rising sun could penetrate and accelerate the thaw.

An exposed hole could be a problem, though. What if a neighboring dog, its owner oblivious to the leash law, found the hole and decided to continue her digging? What if it were to damage the poppet?

She would have to cover it somehow, but in a way that wouldn't attract attention. She returned to the shed, looking for planking when she noticed a black plastic bucket. It was small enough to fit in the hole. If she could weight it down with a brick or stone, maybe the heat-attracting properties of the dark color could work in her favor.

Meg returned to the hole and inserted the bucket, then added two old bricks. As she picked up her trowel and garden fork, she held her palms out over the bucket and quickly released a wish that the bucket would not be disturbed and that the heat of the dawning day would aid her in her task.

And then, quickly, before neighbors started coming outside to leave for work, she returned the tools to the shed and locked up, and then returned to the warmth of the house to get ready for work.

"Rice? You're eating rice for breakfast?" Alicia's slackened jaw and widened eyes proclaimed her astonishment at her housemate's repast.

"Mmmm." Evan swallowed before continuing. "In China and most of the Far East, they don't have specific foods identified with the morning meal like we do. Breakfast is often just a smaller version of the other meals."

He held out his bowl for her to examine. "This is something they call *jook* or *congee*. It's a sort of rice porridge, like a thick chicken-rice soup, with an egg dropped over it. Except that it doesn't have the chicken in it because I'm vegetarian. Want to try it?" He held out his chopsticks.

Alicia shook her head. "Let me get a spoon. I'm not that good with chopsticks and rice." She removed a teaspoon from the cutlery drawer and tentatively took a small portion from the side of his bowl.

"Be sure to get some broth, and some egg, too."

It was salty, hot, and faintly savory, with a thicker, richer feel than vegetable rice soup. "Wow, that's very good. Where did you get this?"

"I made it. It's very easy. You boil rice in vegetable broth until the grains swell to many times their size and then add ingredients like tofu, cilantro. Before serving, you add the egg. I think that the recipe I use is probably an American adaptation of one using 'Century Eggs'."

"Century Eggs?

"Preserved eggs. They're pickled and buried for one hundred days. They're not easy to come by in Danforth. Plain old chicken embryos are."

Chicken embryo! Of course. That's all that an egg was, after being fertilized, but it was the way that Evan said it, with that mischievous look in his eye, that was endearing.

"I can show you how to make it sometime," he said, deftly teasing the fairly gelatinous mixture into his mouth with his chopsticks.

"Yes, I'd like that."

"I usually make the week's batch on Sunday, as I'm reading the papers, but this Sunday I'm having dinner with some friends of my grandmother's. What are you doing on Saturday?"

"Oh, the usual. Going to the bank. Other errands."

"I have to work at the co-op in the morning, but I'm free after that."

"I have some, uh, meditation to do Saturday night, but I'm not busy in the afternoon."

"Okay, Saturday afternoon. It's a date?"

"It's a date!"

"So, how's it going? Just wanted to touch base with you to see if there's anything I can do to help." Maxwell's manager pushed back in his large padded chair and waited for his subordinate's reply.

The chair caught Maxwell's attention, just as much for the status as the comfort. "Nice chair. Is that model available to people at my level?"

"This? No, I bought this myself. Had it delivered."

"Ah." He had heard that UI was cheap, but he hadn't realized *how* cheap.

"So, do you have the lay of the land yet? Any improvements to suggest?"

"Yes, I think I have a good idea of the organization, the policies, and so on. Haven't had a chance to look at individual job performance yet, but that's my next step."

"Good. We're starting to see some profitable quarters right now, but that's no reason to get fat and lazy. I heard you've got a good sense of what's important, what can help this company forge ahead. We'll be looking to you to observe, to make recommendations over the next few months, on where we can streamline, how we can milk this economic upswing for all it's worth."

"Well, if there's anyone who can cut out the fat, I'm your man, and I'm on it."

As she sat at her desk checking her 'To Do' list, Alicia found it hard to focus. What was the name of that soup again? Congele? No, that was French for *frozen*. But it was something that sounded similar...

Evan was so different, and more importantly, so secure in his difference. Alicia reflected that she would be slightly embarrassed if a roommate had quizzed her on her breakfast choice the way she had Evan, but he had been confident, relaxed, and it was she, the observer, who felt odd at the end of it, not Evan.

Why did she feel that she had to conform so much? Alicia smiled at that thought. It wasn't as though she were the poster child for conformity; she hadn't married, she rarely let a boyfriend pay her way, and she had picked a career in a nontraditional field.

Yet, compared to Evan, who walked around in black Chinese slippers and ate rice soup for breakfast, she was Nancy Normal. Then why didn't she feel okay about it? Why the pressure to conform, to fit in?

"Alicia, don't forget bowling tonight." It was Betty, leaning into Alicia's cubicle before rushing off.

Alicia was distracted by Betty's blanched appearance. Except for the dark circles under her eyes, everything about Betty's face was washed out, pale. *Maybe she forgot her makeup.* Alicia didn't wear makeup. She was always struck by the difference when someone who normally did was barefaced. "Huh? Oh, bowling. Yup, got it on my calendar."

"Oh, and it'll be just you, me, and Norma tonight. Frederick's meeting some old basketball buddies."

As Betty pushed away from the cubicle, Alicia noticed how gaunt her hands and arms had become. *She's probably dieting too much.* All of them dieted at one time or another, it seemed, and Betty was no exception. Alicia thought back to recent lunches. Betty had bought a roast beef sandwich and left the bread. And she never snacked, not even when there were leftover donuts after meetings. If Betty was dieting too hard, maybe Norma could talk some sense into her. Alicia wrote herself a note to remember to mention it to Norma.

Picking up her pencil reminded her that she had just started to write an entry for Saturday when Betty had appeared. Opening her calendar, she wrote in small, neat letters:

Rice soup with Evan.

And then she remembered the name— Congee. *Congee.* Like Congo. Like places far away. Exotic. Like Evan.

"Well, I got started on it, but it's going to be slow work." Janith and Rob had called Matricaria to ask about her progress with the poppet. "I didn't want to use the spading fork because I didn't want to take the chance of impaling it like a potato."

Rob laughed. "Well, it would certainly be appropriate if you did."

On the extension phone, Janith asked, "Why?".

"Well, you know, a lot of the vampire legends we have today are connected with Vlad Tepes, or Vlad the Impaler, the bloodthirsty Wallachian ruler who had a thing about impaling enemies. I think it would be poetic justice if we impaled the poppet that represents the vampire."

"Though that sounds very satisfying emotionally," Janith noted, "I don't know if it's wise. Vampires aren't usually killed with garden implements, so all we'd be doing would be cutting the bindings, and therefore maybe loosening the control over him."

"Yes, that's true. Unless you're using a wooden stake to dig with."

Matricaria remembered the willow stake that she had recently re-discovered in the bottom of her ritual bag. "Ah, I'm not using it to dig with, but I *do* have a stake." She recounted how she had found it, a piece of wood removed from a neighbor's tree when it was struck by lightning.

"That could be useful. Hang onto it," Rob said.

"Speaking of loosening things," Janith said, "Rob and I have been thinking about this some more and we wonder if we should dig it up at all. What if we dig it up, and it falls apart as we take it out? Or while we're trying to bind it again with a new cord?"

"I was worried about that myself. I kept wishing that I knew some archaeologists. How would I know if I was getting too close? I kept trying to sense psychically, but with me, that's an imperfect skill at best."

Janith continued, "We also remembered that when we bound him, we made a connection to him. By touching the poppet, we could be reconnecting. That is, we could be calling him back."

"That might explain something. It seems that I could sense the evil near the poppet. I thought that was odd because the poppet should be representing evil *bound*, but if we have a connection through that poppet, and the connection goes both ways..."

"Yes, I think it's just too dangerous to try to dig it up. And what would we do once we had it up? Rebind it? It would probably fall apart in our hands."

"I agree. I think that we should just start with a new one, and this time bury it deeply, in some sort of box or glass jar. Leave the old one where it is."

"What we really should do is make the binding out of steel and store the doll in platinum. But, barring that, an ordinary metal box would provide *some* protection."

"How about one of those strong boxes that they use for important papers?"

"It would be expensive and hard to bury."

"Rob, hon, we could have a vampire here. A little monetary sacrifice *might* be necessary."

"*Might.* We still don't know he's a vampire, do we? The binding seemed to work in the beginning, which makes me think that we might be dealing with a mere mortal."

"If it's the same vampire that Alicia confronted in the lab, is it possible that he was injured in the explosion?"

"Vampires are supposed to be pretty indestructible, right? Bullets can't harm them, knives can't. The only thing that can harm them is a stake through the heart, decapitation, or being in the sun. And that destroys them."

"Okay, but what if there was something in the lab that could harm them, but not quite kill them? Maybe he was injured and now he's getting stronger."

"We just don't know, do we?"

"But at least a metal box would buy us some time."

"How about a cash box, like they use at flea markets and yard sales? It'd be smaller and more affordable."

"Yes, let's start with that. If this thing we're dealing with is just a disturbed human being, it'll give us a couple of years, during which time we can figure out what to do."

"Maybe we should wrap the poppet in plastic, too, before we place it in the box."

"How about aluminum foil? Might last a little longer. Also, it just seems right working with metal instead of plastic."

"Good idea. So we're agreed?" Janith didn't wait for an answer. Instead, she instructed them on the next steps.

"Matricaria, if you could get the box, I'll get the paraffin and binding cord. And the foil."

"Okay. And I'll fill in the hole."

"We should plan to do the new binding on a waning moon. It's waning now. Let's see if we can get everyone here Saturday night."

"I can make it. What about Alicia? Should we invite her?"

"She's not initiated and she's not trained. It would be too dangerous to have her take part. No, I don't think we should. She should stay as far away as she can. Make sure she knows how to cast a circle of protection. On the night we do the ritual, she should be in one. And make sure she's wearing a pentacle or some other protective amulet."

Janith was about to say goodbye when Rob interrupted. "Oh, and one more thing. Let's find another place to bury this one. I know we were thinking that having it on your property would make it easier to keep an eye on it, but we just didn't think that through. It's a two-way link, and you don't want it in your yard."

It was the same Susie. Frederick knew that now. How could he have missed that?

When he met Susie in a bar that day, she was with a friend, but her name was Jean. Alicia was alone when Frederick had seen her in the computer room that day, but Susie *must* have mentioned her to him. He knew that Wesley had.

Maybe he just wasn't paying attention at the time. Maybe he was too caught up in becoming a vampire.

It didn't matter. What mattered now was that Alicia seemed to know, to know that he was the last person to be with her friend Susie when she was alive.

And that was dangerous.

Alicia would have to go. The question was how.

If she were to disappear as Susie did, people might start to put things together. Of course, Frederick could just hit the road afterward— but could he travel fast enough? And having the law after him for murder would seriously curtail his means of getting cash. Robbing gas stations was tricky enough without an all-out search for him as a murderer.

Maybe he could make her his slave, like Wesley did with that old guard, Harry. *Yeah, and she could keep her job and give me cash... I hear those programmers make shitloads.*

But once again, Wesley's previous lack of communication made things difficult. Frederick had little idea what Wesley did to make someone his slave. He bit the person, that was for sure, it wasn't just the biting that did it. Wesley had bitten Alicia, and *she* certainly wasn't his slave; if anything, she became stronger *against* him.

And Frederick had bitten Betty, repeatedly, but she wasn't his slave, either. If anything, *he* seemed to be bending to *her* will more these days. And Susie. Frederick had bitten her. And she had died.

Maybe it was that mind thing. Maybe he should practice on someone. Someone like the tall brunette from the bowling alley.

Matricaria had considered waiting until morning, when it was warmer and when she wouldn't attract attention by walking around with a flashlight, but when she looked out the window, she realized that the light of the moon, even though it was waning, would be sufficient.

Pulling on a dark coat and gloves, she quietly crept out to the shed, this time selecting a spade and a rake. After once again scanning her surroundings for neighbors, she quietly walked across the lawn, realizing as she did that the moonlight that lit her way also lit the back yard as if it were a stage.

No hiding in this light. Just act casual, as if it's perfectly natural to be gardening at this time of night...

The pail came up with a scraping sound, but she didn't stop to see who heard it. Instead, she quickly shoveled in the few clumps of dirt that sat on the hole's edge, and then raked the remaining dirt from the thin, over-wintered grass.

As she did, she could feel the evil emanate, like one could smell the stench from a garbage can on a hot summer day; evil being suppressed, but not extinguished.

And more than a thousand miles away, Wesley felt it, too.

Chapter 23

Meg had urged Alicia to get an amulet of protection as soon as possible. On Thursday night she headed to the House of Astrology. She felt odd asking for it by name, so when Sonny asked her if there was anything he could help her with, she replied, "Yeah, I'm interested in some jewelry. I'd like one of those stars."

A mixture of patience and bemusement hid behind Sonny's smile. "You mean like a pentacle?"

Alicia paused for a second while she planned her next move. Should she play the dumb customer and let Sonny give her whatever spiel he usually gave to the naïve customers? Or should she reveal her seriousness? She chose the latter. "Yes, like a pentacle. Exactly like a pentacle."

He walked back to the desk for the key to the jewelry display without saying anything. As he opened the case, he looked at Alicia as if he, too, were trying to plan his next move. He pulled out one of the medium-priced pendants, a small, finely wrought unembellished encircled star.

"This is sterling. Comes with an 16-inch chain. Twenty dollars."

Alicia winced as she remembered Meg's words: "There's a magical law that says one shouldn't haggle over magical goods..."

She could afford twenty, but it was more than what she usually spent on jewelry. *This isn't jewelry, silly. It's for protection.*

As if reading her mind, Sonny picked up another pendant, a slightly larger one that was obviously not the same quality. "This one's only ten. It's base metal, silver-plated, and so is the chain. If you're just looking for jewelry, this'll do."

Alicia decided to take a chance and expose her motive. "And what if I'm not just looking for jewelry?"

Sonny looked around the store before answering. "Then you might be interested in these."

He returned the base metal pentacle to the display and walked to the back of the store. There, on the bottom shelf, nearly hidden in the right-hand corner, were two discs that appeared to be made of pewter rather than silver.

Sonny unlocked the case. Again, he looked around the store before speaking. "This one— " He handed her a perfectly-cut metal circle. "This one is the Saturn Seal of Protection. It protects against all forms of evil, including hexing, curses, bad fortune, and enemies."

Alicia looked at the strange medallion. On it was a geometric symbol that resembled a large capital 'A' superimposed over a slightly lowered 'V'. Across the center ran a horizontal line. A tiny circle capped the tip of each line.

While Alicia examined the amulet, Sonny handed her another. "This one is the Magic Circle of Solomon, attributed to King Solomon, of biblical times. You've heard of Solomon, right?"

Alicia nodded.

"Legend has it that he was a great magician and that he wore an amulet like this to protect himself from evil spirits. If you're looking for protection from spirits, this is the one I'd recommend."

A customer walked through the door and Sonny called out, "I'll be right with ya."

Turning back to Alicia, he said, "I've got to go take care of that guy. He ordered a book that just came in." He handed her the second disc. Rather crude circles surrounded a central design that featured a diamond engraved in the center with what appeared to be a Star of David at each tip.

Alicia looked from one disc to the other. The first one, rather plain, didn't seem very magical to her. The design was too simple. It was as if there wasn't enough in the design to hold anything in. The second, while more involved, was crude in its execution. As Alicia looked at the circles surrounding the central design of the second one, she realized that they weren't concentric circles at all, but the outline of a snake, its head and tongue visible at the top, just under the hole from which the disc could be suspended.

Neither design appealed to her. *Well, it's not like I'd be wearing them in the open. Meg did say that I'd want something small that I could wear under my shirt.* She tumbled the amulets in her hands, trying to get a sense of the weight. They were both fairly heavy. She could imagine leaning over and having them pop out of her shirt.

"Can't decide?" Sonny was back.

"Uh, not really. I guess I should have done a lot more research. I don't know how to choose these things, but neither of them feel right to me."

"See, you know more than you think!" Sonny surprised Alicia with a little smile. "That's *exactly* how you choose them— by feel."

Alicia was about to ask if that was a little illogical when she remembered that expecting a small circular piece of metal to protect you against a person, a person you thought might be a vampire, was just about as illogical as you could get... *Besides,* she reminded herself, *it's mostly self-hypnosis. If you believe they can protect you, they can. If you don't, they won't. So feelings are a good indicator of efficacy.*

Sonny reached deep in the right-hand corner of the case again, pulling at the draped black velvet, and withdrew another pewter disc. "Ah, I thought I had one left. Here's another pentacle."

He handed her a disc that was of a similar size to the others and whose crudeness of execution lay between the sharp industrial effect of the Saturn Seal of Protection and the much less polished Magic Circle of Solomon, which looked as if it could have been drawn by a child. It was a five-pointed star with magical symbols in each point and in the center. Around the edges there appeared to be Hebrew characters.

"This one feels different. It feels strong."

Sonny smiled. "But? I hear a 'but' in there."

"But it's heavy and big. What if I'm leaning over and it falls out of my shirt?"

"If you're worried about that, don't wear it on a chain." He walked to another section of the store and picked up a small black pouch. "You put it in this and keep it in a pocket. And then on your neck— " he pointed to the jewelry case at the front of the store, and continued, "You wear one of the smaller silver pentacles on a very long chain and keep it tucked in."

Alicia half-wondered if Sonny was just trying to sell her two things instead of one, but what he said made sense. And if there was any power to these, and if her fears about Wesley coming back were true—

"Of course, these are mass-produced. You know that, right? But they're based on real grimoires— spellbooks— and they've been charged in a magic circle. I know the guy who does it. Unless you know enough to make your own, and I'm talkin' casting them yourself, this is the next best thing."

Alicia didn't know how much of it was sales pitch and how much was genuine, but she needed something *now*. "Okay. I guess I'll take both."

"Good choice, good choice." Sonny took the rejected amulets back and locked them in the case. "Let's go get the silver pentacle."

Wesley considered how he would make his next move. If he approached the truck driver in the dark, the man might assume that Wesley was intending to rob him or assault him. If he met him inside, he'd run the risk of being seen.

Out by the highway, Wesley saw a truck slow and then stop to pick up a hitchhiker. He looked down at his own dark suit and white shirt. He didn't fit the stereotypical hitchhiker profile, but perhaps that would work in his favor. Perhaps a trucker would have more pity on a man so seemingly out of his element.

And with his vampire gift of strong vision, he would be able to see the truckers well before they saw him. He could choose which one would be the most likely candidate. And for those who were not, he could step into the cover of the trees and scrub at the edge of the road before the truckers saw him.

As he stepped into the darkness to circumnavigate the truck stop, he kicked something silver. He bent down to pick it up. It was a quarter, a plain old twenty-five cent piece, yet somehow he had seen it differently when he first kicked it.

It had looked like an encircled five-pointed star.

"Hey, buddy. You need help?" The man in the large semi looked down at the overdressed stranger at the side of the road.

It had started to rain, and quite appropriately, the strains of the currently popular "I Love a Rainy Night," blared from the truck radio. Wesley heard the words and smiled. *Yes, how I do love a rainy night.* The driver, seeing Wesley looking at the radio, thought it was a hint that the music was too loud for the older gentleman, and turned the volume down.

Wesley looked away. "Yes, my vehicle's broken down and I was wondering if you could possibly give me a ride to the next exit. I would walk, but the rain..."

"Well, buddy, I'd love to, but we're not supposed to take on riders. Insurance regulations."

Wesley looked in the man's eyes. *But I'm harmless. I'm well-dressed. I'm not some thug by the side of the road. Nice man. Ride. Next exit. Harmless.*

"I could call you a tow..."

As Wesley watched, the man's eyes began to lose focus and he began to sway in small, barely noticeable arcs. Wesley kept up the assault. *Nice man. Ride. Next exit. Harmless.*

"Well, you seem like a nice man..."

Nice man. Ride. Next exit. Harmless.

"I suppose I could give you a ride... just to the next exit." He thumped the heel of his hand against the steering wheel as if he were trying to stamp out doubt— or a voice in his head. "I suppose it's harmless... Okay, mister, but hurry up so no one sees us."

Ride.

Chapter 24

"Hi! I didn't expect you to be home."

Evan was sitting in the living room, playing a bamboo flute, accompanying some unidentifiable Asian music. Alicia couldn't tell if it was Chinese, Japanese, Korean, or some other nationality, but knowing Evan, it was probably Chinese.

"Ah, good evening."

"You play the flute?"

"I'm trying to learn. The fingering is very simple, but it's hard to get the tone right." He blew a few random notes to demonstrate. "Do you play an instrument?"

"Guitar. I haven't played much since I started night school, though. No time to practice and if I don't play for a week or two, I lose my calluses. Then I'm too much of a wimp to deal with the blisters I get from practicing."

Evan looked at the tips of his own fingers. "What you need to do is play long enough so that you get deep ones. Then they don't go away so easily. Here, feel these."

He held out his fingers for her to touch. They were strong and soft, but, as he stated, the tips were deeply callused.

"Guitar, too, huh?" She was jealous. Very jealous. *Isn't there* anything *this man can't do, and do well?*

"I play a little. We should jam. Why don't you get your guitar? I don't have mine with me at the moment, but I could improvise with the flute."

"No, I really don't know any songs, just the ones I've written, and I don't even remember those much."

"You write?"

He seemed interested, very interested, unlike most people, who usually offered a polite, "Oh, isn't that nice?" Alicia thought for a minute that maybe she *would* go get her guitar, but then remembered that she hadn't picked up the guitar since... since... since long before the explosion. *How many things has Wesley changed in my life without me realizing it?*

"I used to write a lot. They're not very sophisticated songs, but I like the lyrics."

"I'd love to hear them." He looked at her, smiling, wide-eyed, encouraging. She wanted to believe that he really cared, that he really *did* want to hear them.

"No, it's been too long. Can I take a rain check?"

"How about Saturday? We could put the rice on to simmer and then sit and play."

She wanted to say no, but he was so enthusiastic. "Okay, sure. That would give me a little time to go over the songs."

"Good. I'd *love* to hear them."

And to her great surprise, she believed him.

Alicia started to leave when she remembered her purchases. "I've been shopping for pentacles." She held them out for him to see. "What do you think?"

Evan put down his flute and leaned over to look at Alicia's outstretched hand. "Very nice. May I touch them?"

"Sure, why not?"

"Just asking. One should always ask before touching another's ritual objects."

"Oh."

"But these just came from the store, right? So you haven't consecrated them yet, have you?"

She remembered what Meg had said about cleansing and consecrating them. She should clean them as she would any jewelry, and then pass them through the classical four elements of which the ancient philosophers thought all things were made: earth, air, fire, and water; except that she should use salt, not soil, for earth.

"No, not yet."

Evan fondled the larger of the two pieces. "Ah, a Pentacle of Solomon."

"I'm impressed! You know your amulets."

"Yes, when I first became interested in magic, I studied the older grimoires first. They're full of amulets and talismans."

Evan examined the smaller of the two pieces. Alicia told him how Sonny had suggested that she carry the larger one in a pocket and wear the smaller one.

"He sounds very knowledgeable."

"Either that or he was just trying to sell jewelry!"

Evan smiled at her joke, not realizing, probably, how seriously she meant that statement, how she often assumed that people had ulterior motives. How rare it was for her trust completely. He handed the pieces back. "Very nice."

Alicia wanted to talk to him forever. It seemed that there was nothing that Evan didn't know or didn't want to know. "If you're still interested in magic, I could ask if there's room in the study group."

Evan smiled, with voice and eyes. "That's very kind of you." He looked genuinely touched by her offer. "I think I'll have to pass, though. I have school and my grandmother isn't faring well. I promised I'd visit her a few times over the next couple of months."

Alicia was unexpectedly saddened. She tried to hide it by keeping the conversation rolling. "Oh, I'm sorry to hear that. Where does she live?"

"The City."

"Fenmore?"

"No, New York. The Big Apple. What's your favorite part of 'the City'?"

"The exit."

"Whh-what?" Evan was chuckling.

Alicia launched playfully into her little diatribe about cities. "Cities are dirty and dangerous. They're an abomination against nature."

Evan laughed. "I grew up in the city."

She was incredulous. "You did?"

"Yes. You seem surprised."

"I am. City people are usually, well, and I know I'm talking stereotypes here, but city people are usually cold, and closed, and sometimes downright rude. You're none of that. You're gentle, and open, and kind."

"Why, thank you." Evan smiled even more warmly than before, leaning in toward Alicia, who had sat down at the opposite end of the couch, and for a moment she wondered if he could be flirting with her. "No, 'the City' isn't bad. You just need to know it. You should come down sometime with me. I'd change your mind."

"I don't know. I'll have to think about that." Was he really inviting her to go to New York with him?

"You should tag along sometime."

To her great surprise, again she believed him. She really believed him.

Alicia reluctantly left Evan to practice his flute. After feeding Moonshadow, she retired to her room with her pentacles. Meg had told her to set up a little altar with the earth, air, fire, and water, which she did, assembling them the best that she could on the top of her dresser.

She had put her full set of glass custard cups to use. One held regular table salt, one held a small tile for burning cone incense, the third held a candle in a candlestick, and the last held tap water. Meg had explained that some witches preferred kosher salt because it was more pure, and that others preferred sea salt because of its direct connection to the sea, but that in the interest of getting the pentacle consecrated as soon as possible, she could use regular table salt. Meg also mentioned that some witches preferred water fresh from a natural source like a spring or brook, but once again, time was critical, so Alicia had used plain tap water.

Alicia had posed the old question that if something was worth doing, wasn't it worth doing well? Or doing right? Meg had confided that although that was true, it was said that with enough practice and talent, a witch didn't need any tools at all. "Let's go with what you have," she had concluded. "After all, witches have been doing that for centuries. It was the ceremonial magicians who insisted on the exact right time, the exact right tools." And so Alicia had gathered what she had, picking up the incense and burner when she bought her pentacles, having the feeling all the time that Sonny knew what she was up to.

She lit the candle and incense, turned off the room light, and stood in front of her makeshift altar. As she had done so often in recent years, she shut her eyes and modified her breathing until she was breathing slowly and deliberately, aware of each breath, aware of *only* each breath.

Feeling that she was ready, she opened her eyes and reached for the small piece of paper on which Meg had written words for Alicia to say while she consecrated the amulet.

She couldn't remember if Meg had said to do them one at a time or together. It was too late to call, and leaving her little altar to make the phone call would ruin her concentration. No, she would proceed as best she could. If it wasn't right, she could redo them.

Picking up the pentacles with her right hand, she dangled them in the incense smoke and intoned,

Air fume and air release,
Cleanse these pentacles, I beseech.

Outside, the wind picked up. The branches of the old catalpa tree in the front yard scraped against the gutters.

She transferred the pentacles to her left hand. With her right, she pinched a measure of salt, dropped it into the water and stirred. She dipped her fingertips into the bowl. As she shook the water onto the pentacles, she chanted:

> Salt and water, as the sea,
> Cleanse these pentacles. So mote it be.

The sound of rain, hard and furious against her bedroom window startled her. Coincidence? Again? *Maybe I shouldn't continue... the next element is fire...*

No, she had to continue. Meg told her that it was important to do all four elements, that the ancients believed that the elements had to be in balance.

Maneuvering herself so that she could jump up and run if needed, she took a deep breath before speaking the final elemental conjuration. Meg had instructed her to speak the final sentence with power, to *command* it, and so Alicia did:

> Fire burn, consume, and bite,
> Cleanse these pentacles, now, aright.

At this, a deafening crack of lightning, seemingly right outside her window, let loose and Alicia jumped backward, tumbling into the corner of her bed. The window shade snapped up, exposing her to the street outside, exposing the outside street to her, and there she could see a storm of a fury not usual for late spring.

But there was one more conjuration to go. Not wanting to break momentum, she ignored the open shade and read out the final incantation with all the might, meaning, and power that she could muster:

> I conjure thee, O pentacles of protection,
> By the virtue of the four elements of the ancient world,
> By the power of all plants and animals, known and unknown,
>
> By heaven and all the stars that rule,
> By the great ball of the sun and the vast face of the moon,
> That thou beist a powerful protection against all mistfortune
> and evil.   So mote it be.

There was one more loud crack of lightning, one loud thunder boom, and then the night was silent, silent except for a gentle thrum of rain against the downspout, and the frantic pounding of her heart.

Chapter 25

On Saturday, Alicia stood in front of her guitar case.

I should warm up first. Though it was the weekend, she had worked late the day before and her finger joints still felt stiff from hours at the computer. Alicia shook her hands out at her side, trying to get the blood circulating and to shake away the inflexibility. Years ago, when she had complained to her guitar teacher that she couldn't play as well after a long day at work, he had shared his own observation that he didn't play very well after chopping wood. Something about the fingers being clenched, she guessed.

She opened and closed her hands a few more times, more out of procrastination now than real need, and then, forcing herself to stop delaying, she lifted the guitar from the battered case, taking care not to smack the finely polished wood of the instrument against the arms of the couch.

It felt so odd to hold it again. At one point in her life, the guitar had been a large part of her daily routine, with practice and lessons, and songwriting, but these days the larger descendant of the gentle lute lay undisturbed in the back of a closet while she busied herself with work, school, homework, and home repairs.

Pressing her ring finger on the fifth fret of the sixth string, Alicia began to tune the guitar. A melancholy enveloped her as she realized how long she had abandoned it. It wasn't that she was such a great talent gone to waste— no, indeed she was barely adequate. It was that the drudgery of work, school, homework, and home repairs had filled her life.

This was not the life she dreamed of as an idealistic youth in high school. Alicia tried to remember what she *had* dreamed of, but it was lost to her at the moment, lost in a fog of vampires and other untidy interruptions in her life. But she knew that her dreams had once included something other than work, school, homework, and home repairs.

Tuning finished, she gingerly arranged her fingers over the correct frets for an A-minor chord. She didn't know what she would play, but it didn't matter; most of her songs started with, or contained, A-minor chords. Her songs were not happy ones. Dirges, Kurt had called them; solemn, mournful pieces of music.

Great! What's Evan going to think of me when he hears these droning compositions?

She strummed aimlessly, trying different chords, thinking that maybe she could whip up a more cheerful song, but she always came back to A-minor. *My* life *is in A-minor*, she mused.

Finally her hand rested on A, and as she thought of Evan and how maybe, maybe after all of the darkness in her life, he might possibly be the one to bring light and joy. She began to sing:

> For me, the spring has come,
> I've cried the winter's tears
> Now I'll have my fun,
> Those months, they seemed like years.

"'Now I'll have my fun'— oh, yeah, that's profound!" Alicia looked around for a paper to write down the words as she chastised herself for the banal lyrics. "It's not great, but it's a start. Just keep going!"

She played the verse again, still not satisfied with the third line, when suddenly the piece took its own shape and rose, like birdsong, into optimism that she hadn't felt in years:

> There's a woman inside
> Waiting to come alive,
> All her hopes and dreams
> To come to pass
> And at last
> She's been waiting,
> Anticipating
> That this moment would arrive.

Dreams coming to pass? Ha! She couldn't even remember what her dreams were! And she wasn't happy about the last few lines; they reminded her too much of the Beatles' song "Blackbird." But again she assured herself that it was a good start. And at least, for a change, it wasn't morbid or depressing.

Moonshadow jumped on the couch and sniffed the tuning pegs, then started playing with the loose ends of the strings. "Moonshadow, no, honey! You'll poke your eyes out." She picked up the guitar and walked to the kitchen. "I guess I really should trim these." It had been the fad to leave the ends long back when she first took up guitar in high school, and she never changed her habit.

Grabbing a pair of wire cutters from the kitchen junk drawer, she continued to address Moonshadow. He had followed her to the kitchen, assuming that she could be going to the kitchen only to feed him. "Isn't that funny, Moonie? You finish high school, and you think you have everything figured out, but even if you do, everything keeps changing."

The only thing constant in life is change... Resistance to these changes causes suffering.

She had seen a poster with those words, attributed to Buddha, at the co-op. What change was she resisting that made her suffer so?

Somewhere, deep in a part of her soul that she had thought was secure from assault or trespass, a terrifyingly familiar voice replied,

"The change that only I can bring..."

"Evan! I didn't expect to see you here." Todd set down the large burlap sack of peanuts and gave Evan a quick hug.

"Just here to do my hours."

"Yes, but I heard you were spending a lot of weekends in town."

"Oh, I see the grapevine doesn't miss a thing!" Evan smiled and then looked down at the floor briefly before looking up. "Yes, Lynnie and I were spending a lot of time together. We both decided it might be *too much* time together and decided to give each other some space. She went to visit a college roommate who just moved to New Haven and I'm just hanging out, catching up on my co-op hours and other things."

"Ah. Well, good to see you. How's school going? How's the apartment, how's Alicia?"

"Good, good. Not so much homework yet, but they've warned us that it'll be getting rough soon. Alicia's great. She's very intelligent, very hard-working. I just found out that she plays guitar. After I get through today, we're going to get out our instruments and jam a little."

"Really? I didn't know she played."

"She said she hasn't played in a while. I think she's practicing today." He grinned.

"That sounds like fun." Todd picked up the sack of peanuts. "I've got to refill the display barrel. There's a customer over there waiting for them. Catch you in a bit."

"Sure. I need to go wash my hands."

Evan lathered with castile soap. Originally he had thought of Alicia as plain and unremarkable, but she surprised him every day. Last week, the toilet had started to run on and without hesitation she had removed the tank top, determined the problem, and fixed it. She came from a working class background, yet she spoke French, played guitar, and had an insatiable hunger for knowledge. And when he flirted with her, the plain, no-nonsense feminist became a playful butterfly, flitting back and forth, parrying and thrusting light jibes and coquetries.

Maybe his discussion with Lynnie the past week had been on target. Time apart might do them good. And maybe he'd spend some of that break time with Alicia.

Of the original group who had performed the first binding, only two members, who had left the coven after graduation, would not attend. The rest of the original party would be there tonight.

The ritual wouldn't start until 8, but Rob and Janith had requested that the coven arrive by 5 o'clock to help set up the ritual space and to prepare for the ritual itself. They would use the living room, which meant moving the couch, coffee table, and other pieces of furniture out of the way. In their small city apartment, the only place to put some of the moved furniture was on top of Rob and Janith's bed, which meant a slow and careful parade from the living room down the narrow hall.

Gabe and Amethyst slanted the couch on its end against the door. It was the only place that it would fit. Placing it there had the added benefit of acting as soundproofing to the door. Patty and Merlin ferried small tables and other items to the bedroom while Sybil vacuumed the vacated space. Rob, Janith, and Matricaria huddled out of the way in the small kitchen, going over their notes for the ritual.

The coven had set up for circle many times before in the three years of training and had it down to a routine. Everyone knew where everything went and what had to be done to prepare the ritual space. The mood was quiet contemplation as they prepared; for although they were often loud and playful when they first gathered, when the furniture moving started, they started their own inner preparation for the task.

Despite the cold, one of the windows in the living room was slightly open, as it always was this time of year, and the sound of tires splashing through puddles from an earlier rain mingled with sirens, horns, and college students out for Saturday night fun. The sweet smell of fresh rain-cleansed air entered the apartment, chasing away the smells of herb teas, pizza, and a touch of fear.

For although they went about their business with calm self-assurance and poise, just under the surface lay a nagging twinge of dread.

After returning from his shift at the co-op, Evan changed from his jeans and sweater to his coarse white cotton drawstring pants and white long-sleeved thermal undershirt. Looking much like a rural Chinese peasant, his only concession to the New England weather was his black knitted wool cap.

Anyone else would have pointed out that it was rude for men to wear hats indoors, but Alicia, remembering that fifty percent or more of body heat can be lost through the head, instead just admired his practicality.

"Congee, Grasshopper," Evan said, imitating a monk in the old *Kung Fu* TV series, "can be made with brown or white rice. Today we make with brown."

Evan put a handful of brown rice in a large bowl and covered it with water. Dropping his David Carradine impression, he continued his lecture on congee. "Some call this the 'Eastern version of chicken soup' because it's very healing. In China, it's common to give it to people who are convalescing, who suffer from digestive upset, or who are weak and have low energy. It's considered very restorative."

He pulled out a large black enamel pot and lid from a low cabinet. As she watched him add water to the pot, Alicia noticed Moonshadow at her feet, rubbing against her legs. "Hungry, sweetie?"

Evan shut off the water and looked at her, then the cat. "Oh, I thought you were talking to me!"

Alicia laughed as she stepped toward the refrigerator, then tentatively gave Evan a playful pat on the shoulder. "You want a bowl of Tuna Deluxe? Hmmm?"

"I think I'll pass, although I hear that tuna cat food isn't that bad."

"I heard that, too. When meat prices went through the roof a few years ago, some low-income elderly were eating cat food because it was cheaper than the human version."

"Another good reason to be vegetarian. Speaking of which, I will now add a tablespoon of flaked seaweed, and a tablespoon of vegetable bouillon granules to the pot. We need to bring it to a boil and then cover it and turn it down to a low simmer."

Alicia was impressed with his familiarity with the kitchen. Joey knew only where the glasses, coffee cups, and forks were. Evan, on the other hand, moved around the kitchen like a chef, knowing exactly what he needed, knowing exactly how to use it.

"In China they often cook the rice for four to six hours. They believe that the longer you cook the rice, the more strengthening properties the congee will have. I just need to do one more thing and then we can get to our guitar session."

Alicia watched as he took what appeared to be dried leather from a small plastic bag and placed it in a bowl. "Dried mushrooms. They'll soak while the congee is cooking. You're not allergic to mushrooms, are you?"

"Allergic? No, I'm not allergic to anything."

"Good. Neither am I. Except death."

Alicia started to laugh, but in the wide, shallow window that looked out over her small back yard, she thought she saw a face, a familiar face. She couldn't make out who, but the eyes, the eyes seemed hauntingly familiar.

"I'm sorry! It was a joke!"

"Huh? Oh, yeah, I know. I just thought I saw something."

Evan quietly let go of the bowl holding the mushrooms and side-stepped into the adjacent dining room and then to the small pantry that led to the back door. He held a finger to his lips, indicating silence, and they both listened. Other than the sounds of clocks and the low hum of the refrigerator, everything was silent. Moonshadow had even stopped eating, and the sound of his identification tag clanking against the bowl had ceased.

Evan slid against the wall and gently, slowly threw back the small security bolt at the bottom of the back door and then released the push-button lock. Carefully he turned the knob, stopping frequently, so as not to make a sound.

Alicia was suddenly aware that she was standing alone in a brightly lit kitchen and the fear she had felt since the BB incident flashed through her. Quietly, she sidled toward the front hall, hoping to meld into its darkness.

Like many who had lived through the energy crisis, she still lit only the rooms in use, so the safety of darkness was only one room away.

In the pantry, she could see the white outline of Evan opening the back door. *Wow, he's good. I didn't hear a thing. But he's wearing white! He'll practically glow in the dark!*

She wanted to call out to him, run over to him, but she was frozen in place in the cover of the hall. Time stretched interminably as she chided herself for being a coward. She flashed back to the last time that she had let someone put his life on the line for her. It was the guard at Theoretic, and he had never been the same.

Resolving that it wouldn't happen again, she quietly opened the glass door to the living room. Tiptoeing toward the back of the house, she reached the dining room and then the pantry, all in darkness. Approaching the back door, she encountered a ghostly shape.

As she bumped into Evan, she gulped air, but did not scream— Alicia never screamed— and jumped backward.

"It's only me," Evan assured her.

"Whew. You scared the daylights out of me. See anything?"

"Nothing. Not even the moon. It's very dark. It must be the clouds."

"Or maybe the moon hasn't risen yet?"

Evan didn't seem to be as relieved as he should have been at her possible explanation.

"No, it's unnaturally dark."

"Did you *feel* anything out there?"

Evan studied her for a moment before replying. "Yes. I don't know what, but I *did* feel something. What's that line from Macbeth? 'By the pricking of my thumbs, something wicked this way comes.'"

They stood for a moment, both motionless, eyes darting from window to window. Nothing. Finally Evan shrugged his shoulders and retrieved a cup of tea from the kitchen counter. Motioning toward the living room, he said, "Shall we?"

Not really sure that the danger had passed, but not knowing what else to do, Alicia entered the living room and took a seat on the couch. Evan sat cross-legged on the floor next to the coffee table.

Alicia could smell the strong smokiness of Evan's Lapsang Souchong tea. "It's an acquired taste," he had told her, and she couldn't agree more. He said that it reminded him of campfires and woods; she said that it reminded her of a house fire many years ago. *Okay, so you don't drink beer because it reminds you of your father and you don't drink lapsang souchong because it reminds you of the fire. Maybe it's time you started making new memories for things!*

"Evan, would you mind if I had a cup of that tea?"

"This? I thought that you didn't like it."

"I don't— not yet. I think I need to give it another try."

Evan leapt to his feet.

"Oh, no, I didn't mean for you to get up," Alicia said, moving the guitar off her lap and starting to rise.

"No, sit. I'm up already. I would be honored to serve you tea." At that, he made a long, low bow, and backed out of the room, smiling broadly.

Alicia put her guitar back on her lap and studied the lyrics on the paper beside her. She ran through the chords quietly, trying to stay her hands from shaking. It was a simple song; A, and then A-minor (of course), and A-minor slid up and down the frets a bit. *You can do this. It's simple. Just sing a couple of verses, ask him to play something, and before you know it, it'll be time to go upstairs and cast the protective circle.*

She tried the chord progression one more time and was surprised to see the cup placed on the floor beside her feet. She hadn't even heard Evan enter the room. As she looked up to thank him, she noticed that he was no longer smiling.

"When you said you saw something in the window," he began, "Was it a face? A very pale face?"

While the driver snored in the sleeper compartment located directly behind the cab, Wesley read a discarded copy of the day's newspaper. He reflected on his short stay in the Crescent City. It had been a mix of good and bad, as all life was. Overall, he decided, it was a good experience.

It had allowed him to restore his energy, plot his return, and, he thought, as he turned the page with both hands, it had allowed him to grow anew his severed arm.

"Did you get a good look at it? I thought it looked familiar, but I couldn't see it well enough."

Evan shook his head. "No, it was very ethereal. I could see the yard through it. At one point I thought that maybe someone was behind me and I was seeing his reflection in the glass, but I spun around quickly and no one was there."

He knelt in front of her and put one hand on her knee. "I have a confession to make. When you first told me the story about the vampire, I thought, well, not that you weren't telling the truth, but that you were misinterpreting things that you saw. I thought that there was a logical explanation for everything you saw— "

"So did I."

"—even if it was just that you were getting psychic impressions rather than actually seeing things. Maybe that's still true. Maybe that's what happened to me. But now I know that whatever you saw— whatever *we* saw— it had bad intentions, and that we should consider doing something to protect ourselves."

Alicia told him about the circle that she would be casting around herself and the ritual that would begin at eight.

Evan gently turned Alicia's left hand around so that he could see the face of her watch. "Seven-thirty. I don't think he's going to stay outside for another half hour."

Alicia trembled. Her house, her one safe refuge from the world, was it really that vulnerable? "Wait, isn't there a belief that vampires can't enter unless they're invited?"

"Yes, that's true, but didn't you tell me that Matricaria told you that he manifested in their circle the first time they tried to bind him?"

Alicia nodded. "Yes, she said that."

"Okay, so either someone invited him in without their knowledge, or the legend isn't true."

"Yes..." Alicia looked at her watch again, having forgotten the time already. Seven-thirty-one. "Mat told me that they wouldn't take the phone off the hook until just before the ritual started. Maybe I can call and ask."

"I'll be right back."

With that, Evan disappeared up the stairs, taking them in twos and threes, grabbing something from his room and returning so quickly that he didn't even see what was waiting in the shadows.

"Hon, it's Alicia," Janith called. Rob went to pick up the extension phone while Matricaria positioned herself near Janith and the other phone.

"Okay, I'm on. Hi, Alicia."

"Hi, Rob."

"Okay, so what were you saying? Something about a face in the window?"

Alicia explained what she had seen and how Evan had seen it, too. Janith covered the mouthpiece of the phone and asked Matricaria, "Who's Evan?"

"Housemate."

"...And then I brought up the point that vampires can't enter a house unless they're invited, but Evan pointed out that Wesley had manifested in your apartment. Is there any way anyone could have invited him in?"

"We don't know him. How could we have invited him in?"

"Rob, honey, I think that's the point. Were there any strangers in the apartment before we did the binding?" Janith asked from the other phone.

"Remember, that was a long time ago. Let me think..."

Next to Janith, Matricaria prompted, "Any repairmen? Phone workers?"

Behind them, Gabe stood, gloom washing over him like a dirty waterfall. "Uh, Janith?"

Janith and Matricaria turned together to look at Gabe. "There was this one guy who said that the landlord sent him to check for a water leak. You guys were at the store. He said he just needed to look in the bathroom, and that's all he did. I didn't know. *I didn't know.*" There were tears in his eyes.

Matricaria put her arms around Gabe to try to comfort him. "Did he look like the man who manifested in our circle?"

"I don't know. I wasn't paying attention."

Janith laughed, "You, Gabe, not pay attention to a *man*?"

Gabe wiped his eyes with his sleeve.

"I wasn't interested. He was older— too old for me."

Alicia breathed a sigh of relief as she looked up at Evan, who was watching with great concern as she spoke to Janith.

"Ah. Okay. I'm sorry to hear that, but at least that means we don't have to worry. Yes, okay, I will. Still at eight? Okay. Thanks. Goodbye."

Evan cocked his head in a humorous, puppy-dog way.

"He was invited. Someone in their group invited him in, thinking he was a plumber."

Evan exhaled, closing his eyes and dropping his shoulders with relief. "Thank gods!"

"Janith thinks that I should still do the circle of protection at eight, so I'm going to do that. Do you want to join me?"

"No, I think I'll stay down here and do some martial arts practice with my bo." He showed her what he had run upstairs to retrieve, a thick four-foot long ash stick, smooth and polished, with its slight nicks and scratches lending a fine patina. "Some believe that staff fighting techniques were developed when peasants were prohibited from carrying weapons. The resourceful peasants developed a fighting system using traditional farming implements like hoes and rakes."

He twirled the bo like a parade baton and then flipped it over each shoulder, grabbing it with the opposite hand, squatting as he did, so that the bo would clear the ceiling. Again, Alicia was impressed.

"But that's just a stick. Vampires are stronger than humans."

Without a word, Evan flipped the stick so that it faced her like a spear. Looking down, she realized that the ends were very slightly tapered; had he been serious, he could have used it as a stake.

"Oh," she said, smiling. "I get your point."

Chapter 26

Rob looked at the altar, mentally checking off a list. Binding cord, wax, herbs, incense, charcoal, poppet. Everything appeared to be there.

They would do it again. Bind the vampire. Would they be successful this time? They had to be.

Maybe Janith was right. Maybe this situation was bigger than they were. Maybe after they did this ritual, he and Janith should call Sumner and Tania, their teachers, and ask their advice on what to do next. Maybe they should get a few covens together, for more power, more strength. Maybe they should have done that already...

No! Too many maybes! Doubt, be gone! Rob knew that for a spell to work, a witch or magician had to have belief and strength of will. Even the smallest doubt could sabotage the work of the coven.

Doubt, be gone! We WILL prevail!

Alfred took his TV dinner and glass of wine to the sitting room. 'The Wizard of Westville' had just returned from reading at a psychic house party an hour ago and he was exhausted. It had been a stereotypical suburban party; the women, well dressed and coiffed, anxiously wanting to know if their children would succeed at school, if their husbands had been faithful on those weekend fishing trips last summer; the men wanting to know if they should invest in a certain stock... and some wanting to know if their wives suspected what went on during their fishing trips.

He arranged his meal on a TV tray and then leaned back, running tired hands through his thick, pale hair. "Well, it's important to them, right, Tituba?" he said, addressing the voodoo doll on the bookshelf.

Regardless, it had gone well. He had managed to avoid painful truths, instead counseling them on ways to improve openness and trust with their spouses and relaying methods for encouraging a reticent child. He had kept each reading short, and that helped. It didn't give him enough time to connect deeply enough to see things that might upset the subject. A few had made appointments for full readings later. That's when he'd tackle the difficult insights.

But he had read for almost two hours, and it had taken a lot out of him. Leaning his head back, he made the mistake of closing his eyes "for a second," and quickly drifted off to a troubled sleep.

After the phone call to Meg, the musical jam that she and Evan had planned dissolved. It was hard to think of music when outside an unknown terror was waiting, watching.

"I'm not going to wait. I'm going to go upstairs and cast the circle now."

While the coven started the ritual, Alicia had planned to find a suitable spot in her room to sit comfortably and go into a meditative state. She would surround herself with protective energy, as Meg had taught her. She would cast a circle of salt, don both pentacles, cross her fingers, and not leave the magical protection of the circle until the first strong light of dawn pierced the horizon.

She felt vaguely uneasy about leaving the living room— and Evan— but all of her supplies were upstairs: the salt, the water, the second pentacle. And though the vampire was surely targeting her, was it irresponsible to leave Evan on his own, unprotected?

"What about you? Are you going to be okay? I feel wrong abandoning you."

Evan put a gentle hand on her shoulder. "Would you feel better doing the circle down here?"

Alicia leaned into his touch. "You read my mind! Yeah, I would, but everything's upstairs."

"Bring it down here." He gently rubbed her shoulder. "Need some help?"

"No, I think I can get it all in one trip. Be right back."

"Okay."

As she turned to go, Alicia, being Alicia, couldn't help but think of the practical.

"Evan, maybe you should turn off the congee?"

The coven stood together mutely, in a circle, holding hands, eyes gently closed, each one of them breathing slowly, deliberately. Inside the small apartment, all was silent. Outside, the world clattered, honked, and screeched, but it seemed miles away for them, miles away.

Janith squeezed the hands of the people on either side of her, opened her eyes, and announced:

"Okay, folks, let's boogie!"

Grasping the round ball atop the newel post at the bottom of the stairs, Alicia could feel an undercurrent or vibration in her palm. Her logical mind assumed that it was something physical, something mechanical— like a low oscillation from the furnace— and dismissed it. As she bounded up the stairs, having let go of the post and handrail, she could still feel a slight palpitation from when she had touched the post.

At the top landing, she noticed it in her other palm, too, and it strengthened as she approached her bedroom door.

Alfred quickly plunged into a deep dream state, more quickly than sleep psychologists would have us believe was possible. His eyes moved rapidly, his breathing and heart rate increased, and his body fell into a state of paralysis.

In the dream, he was walking down a city street late at night, when he noticed two birds in a small alleyway to his left. One was much larger, so much so that he thought it might be a mother and baby. Wondering what birds were doing awake at this time of night, he stepped closer to investigate.

The birds looked like red-winged blackbirds, with shiny ebony feathers, but their wings, which normally would have had red and yellow epaulets and tips of white, were *all* red, and as he leaned closer, he could see that the red was blood.

As he withdrew in shock, the larger of the birds turned to look at him with fiery, piercing eyes, its beak opening to reveal— quite unnatural for a bird— a row of teeth.

A row punctuated by long, sharp canines.

Dangerous and menacing, it stared, but not quite so dangerous and menacing as the smaller bird, the baby bird, who, after baring its own sharp fangs, took one quick jump, flew up and bit him savagely on the neck.

The coven released their held hands and stepped into position; Rob and Janith at the altar, and Matricaria slightly behind them. Once again, because she held the connection to Alicia, she would be instrumental in helping them focus their energy toward their target.

From beneath the altar, Janith withdrew a sword from its metal scabbard. With grave determination she lifted it. Candlelight glinted off its steel blade. It was a beautiful weapon, with dark wood handle, crescent-shaped brass guard, and brass coin-shaped pommel engraved with a pentacle. It was a symbolic ritual weapon used only in the circle, and never as an instrument of violence, never to cut.

As Janith lifted it and drew in the power, she said a silent prayer to whatever gods may be that her injunction would hold, that on this night she would not have to resort to the violence that was taboo.

Slowly she circumscribed the ritual area with her sword, all the while intoning in a measured, deliberate voice:

> O thou circle, be thou a boundary
> Between our world and the worlds beyond.
> Protect and preserve us.
> Strengthen and sustain us.

When she returned to the point at which she had started, she kissed the blade and replaced the sword in its scabbard.

She stepped to the center of the circle, stretched out her right hand, the first two fingers pointing to the ground as she spun and delivered another address to the circle that she had just inscribed:

> Circle of power, this charge I lay,
> Shield us all who in thee stay.

Behind her, standing close, the coven mimicked her actions, spinning with her, directing energy with her, enforcing the shield that would protect them during this dangerous operation.

They knew that Janith and Rob would ask them again ritually, as they had the first time, if they understood the dangers and wanted to continue.

But they also knew, each one of them, that this was a mere formality. Not one of them would dare step out of the circle now, for whatever it was that haunted them would have felt the vibrations of the circle being formed, and would be drawn to it, like metal to a magnet. And meeting the wall of protection that the circle had just created, whatever it was that troubled them would be left to rage outside the circle.

No, no matter how dangerous it would be to be in this magical circle, it was certainly much more dangerous to be *outside* it.

Caught in the cerebral puzzle of what could possibly be going on with her neurological system, Alicia failed to notice the shadows in the far corner of her room.

One of the them was Moonshadow.

And, Alicia being Alicia, she saw Moonshadow before she saw anything else— before she saw the vampire standing before her.

"That soup smells good. What did he call it?"

From under the altar, Janith retrieved two nested enamel pans. The top one contained melted paraffin. The bottom contained boiling hot water, to keep the paraffin soft.

"Okay, what do we have?"

They had decided to add herbs this time, to strengthen the spell. Matricaria opened a square of silk holding dried, light-green leaves, whose furry surface was still discernible. "Mullein. I read somewhere that it has an overpowering effect on demons. Vampires are a type of demon, right?"

Janith removed the top pan and placed it on the rug. "For our purposes, yes. It's worth a try."

"By the way," Rob added. "We tried some herbs in wax once before, but we put them in while the wax was still melting on the stove. They fried to a crisp. This time the wax should be cool enough not to fry it, but warm enough to release its essence."

The coven watched intently as Janith stirred in the herbs with a wooden spoon. "Yes, it seems to be okay. They're blending in fine."

"We could also use essential oils, if we had to, right?" Amber asked.

"Yes, we could. We didn't have anything on hand that fit the bill as well as mullein, though, and that we had only as a dried herb."

"Okay, time to shape it. Who wants to volunteer?"

"I'll do it," said Gabe, coming forcefully out of an uncharacteristic period of silence. "It's my fault that the bastard got in the first time. Believe me, I've got plenty of intent to work into the shaping."

Alicia couldn't scream. All her life she had repeatedly had the same nightmare where she faced various dangers and never, never, could she scream. Here was the nightmare embodied.

But she *could* talk.

"Frederick! What are you doing here? How— "

"Y'know, you shouldn't leave windows open when they're right over a roof. Shimmy up the drainpipe. That's all it took."

Alicia looked past him, to the open window that overlooked the front porch.

"No, but you, you're not supposed to be able to—"

"Oh, you mean, *who invited me*, huh? My good pal Joey invited me. Remember Joey, your old roomie? The one you used to work with at Theoretic? We go way back. Used to see him at the bar downtown after softball games. Late after softball games. So, how's he doing? He was moving boxes when I saw him. Just a few nights ago. He invited me in for a beer. He didn't tell you? Aw. He must have forgotten. Yeah, I'm *sure* he forgot." With that disclosure, Frederick's gaze turned hard.

Alicia looked away quickly. Frederick only laughed.

"Yeah, you had your suspicions about me, didn't ya? What, did your friend Susie tell ya?"

At her friend's name, Alicia looked up at him, unable to stop herself.

"Oooh, hit a nerve, did I? Yeah, your friend Susie. Your *good* friend Susie. Now that I think of it, she mentioned you. Mentioned you a lot. How you were busy. Always too busy. Too busy for *her*, anyway. Or was it that you thought you were too good for her, huh? Had your fancy job and your night school? Couldn't spend time with low-lifes like her, huh?"

"NO! She didn't really say that! How could she think that I thought she was a low life? I respected her, I admired her! I just— "

"Just didn't have time for her, huh? I tell ya someone else you didn't have time for."

Frederick looked down at Moonshadow, who was crouching on the floor staring up at him. The cat had been flicking his tail rapidly, first just at the tip, but as the vampire looked down, the flipping became more rapid, more brusque. Moonshadow's ears flattened back and he lowered his stance even more, emitting a low-pitched growl. His tail, now bristling, stopped flicking, and instead arched in a display of defense.

"Yes, your precious little kitty!" With preternatural swiftness, Frederick scooped up Moonshadow with one supernaturally strong hand.

Alicia had no problem screaming now.

"LEAVE HIM ALONE!"

The middle-aged Wizard woke with such force that his TV tray went flying and his heart contracted in an agonizing spasm.

Any normal person might have thought it was just a bad dream, but Alfred had lived a life in communication with the unknown, with esoteric symbols. It may have been a bad dream, but it was not *merely* a bad dream.

He sat back to catch his breath and to try to make sense of it all. Across from him, Tituba had left her perch on the shelf and now lay on her stomach, with her head up, like a baby learning to crawl. Any normal person would have seen just an inanimate object jarred off the shelf when Alfred jerked awake, but Alfred had lived a life in which everyday events might be omens that could portend the future, or symbols that would trigger his psychic senses.

"What are you trying to tell me, Tituba? Who is she?"

The word *she* came out of nowhere, and flashes of intuition rapidly flooded his mind. Yes, it was a woman, and a woman he had read not long ago. Closing his eyes and trying to relax, he waited for the next image...

Yes, it was the no-nonsense woman with the long flyaway hair. Alicia. And she was in mortal danger.

Alfred sprung up from the couch and grabbed his schedule book from the table next to the phone. If he had written down her number, he could call her. But as he thumbed through the pages and found Alicia's name, he found that not only did he not have her number, he did not have the time.

His solar plexus contracted sharply, telling him that whatever was happening, it was happening *now*, and there was no time for phone calls.

Alfred hurriedly set himself at his reading table, pulling back a black velvet cloth to expose a large crystal ball. His hands shaking, he lit a small candle and cone of incense. Quickly setting himself into a meditative state, he stared deeply into the ball. A swirl of smoke that formed before his eyes— smoke not from the incense, but from his inner self— told him that he was well on the way to psychic vision. He pictured Alicia as he remembered her from her visit, and the swirl of smoke changed to a dimly lit bedroom where he saw Alicia, a vampire, and a snarling, hissing cat.

Show a news report of thousands dead from famine and many will just sadly say, "That's too bad" or "That's life." But show a defenseless animal in danger, and a deep need to nurture and protect kicks in.

And so it was with Alfred, whose own cat he had loved so much that he had it preserved by taxidermy. Looking into the crystal ball, he watched in horror as Frederick reached for Moonshadow.

Drawing from deep from within him, from the deep reserves of his soul and a lifetime— or more— of magic, Alfred jumped up, pointed a finger so forcefully at the crystal ball that he could have shattered it with a thought, and yelled,

"STOP!"

Downstairs Evan moved gracefully through some warm-up tai chi chuan forms. Then, picking up his staff, he practiced short, forceful lunges as he concentrated on moving the *chi*. As he worked on refining his technique, he willed all else from his mind while remaining alert to his surroundings.

He was deep in this state of awareness when the sounds jarred him into action— Alicia's scream, followed quickly by Moonshadow's piercing yowl.

Bounding up the stairs three at a time, his long legs and adrenaline had him at her door just as *Frederick* howled... in pain.

Gabe laid the wax poppet on a black cotton square in the center of the circle and peeled the excess wax off his hands, dropping it into the pan.

"Good job, Gabe!" Janith complimented him.

Gabe smiled, a coquettish grin they knew well. "If anyone knows the shape of a man's body, it's me."

They all chuckled softly, glad to have a little humor provide a brief respite during tonight's dread working.

Rob stood up and the coven did the same. They all joined hands. After years of study together, they knew the routine, even though tonight it would differ from their normal ritual practice.

"We're going to streamline the oath a bit. If you agree, you will all repeat it after me, in unison. If you feel you can't do it this time, let go of the hands on either side and step back and wait. After the oath is over, we'll let you out of the circle. No one will blame you if you go. By doing this binding, you are binding yourself to the subject— to the vampire."

Janith also addressed the group, her voice strong, intense, and deliberate: "Remember that together we are strong, but if even *one person* doubts, we are *all* in danger. As your High Priestess, I am responsible for all within my circle. I won't see you unwittingly stand in harm's way. Confirm to us now your will to stay and your courage to do the work, or leave this circle with our blessings."

Rob began the oath, "I, Rob, do affirm..."

Frederick being Frederick, he had grabbed the cat without thinking, clasping Moonshadow in the middle of his back, not realizing how agile cats could be.

He also failed to read the signs that the cat was transitioning from defensive to offensive mode. Moonshadow's ears had rotated completely back and his pupils had dilated so much that his beautiful deep emerald eyes appeared completely black.

While raising Moonshadow to his mouth to deliver the bite, Frederick was assaulted by the furious batting of fast furry paws, claws unsheathed and extended.

Nothing was a match for a vampire's speed— except maybe a terrified cat.

Yowling maniacally, Moonshadow raked deep red furrows in Frederick's cheeks and nose, and although vampires could heal, that didn't mean it didn't hurt. Frederick, in return, howled in pain, which caused the frightened cat to fight harder for release.

Angry now at the furious animal in his hand, Frederick leaned down for the bite, but he had barely pierced the thick Persian coat and begun to drink when he was struck by a swift, thick stick, connecting roughly in the area of his bladder.

Stunned, he raised his eyes and saw Evan, feet flat on the floor, back straight, bo pointed directly at him, with a fierceness in his eyes that rivaled the cat's.

Moonshadow, flesh torn from his neck, bleeding profusely, took advantage of this momentary distraction and wriggled out of Frederick's hands, leaving the men to their face-off.

Not one of the coven chose to leave the circle. All affirmed, with strong, determined voices, that they would assist.

Janith thanked them as she squeezed the hands on either side of her. "We're going to raise the power over the poppet as we name it. For this part, we're going to circle clockwise, as we always do, okay?" The coven nodded.

She stepped back one step and then closed her eyes, taking three measured inhalations and exhalations. Once again, the coven, so accustomed to the routine of ritual, did the same.

At the end of the last breath, she began the chant. The coven accompanied her as she did, standing in place, but swaying ever so slightly as the power built.

> Long ago, in days gone past,
> When shadows ruled the land,
> The people gathered far and wide,
> From hill and dale and strand.
>
> Gather we now as long ago,
> The circle strong, unbroken.
> Hand in hand, in twisting dance,
> As magic chant is spoken.
>
> Gather we now as moon rides high
> And incense smokes and burns,
> Energy courses through our veins,
> And the Old Power returns...

It certainly has, Janith thought. *And not necessarily all of it for good.* She thought of Wesley, his power, his presence.

And spring. How things return in the spring.

The coven stood still, repeating the deliberate breathing, as Janith now spoke their intentions:

> We name this doll Wesley.
> What we do to it, we do to him.

Tugging on the person to her right, Janith led them in a circle, led them in repeating the naming. Faster and faster they circled, their speech quickening, hair and robes flying, until at last Janith brought her hands down, pushing the energy with her palms, driving it deep into the poppet.

Frederick stared, mouth agape, at the figure before him. "Aw, c'mon, man. You can't be serious. Do you know what I am?"

Evan did not respond. He stared straight ahead at Frederick, intensely aware, yet seeming totally relaxed, like one of the great cats. Like a panther ready to spring.

"C'mon, Kung Fu man, give me your best shot." Frederick was laughing now, arms bent as a boxer, feet spread lightly apart. "Look at you— pajamas and a beanie! Woo! Yeah, I'd like to see you walk into a bar like *that*!"

On the other side of the room, Alicia watched, astounded. Her cat had just been mauled while she had stood there helplessly and watched. And now she was letting Evan put himself in danger. Her mind flashed back to the night of the explosion, when she had let Rick, the guard, enter the room first; had let him enter, knowing full well what could be waiting for him. And now she was letting Evan stand off against a vampire, a battle he *couldn't* win.

The vampire was circling Evan now, bobbing and weaving, but Evan calmly faced him, elegantly pirouetting, following his moves, never letting him see his back.

The vampire was fast, too fast, and he kept circling.

What if Evan gets dizzy and trips? She had to do something, anything, and soon!

Alicia looked around the room for a weapon. She had no idea how to fight, and certainly didn't have the reflexes or strength. She had moved slowly through life, her reaction time slowed by the mental process of trying to analyze every situation that she encountered. No, she definitely couldn't fight him, but maybe she could distract him long enough so that Evan could— could fight or run away.

Okay, what do I have in here that's heavy? The only shoes she wore were sneakers, and they weren't nearly heavy enough. *Too bad we aren't downstairs. I have an iron skillet that would really do some damage.*

Think, think! You've got back problems. What is there in this room that pains you to lift! THINK!

And just as Frederick stepped in toward Evan, she found the perfect heavy object:

Her pocketbook.

It began as a tingle, but in no time his regrown left arm was caught in a paroxysm of pain.

Wesley was not used to pain. Vampires, being immortal, were immune to diseases and the effects of aging. The pain in his arm, therefore, caught him off guard.

It must be otherworldly in nature, he decided, and with just a second or two of concentration, he confirmed his diagnosis: The coven! They were attempting to bind him again!

He tore open the curtain separating the truck's cab from the sleeping compartment. Seizing the driver by the throat, he squeezed just hard enough to show that he meant business. "I am going for a walk. You are not to leave this truck except to relieve yourself, and even then, use the side of the road and return immediately. Do you understand?"

The driver, who could not talk at this point, merely nodded.

"When we do the binding, remember that we need to bind him from causing harm to *anyone, anywhere.* Make sure that you hold that in your mind. Otherwise, we protect Alicia and leave the rest of the world vulnerable."

The coven murmured their assent and took their places kneeling around the poppet, which rested in the center of the circle.

"Mat, what is it?" Janith looked with concern at Matricaria's pale, wide-eyed face.

"I don't know, but I do know that something's happened."

"Oh, gods. Let's hurry!"

Rob sprang into action. With one hand he grabbed the black cord they'd use for binding. With the other, he picked up the poppet. "What are the words? The words?" Unflappable as he usually was, he was panicking this time.

Matricaria took the poppet and cord from him. "Allow me!"

Rob looked at her as if to say, "Are you sure?".

Answering his unuttered thought, she replied, "She's my friend and my student. Let *me* do it. I'm involved already. No need for you to reactivate your involvement."

Rob nodded once and leaned back on his heels. Matricaria began the binding.

> Creature of night, we bind thee.
> You cannot harm us! You cannot harm us!

Janith look the lead, standing up and leading the group in a counter-clockwise circle, as she had when they first joined hands against the vampire. Together they chanted with Matricaria, blindly parroting her words, forgetting that they were to protect *all*, saying only the words that would protect Alicia and them alone, sending all the energy they could muster, imagining an unspecified dark shape called Wesley, and imagining a wall between them and him.

As they had done before, they stepped up the pace, dancing faster and faster around the circle, stamping the floor at the word "cannot." The circle widened as their sweat-moistened palms and centrifugal force allowed them to slip away from the center.

At the center, only Matricaria remained, wrapping the doll with a strength and a vengeance so fierce that her knuckles glowed white in the candlelight. As she wound the final strand, she stilled her hands, willing in all her energy and power. Around her, the coven, on their final line, dropped to the floor beside her, likewise forcing all their power and energy into the poppet:

> YOU *CANNOT* HARM US!

As Alicia reached for her impromptu weapon, Evan quickly, forcefully lunged. But Frederick, although he knew nothing about Eastern martial arts, had had his share of bar fights and knew how to block. With his vampire-gained speed, he quickly brought up his right arm, blocking the lunge and snapping the bo in half.

At that very moment, Alicia wrapped both straps of her pocketbook around her hand and rushed Frederick, swinging as she ran. She caught the vampire on the left temple, knocking him only slightly off balance, but off balance enough for Evan to step forward and flip the sharp end of the split bo in front of him as he had demonstrated to Alicia, this time driving it deep through the vampire's heart.

Wesley had left the cab to pace, to rage furiously at the witches who dared try to restrain him. The witches who *were* restraining him.

More than a thousand miles away, they had reached into the astral, the plane of existence where the vampire spirit dwelled, and had curtailed his activity. He would still live, still kill to live, but he could not harm *them*.

"You are correct. *I* cannot harm you. But there are many other vampires in the world. And I do not walk alone."

And in the haughty, overconfident manner of a man of his time and station, Wesley pronounced:

"And I *will* return."

At first Frederick didn't react. Then, very slowly he glanced down at the stake through his heart and the thick, tarry blood oozing from the wound like pitch. He looked as if he couldn't quite believe it, didn't quite know what to make of it. Gingerly he poked a finger in the ooze, then looked up at Evan.

"Hey, well done, Kung Fu Man. Didn't think ya had it in ya. Of course, you couldn't have done it if a *girl* hadn't helped you."

Maybe Frederick had expected Evan to take offense, to charge at him senselessly, to get close enough for Frederick to rip and rend his neck as he had done to the cat, but he knew nothing about discipline and the martial arts.

Evan stood his ground, relaxed and alert, eyes on Frederick, not reacting to the intended insult.

"The point is, if you'll pardon the pun, " Evan said, "We did it. We did it, *Vampire Man*."

Alicia, who had fallen with the force of her swing, and had then scrambled out of harm's way, watched from the edge of the bed. Was it her imagination, or was Frederick withering before her eyes, like roses caught decaying in time-lapse photography?

He was leaning against the wall now, pulling at the splintered bo in his chest. She worried that he might pull it out, but Evan had picked up the other splintered piece and she knew from Evan's previous demonstration that even if Frederick were able to pull the first half out, Evan was capable of plunging the other half deep into his heart.

As she watched, Frederick's complexion, already pale, turned an ashen gray. His teeth were clenched in a display of agony as he slid down the wall, coming to rest sitting on the floor. His feet splayed out limply in front of him and she knew at that moment that she and Evan had succeeded, that Evan had landed a fatal blow.

They watched, silently, for long minutes, neither one daring to move, as Frederick's skin turned the translucent parchment color of old age and then literally flaked off, leaving only a skeleton that, too, flaked and disintegrated before their eyes, leaving only dust on the carpet. They stood transfixed until Alicia broke the silence.

"Oh, my God. Moonshadow!"

It was as if the universe sneezed. There was a brief, quick, rift in the astral, and then nothing.

Wesley, who had settled back into his newspaper after his brief tirade in the parking lot, looked up, knowing that he would not see anything, but knowing, too, that he had to mark a passing.

Frederick was gone.

They were as one, all of them kneeling on the floor, each of them reaching into the center of the circle, hands on the poppet, pushing their energy into it, into the earth far beneath the apartment.

There was a palpable sense of release, and as they tried to regain equilibrium, Janith spoke quietly. "Where are the cakes and wine? We need to ground."

An immediate wave of nausea hit Alfred the Wizard after he sent the energy ball. A wave so powerful that he slid back into his seat, sweating profusely. His heart was pounding, as a strangling band grew tighter across his chest.

He reached desperately for the telephone.

"Moonshadow? *Moonshadow?*" As Evan looked in the rooms upstairs, Alicia flew downstairs, searching frantically for her wounded cat. She followed a trail of blood that dotted the stair treads into the kitchen and then through the open door to the basement.

The trail stopped at the bottom of the stairs, but she knew where he had gone. As quickly and as quietly as she could, she started removing the boxes under the cellar stairs one by one until she saw a protruding tail... soaked with blood.

She crouched down, wanting so desperately to toss the boxes aside and snatch her wounded kitty from his hideaway, but she knew well that a cat's innate fear of quick movement and loud noises meant that she must move slowly, carefully.

She made the chattering, squirrel-like sound she always used when trying to soothe him and peered into the dark. He was sitting upright, paws tucked tightly against his body, with his ears out and almost parallel to the ground. His breathing was rapid and shallow, and he was in obvious pain.

Alicia spoke to him softly, trying to allay his fears. She knew that an injured cat was a dangerous cat. She called out to Evan for help.

"Evan! I found him. Can you bring me a bath towel?"

She listened carefully until she heard the sound of the linen closet opening upstairs, and then turned to Moonshadow. "It's okay, honey, it's okay. Mommy's going to take you to the vet and you'll be okay, all right?"

But for all her cooing and comforting, she knew the awful truth: Moonshadow would most likely die.

"I've got to call the vet's to let them know I'm coming. You stay right here, okay, Moonie?"

Alicia ran up the stairs as fast as she could, leaving Moonshadow to fend for himself.

He looked up at her departure, blinked, and then made a half-hearted effort at grooming, not because of pride or good manners, but because that's what cats do to comfort themselves. Feebly he licked his paw, and, spreading his toes, made an attempt at reaching what had splattered there when he had raked his claws across Frederick's face.

Tried to remove the blood, the unholy blood, Frederick's blood.

"Operator, connect me with the Westville police. I think I'm having a heart attack."

The Wizard clutched his chest with one trembling hand as he held the phone with the other. The burst of energy he had sent into the crystal ball was more than he had sent in years, and he wondered now if a man his age should have done something like that.

Alfred gave his address to the police, hung up the phone, and leaned back, trying to relax. Like so many others in his profession, he knew how to heal, but healing oneself was always hardest. A wave of pain hit him. He breathed through it, willing his heart to relax, willing the pain away.

He should call someone. Someone in his coven. As he reached for the phone, another wave of pain hit.

Evan came racing nimbly down the stairs and handed Alicia a bath towel as she stood at the kitchen phone, talking to the vet's answering service. "Yes, about fifteen minutes. Thank you."

She hung up and indicated the door to the basement. "He's down there."

She led, with Evan following light-footed behind her.

At the bottom of the stairs, she knelt quickly, gently draping the towel over Moonshadow's body, and slid him across the floor toward her.

It was too late. Moonshadow was dead.

After the main body of the ritual, the coven always ritually shared cakes and wine, while still in the circle, to help reconnect them to the physical world and to end the altered state that ritual produced.

The cakes weren't really cakes in the American sense of dessert cakes, but instead were cookies baked by one of the participants. They had been called "cakes" in the rituals passed down to them from their teachers' teachers, and their teachers before that, and so on, so cakes was what they called them.

The process of eating diverted leftover energy to the process of digestion and reinforced the social bond among group members. It also restored them physically after expending so much energy. Tonight they desperately needed that.

Normally the group would also discuss what had happened, what they saw, and how they thought the ritual went, but tonight they agreed that silence was called for, that they should release the spell into the universe and then let it go. And tonight they were all so willing to do that.

Alicia picked up the limp body of the cat who had been her constant companion, sometimes her *only* companion, for the last seven years. She squeezed him tightly to her chest.

"No, no, not my Moonie!"

But it was obvious as she held him that it *was* her Moonie, and he was dead. His tongue, whose tip only barely peeked out from between his lips when he was sleeping, and hid completely when he was awake, now lolled out of the side of his mouth at its full length. His amazing feline tongue ... washcloth, comb, and towel ... now useless. It was so pale that it was no longer pink, but instead a sickly gray. His soft, padded feet that she used to warm in her hands on winter nights would never warm again. She cupped her hand over a front paw, but even the spongy resilience of his toe pads was gone.

His eyes, still open, were glassy and starting to cloud over. No longer the wise windows to the soul of her faithful friend, they changed to the soulless look of a fish on ice at the local deli counter. His body, normally so warm and soft, was growing cold and stiff. And the purr that usually vibrated through Alicia's breastbone whenever she held him was gone, dreadfully gone.

Alicia rocked back and forth, holding his lifeless body to her chest, her normal reserve abandoned, crying, sobbing, wailing, like a peasant woman from a far-away land keening a lament for the dead.

Evan stood by, motionless, knowing that there was nothing he could do to comfort her. Knowing that she was inconsolable.

Chapter 27

The EMT who took the call knew Alfred. His wife had been a regular client of the Wizard for years. The medical technician looked sadly at the man with the oxygen mask who lay in involuntary repose on the stretcher. Alfred would be okay. He would make it. He had had a heart attack, but the EMTs had arrived quickly and now Alfred seemed to be stable.

At the hospital, they transferred Alfred to a gurney, and the EMT returned to the ambulance. His partner was smiling.

"What's so funny? He's a nice guy. My wife says he's a real sweetheart."

"I know, I know. I just wondered. He's a psychic, right?"

"Yeah, so what?"

"Didn't he see this coming?"

"They don't see everything, y'know. They don't see everything."

When Alicia had stopped sobbing long enough for Evan to speak to her, he delicately broached the subject of burial. Had it still been the dead of winter, they could have wrapped the small limp body in the towel and left it in the shed out back for a day or two, but now that the sun was growing stronger, they couldn't count on using the great outdoors as their walk-in refrigerator. They'd have to deal with the body soon.

"Have you thought about how you'd like to prepare Moonshadow for the afterlife?"

"Afterlife?"

"Yes, for his journey to the Otherworld."

"But I believe in reincarnation."

"The two don't contradict. After leaving this incarnation, the soul goes on a journey to the Otherworld, where it rests and reviews the lessons learned in this life."

Alicia swallowed hard and accepted the tissue that Evan had seemingly magically produced. "What do the Chinese do?"

"Well, they had an interesting practice at one time. I don't know if they still adhere to it, but they used to have two burials. The first would be a temporary one, in a shallow grave. During this time, they believed that they could ask favors of the dead. After seven years, they would dig up the body. The bones, or bone dust, would be placed in an urn and then entrusted to the family vault."

"No, I don't think I could bear to dig him up, and a shallow grave wouldn't be too good in this climate. A frost heave might disgorge him." She looked at Evan and laughed, a short, choking laugh. "Disgorge? Where did I come up with *that* word?"

"Yes, it does produce an odd image."

Alicia started to giggle self-consciously. "I'm sorry, but I have this image of the earth puking up bodies."

Evan started to chuckle, too, and in a few minutes, they were laughing uncontrollably, falling into each other in hysterics as they released the tension, the sorrow, the horror of the evening.

Their laughing died down and they found themselves facing each other, tightly embracing; the warmth of their bodies triumphing over the cold reality of death. Desire for the expression of life triumphing over the expression of mortality.

With utmost gentleness that belied a fierce passion, Evan kissed Alicia fully on the mouth. She responded with equal enthusiasm, born more of a desire for closeness than from a rage of lust. Having escaped death so narrowly, watched a vampire disintegrate before her eyes, and seen her closest companion die, what she wanted now was closeness, an affirmation of life in the environs of death.

She needed to bond, to bond so closely that she not only touched, but melded.

With Evan.

"What should we do about Moonshadow?"

He smoothed her hair with his long, sensuous hands. "It's too dark to bury him now. We could cover him and do it tomorrow, okay?"

Alicia didn't like the idea of leaving Moonshadow unburied, alone, exposed, but Evan was right; it *was* too dark. And right now Moonshadow would have to wait. She needed Evan.

"Let's get some sleep."

Looking at him through tear-welled eyes, she said, "No, I can't sleep here."

"We could put him in the shed."

"No, it's not him. It's the vampire... dust..."

Evan held her closely for a minute, rubbing her back with his hands, rocking gently. "We can get a room for the night."

"You mean in a hotel?"

"Yes, a hotel. Or motel. There's one on Route 9 I stayed at when I first moved out here."

"H-how expensive are they?"

Evan pulled back a little, brushing her hair away from her face. "Not very. Not the ones around here. I've got some money..."

"I've got some. Would they take checks?" She knew that they probably would, but she was stalling for time while she tried to adjust to the idea. A hotel? Certainly there was someone she could call on. Carol. Or Betty. She really should be putting money away for home repairs, not spending it on hotels. Not in her own town. It seemed almost sacrilegious to pay for a room in your own town.

As if he sensed her objections, Evan continued. "It's not that much money, not split between two people. I think you need to get away from here, to go somewhere safe."

"Maybe I can call Meg."

"They might still be doing ritual. She might still be in town."

"You're right." Alicia struggled to convince herself that it was okay, okay to spend the money.

"If you don't want me there, I can stay in your car."

"Oh, no. No, that's fine." How do you explain a fear of poverty so strong that it defies logic? A fear of spending lest there be nothing left for emergencies. Yet, this *was* an emergency. "You're right. We need to get out of here."

Tenderly Evan draped the towel over Moonshadow's cold body, tucking the ends gently under the departed pet. "We'll be back in the morning, okay, Moonie?"

Alicia was touched by the way he treated Moonshadow, by the caring, the respect, and she knew now that she could never love a man who didn't love animals, who didn't know the unbelievable bond between human and animal.

She ran her hand over the towel, feeling Moonshadow's cold, rigid, form. No more purring, or turning over on his back with his front paws against his chest in that silly display that she called his baby seal pose.

Her eyes teared up again and she fought hard against the sob that was building inside her. "Let's go."

Chapter 28

Alicia drove to the hotel on Route 9. She stood silently at the registration counter as he handled the details, relieved that he had taken the lead. She had no idea how to book a hotel room or what kind of room to ask for. Evan seemed to know the process well. Maybe too well. Was he used to taking women to hotels?

"And then you take the first corridor on your left after the elevator. Do you need help with your bags?"

"No bags. Thanks."

Evan put a hand on Alicia's shoulder to guide her toward the corridor. She was relieved to notice that she wasn't insulted, didn't feel patronized by his gesture. But that confused her. Why didn't she? Was it because she really needed guidance? Was she losing control again? Her neck twinged as she remembered Wesley, the bite, the obsession. *Not again!*

"Are you okay?" Evan was jiggling the well-worn key into the room's lock.

"Yes. Just a little dazed."

"I think we'll both feel better once we get inside."

"But it's just a room. It can't stop a vampire."

"No, it can't. But he's gone now, remember? And the coven did the ritual for protection. We'll be okay."

Mustiness and stale cigarette odor greeted them as they entered the room, an unpleasant smell to even a smoker like herself. Alicia expected the worst, but the small bathroom looked clean and the bed was neatly made. In the weak illumination of the overhead light, the walls looked a little dingy, but there were no holes or water stains.

Evan was opening the small closet by the door as he spoke. "Why don't you shower and I'll see if I can find an extra blanket to make up the couch."

"You don't have to sleep on the couch. I don't want to be alone."

Evan stopped his search of the top shelf and turned to her. In that spare, elastic moment Alicia worried that he might reject her, might refuse her, might say, "Thanks, but I don't find you attractive." Her apprehension of rejection far outpaced the fear of the terrifying creature that had disintegrated in her bedroom earlier that night.

She watched, helpless, as he turned and placed his hands on her arms and drew her close to him, an act that she was sure would be followed by a polite dismissal.

But then, in a moment that would later seem more unreal than a vampire turning to dust, he kissed her.

Alicia and Evan made love through the long and anxious night, clinging to each other as if drowning, waiting for the break of day. And when dawn came filtering in through the partially closed drapery of the hotel room, it found them nestled together, sleeping soundly.

Alicia woke before Evan. Her first thoughts were of Moonshadow lying on the rough dirt floor of the basement, under the stairs, and then the vampire, who had turned to dust in her bedroom. How did her house, in so few hours, go from being her life's dream, her refuge and strength, to a vault of terror?

The force with which her heart pounded as she lay there cuddled next to Evan wasn't imaginary, for the thumping in her chest woke Evan up.

"You okay?"

"I was just thinking about what happened last night."

"Maybe we shouldn't have— "

She laughed and nuzzled into his chest. "No, not that. That was okay."

"Just okay?"

"Well, more than okay." She kissed him gently on the lips and rubbed his upper arm as he sat up.

"Well, you *did* have some distraction..."

She smiled up at him. "Yes, that I did. But I won't have distraction around the clock."

"No, that's true. You need to cleanse the place."

"What, like with bleach?"

"No," he laughed ever so gently, poking her in the side playfully with a finger, "Although that might not be a bad idea. I was talking about smudging."

"Smudging?"

"It's a Native American tradition. White sage is gathered and bound in a bundle, which they light, and then use the smoke from it to cleanse and purify an area."

"Never heard of it."

"I learned about it in New Mexico."

"You've traveled a lot, haven't you?" *So that's how he knows about hotels.*

"Yes, I guess I have. And you?"

"No, not much at all." She wanted to pick his brain, hear all about the wonderful places he had been, but she couldn't banish the images of the pile of vampire dust and Moonshadow lying dead on the floor from her mind. "I'd like to take care of Moonshadow, if we could."

"Definitely." He stroked her cheek with his hand. "Have you decided what you want to do?"

"I was thinking about what you said about the afterlife. I'd like to make him comfy." Her voice started to break and she choked back a sob. "I'd like to find a box large enough for a nice, soft towel for him to lie on. And put in some dry food and some catnip and one of his toy mousies for his journey." She stopped to wipe her eyes. "And maybe a small picture of me, so that he can remember who I am and how much I loved him."

She was crying now, and Evan leaned over, reached around, and held her close. "I'm sure he knows."

Trying to regain control, she sat up and took a deep breath. "Okay. And we need to clear out the vampire dust. Maybe that'll help get rid of this feeling that the other shoe's going to drop."

"Maybe you could call the coven and see what they suggest."

"That's a good idea. I almost forgot about them."

"Yes, I noticed. You seem to always assume that you're in it alone."

Alicia looked back at him tearfully. "Usually, Evan, I am."

He pulled her close again. "Not today, you're not."

Alfred woke early, though not of his own choosing, although he probably would have woken on his own even if the doctor had not waken him during early morning rounds.

Yes, it had been a heart attack. He had known that he was risking one, sending energy like that, but he couldn't help it. He couldn't stand by and watch Alicia and her cat exposed to danger like that. He would have to call

Norma when he got home, and ask for Alicia's phone number. He wanted to know what happened during the time that he was wracked with pain, desperately trying to summon help, unable to watch the scenes unfolding in his crystal ball.

And he would have to tell her about the vague sense of impending doom that still lingered over him like the stale smell of antiseptic and death that clung to him and everything else in the coronary care unit.

His doctors would tell him it was a normal emotional reaction to a heart attack, but Alfred knew differently; Alfred, who had lived a lifetime reading these signs, knew that the curtain had not yet fallen on this tragic play.

Back at the house, Alicia found a box that would be just right for Moonshadow. It was long and wide enough to fit his slight body, with room for a fluffy towel and supplies for the afterlife, yet not so large that it would require too much digging for the burial.

Outside, Evan had dug a small grave in the southwest corner of the yard, next to the fence. Alicia had planted vegetables there the previous year, so the earth was relatively easy to dig, but she was grateful that Evan had volunteered because right now she didn't think she could deal with the pain.

Evan finished digging and joined Alicia in the basement where Moonshadow lay. Gently she lifted his lifeless body as Evan slid the box beneath it. Together they arranged the food, catnip, and toy mousie around him, Alicia telling Moonshadow how much she loved him, and pointing out the supplies for the trip. She stroked an unbloodied area of Moonshadow's silky fur and closed the box. It was not lost on her that Evan was there for her, for Moonshadow, for them both. It was the closest thing to a family that she had experienced in a long time.

Evan helped her to her feet and together they exited the basement through the bulkhead door, which groaned and squealed as she pushed it open for the first time in the season. Normally the exit from the dark basement to the back yard would have been blinding, but the day had turned overcast and a stiff wind forecast a possible shower. They emerged without blinking, without noticing much change from the darkness, the darkness that had so long pervaded her life.

Together they laid the box in the hole. Evan was kneeling next to Alicia as she delivered her tearful eulogy and final instructions for the passage. "Moonshadow, you were such a good and sweet cat, always there for me.

Even now, you died protecting me— well, some would say you died protecting your territory, but you died, and you died because of me, and I am *so* sorry."

At this she broke into a heartbreaking sob. Evan gently hugged her as she struggled to regain her composure. "You weren't the first to die because of me, but maybe, if the coven was successful, you'll be the last." She stopped to wipe her eyes and blow her nose. "Moonshadow, may the small gifts I've left for you comfort you in your journey to the afterlife." Remembering mythology that she studied in high school English, she continued "May you arrive at the other side of the River Styx rested and refreshed, and may bowls of sweet cream and plates heaped with tuna be waiting!"

She smiled with all the hope and joy she could muster and threw the first handful of dirt onto the box that was Moonshadow's coffin. Taking this as a cue, Evan rose and shoveled in the rest of the earth, as Alicia stood and dried her eyes.

Yes, Moonshadow. May your death be the last.

Back home, Meg waited with growing alarm for someone to answer the phone at Alicia's house. Alicia was supposed to call her to let her know how it went during the binding, but she never did. And now no one was answering the phone.

Maybe she's not up yet and doesn't have a telephone in the bedroom. No, that didn't make sense. Alicia would definitely have a telephone in the bedroom, in case of emergency, even if she had to wire it herself. *Maybe she's in the shower.* That made more sense.

She would try again in a few minutes. And try not to worry while she waited.

"Oh, no. Your congee!"

"It should be okay."

"Really?"

"A little fermented maybe, but okay. Hungry?"

Alicia wasn't, really, not after burying her closest companion, but she wanted to please Evan, and even more, she really wanted to try the congee, a full bowl, just to immerse herself in its flavor, in its creator's life.

Evan took the pot to the sink and trickled water into the thickened congee while he stirred with a wooden spoon. "It wasn't hot enough in here for it to ferment. This should be fine, especially after we add some flavorings."

Without really leaving his place, he stretched his long legs and reached for the refrigerator. Alicia watched, not quite knowing what to do with herself. She wanted to wrap around him, feel his warmth, his soft skin, his strong hands, but she had always hated clinging types, and she was sure that he did, too.

Evan pulled scallions, carrots, and soy sauce from the refrigerator and placed them on the counter. He looked deeply into the refrigerator, then pulled away, apparently not finding what he was looking for. He shut the door and stepped to the other end of the counter. "Mushrooms look good!"

"Oh, that's right! You put them in to soak."

Alicia timidly crept up behind him. With one hand, Evan emptied the mushrooms into the pot. With his free arm, he pulled Alicia close to him and rubbed her back.

"Can I help?" She asked, needing something to do to keep her from adhering to him like a burr on a pant leg after a walk in the woods. She didn't want to cling.

"You can slice the carrots. Make them very thin. These are organic carrots, but you still should wash them."

He handed them to her and she pulled away, regretfully, to find a cutting board. Together they chopped vegetables in silence until Evan walked across the room to the radio. "Mind if I tune this to an NPR station?"

"Go ahead. What's that?" She had only known the local rock stations on the FM band, and the local news and weather station on AM. She had a feeling that it wasn't either of those.

"You've never heard of NPR?"

"No."

"Ah. National Public Radio. It's a loosely organized public radio network of independent member radio stations. They buy programming from a private, not-for-profit corporation. It's been around for about ten or eleven years. I started listening to it in college."

Alicia cringed a little at the mention of college. Although she was going to college nights, could her education ever compete with that of a day school? Surely the missed cultural enrichment of campus life would make a difference. Make her different. Would she always be such a misfit? No matter what she did, she'd always fall short somehow.

She steered her mind back to Evan to hear him speaking enthusiastically about the radio network's cultural programming, its political discussions, its diverse music—all of which Alicia had never known existed. He spoke disparagingly of the commercial rock stations, not realizing, she hoped, that that's what she listened to. Something in his voice, in his intonation, and his delivery soothed her, though, and she started to find herself not feeling ashamed or belittled, but uplifted and improved, by just his conversation.

Evan's world was so different from hers, but now instead of feeling the rage against the bourgeois that she felt in her high school days, she was fascinated by their wider world.

And part of it, she realized, was the way Evan presented it to her. Obviously, he was a man of experience. He had traveled widely, and studied well, but in the short time that she had known him, he never made her feel she was beneath him. Instead, he seemed happy to share his knowledge with her hungry mind.

The ringing telephone interrupted her contemplation. She put down the knife and answered the phone on the second ring. It was Meg.

"Are you okay?"

"Sure, why?" Alicia sat on the floor in the hall, the long cord of the phone easily reaching to the small alcove where she customarily sat to talk.

"Well, you know, the ritual. I was wondering if there were any side effects."

"Oh, my God. That's right!" She was so distracted by Evan that she had, for the briefest second, forgotten the horror of the night before, let alone the ritual that ran in parallel. "Well, we killed ourselves a vampire, and..."

It was easy for her to tell the details of Frederick's demise, but she choked on the telling of Moonshadow's death and subsequent burial.

"Oh, Alicia, not Moonshadow! That must have been so terrible!"

"Yes, it was. Surreal." She started to cry again, but caught herself. "I think we gave him a good sending-off, though."

"Do you want me to come over?"

"No, that's okay. Evan's been very, uh, *helpful.*" She whispered the word, hoping that Meg would notice her odd inflection and read between the lines.

"Helpful, huh? That's great! Are you going to be okay, though? I mean, I know he staked the vampire, but, well, what if it's not completely gone, or what if another shows up to investigate? Do you want one of the coven to stay there with you?"

Meg was right. She didn't know yet if everything was over. But Evan had shown courage, strength, and quickness of thought, and those attributes would be priceless no matter what the situation. Besides, he, too, had studied the occult, and he had studied Eastern mysticism and martial arts. If anyone was a candidate to be her guardian, it was Evan.

"I think Evan's up to the task. He's actually had training, and he's not afraid."

"All right, but call me if you need me, okay?"

"Okay."

"And Alicia, uh, I don't know how to say this, but don't get so caught up in the moment with him that you're not paying attention to your surroundings. There'll be plenty of time for that later, after we're sure there's no rebound from this."

"Yeah, I thought of that."

As she spoke, Evan gently sank to a squat and handed Alicia a bowl of congee. Holding her hand over the phone, she whispered, "It's Meg."

"Invite her over for congee."

"Really?"

"Sure, there's plenty."

He spun up to standing and walked back into the kitchen. Alicia felt ambivalent about having a guest interfere with her afterglow with Evan, but it would be good to have Meg here, to help with the smudging and protection.

"Meg, have you ever had congee?"

Alfred tossed and turned in his hospital bed. Something wasn't right. He knew that the energy had hit its mark and that Alicia had survived, but the heart attack had pulled him away from his crystal ball before he could see the events unfold in their entirety.

He had tried to call his coven after he called the ambulance, but it was Saturday night, and the first two members he had called weren't home. He needed their help, not just for himself, but for Alicia.

Though their physical telephones didn't have answering machines, their psychic ones did, and each one suddenly felt a stab of worry about Alfred and tried to reach him. Not being able to reach him at home, they called each other, and eventually called the hospital. Having found him there, they immediately started a healing circle and held a vigil through the night. It was only when the hospital upgraded his condition to fair that the coven closed the circle and got some sleep.

Alfred had spoken to them just an hour ago, explaining the situation and asking them to direct their energies now toward Alicia, but he had little to go on. He didn't have Alicia's phone number, so he couldn't call her. Norma, his only connection to Alicia, wasn't answering her phone. She most likely was out, probably at church for the day.

All he could do now was wait. Wait, and ask that the coven send general protection energy to Alicia, wherever she might be.

"That bastard! How could I be so stupid? How could I be so *fucking* stupid?" Betty sniffled as she tried to talk on the phone and wipe her nose at the same time.

"What happened?" Carol asked.

"He didn't show up at all last night. He said he'd be here around 7:30 or 8. I waited all night, and he didn't show up, didn't call."

"Maybe he's been in an accident or something?"

"I called the hospitals. Nothing. Carol, I don't even know where he lives. After he said he wanted to get a place together, I stopped pushing him for details. I thought everything would be okay. He's probably screwing that brunette he was staring at in the bowling alley the other night."

"Oh, Betty. I don't know what to say. He could have at least called. I hope you're wrong, but it doesn't sound good, does it? I mean, he never told you everything, always came and went as he pleased. I hate to say it, but I wouldn't take him back if he *did* show up— not unless he had two broken legs and all his dialing fingers were broken!"

"You're right. You're absolutely right. But I love him. I really, really love him." She was sobbing now. "I don't... I don't know how to describe it, but, but he made me feel like no other man ever did. It was as if he consumed me."

"Wow! How poetic!"

Betty laughed.

"That's so sad." Carol tried to bolster her friend's feelings. "I know this won't help, but you're still young, you're attractive, you have a nice figure, there'll be other guys."

"But not like Frederick!"

"Maybe that's a blessing?"

"Yeah, yeah, I suppose you're right. Oh, God, Carol, will I ever learn? The smooth ones are the bad ones. I should go for Joe Average. Y'know, the guy next door. Someone who won't love me and leave me." She sighed heavily. "Thanks for listening, Carol. I hope I didn't wake you up. Norma's not answering her phone and I just had to talk to someone."

"No, I was up. I usually don't do much on Sunday mornings. I think Norma goes to church."

"Yeah, that's right. I forgot. Well, thanks again. See you tomorrow."

"Okay. You take care of yourself."

Betty hung up the phone, slumped back on the couch and then curled up in a fetal position, listless. She had had such high hopes for Frederick.

Maybe he'd show up later. No, she didn't think so. She didn't know why, but she felt with certainty that this was the end.

Deep in her neck, a painful spasm caused her to flinch protectively. Instinctively, she brought her hand up to the pain.

Frederick. Gone. She'd miss him.

Some years an early summer immediately followed winter, or so it seemed. The balmy, beautiful spring days were followed by cool, wet, weather.

Yes, this year spring seemed to be holding in the reins, Meg thought as she stepped out of the house to the overcast day. The wind was mild and steady, the clouds moved readily through the sky, and all around was a sense of becoming, a sense of change, but not a sense of the promise of spring.

As she drove south toward Alicia's, Meg thought about what Alicia had told her. She probably should have called Rob and Janith before she left the house, but she wanted to get to Alicia's quickly. Someone needed to be there with her. After all, Alicia hadn't known Evan very long. He was just a friend of a friend. Was he really as capable as she seemed to think he was? Was he even who he said he was?

Though she hadn't mentioned it to Alicia, Meg had begun to wonder if he wasn't an agent of Wesley's. Destroying Frederick would fit in nicely with that theory: the only person who could be a real threat to a vampire was another vampire. With Frederick out of the way, Wesley would have less to impede him.

Watching for cops, Matricaria drove just slightly over the speed limit and glided through every yellow light. Maybe Evan wasn't a double agent, but there was something about all of this that still made her very uncomfortable.

Uncomfortable, even though her ritual bag with all her magical tools and a sharp wooden stake lay within easy reach on the passenger seat.

"Hi, c'mon in."

Three months ago, Alicia would have just said hello and left it at that, but in their recent meetings she had noticed that the study group and the coven all greeted each other with a hug, so that's the way she greeted Meg now as she opened the door.

She shut the door behind Meg, and turned around. Evan was standing at the end of the hall, feet together, bowing gracefully.

Alicia didn't know whether to be embarrassed or proud of her strange roommate. No, make that *lover*. A thrill of excitement ran through her as she mentally repeated the word: *lover*. Evan was her *lover*.

"Uh, Meg, this is Evan. Evan, this is Meg."

He spoke what she assumed was a greeting in what she assumed was Mandarin, and then added, "Congee?"

Meg was gracious, returning his bow. "I'd love some!"

"Follow me, please, m'lady."

Alicia was a little lost. She didn't have visitors often, and when she had, she had been very informal, ignoring the finer points of manners, hanging on to her rebellion against the Establishment, the middle class, and all that it represented, but here was Evan, acting so much the polished host, and to her it seemed nice, seemed *desirable*.

"Uh, Meg, shall I take your coat? I don't want—" Alicia stopped, and tears welled up.

"Are you okay?" Meg asked, placing a hand on Alicia's arm.

"I'm sorry." Alicia pulled a tissue from her pocket and wiped her eyes. "I was going to say that I didn't want Moonshadow to get fur on it. I guess it's going to take a while to get used to the fact that he's not here."

Meg pulled Alicia to her. Evan, hearing the sobs from the hall joined them in the hug.

Alicia wanted to wail, not just for Moonshadow, but for the innocence that disappeared once she realized that vampires were real, but the part of her that demanded she stay in control was fighting back. She could cry later. Right now she needed to talk to Meg.

"I'm okay. It's just going to take time."

"I have cats, too," Meg said, more to Evan than to Alicia. "I know how it is. They become your family."

Family. What family did she have? No parents, no siblings. And now, no cats.

But now she had Evan. And she didn't want him to think that she was a crybaby. Gently she pulled away from them both. "No, I'm okay. Really. Thanks."

"Congee?" Evan asked again.

"Let's go to the living room," Alicia urged, pushing open the multi-paned glass door that separated it from the entrance hall.

Meg followed her and sat on the couch. Seconds later, Evan arrived with a bowl of congee on a tea tray, looking very much the Chinese waiter, Alicia thought.

He placed the bowl on the small end table next to Meg and bowed again, palms together as in prayer, tea tray slipped under his arm.

"Thank you." Meg smiled and dug into the bowl with the chopsticks.

Alicia noticed her dexterity. *Am I the only one in the world who can't use chopsticks with rice?*

"Ooh, this is good. Alicia tells me you made it yourself? I'll have to get the recipe."

Alicia joked, trying to lighten the sadness she had brought upon them in the hall, "I think we can leave out the part where you let it soak overnight while you kill a vampire."

Meg looked up at them both, smiled, and then returned to her congee. After a polite mouthful, she spoke. "So what happened last night?"

Alicia sat down and began to tell the story, how she had encountered Frederick in her bedroom.

"Frederick? I meant to ask you about that. Didn't you tell me his name was Wesley?"

"No, Wesley's a different— uh, person. Frederick. Frederick is the one who..." She started to choke on her words again. *Alicia, stop it! It's over. There's nothing you can do. Tell the story.* She shook her head and took a deep breath, regaining control. "Frederick was my friend Susie's boyfriend before she disappeared. I think he killed her. I *know* he killed Moonshadow."

"But what about Wesley?"

"I don't know about Wesley. Maybe the disturbance I was feeling was Frederick. Maybe Wesley really was destroyed in the explosion."

Meg flopped back on the couch. If Wesley was already gone, their binding did nothing, but nothing was okay. And this Frederick, who came out of left field—well, he was gone. "That's a relief, then. We had the wrong vampire, but thanks to you and Evan, he's gone. But are you sure that Wesley was already gone?"

Evan spoke hesitantly. "Wait, what was it that you said the Wizard said? 'He does not walk alone'?"

Alicia looked at Evan and her face paled. "That's right. The Wizard didn't seem to think that Wesley was gone. And he obviously wasn't walking alone. There was Frederick."

"Well, if our binding worked—"

Evan interrupted. "If? I thought that, for a spell to work, you had to believe beyond all doubt that it *would* work. That is, no 'ifs'."

"Evan, you sound like you have had some serious training."

Evan smiled at Meg and Alicia found herself starting to feel a little jealous. *Stop that! You've only slept with him once! Where's the Alicia who didn't believe in possessiveness? And maybe he smiles at everyone like that... Wait, if he does, then maybe the way he looks at me isn't anything special... Maybe I don't mean as much to him as I think I do... Stop it! Negative thoughts, I banish you!*

Evan and Meg didn't notice Alicia's little lapse in attention. He was busy telling her of his experience; Meg was busy remembering names and asking about different groups.

Alicia didn't want to interrupt them, but she felt that if she didn't, she'd spiral further down into her negative thoughts and jealousy.

"So, I have this pile of vampire dust in the bedroom. What do you think I should do with it?"

"Normally, I'd say bury it, but since vampires crave the dark, I'd say scatter it on the lawn where the sunlight can hit it." Meg craned her neck and looked out the front windows. "We should probably hurry, though. It's clouding up."

"But it shouldn't matter if the sun is still technically up, right?"

"I don't know. Think of a solar eclipse. The sun is still there, but the ancients felt that all sorts of evil could still occur because the face of the sun is hidden and its influence is blocked. How do we know that vampires can't walk if there's a good-enough cloud cover? Before Alicia told me on the phone this morning that you two actually killed one, I still wasn't certain they existed."

"Then how could you have done the binding?"

"The same way I can read fiction. What's the expression? 'Willful suspension of disbelief'?"

"Yes, Samuel Taylor Coleridge, I believe," Evan said, obviously proud of his own knowledge, and a little too impressed, Alicia thought, with Meg's.

"Coleridge, that's right. But yes, I can cast a spell on a creature I'm not one hundred percent sure exists by willfully suspending my disbelief long enough to do it."

"Wait. Nothing happened with the dust last night. Why should we worry about it now?"

"According to some legends, vampire victims don't become vampires until the next moonrise. If Frederick's not really destroyed, maybe he wouldn't rise again until the next moonrise— tonight. Why take chances?"

"I'll get the dust pan and brush." Alicia stood up and went to the cellar stairs, where the dustpan and brush were suspended from nails on the wall just inside the door.

"Do you have a vacuum cleaner? We'd have to destroy the bag, but it might be better."

"What about particles of dust clinging to the inside of the hose and nozzle?" she called from the kitchen.

"They're removable, right? We wash them, outside, so that the dirty water stays outside. And we can leave the vacuum out for a day or two. I thought I saw a shed out there. Is that yours?"

Alicia nodded. "Yes, it is."

"Good. We can leave it in there. The sun will get to it through the windows, but it'll be protected from rain."

"Okay. I'll get the vacuum cleaner. Evan, can you get a pail and some rags from the basement, by the utility sink? There's a garden hose in the shed we can use as long as it hasn't been eaten by mice over the winter. I emptied it before I stored it, so it shouldn't have frozen."

They dispersed to carry out their tasks, Meg following Alicia to the hall closet for the vacuum cleaner, and then upstairs, for Frederick.

Meanwhile, the guardian sun sank just a little further in the sky.

They took care, vacuuming Alicia's room and the cellar meticulously, cleaning the same spots over and over. Using several changes of hot soapy water, they washed the vacuum and dust pan, and then decided to do the same to the cellar and bedroom floors. They finished just as the sun lowered to the horizon.

Meg suggested that they all bathe and wash their contaminated clothes immediately.

"You don't have a septic tank, do you?"

"No, town sewer. Why?"

"That's better, for our purposes. The remains and dirty water will be carried out of the house and diluted so much that it couldn't cause any harm. I don't even know if it's possible for the dust to be harmful anyway. We really don't know how much vampire lore is sheer imagination and how much is based on fact, but it's better to be cautious. Let's get started."

Evan showered while Alicia foraged for a change of clothes for herself and a set of clothes to lend Meg. She knew she had a sweatsuit that would fit.

She had left the window slightly open after they vacuumed, and a fresh, spring smell greeted her when she returned for the clothes, though the air was getting chillier with the setting of the sun. Placing her hands on the sash, she looked out on the asphalt shingles that covered the porch roof. She thought that she saw pawprints there, in the fresh dew. *It's probably that Siamese cross-breed that used to tease Moonshadow by sitting on the roof outside the window. Darn! I wonder if he got in...*

Softly she called out, "Here, kitty, kitty, kitty," and then made the smacking sound with her lips that seemed to work with most cats. She waited, silently, hearing the water splash as Evan showered, and Matricaria's voice as she spoke to Janith from the kitchen phone downstairs. Not hearing any response from the Siamese cross that she thought might have entered the house, she tried again. Pursing her lips together, she made the smacking sound, and then the chittering, squirrel-like sound, that she always employed to calm and soothe Moonshadow.

"Here, kitty, kitty, kitty."

Nothing.

She made the smacking sound.

Nothing.

She made the chittering, squirrel sound.

The bottom of the bedspread stirred softly, and there—

"Oh, my God— "

"Yes, we cleaned the vacuum cleaner and the hoses and we're going to shower and wash our clothes. Evan's showering now, then me, and then Alicia... I don't know. I'll ask her. Hold on."

Meg put her hand over the mouthpiece of the phone and walked to the foot of the stairs, untangling the long coiled cord as she went. "Alicia? Alicia?"

She waited for a response, but all she could hear was the sound of the shower.

"Hold on. I think she has the door closed. I'm going to put the phone down. I'll be right back." Meg gently put the receiver down.

"So, what do you think?" Rob asked Janith as they waited for Meg to return to the phone.

"I don't know, but I've got that feeling that something isn't right. There's something they— we— have overlooked."

"Moonshadow!"

There, on the floor, emerging from beneath the bed, head poking out from under the hem of the chenille bedspread, was Moonshadow.

He was a bit bedraggled, his beautiful white fur gray with dirt, his claws clogged with dark brown mud and clumps of tan New England clay, but the most disturbing part of his shabby appearance was his face.

Moonshadow had been a beautiful, silver-shaded Persian cat, but not one of the more recent Peke-faced Persians with their flattened faces that gave them the appearance of a permanent scowl. His was a sweet, classic cat face with a mildly protruding nose and a tiny pink bottom lip.

But that was not what Alicia saw tonight. On the floor in front of her sat a monster, its clear emerald eyes now a deep cinnabar, its soft tufted paws matted with what could only be blood.

Moonshadow's delicate tongue, which she had seen lolling over the side of his mouth after what had appeared to be his last breath, snaked out over curled lips in anticipation of what she dared not think, and the tiny mouth opened to reveal grossly enlarged canines ...

...covered in blood.

As Evan turned off the shower and reached for his towel, he found himself wondering what Lynnie would think about the vampire. He was the one who had suggested that they spend time away from each other, but they were still friends and he was sure that she'd want to hear about *this*. He'd have to call her tomorrow.

It never occurred to him to think how Alicia would feel about him staying in touch with Lynnie; after all, it was just a phone call. And what had happened between him and Alicia the night before didn't bar him from calling an old friend.

As she arrived at the top of the stairs, Meg heard a low growl. A cat owner for many years, she could tell by the volume and timbre that this was not a typical growl; it was a fierce, *dangerous* growl.

Could vampires change into animals? Legend said they could change into wolves, the "children of the night." Had Wesley, knowing Alicia's fondness for cats, returned as one?

It was a little far-fetched, but once one accepted the fact that vampires existed at all, and that their bodies defied the laws of physics, *anything* was possible.

She knocked on the bathroom door to her right. "Evan! Get out here!"

Not waiting for an answer, she continued to Alicia's bedroom. Alicia stood with her back to the door, facing the spot where Evan had extinguished Frederick, and there, where Moonshadow had launched his last, desperate battle, sat—

Without taking her eyes off the cat, Alicia spoke to Meg behind her. "It's Moonshadow. He's a vampire."

"Are you sure? It might be Wesley, taking the form of a cat, to win your trust."

"No," she said, shaking her head in pity, tears starting to well in her eyes. "No, he certainly wouldn't win my trust, not looking this way."

Meg edged closer, and the creature that once was Moonshadow turned in her direction, its dainty tufted ears flattened hard against its head. It was curling around to face her, hissing, and baring its awful teeth.

And now they could see that even its broad little chest was covered in blood.

Downstairs, the kitchen phone handset lay on the hall floor, receiver pointed to the ceiling, picking up the noises from the room above. On the other end, Rob and Janith listened, with increasing alarm.

"Rob, did you hear that?"

"Yes, yes, I did."

"There's something wrong. That sounded like Matricaria."

"I'm going to try to get her attention." Taking a deep breath, drawing on his few drama classes, Rob projected loudly into the phone. "Matricaria! Alicia! Are you all right?"

In the hall now, clad only in his drawstring pants, Evan heard the noise from the earpiece of the phone downstairs— and the growl and hiss of the angry cat in the room to his right.

Looking into the room, he could see the light from the upstairs hall reflected on the shiny white fangs. Immediately he grasped the situation.

Returning to the stairs, he leaned over the rail and yelled, "Send energy. It's another vampire!" and then quickly took the several steps into his room where he retrieved the remaining piece of his split bo.

Within mere seconds, he was standing at Meg's side, bo at the ready, staring down a vampire cat.

Rob virtually flew out of the bedroom where he had been using the extension phone. He ran to the living room, where Janith was digging wildly through the crammed coat closet.

"Hon, *what* are you doing? We don't have time!"

"The sword, Rob, the sword. Somehow I know that we need the sword!" She reached back and grasped something, and then, pulling it out, Rob could see that it was, indeed the sword.

"Okay, I trust your instincts. What now?"

"She's to the west, right? Let's face west, and send all our energy out through the sword."

"Protective?"

"No, this time *destructive*. That bastard has to go."

Alicia was sure that the vampire cat was going to spring at Meg, but Evan's appearance had distracted it so that it now turned to face Evan. Evan returned the stare, calmly, resolutely.

He shouldn't stare! Alicia noticed a familiar loosening of the muscles in Evan's face and body. "Evan, don't stare at him! Vampires can hypnotize... And cats see a stare as a challenge."

Evan blinked hard, twice. He focused his gaze higher, above the cat's head, and resumed his alert stance.

Behind him, Meg was thinking aloud. "We've got to distract it. And unfortunately, the best candidate is the person in front of it." She was looking at Alicia.

This was the third time that innocent people faced death because of the vampires that Alicia— however involuntarily— had brought upon them. She could not shirk her duty. She must destroy the companion whose death she had mourned only a short time ago.

"Moonie! Moonshadow!" Alicia squatted and extended an upturned hand.

It turned its head slowly to look at her, its body still in a tight crouch facing Evan.

At that moment, Evan struck with the bo, aiming for the vampire cat's chest, but he wasn't fast enough for the agile feline. Moonshadow leapt for Evan's throat as the bo missed its mark and rattled, useless, to the floor.

Miles away, Janith quickly raised her ceremonial sword to the west, both hands firmly on the hilt. She planted both feet firmly on the ground, hips' distance apart, as she intoned:

I conjure thee, O Sword, who was made to serve me as a strength and defense in all magical operations against all mine enemies, visible and invisible, to fulfill now your purpose.

I, Janith, Priestess and Witch, command thee to pull the power of sun, moon, and stars, to aid those who aim to defeat and destroy the creature, real or imagined, mortal or immortal, that pains and endangers our coven sister Matricaria, her friend Alicia, and the man who stands with them against the foe.

Rob stood behind her, arms outstretched in front of him, semi-circling Janith, pouring his magical energy into the sword's blade. In the darkness of the living room, the sword seemed to mist over, to pulse and then glow with a faint blue light as they willed their energy into it.

When it felt as if she could send no more, Janith shot one last push of energy through the sword with one final, powerful incantation:

SO DO I COMMAND THEE!

Outside, unpredicted lightning and thunder crashed through the fine damp night, and the world beneath it trembled with the power.

"Moonshadow, NO!!" Alicia was upon the animal now, grabbing the scruff of its neck, which, had it been a living cat and not the foul demon that it was now, would have activated an instinct to go limp, as kittens do when their mother carries them thusly.

Moonshadow turned to face her with a snarl. She tried to lift him up, but he was too strong for her to pull off, and his claws were sunk deeply into Evan's shoulder and chest. As Alicia pulled, she could hear the intake of breath and clearly see the plain in Evan's face as the claws, now deadly talons, dug deeper into muscle.

Despite the pain, Evan, too, struggled to remove the enraged demon. With his right hand, he tried to force Moonshadow away, and with his left, though the pain in his shoulder must have been excruciating, he tried to assist Alicia in pulling off the cat.

Neither could budge the infuriated beast. Though only seven pounds, it could have weighed seven *hundred* for the sheer force that it exerted. Bright red rivulets of blood flowed from Evan's neck, shoulder, and chest. With no human hands able to restrain or impede him, Moonshadow turned back to

Evan's neck, lapping the still-warm blood that pooled at Evan's collarbone, and then opened his jaw wide for another bite—

He could have bitten, and no one could have stopped him, but, miracle of miracles, he was distracted.

Moonshadow stopped mid-bite to look as Meg re-entered the room. In the commotion of the attack, as Evan had raised his own weapon, she had slipped downstairs, where her worn canvas ritual bag lay next to the front door. From the bag she had swiftly withdrawn a sharpened willow stake, a stake formed when lightning had severed it from a large willow tree in her yard; when the strength and power of light, of the sun, of good, had yielded a magic-blessed willow stake which she now drove deep into the vampire cat's chest.

"Bast, forgive me!"

Meg watched as the frenzied cinnabar eyes of the demon vampire cat blinked shut and then opened, the gentle emerald eyes of Alicia's beloved sweet pet returning.

Alicia felt the mass of taut raging muscle beneath her hands collapse into the soft, cushy fur that she used to nuzzle against her cheek, the soft cushy fur of a breed known for its gentleness and peaceful disposition.

Evan felt sweet release from pain as the sharp talons retracted and withdrew from his shoulder and chest.

Meg, Evan, and Alicia stood silently as Alicia renewed her grip on the scruff of Moonshadow's neck. Tenderly she pulled the cat away, hugging him one last time to her bosom as he slowly withered, and, like Frederick before him— Frederick his sire and master— Moonshadow turned to dust, coating Alicia's clothing with his remains.

Chapter 29

Alfred turned on his side in his hospital bed and looked into the darkness outside his window. The lights of the city of Worcester still greeted him, but there was something more luminous, something less threatening in the scene before him.

And he knew, as a man with his talents would, that the energy that he and his coven had been sending for Alicia's aid, had been well-used, and that the threat had been quelled.

But he also knew, deep inside, that this was only one of many threats. That these innocent people, unwittingly drawn together by the world of computers, were now bound as warriors to defeat an evil as old as time.

And he knew, though he pondered whether he should ever tell them, that their battles were not over. That though there may be a lull in the fighting, the war of good versus evil was eternal.

"May the gods guide and protect them," he whispered, and then rolled over on his back for a well-deserved nap.

"What's that noise?"

Alicia, Meg, and Evan listened intently until Alicia identified it. "A phone's off the hook. Did someone leave the phone off the hook?"

"Oh, my gods," Meg said. "It was me. I was talking to Janith and Rob when all this started. They must have hung up."

"Yes, I yelled to them when I came out of the bathroom." Evan said.

"I'll go call them and tell them we're okay. We *are* okay, right?"

Alicia nodded, a stray tear trickling down her cheek. As she moved her hand to wipe it away, dust from Moonshadow's remains floated to the floor.

"You should probably take a shower," Meg suggested. "Step in fully clothed, and wash until there's no more dust," she reminded her.

"I'll get the vacuum," Evan volunteered. "One more time."

"And I'll go make that call. You're okay, right?"

"Yes, I'm fine."

Alicia looked at Evan. "You should shower, too."

Meg shook her head. "I don't know, you look a little faint. It might not be good to shower now. I'm worried about you fainting." His wound had clotted, but he seemed unsteady on his feet.

Evan pulled Alicia to him and looked at her tenderly. "Maybe we could shower together? You know what they say, 'Save water, shower with a friend'?"

Meg smiled. Trying to leave them with a little privacy, she offered, "Yeah, that sounds like a good idea. I'll grab the vacuum after I speak to Janith and Rob. You two going to be okay?"

Alicia nuzzled into the uninjured side of Evan's chest. "We'll manage."

Meg descended the stairs and picked up the phone from the floor. As she did, she caught sight of the clock in the kitchen. It couldn't have taken more than a half hour for all to transpire, but it seemed longer, so much longer.

In that short thirty minutes, they had each faced their own deaths, made decisions that would prevent or possibly cause the deaths of the others, and tested their beliefs in a world that most people didn't even know existed.

And now what? Were there more vampires? Did it end here? Did life go on as usual?

Of all the questions racing through her head, that last one was one that she knew the answer to. Life would *never* go on as it had before. Life was forever changed.

Chapter 30

Monday morning. Spring. New England. The fresh scent of green and growing things rises in the strengthening sun. Traffic toward Fenmore increases steadily on the Mass Pike and the smell of exhaust mixes unpleasantly with the smell of donuts and powdered sugar as commuters stop at Dunkin Donuts for their morning fix.

In downtown Danforth, Evan, newly minted vampire exterminator, warms restorative congee in a shallow saucepan, practicing his tai chi forms before school. A gauze pad with a non-adhesive surface is taped securely to a spot on his bruised neck. Smaller bandages with first-aid ointment cover cat scratches on his chest and back. He is paler, weaker, than usual, but he is alive. Miracle of miracles, he is alive.

Upstairs, Alicia, vampire co-exterminator, showers. She feels hollow, spent, but as the sun brightens a dreary Danforth, she feels a rising optimism and is thankful that she, too, is alive.

In a beautifully restored colonial house on the north side of town, Meg/Matricaria, another newly minted vampire exterminator, feeds her cats and thanks her gods that they, unlike poor Moonshadow, are *just* cats.

And their world, forever changed, is still a Monday morning world, the start of a new week, forever the same.

And they, forever changed, will step forward, into the Monday-morning world. And no one, not the cop directing traffic on the corner, not the clerk at the local convenience store, nor the garbage collectors who have pulled up in front of Alicia's house and noticed that she forgot to put out the trash, not their co-workers or families, will ever know how different this Monday morning is, how much life has changed in the last twenty-four hours.

And how much it has yet to change.

Author's Notes

Place Names

Locals might have noticed that Danforth bears an uncanny resemblance to Framingham, Massachusetts. So why didn't I just call it Framingham? Writers are often advised that if you set your novel in an existing town, readers will expect the details to be perfect. Any slip up— for example, making a street one way the wrong way— will cause you to lose credibility in the readers' eyes. By calling my town Danforth, I give the hint that it just might be Framingham (Framingham was called Danforth Farms early in its history), but I also say that it's a different Framingham. Some of it is a Framingham of my own making; some is a Framingham of the past. Not the past of the original Danforth Farms, but circa 1980-1981. And since it's in the past, it's a Framingham of memories, and memories are, by their very nature, imprecise.

I had a similar problem with Brighton, Massachusetts, the location of the coven. Once again, my perceptions of Brighton around 1981 are going to be very different from anyone else's. Finding an alternate name for what is actually just a neighborhood of Boston was a little more difficult than finding a pseudonym for Framingham. After a few internet searches, I couldn't find any information on earlier names for the neighborhood. Not having the luxury to spend a lot of time on historical research— I've got to finish this book!— I decided that I would perform a search on early names for Brighton, England, since the settlers of the Boston neighborhood were probably thinking of that town when they named it. I found references to Brighthelmston and Bristelmestune. Great! Not really names that roll off the tip of your tongue, right? So I emailed my friend Helen, who's studied old English and old Welsh. She came up with *Bristelton*.

And renaming Boston? Boston was named after Boston, in Lincolnshire, England. The name was said to be a corruption of "St. Botolph's Town" and indeed there is a St. Botolph Street in Boston, Mass. The name "Botolph," though, doesn't roll off the tongue very easily, and I already have a few tongue-twister names for the witches (for example, Matricaria). Why not name it Shawmut, after the original native settlers? To me, Shawmut gives a sense of the land itself, not the city as it endured "civilization" over the years. So, I settled on *Fenmore*, a combination of Fenway and Kenmore, two Boston neighborhoods I had in mind as I was writing.

Other place names I used in this novel are Ashton (Ashland), Elliott (Natick), Hoppersville (Hopkinton), Westville (Westborough), and Lake Harmony (Framingham's Farm Pond).

The Magic

I've done a lot of research on the magic— or, as the witches often spell it, to distinguish between this and the illusionist variety, *magick*— and tried to make the magic, chants, and spells similar to those that are reported to have been in use by traditional witches around 1980-81. But I find, the more I write in this series, that I need to modify things, not just to fit the story, but to avoid copyright infringement, and to give a broader view of the practices of the time. So I've paraphrased and invented, all the while attempting to make my inventions fit the spirit of the practices.

The Food Co-Op

There actually was a food co-operative in Framingham, but I remember very little about it. I remember the shopping plaza where it was located, but I don't remember what was there before the co-op, so I picked a second-hand furniture store. (I think the furniture store might have been *after*, but, hey, this is fiction.) I created the details of the Danforth Co-Op from information I gleaned from web sites of current food co-ops, some of which mentioned their early histories.

The Wizard of Westville

Many years ago there was a gifted psychic a few towns west of me. The character for the Wizard of Westville is based on him. Since my memory is faulty, I'm sure a lot of what I wrote won't ring true for the person I based him on, but I intend no disrespect. I've also deliberately moved things around to suit the time period. The man was a gifted psychic, even though I find his later declarations that all witchcraft is evil to be a bit sensationalist, and untrue.

The Tarot

When constructing the scenes and writing the interpretations for the tarot readings, I used the Rider-Waite deck and *The Tarot Revealed* by Eden Gray. I chose this deck and this book because they would have been the tools that a coven would have used at that time. In recent years, newer decks with broader and different interpretations have been published, but, as I said, the Rider-Waite deck was a better fit for the time period.

Alicia's Parents

Since new writers are often counseled to "write what you know" and many novels are autobiographical, you might wonder if *my* parents died in a car crash. No, they did not, but I did lose my mother as a child and then my father and stepmother as a young adult. I felt that the resulting sense of isolation, of needing to count on oneself first, would be a handy character trait for Alicia. And likewise, I felt that being an only child would be a good character history. In real life, I'm not. I have a brother (and nephew and niece) and don't feel isolated at all.

Cigarettes

Yeah, Alicia smokes in this one. A lot of people did at the time in which the novel is set. I remember smoking at my desk at this time period. It happened. I'm not condoning it, just reporting it.

Bast

Late in the story, Meg says, "Bast, forgive me!" Bast is the ancient Egyptian cat goddess.

Acknowledgements

My dear husband and our two elder cats (now just one), for their patience and support through both *Darksome Thirst* and *The Old Power Returns*.

T. Rose and Cullen Quinn of T. Rose Karate Studio, in Northboro, Massachusetts, and Nancy Quinn, for walking me through Evan's work with the bo staff.

Amy, Paul, Ed, Kathy, and Colleen for their continued encouragement. Ron, Renee, Richard, and Justine for the same. (Hi, young master Tom!)

The "lunch bunch": Nancy, Tom, Doug, Keith, Bob, and John, for sharing their memories of bowling.

The writers at the New England Chapter of the Horror Writers Association (www.horror.org/ne), for their continued support and suggestions, especially Michael, Laura, Don, Stephen, Jack, John, Rick, Dan K., John, Holly, Daniel, Lauren, Paul, Trista, and Dan R.

Xanna and Jimahl, my fellow writers, and Fran D., for their support and insights.

Michelle C., poet extraordinaire, for her continued support.

Indigo, Collin, Rekhetra, John from the UK ("Specialist Consultant to Best-Selling Authors"), Sr. Xarisma, Callisto, Darkwillow, Lady Bronwyn, Rhiannon, Susan, Raven, and Arianrhod for their online discussions of poppet magick.

Aria, Bran, Debbie, Starspawn, Berta, Pat R, Rowanne, and Shamash for their memories of Brighton and its eateries.

Readers of *Darksome Thirst*, my first novel, for encouraging me to keep going and for their helpful feedback.

Finally, to Shadow, my real-life Persian cat of many years ago, and Watty-Girl, the model for Luna, who left this earthly plane a few months after I wrote the final scenes with Moonshadow, I give my heartfelt thanks for being my kitty companions. You are missed.

About the Author

A computer professional by day, at night Morven Westfield's most likely to be reading non-fiction on the supernatural, novels involving witches or vampires, or books on the craft of writing. In her spare time—when there is any—she likes travel, beading, and nature walks. Although she prefers sitting at the keyboard to actually moving (grin), she practices yoga, takes walks, and rides a bicycle now and then.

Interested in the supernatural since 1969, Morven started writing the first sentences of *Darksome Thirst* approximately nine years later, as she fought off sleep as a second-shift computer operator. Never able to devote herself full-time to her writing, she shelved the novel until 1999. That same year she discovered the Horror Writers of America (HWA), which gave her the inspiration to pick up where she left off. Life intervened—as it often does—and it was four more years before she finally completed the publishable manuscript.

Darksome Thirst was published in June 2003. Morven started working on *The Old Power Returns* in December of that year, but found herself procrastinating. Finally realizing that the fear was based in the legendary "sophomore slump," she searched for something to force her to "just do it." That something was National Novel Writing Month (www.nanowrimo.org), held every November, where writers sign up and vow to complete a 50,000-word novel in one month. Laying aside the initial start to *The Old Power Returns,* Morven began a fresh file and completed the second half of the draft on November 26, 2005.

Married with one cat, she lives with her husband, also a computer professional, a pragmatist who is mildly amused by his wife's interest in things that go bump in the night.

Morven is planning future novels in this series.

If you have access to the Internet, you can look for news about her books on her web site at **www.morvenwestfield.com**.

Ordering Information

Want to order additional copies of this book, or copies of the first in the series, *Darksome Thirst?* You can order Harvest Shadows titles from your favorite bookstore or from many online sources including Amazon.com. For other outlets, use your favorite search engine to search for the title or visit the Harvest Shadows web site at
www.harvestshadows.com

If you do not have access to the World Wide Web at home, try your local library. If you are still unable to access the Web, write to the following address and request current pricing and ordering information.

Harvest Shadows Publications
PO Box 378
Southborough, MA 01772-0378, USA

Books Published by Harvest Shadows Publications

The Old Power Returns
by Morven Westfield
(Fiction. Retail price $15.95)

In this sequel to *Darksome Thirst*, Alicia and Meg meet again and discover that the saga of Wesley and Frederick is not yet over, and that when the Old Power returns, it can be good power— or bad.

ISBN-13: 978-0-9741740-7-5   ISBN-10: 0-9741740-7-6

Darksome Thirst
by Morven Westfield
(Fiction. Retail price $14.95)

A rather geeky young woman must resolve the difference between what her logical mind tells her and what she is actually experiencing. Meanwhile, in another part of town, fledgling witch Matricaria has begun to receive psychic messages— vivid dreams and tarot card readings— that point to a terrible fate for someone near her. She and her coven attempt to decipher the symbols, hoping to prevent a tragedy. Soon the lives of these very different women intersect.

ISBN-13: 978-0-9741740-3-7   ISBN-10: 0-9741740-3-3

The Song of an Emerald Dove
by Xanna Vinson
(Fiction. Retail price $15.95)

Mother Earth has been imperiled and is trying to ask for help.

A group of wiccan women devote themselves to the puzzle that is laid before them by the sentient Earth, as they strive to save all they love from a prophesied doomsday. The messages are real. The women are willing participants. But can they decipher the puzzle and act in time?

"Authentic and inspiring." Dolores Stewart Riccio, author of *Charmed Circle.*

ISBN-13: 978-0-9741740-5-1   ISBN-10: 0-9741740-5-X

A Voice in the Forest: Spirit Communications with Alex Sanders
by Jimahl di Fiosa
(Nonfiction. Retail price $17.95)

Ten years after the death of the founder of Alexandrian witchcraft, a handful of witches camping at a secluded site in New Hampshire began experimenting with a spirit board. An entity responded and identified itself as 'Alex Sanders' and then proceeded to prove that claim to them.

ISBN-13: 978-0-9741740-0-6   ISBN-10: 0-9741740-0-9